The
SILK ROAD
AFFAIR

The
SILK ROAD
AFFAIR

A Novel

Larry Witham

ARCHWAY
PUBLISHING

Archway Publishing books may be ordered through booksellers or by contacting:

Archway Publishing
1663 Liberty Drive
Bloomington, IN 47403
www.archwaypublishing.com
844-669-3957

ISBN: 978-1-6657-4906-0 (sc)
ISBN: 978-1-6657-4907-7 (e)

Library of Congress Control Number: 2023915888

Print information available on the last page.

Archway Publishing rev. date: 09/26/2023

PART ONE

1

Vienna

COUNT ARNOLT SHÖNBERG felt all the weight of his seventy years. He watched the workmen in blue coveralls trundle the last of the four crates off the villa porch. He should be feeling light, freed of a burden. Instead, he imagined muffled screams coming from the crates, the scream of the Degas, the Monet, the rare Tang Dynasty scroll. They were all leaving the little town of Eisenerz near Vienna, their adopted home.

The old Shönberg estate had ended in ruin. The properties had to go, piece by piece. First some land, now the paintings. After the paintings were gone, so would be the villa where he stood.

"You can't live forever," he sighed. Everywhere in old Europe, it seemed, old estates, old collections, were on the auction block.

"Count Shönberg," a man in a trim suit said. "We'll need you to sign some papers if you will."

The man was a Swiss, an art agent. His business card and the contract said Silk Road Company. According to its brief, the organization specialized in placing artworks in museums. The agency had found the count's collection, made a good offer, and was shepherding through the deal. It was transacted through Swiss banks—very low profile, avoiding taxes, and this sort of arrangement appealed to the count.

The count had not gained so much attention in a long while. Another firm, Omni Art Global, had also been trying to reach him. Silk Road Company got to him first.

"Where do I sign?" the count said.

The agent handed the documents on an aluminum clipboard. "Here, here, and here," he said. That done, the agent gave a thin smile. "And you have the provenance papers." Those were the documents that traced all past ownerships of the works. The count had a thick envelope. He handed it to the art dealer.

"It's been a great pleasure, Count," the man said with a slight nod. "You've made the right decision."

"Yes, yes, of course," the count said. "My family will be pleased."

The love of art had evaporated among the Shönberg clan. Not the love of euros. The count's two sons, a daughter, and assorted nieces and nephews agreed. They needed money, not heirlooms. The count's wife was the only one who treasured the twenty-six paintings, collected over four generations. Now they were in the four reinforced crates, out the door.

The morning sun had risen above the mountainous skyline, bristling with tall pines. The little town of Eisenerz, with its St. Oswald castle-church, steep hills and valleys, fifty miles from Vienna, had been home for the Shönbergs, a very minor nobility, as far back as the Austria-Hungarian Empire. The family had been proud of the little collection, especially its diversity. Some French academic work, such as the Delacroix and Chardin, French Impressionism including a Millet and Courbet, and then some Austrian works, a Klimt and Kokoschka. And the wonderful Degas, *Portrait of a Sad Woman.*

Then there was his prized ancient Chinese painting, a magnificent landscape of rippling mountains, a stream, bamboo, cranes. It was from the Song Dynasty, more than a thousand years ago, painted in a dark, subtle ink wash by Master Guo Xi.

His thoughts were interrupted by a voice from behind him.

"Count, thank you again." It was the young Chinese woman who accompanied the Swiss art agent. She had inspected the paintings and inventory list.

He turned to her and nodded with a weak smile.

"Your beautiful art is now for everyone," she said in perfect German.

"I hope I've been helpful," he said. "The world is moving so fast now. I can be a bit slow."

"All went perfectly," she said.

She then handed him a little package. "It's a gift. Black Jade Tea." She also gave him a business card, with the black embossed title Silk Road Company, and below that a beautiful gold Chinese calligraphic character. Its glittering beauty struck the count.

"What does this gold symbol mean?" he asked.

"It says Fenghuang Zu, which means Phoenix Group. The emblem of our mother company," she said.

She turned to leave. The retinue had come in a BMW and two moving vans. As the rising sun began to glint off the tall front windows of the villa, the fleet started its engines, moved slowly out of the circular drive, and headed down the road for the autobahn. It was headed for the Vienna International Airport, the count assumed.

The count waved goodbye. He could use a cup of hot tea, perhaps then a nap.

LATER THAT MORNING another BMW arrived at the count's home. From the front seat, a well-appointed Chinese man appeared and shuffled to the villa's front door. He rang the bell, and the count came down to see who it was. The man, with a smile, greeted the count and got down to business, handing him a card. "We've been eager to talk to you Count Shönberg," the man said in passable German.

Shönberg looked at the card. Omni Art Global. He said, "I'm afraid you're too late. A Silk Road company just paid for the collection and took it away."

Paid for? Taken away? The man's face went ashen. With a flick of his hand, he took back the card, pivoted angrily, and returned to the car, which sped off, spraying gravel.

These art people, the count thought. So aggressive.

AT THE AUTOBAHN, the three vehicles with the count's collection approached the interchange. The choice was between Vienna to the east and Salzburg to the west. They turned west. The Salzburg airport, a hub of vacationers, ski buffs, and the jet set, was gateway to Austria's pleasure world, nestled by the Alps and villas. Springtime was ending, the snowy mountains in their last stages, and the airport would be clogged, wrapped in celebratory confusion. Lots of private jets and charters. Naturally, customs would be lax.

With the phenomenal speeds of the autobahn, the three vehicles arrived in an hour. Rather than report to the main terminal, they headed to the private airplane venue. The vehicles pulled into the loading area, where a small transport jet was parked.

"May I see the paperwork, please," the airport agent said. Chartered to Berlin, it said. The contents were personal belongings for a family move. Strange that the crates had Chinese characters stamped here and there, the airport agent thought. How the rich live. The shipment was approved, and the blue-clad workmen loaded the crates into the private jet.

The Swiss art agent tipped the workmen with some euros. Then he and his Chinese assistant boarded the jet. Soon enough they were airborne. Halfway through the flight, the co-pilot radioed the Salzburg Airport.

"Changing course," he said. "Now due south to Budapest."

The change was logged and confirmed, and the jet bearing the twenty-six works of art set its sights across Hungary. Airport governance there was even more lax than in Salzburg. The jet landed, ferried in, and pulled up behind a larger jet. The four crates were transferred.

The work of the Swiss agent was done; another acquisition for the Silk Road Company.

"We're getting good at this, aren't we?" the Chinese woman said to him.

"Always a bit tense, but it always seems to work," he said.

"Until we meet again," she said.

He gave her a faux kiss on both cheeks, and she turned to enter the plane. It was off the ground in another ten minutes. She sat back in comfort for the five-hour trip. Long distance and comfort, that's what the jet was built for. The co-pilot plotted the course to a point in a far-off desert, a little more than three thousand miles. Then he'd land at Urumqi, People's Republic of China.

2

Washington D.C.

AT HIS OFFICE on Dupont Circle in Washington, private investigator Joseph Castelli—aka, Castelli and Associates—took the phone call mid-morning. It lasted longer than he'd expected. "Yes, sir, okay," he mostly said. "Uh-huh . . . no kidding." His yellow pad was out now, filling up with notes.

He was thinking, *There's always something.*

Which was good, since this was the kind of intrigue that Castelli enjoyed. The third decade of the twenty-first-century had arrived, and he wasn't getting any younger. His own boss now, he no longer did the heavy lifting of his youth: the NYPD, first patrol, then detective, up to lieutenant, and then something new—America's first "art cop."

The odd designation had begun abroad. Around 1970, the profession of "art police" was invented in Italy, the Carabinieri Command for the Protection of Cultural Heritage. Then the idea spread to the Levant, around the Mediterranean, within the United

Nations, giving rise to experts who tracked an illegal trade in art and antiquities that had grown rampant—and international.

For a time, Castelli was that man in New York City, eventually working both municipal and federal. With each year, the inter-agency frictions took their toll. That's when he decided to go independent, where he could still do his duty to God and country. Now he ran a go-to operation, a service to government agencies that wanted to keep their hands clean. He was their fixer. He recruited experts of quality, finding the right people for a given job.

The phone call actually had two voices. It was a secure conference call with the Department of State and the CIA.

"Too much is going on right now," the State man said. "We'd like to outsource this particular investigation." Usually, this meant Washington was in some delicate diplomatic limbo with another country. Even using the CIA might stir the waters a bit too much, and that seemed to be the case on this occasion.

"We're looking at stolen American art going to China," the State man said. "In particular, you've probably heard of the theft at the Gardner Museum up in Boston." It had been called the "art heist of the century."

"Back in 1990, if I recall," Castell said. "That was more than thirty years ago. Has something new turned up?"

"Yes and no," said the State official. "What we've got is a red flag in Europe. It may be something." He reminded Castelli that while the Gardner Collection, made up of thirteen items, was not a national treasure, it had long been a black eye for the FBI, even after countless tips came in from overseas, mostly that it was done by the Irish Republican Army, with the art floating around in the black market.

Castelli asked, "Why aren't you using the FBI or Europol? The FBI does liaison overseas." From his experience with the New York bureau, he knew that G-men couldn't trump the police in their own countries—unless it could be done unawares.

A kind of frustrated sigh came over the phone. It was a woman's voice. "I'm with CIA Mr. Castelli," Lucy Anderson, a deputy director, said while not offering her identity. "We've considered that, but it would complicate things. Best to work around them for now." She did not elaborate, except in her own thoughts: Europol was the cooperative police system set up by the European Union in 1999, and it was active in tracking art theft and fraud. It did not take kindly to intrusions by CIA interlopers, or any independent operatives, indeed, the very sort of thing they were asking Castelli to line up. Anderson also had a particular FBI name in mind: Senior Special Agent Hargrave. The original agents on the Gardner heist had retired, and the Washington file had been put under Hargrave's authority. Hargrave had spent time in Europe as FBI liaison with the Europol set-up, and he was apparently still thick with those contacts.

By all accounts, Hargrave viewed himself as occupying a stage all his own, believing he was a synonym for the Gardner case.

"Anyway," Anderson continued, "all FBI activity abroad is under the state department, and state's on our side. There's a history, and, well—"

"I understand the 'history' dilemma," Castelli said. He was well aware of the potential thicket of inter-agency politics "Okay, so you mentioned a red flag."

The man from State said, "It's one of the Gardner pieces, a Vermeer painting. We want to pin that down. We also want to get a reading on the big picture, the illegal art trade with China. State has its own cultural-exchange program going on with China right now. We'd like to do this probe without sinking all the other peace-making initiatives."

"I see," Castelli said. "That's our specialty."

CIA's Anderson explained a few things about the case. "For a start, there's a few people we'd like you to meet. Three people in particular."

Castelli knew the drill. He hoped it was not too complicated. Too many cooks.

Anderson said, "First, one of our old China hands, CIA, name of Mark Hepworth. He's here in Northern Virginia. Then we've got London, someone you need to meet over there."

There was rhyme and reason to this, Castelli thought. The British were in the thick of art-and-espionage, and not always in happy ways. Back during the Cold War, Sir Anthony Blunt, Keeper of the Queens Pictures, had operated as a Soviet agent. One day, he just vanished into the black hole of Moscow. There was even a rumor that a former head of Christie's, the London auction house, had been a Soviet spy, the "fifth man" of the so-called Cambridge Five.

"Still with me?" Anderson said.

"I'm getting it down," Castelli said.

"In London, we want you to see Arthur Morris, former MI6, a specialist in Chinese art. We'll give you all the contact information, give both Hepworth and Morris a heads up. It's a little tricky with MI6. We're not always on the same page, but we'll get this cleared."

"Right," Castelli said. "And you mentioned a third person."

"For the actual operation, we're recommending one of our own operatives, an independent, a Chinese woman. She's an expert in the art world, China, that sort of thing. Name of Grace Ho."

"Okay," Castelli said.

"There actually will be a fourth person," Anderson said. "Of your choosing. We want you to find Miss Ho a partner, an American. Ideally someone with the right cover, knows the art world, reliable."

In a flash, Castelli knew who that could be. He wouldn't say right now.

"Okay, then," the State man summarized. "This may involve some travel. The door's open, wherever they need to go, even China. Sky's the limit. Funding has been appropriated. Let us know when you've got your two agents ready to go."

Castelli knew this was going to take some planning. At least the bureaucracy part was over. They'd left it in his hands.

By mid-day, two confidential files arrived at Castelli's door. A military courier made the delivery. Having looked cursorily at the bulk and detail, Castelli could see that someone in government had been thinking about this for a while. Now it was, as they say, "actionable." Through the evening his eyes consumed the reading matter.

For thirty years, the FBI had received countless tips and leads on the Gardner theft, but most were frauds seeking the reward. The plausible ones were all dead ends. This new one, a new "red flag," was deemed fairly solid, but would need, as usually preferred, a tiptoe investigation.

The item in question, the Vermeer painting, was two-feet square, titled *The Concert*. It had been spotted. The other twelve pieces— three Rembrandts, a Monet, an old European landscape, five Degases, a Napoleon-era filial, and an ancient Chinese bronze cup from the Shang Dynasty—were presumed to be somewhere in the vicinity of the Vermeer. More precisely, the Vermeer had turned up in Spain, then Budapest, apparently headed for China. Something called Silk Road Company might be involved.

Castelli read more of the dossier. He was also recalling something of the bigger picture, the political maze that he—namely, his two agents-to-be—might be navigating. Unavoidably, this would get into the political weeds of Washington. This immediately brought to mind what the CIA's Anderson had said about one lose end, namely Special Agent Hargrave, who would probably be watching them with a gimlet eye. If Castelli knew the FBI, and he did, he wouldn't be surprised if Hargrave used his European contacts to watch their every step.

Then there was the geopolitics to consider. From the American side, the Department of State had what was called a blue team and red team, rivals as the names suggested. One was soft on China, the other hawkish and hardline. Whatever U.S. policy emerged, it was cobbled together with these two groups at each other's throats.

Then, from the China side, the whole question of "cultural property" had become central to current diplomatic tensions. A hundred or so years back, during the Qing Dynasty's "open door" policy with the West, the motley armies and diplomats of England, the U.S., France, and Germany had essentially bought up, or pillaged, a treasure trove of art objects from China during a one-year occupation of Beijing. That was around 1900. From the Western point of view at the time, it was justified. The Qing Dynasty, the last imperial regime, had sided with the Boxer Rebellion, and the Boxers had attacked the large Western community and its legation compounds in Beijing. Now that China was a global power, the cultural slights of the "Century of Humiliation"—which included the opium wars—was not forgotten.

Finally, there was the American President himself. He was a conservative Democrat from New England, a long-time hawk on Russia, but seemingly wait-and-see on China. He kept Congress on its toes, if not in some confusion, according to the headlines. Castelli read one pundit saying he was actually an Independent; neither Democrat nor Republican, neither left nor right. Another wag called him leader of the "Experimentalist Party." Castelli couldn't grasp how this China job might pan out with the White House, if it every reached that level. Not his worry, he hoped.

Into the evening, he began to consider more government files and some of his own records. Then he turned to the resume of Grace Ho, the recommended operative.

"Has a nice ring," Castelli said out loud. "Grace Ho." He liked that she was an independent contractor, just like himself. He worried that, in her early thirties, she was a bit young.

Ho was a resident of Northern Virginia. Impressive government service, covert mostly. Second generation Chinese, American citizen. Multilingual, trained by the Marines and adept at the "culture" controversies. Then there was her current cover. Martial arts instructor. Visiting lecturer in Chinese language. And finally, former research fellow at D.C.'s vaunted Asian art complex, the Freer Museum of Asian Art on the Mall.

Having read through, Castelli sat back. He already had the second agent in mind. One Julian Peale. His mind skipped back. They'd worked a Russian caper together. Miss Ho and Mr. Peale, he wondered. Could this possibly work?

JULIAN PEALE'S FOOTSTEPS clicked over the stone floor of the Freer Museum complex as he pushed open the glass door. The noon sun of late spring fell across his face, a delight after spending three hours at a hard desk in the basement library, leafing through dense academic books on Chinese art. But he did enjoy looking through the Freer Collection of historical Chinese paintings. His doctoral work gave him access.

For the past two weeks, a traveling exhibit, the "Celestial Face of China," an extravagant dog and pony show organized between the state department and Beijing, had been drawing big crowds to the National Gallery on the Mall. From his vantage on the Mall's sandy pathway, Peale could see the giant banners hung over the National Gallery's main entrances. The vast rooms inside had been virtually cleared, then filled up like a Mandarin palace, displaying the glories of millennia of Chinese art. It made the Freer Museum collection look like a footnote.

Peale took a bench by the path, put down his satchel, and pulled out a sandwich. He was taking measure. Another few hours, or call it a day? For now, he relaxed. He gazed down the great Mall with its walls of museums, one of them quite old, the red-stone Smithsonian Castle, and the rest of a similar type, built variously of white sandstone, granite and marble, cut and shipped from as far as Maine and as close as Maryland.

A few years back, he had left New York, where he worked at Medici Studios, a staff restorer, working with the old Italian patriarch, Leo Medici, now in his dotage. Peale couldn't seem to settle down, excepting of course his marriage. He and Priscilla had moved into his old family home, a welcome inheritance. For all his wanderlust—Naval Academy, intelligence duties in Afghanistan, "art detective" work in New York—here he was, back in the city of his upbringing, a hometown boy.

Like the day itself, his life had mostly experienced fair weather, though he always seemed to need a new challenge to keep the darkness at bay. Amid those kinds of choices, he wondered if he'd ever settle on something permanent. Maybe it would just be a tax-paying member of the middle class. Some days he felt like he was slumming, slipping back. On others, his reasoning went fruitlessly to and fro. New ideas constantly flooded his brain. They usually ended up in a drawer, never to surface again. At the least, with his long-ago course credits from the Naval Academy, he'd done a master's in art history. Now it was on to the Ph.D. And even with that he was admittedly getting bored.

He crossed his legs and crumpled the sandwich wrapper. Just as he reached for an apple, his cell phone rang.

"Hello."

"Julian Peale, this is Joe Castelli. Long time."

A slight thrill rippled through Peale. It was a while back, but Castelli's voice produced an instant replay of their adventures together. "Hey, detective Joe, long time indeed."

"Actually, lieutenant now, retired. Can you talk?"

"Sure," Peale said.

Caselli explained that in effect he wanted to know if Peale was recruitable for an art-related investigation. Some foreign travel would be involved. It took a while to explain, and Peale held his peace to hear out his old co-conspirator.

"So you're what, CIA now? State?"

Castelli said, "Independent contractor."

Peale knew all the implication from his time in the Navy. From the end of the Cold War, the old trade of HUMINT—human intelligence—was supplanted by electronics, computers, and datamining. Now, however, everyone was hacking everyone. At the same time, after the 2001 terrorist attacks on the World Trade Towers, U.S. intelligence services expanded their reach through "soft" operatives, that is, citizens and independent contractors. All of this required a return to the old world of eyes on the ground, if not brush passes and dead drops. A kind of "citizen spy" had been reimagined. That was almost two decades ago, and Peale had lost touch and didn't know how that was working out. But here was Castelli, apparently part of the new game.

"Yeah, I'd like to hear more," Peale said. "Time and place?"

"One thing I should make clear at the outset. If this is a go, you're going to have a partner, which I'm working on. You'll need someone who speaks Chinese, knows China inside out. She will . . ."

"She?" Peale said.

"Yeah, *she*. She trained in the Marines. Apparently had field experience. A good deal of security clearance."

"Single?" Peale asked.

"Around thirty. Engaged to some American guy in the Foreign Service." Castelli laughed. "They say she's a phenomenon."

Peale was no chauvinist. He'd brushed shoulders with "military ladies" for years, going back the Naval Academy, right down to the trenches of Afghanistan. Now in his relatively old age, his relatively new marriage—following his long-ago divorce, thanks to the Afghanistan fiasco—was all he needed. He was born in the mid-1970s, a time that seemed to put him a few generations apart from the end of the eighties, when Ho was born. Culture and technology were changing rapidly. Sure, he could work in the field with a younger woman. "Sounds interesting," he said. "Right away?

"*C'est la guerre*, my friend."

"Well, since you put it that way."

"A week or less," Castelli said. "Meanwhile I'll send you two files. One on the case, one on a Miss Grace Ho."

PARKING AT THE Virginia strip mall was tight. Once Castelli found a spot, he set his eyes on the nondescript storefront bearing the sign Apex Martial Arts. This was a recruitment that called for a face-to-face. Miss Ho had been informed of his arrival.

As he entered, he saw a small office set in the corner. Beyond was an open door frame, from where he heard a loud slap-like noise. He smelled sweat and Lysol. At the desk he said, "A Miss Ho please."

"In there," said a young man in a white dojo.

Entering, Castelli saw a tall Asian woman squaring off with a man, both in white outfits. Apparently they had just come out of a tussle, and were back at it. Suddenly, the man's foot swung upward toward her head, she blocked it with a forearm, pivoted, and with her left leg hit one of his knees. Off-balance, he was down in a moment. *Womp*!

Castelli then heard a faint "Arghhh." The man was up again, but

Ho caught Castelli in a glance, and she said, "Enough for today." A little bow, a shaking of hands, and she gave her partner a pat on the shoulder. She grabbed a towel, mopping her neck, her fingers combing her hair. She headed for Castelli.

"Quite a move," he said.

"We do mostly soft here," she said. "Soft means you use the opponent's move against him, like pulling, turning. That was a hard move, where you actually kick or punch." She smiled. "That's what he wants to learn."

Interesting, Castelli mused, as he pictured himself, getting old and in modest shape, out there on the matt with a nimble young woman. "You must be in great shape," he said, a comment he wished he could withdraw, adding quickly, "It's all about the mind, as I understand it."

"Concentration helps." Ho was taking off her white dojo top, exposing a message T-shirt that said, "*I* am your Yellow Peril," the front view of a fist below.

"Right," Castelli mumbled to himself. She was an attractive woman, in a tomboyish way, slim, her upper arms with taught muscles.

Ho had been contacted by her channels in government, and was open to this first consultation. She, too, was an independent. She taught martial arts, lectured on Chinese language, and retained her ties with the Freer. But it was all by her own schedule. She could take jobs that interested her, or that her former superiors "highly recommended," given her patriotic call, her signed security agreements, and, yes, a retainer salary.

She too had been sent the dossier and had time to consider. By the time Castelli had arrived, she was mostly in, but wanted to meet her proposed partner before clinching the deal. In truth, she had found that teaching and reading could become an arid pastime, even humdrum. Some field action was always welcome. As she would later learn, these were also Julian Peale's sentiments exactly.

FOLLOWING HIS DIRECTIVE, Castelli had set up a group meeting with Mark Hepworth, the old China hand formerly on the CIA's Asia desk. The meeting was scheduled for the next Monday.

Hepworth was of a kind, one of the many government retirees who now filled the suburbs of Washington. Since leaving the CIA, he'd written several white papers on the current regime in Beijing. One of the documents addressed cultural exchanges.

Appropriately, for their tete-a-tete, they all converged on the Golden Harvest Chinese restaurant in Reston, Virginia. The restaurant was a surreptitious favorite of old China hands. They all met in the lobby—Castelli, Peale, Ho, and Hepworth—shaking hands, saying hello. They repaired to a back room and Castelli suggested they order first.

Ho was clearly the most vibrant of the bunch. She had drawn back her mid-length hair, put on something in white business attire, carried a document-sized red silk purse, and wore flat black shoes. By comparison, Peale felt he'd dressed too down, suddenly making him aware of his appearance. It was what it was. Hepworth, in a casual gray suited, wielded a large, brown, accordion folder. Castelli arrived hands free, relying on what he believed was his photographic memory.

In came the tea pot and cups and the small bowls of turnip and spinach. They gave their orders, and soon after, the four steaming main courses arrived. With delicate side glances, Peale and Ho were sizing each other up. To her, he seemed a bit old, rough around the edges and perhaps over the hill; he was struck by her youth and presumed lack of experience making battlefield judgments. And then there was the cultural divide, which showed up quickly. Ho and Hepworth clutched their chopsticks. Castelli and Peale reached for their forks.

"We can already see who knows China best," Castelli said.

"We're creatures of habit," said Ho, smiling at Hepworth.

"Took me years, but I've gotten it down," the old scholar-spy said.

As eating wound down, Castelli raised the curtain. "I think we're all up to date on the background. We have a specific concern, tracking down the Vermeer painting, the red flag, and something called Silk Road Company. In addition to that, our beloved government wants a handle on the broader issues, the art trade with China, legal and illegal. Then we'll finish up with some plans of action." Then he gave the floor to Hepworth.

"Thank you," Hepworth said. "I hope I can be helpful." He was actually thinking how nice it was to be back in the spy business again. "In the past decade, China has changed dramatically, and not in ways most people think," he went on. "We see it today as an economic powerhouse, manufacturing going out, natural resources and investment coming in. It can easily obscure the radical changes after Tiananmen."

That was in 1989, when Beijing put down a mass protest in Beijing's Tiananmen Square, a vast public space extending from the ancient Tiananmen Gate and Imperial Palace grounds, and all of it a stone's throw from the China's "White House," the Zhongnanhai. The crackdown killed unknown thousands and spread to many cities. It also came as the Soviet Union was falling apart. Under such shock treatment, China had reversed its political liberalization and brief experiment with openness, even though on the surface it was still all business.

"The difference was that now the Party had insinuated itself up through all the ranks of society, asserting a kind of ideological control not seen before." The Party meant the Politburo, he continued, which was a kind of pyramid. "There are twenty-five members, usually divided into factions, but then, ruling over that body are the nine members in the Politburo's Standing Committee. They also reflect the factions, their power bases. This is the black box for Western Sinologists. How does the Politburo make policy?"

Ho said, "But we do know that at the tip top is the general secretary, Ren Jinuah."

"That's true," Hepworth said. "More than anyone, he's enhanced central Party control. Before his time, China was losing a grip on its chaotic free market. Its bureaucracy was larded. Now it's been winnowed back, with the Party insinuated into every province and board room. And at the top is Ren. He's near the end of his second five-year term. He's hoping to change the rules, get a third. Some think he's going to really change the rules, get chairman for life."

"What about the factions?" Ho asked. "Isn't there some pushback?"

As Peale looked on, noticing Ho's animation, he had the strange feeling that they were like contestants in a quiz show, he an Old Father Time and she a Young Turkess. Both were eager to display their knowledge on things Chinese, but only she was scoring the points. It was a fleeting thought. Anyway, Hepworth was mostly filling the space with his erudition, and Peale was happy to be a spectator for now.

"Ah, the factions," Hepworth said. "You could not argue that the Politburo is utterly united. It's always riven, one part dominant, other parts acquiesce. In my time, perhaps even now, a group was called a 'faction' if it was a bit independent. If it's a rival, they slighted it as a 'clique.' The Politburo's stated goal is to be Leninist, centralize on top, but don't let things centralize out on the wings. You don't want those wings—the provinces, businesses, cities—to gain independent power. Instead, keep them separated. So as to factions, it's still hard to control. Factions in the top and out in the wings. So a General Secretary will push hard to tie everything to Beijing, up the ranks with omnipresent and loyal Party operatives."

Ho said, "Reporting to Ren Jinuah."

Now Peale had a question, hoping to get a better grip on the narrower topic that defined their mission. "How would you say this effects the art market?"

"Yes, of course, Hepworth said. "That's what this is about, isn't it."

All of them had been through Art Market 101, one way or another, and the terms were familiar. The black market was criminal activity, theft, and extortion. Floating above that was the gray market. Not quite criminal, but unregulated, taking on a thousand forms. In the art world it was comparable in size to the world's illicit drug trade.

"And where, in your opinion, does the Party fit in?" Peale asked.

"You may be surprised at this, but the Party, government officials and even the PLA are very active in China's gray market. Everyone knows it's there, I suppose. It's an inherent piece of the booming economy. You can be sure the Party has a hand in it, for whatever reason."

"So, do you think General Secretary Ren Jinuah has a hand in this?" Peale asked.

"Clearly, China has a soft power strategy, and it must include the art world." Everyone at the table knew the difference. Hard power was military and economic. Soft power, as famously defined, was "getting others to do what you want without using force."

Peale was skeptical that soft power really made much difference, having seen what military force could do. All the art market talk, however, was forcing his mind back to his art history studies.

A couple of shrewd art dealers in France had cornered the market on some unknown "sloppy" painters there. Through clever marketing, later generations in the West were obliged to utterly love Impressionism. During the Cold War, the state department, with visions of the "American Century," promoted New York Abstract Expressionism across Europe, an alternative to Soviet Socialist Realism. That had worked too. So maybe there was something to soft power—but was it real power? he wondered.

"I may be out of line here," Peale said, "but does anyone really think that China's soft power is going to take over the world?" He'd been trained in the Cold War philosophy of "containment" and balance of power. He'd also seen in Afghanistan, America's longest war, that a bad actor nation can harm the world piecemeal—in the Afghan case, exporting opium and harboring terrorists—but it couldn't take over the world, nor could its culture be changed root and branch. After offering this summary, he added, "I imagine China's the same."

Ho suddenly chimed in, surprising Peale. "We're not talking conspiracy theory, Mr. Peale. We're talking historic change, and about China currently having the advantage. I know, some flashy book titles say China will 'rule the world,' but that doesn't mean there isn't truth to the notion. China's massive population, its financial system, its centralized politics, and its cultural resources, are moving outward, probably like nothing since the British Empire. Anyway, I accept Mr. Hepworth's premise. Soft power is extremely consequential, especially over time."

Quite a lecture, Peale thought to himself. She was Chinese, however, so by rights she could certainly hold such a strong opinion. "I do concede that the future will probably have one superpower, but I can't see China as—"

Castelli cleared his throat loudly, eager to swing the conversation to the focal point. "The Vermeer, the stolen painting, is our thing," he said, looking at Peale and Ho. "Mindful, though, that the government also wants to figure out what you call the soft power, with the art, without disrupting the diplomatic front. Hopefully, the Vermeer will lead you to that bigger picture. But our brief is not to fix the power balance of the world."

Hepworth sensed the awkwardness in the exchange between Peale and Ho, so decided to insert a conciliatory, if not much happier, topic. "Of course, we must be mindful that the Chinese Communist Party does have its eyes on the art world. It wants to be an economic hegemon, but also a cultural hegemon. I can only quote Chinese ruler Deng Xiaoping's from the seventies, 'Hide brightness, bide time.' Beijing today may be bright in economics and military, you known, 'Made in China 2025,' the whole Belt and Road initiative. But I think on cultural strategy, it's hiding the brightness, at least for now."

The concept matched what news reports had been saying for a few years about China's grand strategy. The Politburo had called it "China 2049," a goal that marked the centenary of the People's Republic of China.

After a time, Castelli wanted to sum up. To get behind the scenes on all this, he said, Peale and Ho would have to put in some mileage. "Prepare yourselves for overseas travel. London first, maybe mainland Europe, then take it from there. The government will issue your visas, passports, each with alternative identities. Then you're on your own."

"Any other assets?" Peale asked, referring to fellow spies abroad, often helpful when the chips are down.

"Not as many as China has here," Hepworth said with a laugh.

China and the U.S. both had one embassy and five consulate in each other's backyard, but when it came to assets, no comparison, he said. "We have maybe thirty thousand Americans in mainland China at any one time. Students mostly. Sounds like a lot. It is a lot. Then China. It has a third of a million college students in America, then businesses, thousands of tourists."

"Beijing's eyes and ears," Peale said.

"True, true," Hepworth said. "I think you'll be given reliable assets of ours in China, if your work takes you that far."

Castelli said, "Case by case, we'll hook you up." He was beginning to worry whether Peale and Ho would get along.

3

Urumqi, China

AT NEARLY THIRTY-THOUSAND feet, Quang Daiyu felt invisible. She sat in the back seat of the single-prop jet, the newer Primus 150, "Made in China," a design bought out from an American firm. Like an arrow, the small craft cut through the buffeting winds over northwest China, a virtual desert land.

Across from her sat the solemn Liu Hui, her shrewd right hand, a young man who always wore a suit. In ancient calligraphy, the surname Liu came from the Han Dynasty and meant "kill," while his first name read as "clever." Quang viewed the first name as suiting him best. Next to her sat an older man, his temples slightly gray, quiet in his dull green uniform of the People's Liberation Army. She called him by his first name, Zhang Wei.

For several years, they had helped her navigate the country's surveillance society, stay as invisible as possible, which might seem contrary to the Chinese way. China's symbol was the dragon, a bright conspicuous beast, active, fiery, big-eyed. That was what China's general secretary, her uncle, Ren Jinuah was trying to be. Not her, though. She favored a byword born of modernizing China as it prepared patiently to seize the world stage. "Hide brightness, bide time."

Quang brushed back her silky dark hair, still black as coal in her late forties. Her name, Daiyu, meant black jade, and in this her adoptive parents had chosen well.

The flight was due to land in China's far northwest "autonomous" region, Xinjiang, the largest designated area in China, far larger than any of the official twenty-two provinces. On a map, Xinjian was a land above the Tibetan mountains, poised between China's two great deserts, and squeezed up against Russia. Through the deserts, skirting the mountains, and across strings of oases, ran the many sinews of the ancient Silk Road, many paths from East to West.

Quang was on business for her company, Phoenix Group, with its Silk Road Co. While the Communist Party tried to keep control of entrepreneurs, her ventures continued to move like water among a thousand pebbles. She did not need to wear the "red hat," the Party imprimatur required of all state-owned or co-op businesses. She did not have to be a private sector behemoth either, like the entrepreneurial millionaires who built Shanghai's skyline, or who ran the financial districts in big cities. She'd set up a Party of her own.

At her side, Zhang Wei took out a boxy travel case. It contained a large thermos. "Some tea before we land, madam?" he asked.

Quang looked at her empty cup, a fine piece of antique China. She shook her head, raised her hand palm out. "When do we land?" she said.

"Very soon, I think," Zhang Wei said.

With a small sigh, she calmed herself. She'd much prefer to know the precise minutes. Anyway, what would she do without the graying, fiftyish Zhang Wei? He was reliable. Trustworthy. He'd gone the course with her for years.

Her hands shook a little, but the tea, the Gold Tea, would help. "Oh, well, yes, Zhang Wei, some of the Gold Tea please," she said.

Gold Tea was a specialty in her Black Jade Tea brand, a small branch in Urumqi, part of her Phoenix Group. It was one more way, one more cover, for all her shipping exploits. There was something sublime about tea, growing it, drinking it. One of Quang's little joys. Years earlier an old herbalist, a medicine woman, had helped Quang with her failed pregnancy, and taught her the art of growing tea, making hybrids, ancient formulas for various purposes. Quang put it to good use. She built her business. For today, the Gold Tea would elevate her mood.

From the special thermos Zheng Wei poured the Gold Tea, which still steamed slightly. After a few sips, Quang's mood was better. She said, "Have you enjoyed the flight?"

"Always," Zhang Wei, a hint of a smile. He was used to taking orders. He always warmed to her at such personal moments, rare as they were. She could have been a PLA colonel.

As the plane descended, it met the headwinds of the north. Over the centuries they had carved out the shapes of the desert. The plane jostled, but cut through like a scissor on silk. Quang's business had its headwinds, but nothing she could not handle. She fingered the cup in her hand. Such items were a large part of her inventory, crates of ceramics that bedazzled the West. There were also bronzes, stone figurines, and jade jewelry. They generated revenue, even multi-millions, but she viewed them as trivial things, mere crafts, mass produced now and in ancient times. Her love was for the paintings, both Chinese and Western, and with her profits it was these she sought, especially the works the West had stolen from China. *The West had taken from China, and now China is taking back.*

For her the brush—not the forge, pottery wheel, or chisel—was the essence of China, from its calligraphy to its painting. The brush—pressed down for the bold stroke, lifted expertly for subtlety. Ink and water flowing, like nature itself. Her companies had many names, but she had one of her own, Qishu: Qi for "wondrous" and shu for "brush." *The Wondrous Brush.*

Descending still more, the pointy-nosed Primus banked softly to the leeward. The winds skidded off the nearby Tien Shan Mountains, not the tallest in China, but by far the longest east-west range in the world, running across west China and Central Asia.

Quang took her last sips of the Gold Tea. With its taste, its effect, she went into a reverie. In that elevated state of mind, her thoughts always sought the essence of China. Her younger years had brought turmoil, beginning with uncertain family roots. Then there was her brief student life in America. At that impressionable time, her emotions were put into a whirlwind by the great upheaval, the Tiananmen Square massacres of spring 1989, the "June Fourth Incident," as the government now called it. She was not there, but when she returned to China, smothered in a political crackdown, her loyalties were confused. She could not find an anchor. She finally found it in her personal ambition, first in knowing the essence of China, its art and cultural legacy, and second in creating her own citadel of success, even power.

Today, Quang's trip from Shanghai had covered a bit over two thousand miles, seven grueling hours. There was one stopover at the midpoint of Lanzhou, capital of Gansu Province, next to the great Tibetan Plateau.

The plane circled Urumqi Diwopu International Airport, then descended to the airstrip, rolling to a private PLA-secured gate. She looked out the window, spying another aircraft parked in the apron. That was hers too. It was her transport plane, a Shaanxi Y-8, that old PLA mainstay. Built on a Soviet design, it could travel three thousand five hundred miles nonstop. It could carry shipments to and from the West, to and from Urumqi and Shanghai. And it was very busy in the past few years.

She had chosen well with Urumqi. It was at the very center of Asia, the point farthest from all oceans. In air miles, it was also the closest point to Europe. It was an old desert passageway on the Silk Road, a cut in the great Tien Shan Mountains. Now it was the capital of Xinjian Province, and to her mind a properly godforsaken place.

There was a saying of old and Quang knew it well: "The mountains are high. The emperor is far away."

AT THE URUMQI airport a black sedan was waiting for her party of three. It whisked them out of the airport and into Urumqi, past the imposing red-rock cliff that jutted upward in the city—with its ancient tiered, temple on top—and into one of the industrial areas.

The city had spread in a vertical shape, downtown at the heart and the industry in the north. In the south were the great squares— the Grand Bazaar, Hong Shan Park, and the People's Park and People's Square. The black sedan headed north for the industrial sector, grazing off the edge of the rectangular high rises of the inner city. Quang could see the tall, silvery building that housed the State Security Ministry. Yet for all its height, it could not see her.

Farther north, just outside Urumqi, Quang had her own tea farm in the watershed of the Tien Shan Mountains, two acres of green houses. The desert region was not known for growing tea, a crop of the humid south, from China to India. She had conquered even this. With the greenhouses, her horticulturalist, a talented chemist, had cultivated their brand, but also a hybrid, the Gold Tea. A tea of reverie.

Driving through Urumqi, the air was thick with smog, rising

from industry: high tech, heavy manufacture, and gas and oil production. Soon they were at her Phoenix Group warehouse. All was quiet. The front bore the company name, but it was otherwise nondescript. The façade was brick, matched with gray masonry and a silvery entry overhang, a low building with an underground matrix of rooms.

As they exited the car, a man in a green uniform came out to greet them. He saluted. He opened the door and the threesome walked in. Two other staff were in the lobby, standing stiffly, as if a royal visit was at hand—routine since ancient times for any senior figure.

"Welcome back, Madam," the supervisor said. "We look forward to your visits."

She nodded, glanced pleasantly at the other staff. "Please take the two empty suitcases downstairs," she said, pointing to their only luggage.

Quang turned and headed down a hallway, everyone else in tow. Soon they arrived at the elevator, one taking her down with her three-member party and the supervisor. There was a second, a larger freight elevator, but the others repaired to a stairwell, meeting up in the lower lobby.

"We will be an hour or so," Quang said to the supervisor.

He straightened, nodded, and then signaled to the staff.

The door had a computerized lock. It also had a humidity control, with a digital pad outside the room and its twin inside. Quang pressed the number pad eight times, her memorized pass code. It showed up as eight red-lit asterisks in a row. With a beep, the door unlocked. Quang and her party went inside, bringing in the two suitcases. It was cool and dry.

The lights came on automatically. Before them stood a state-of-the-art storage room, not so much equipped like a museum restoration laboratory, but with the same aura. There were two large work tables and beyond them large shelves. Then an area for stacked cases. The fiberglass ones were designed with soft, but firm, spine-like dividers inside that safely held two dimensional works of art. Others were in the old and inconspicuous wooden style. They looked like industrial crates, some stamped with Silk Road Co., others Black Jade Tea. Boxes of tea flew under the radar in China, for obvious reasons. In practice, all of the crates were unassuming among the legions of shipping boxes at airports, especially in Urumqi.

For all its utility, the room also had a handsome wall with a large glass display case. In this Quang liked to mount samples of her recent acquisitions. The supervisor, dipping into a recent shipment, had put up a tall silk scroll painting, always hoping to please Quang with a new artwork that had arrived. Now the case held an ebullient landscape in ink and wash titled, *Celestial Mountains, Loyal River*.

Quang stopped to look at the artwork, a masterpiece, done by the hand of the great Song Dynasty master, Guo Xi. So much native art, now in either China or the West, were actually antique copies. The one before here was certainly an original. It came from an Austrian collection, she had been informed.

Already, her suited assistant, Liu Hui, was walking about the crates and shelves. It was a general inspection, as usual.

"Let's begin," Quang said. "Include the Austrian collection."

Zhang Wei was standing by, ready to lift and move. Some new acquisitions had come in over the past month: Germany, Hong Kong, even Brazil, and a few from the United States. Some artworks were sold by collectors, others given up by cash-strapped museums, the dreaded "deaccession," every museum's shame: selling art that long ago had been donated, usually by long-dead millionaires.

One by one, a half dozen crates were rolled over to the table. As each was opened, a variety of paintings were removed. They were unwrapped and put on the table for Quang to inspect. She was silent throughout. A half hour later, after many second thoughts, she said, "I'm very pleased, you may put them back." Her attention seemed to wander a bit.

She thought about the American collection, with its Vermeer and ancient Shang Dynasty cup. She liked to surround herself in Shanghai with such superlative things, but her business mind, her calculating mind, was a brake on such fancies. The storage area at this building was getting crowded, and more shipments were coming in. It was probably time to transfer many of the artworks to the larger tea farm storehouse, which was both large and secure.

"Let me see that Austrian collection again," she said.

One of its prizes, the *Celestial Mountains, Loyal River* painting was already on display. From the Vienna case, the other works were again set on the table. Quang moved past each, thinking.

"This one and this one," she said. A Corot and a Monet. She was in a French mood today.

"A fine choice," Liu Hui said. He turned to Zhang Wei and said, "We are taking these two. The others stay."

As Zhang Wei, in his efficient military manner, began to put everything in order, Quang fought a temptation. The allure of the American collection was tempting her. *Take something back to Shanghai?* No, she resolved, it must stay together, await a plan.

"Is that all, Madame Quang?" Liu Hui finally asked. This had been a long trip for a two hour visit, so he wanted to make sure. She was always on the move. Her mind could change like the weather. More and more was coming in, more going out.

"You'll be staying behind, Liu Hui," Quang said.

"Yes, as planned," he said. There was inventory to inspect, a staff to be reminded of who was in charge, cash bonuses to be distributed.

"I think it's time we move more to the tea farm," Quang said.

"Take the American collection and the ones from Vienna over there. You can judge which other crates should go."

"Yes, Madame," Liu Hui said. "There is more space, and we've improved the storage climate." Artworks such as these needed a cool and dry environment.

"Very good," Quang said.

By now, Zhang Wei had the two paintings, a Monet and a Corot, snug in the larger of the two suitcases. This time, a second was not needed. All would fit back in the Primus 150, and they'd soon be off. Over time, the other crates would be shipped by the other airplane, the Shaanxi Y-8 transport. Zhang Wei enjoyed some of those flights, a plane full of many kinds of crates. For today, however, they'd jet their way back to Shanghai, taking an overnight rest stop in Lanzhou, a Yellow River gateway to China's heartland.

Outside the inner room, back out in the lower lobby, Quang thanked the supervisor of the Urumqi facility.

"We are all very pleased with the situation," she said. "Mr. Liu Hui will remain in Urumqi for a few days. He'll treat you well."

"Yes Madame Quang," the supervisor said. "There's a lot of work to do."

Quang and Zhang Wei were driven back to the airport, where the Primus 150 had been refueled and the pilot refreshed. Soon the sleek white aircraft was off the tarmac, circling Urumqi. Quang looked down at the desert city, its mountains and oases, a city of 3.5 million mixed inhabitants. She'd have some Gold Tea and think about how different the two China's were, Urumqi in the west, and in the east, Shanghai, city of glitter, wealth, skyscrapers and mischief.

Rising in altitude, the Primus 150 navigated the desert winds. At such times, Quang felt that she was doing the same. As China spread its influence around the world, there was great competition at home, a hothouse of rivalry, headwinds of another kind. To get to the top, above the turbulence, Quang had to rise above her chief rival, Omni Art Global. It was not only a wing of the Party, but a branch of the People's Liberation Army. It had PLA budgets. Not least, it followed a Party agenda and was headed by Madame Soong Wei, the wife of a former general secretary.

They were two dragon ladies, Quang often conceded, but only one of them had a family secret. And that was Quang's family secret, which for now she hid from brightness, biding time.

AS THE PRIMUS 150 began to breach the horizon, leaving Urumqi behind, a bomb exploded in the People's Square. It was a blast outside the Party building, shattering some of its façade. Fifteen minutes later, another blast took place at the edge of the Grand Bazaar, marring the façade of a trading company. There, when the smoke had cleared, no one was injured. Amid the building shards and black soot, the company sign hung down, Omni Art Global.

4

Washington D.C.

GRACE HO ARRIVED at Peale's house at 8 p.m. on a Tuesday, about a week after the restaurant meeting. Castelli had worked out all the official arrangements. He had also recommended, to each privately, that a second more informal meeting, a kind of war room over coffee, might help them iron out some wrinkles, personal or philosophical, in their joint operation—to become of "one mind," as he put it, at least as much as possible.

She parked, paced to the door and rang the bell. Peale's wife, Priscilla, answered.

"You're right on time," she said.

"Easy to find," said Ho.

It was not an awkward first encounter, but naturally Priscilla sized up her husband's new partner, as did Ho with what Peale had called "the wife."

Peale came from the kitchen, expecting to keep the session a bit formal. "Miss Ho, thanks for coming out. This will just take an hour or so."

"Be careful," Priscilla said, "He operates on Julian Time."

"Julian Calendar," Peale said. "Foundation of Western civilization. By the way Grace"—he surrendered to a more personal touch—"that reminds me, if we get as far as China, do they do everything on the Western calendar, or use the lunar calendar?"

"Western on all the important things, politics, business, military," she said. "There's still the zodiac, though. That folk tradition remains strong."

"You mean like, what's your sign?"

Priscilla said, "He used that line to pick up girls in the Navy."

"It worked," Peale said.

Ho didn't smile, which Peale noticed. She said, "Well, if you want to get personal, I go by the Rat, but I have my best energy, do my best work, when the Goat is rising in the Monkey."

With relief, Peale caught a glimmer of his partner's sense of humor, since there was little else he knew about her. Chinese people were generally reserved, in his estimation, and despite Ho being evidence of that dictum, she might have a hidden wit. As he learned in Afghanistan, wisecracks, sarcasm, and jokes had gotten American GIs through a lot in the past century.

Priscilla didn't often see her husband in a business setting, but the new job, and the night's encounter, made her look at him in a different light than usual. He didn't have the distinctive looks of even a movie extra, but there was something. He was a bit above average height, his features ordinary, excepting for his slightly crooked smile. His furrowed brow could be delightfully sinister. His unruly brown hair would not keep a part. Above his erect bearing were his wide shoulders, like a coat hanger, and his cold-weather limp was almost imperceptible. Known only to Priscilla, he had clusters of welts and

scars on his abdomen and thigh. "Mementos from Afghanistan," he
called them.

Priscilla had just put on some coffee, so she invited Ho to see
the vista out the back of their house, since a full moon was rising.
The Chesapeake Bay met the mainland like a hand with a thousand
crooked fingers, and one of them was an inlet off the back yard. The
moon was reflecting in the darkening water. Here and there little
white boats wafted on other people's docks around the shore.

"Enchanting," Ho said. She was reluctant to invite anyone to her
condominium near the Virginia freeway.

Peale headed in the other direction for a moment, catching some
cool air on the front porch, letting them have woman-time. A glow
was over darkening Annapolis, and its spires—the capital, a church,
the Naval Academy dome—caught some of the light. The small city
was one of the brains of the Navy, while one hundred fifty miles
south, in Norfolk, Virginia, was the brawn. Peale had shipped and
flown out of there a few times. All around Washington was that mix
of civilian and military, government and business, sometimes called
the "military industrial complex," other times the "beltway bandits."
He had happily served his country, as did Ho in the Marines, best
he knew. Now he was content to be independent, but could only
guess at Ho's outlook.

"Coffee's ready," Priscilla said.

Peale and Ho got a cupful in the kitchen and went to a front
room with its low table and two soft chairs, one beige the other
black. Ho chose the latter, making her muted yellow coat a kind
of accent in a sea of black, the color also of her slacks, hair, and
eyes. Several folders lays on the table, one bulked up with passports
and other items. Normally, such projects as theirs would have been
hatched in a secure military facility. Now it was Peale's living room,
typical of a HUMINT operation, a throwback to the old days of

face-to-face talks and shredded documents, which could not be leaked, hacked, or tracked electronically.

Each was given a brief bio of the other that offered some basics. Neither had a traditional rank in the military. They had served as "specialists."

Her bio read: Ho, Grace. b. 1988. Parents: Emigrants, China. Marital Status: Single. Ed: University of Chicago (non-completion). Service: US Marine Corps. Career: USMC Intelligence Branch, China-US Trade/Security Task Force. Languages: English, Chinese, French. Current Status: Independent, Martial Arts Instructor, Visiting Lecturer (Chinese Language), Visiting Scholar Freer Museum. Intelligence Skill: A. Character: Reliable, intuitive.

And his: Peale, Julian, b. 1975. Parents: Naval family. Marital Status: Divorced, Re-Married. Ed: Naval Academy. Seals Training (early withdrawal). Service: Navy Intelligence, Afghanistan, D.C. Languages: English, some Russian. Career: Military service, Independent contractor, NYPD-FBI-Customs Task Force. Medici Studios NYC. Current: Independent. Intelligence Skill: A. Character: Reliable, creative.

It was good material to spark inter-service wisecracks between them, if they wanted, but the serious part was their "reliable" status. As a traveling pair, they were well suited to come off as authentic Sinophiles. He was indeed the doctoral researcher, she the language expert. For this job, those were also their *personas de guerre*, as Ho had called it.

"So, Julian, why did you sign on to this?" Ho asked, surprisingly blunt. "Neither of us is under any government command. No job to lose. Pay is nothing to speak of." And, as they both knew, they could quit anytime—though neither viewed one's own self as a quitter.

"I like working with Castelli," Peale said. And he hoped he'd like working with her. "I was in intelligence, and we like puzzles, especially solving them. A bit of family background also. My grand-father was a 'monuments man,' U.S. Army, recovering European art treasure from the Third Reich. But we had some mishaps in Afghanistan, and I'm not looking for another Purple Heart, be-lieve me."

The unexpected comment about his wounding in action strangely touched Ho, a first in the company of Peale. She knew her own self, rarely prone to emotion, though at times she juggled too many at once. "I respect that," she said. "You strike me as in tip top health."

"I try. Not getting any younger." This raised the issue of their age difference, nearly fifteen years. "And yourself? Any interesting motives? Obviously, your language skills will make all the difference, if we get to China."

"Well, like you, I have a few loyalties. I was given good training, and for my relative youth, quite a few interesting assignments."

Peale sensed a modest brag. Nothing wrong with that, except that it lacked detail. "But now independent?"

"Like yourself, as I understand."

"Can quit any time."

She nodded. "So, your wife lets you run off like this?"

Was that a curve ball? "She's used to me disappearing. Anyway, absence makes the heart fonder. And what about you?"

"Marriage on the horizon," she said. "Fiancé in the Foreign Service. He's American, a great guy. Scotch-German ancestry, which I still have to figure out."

To mellow the exchange, Ho decided to seek some common ground more appropriate to professional activities. Both she and Peale had circulating through the Free Museum on Asian art as researchers, so she probed what mutual bonds that might evoke. "What's going on at the Freer these days?"

"A lot of back ache," Peale said. "The library's got the hardest chairs."

"I mean with the Chinese curators. I see that it's a project endowed by several of China's state corporations. I've been told the curators come over from the China embassy looking for lost art from China."

"That and conservation, I think. It *is* a little strange."

Stranger things had happened in U.S. diplomacy, but this one was for the books, he suggested. Washington was trying to make amends for Western pillage of Chinese art in the past, and had allowed Beijing to finance a new wing on the Freer for the Chinese curators' work. On site once, Peale had joked that the Chinese largess should go for softer chairs for researchers—a joke that was not appreciated by the Freer staff.

"And just look at the Mall for the past two weeks," Peale said. "Most of the National Gallery was cleared out to make way for that traveling Beijing exhibition. 'Celestial Face of China.' Flags waving, glory to China." His point, he emphasized, was not that art from China was uninteresting, quite the opposite. It was beautiful. "It's the politics that's unusual, kind of a kowtow by the U.S."

They were still getting a grip on the soft power angle of all this, how China wanted to use the history of art, or the accumulation of art, to gain one more step up the global ladder.

"I suppose it's just like France has the Louvre, a worldwide brand name as well as a tourist draw," Ho said. "Or like blue and white Chinaware. It's everywhere, a global brand." Naturally, she was wondering about Peale's mastery of things Chinese, from the history to the art, if not the language. The topic covered three or four millennia, a few hundred emperors, maybe forty or fifty dynasties. Constant changing of address, lots of little wars. Names of personages constantly changed or multiplied.

"I'm getting there," Peale said, addressing her concern. "Knowing a few main dynasties well is as far as my brain takes me. I'm best on the Chinese painting. Not much interested in the dishware."

"Ahem," Ho said, a tiny glimmer of humor. "Ancient pottery, please. When you say 'Ming vase,' you have to do so with a little reverence. Otherwise, you'll offend half the curators in the world."

"Point taken," Peale said, noticing the dry humor that lurked behind her reticent surface. "I'll just say China nick knacks."

"Anyway," Ho said, "It is a valid distinction." She noted that during America's first world's fair, none of the Chinese art—being deemed craft—was put in the Fine Arts Pavilion. The only item was a portrait painting done by an American painter of the Dowager Empress Cixi, the last imperial ruler of China. She added, "Pronounced '*Zhee*.'"

Now that their paperwork was in order, Peale was thinking geography. He had spread a map on the small table.

"When I was in Afghanistan, there was a lot of in and out of western China, especially its main city, called Urumqi," Peale said. "That's also the shortest route from Europe, a fairly active trade route. The name is supposed to mean 'beautiful pasture,' but out in the desert, I don't know."

Ho said, "Back in imperial times they called that city *Tihwa*, which translates to 'To Enlighten Uncivilized People.'"

Quite the young historian, Peale realized, and wondered if she was showing off. Anyway, he still had visions of Afghanistan, and could probably see her point. "A lot of hell holes out there in the desert."

Between them, only Ho had been to China, though she was being mum, not to say mysterious, about that. If the trail took them there, their cover story fortunately had some fortuitous basis in fact. On the face of it, they were just two Sinophiles, lovers of Chinese art and culture, wide-eyed travelers and learners—and least of all American spies.

"I wonder about one thing," Peale said.

"Yes?"

"I wonder why much of this investigation isn't done by telephone, for example, calling around to Europe, well, probably not to China."

"I think they want us to get a sense of things, a little HUMINT rather than just hearsay. We might even find new things. New leads, right?"

"That seems to be the directive," Peale said.

On the road, Castelli was their contact, and when needed he would send their findings or requests up the ranks. Their flight was set for two days later.

And there's something she's *not* telling me, Peale thought.

5

Shanghai

THE SHANGHAI SKYLINE sparkled tall and spiky, its odd assortment of towering buildings a new icon for travel brochures and postcards. The U.S. trade delegation had been there for a day after spending three in Beijing, an event of worthy note. The U.S. Deputy Secretary of State for Cultural Affairs was one of its two top officials. Things had been quiet in the capital. That changed on the delegation's final ceremonial visit to Shanghai, their point of departure.

Many of the American business delegates had already left. The delegation also included a number of curators from major American museums with Asian collections, the Freer Museum in Washington included. They were given a tour, reminded often of the "Century of Humiliation," when the Imperial City lost much of its artistic treasure to the West. The guilt-ridden American curators listened, though always quick to note that as a goodwill gesture, curators from China were currently visiting American art museums to take stock.

"The Freer is an excellent example," one American emphasized. Others mentioned their museums as well, a true people-to-people, peace-making, America-to-China gesture, a reconciliation of a conflicted past, the time of China's first "open door" policy.

To add some diplomatic pomp, the Chinese gave a few top officials a Shanghai "cultural tour," first to a few historic sites, then to the great National Museum, the second largest repository of historic art after Beijing.

That's where the commotion began.

In the square outside the museum, more than a thousand protestors had gathered, seemingly with spontaneity, but surely organized by the Propaganda Ministry of the People's Republic. Mostly young, they were the generation educated by the Party, now willing to do its bidding—their education and jobs relying on a mutual pact.

There were shouts and chants, a kind of collective hysteria. The police, garbed in blue slacks and light blue tops, put up a good show of restraining the government-approved crowd. They let a few megaphones slip by. "Give us back our treasures," came the chant. Banners went up with the same words, two of the largest in English. The state media's cameras flashed. When the U.S. delegates were brought out of the museum, the chorus of resentment rose in volume, filling the warm air with a kind of frenzy.

At the entrance of the museum, the Chinese officials shepherding the U.S. delegates gave sincere apologies. Still, the way the limos were parked, the delegates were in the open air, with a clear view of the protest, for at least four minutes. Enough time for an impression. As the vehicles moved off, the crowd—still more conveniently—somehow broke through the police cordon. It snaked around the moving-out cars, which were now exposed to a half block of protestors and signs not twenty feet away.

"We have a very patriotic youth," a Chinese official said to the

U.S. Deputy Secretary inside their limo. "We've asked for good behavior always, but—"

"I understand completely," the deputy secretary said. He was in an Ivy League college during the Vietnam War protests. "It goes with youth." He, of course, knew well the history of Western intervention in China. All those "treasures," as the banners read. He could not deny it. He saw their point of view. He also knew that China's government, at that moment, was treating them to a bit of international street theater. Back in Washington, he would find that a picture of the limo and crowd had been front page on the *People's Daily*, China's largest official paper.

FROM HER TWELFTH-FLOOR office, with its grand window on Shanghai, Quang Daiyu could see the demonstration across the river.

"A paper tiger," she said to herself, turning back to her desk. It was set opposite the window in her spacious office. "Theater is not enough. I want to do things." If the Party cliques were not up to it, then she certainly was.

After all, this was modern Shanghai. First it had been the home of Chinese pirates and Western traders, then the home of Maoist radicals. She was only the latest accent.

Her office was spare. Its walls bore only two ornaments, a large elegant hanging scroll—a twelfth century Song Dynasty landscape by an early master—and over in a corner, a tall upright folding screen. Its design was one of blossoms, branches, and birds, a colorful creation of the Qing, China's last imperial dynasty. Back toward the office entrance, there was also a hallway and door that led to her apartment.

She had another small residential apartment amid a leafy street in Old Town Shanghai, a life that suited her self-image as a modern-day dowager. Not widowed, though, nor ever married. She imagined herself as a kind of dignified aristocrat of her own making. For a brief moment, the memories came back: a casual love affair long ago, a stillborn miscarriage, working with the old herbalist, closing her heart to a normal life. She became like a dowager—and because of this, she learned herbalist arts. She began her tea company, her Black and Gold, her experimental teas. The wizened old herbalist had also told her about another ancient practice; she called it "bronze" tea. It was a specialty of imperial household intrigues, grown in soil with cyanide: a poison tea. It was said to be uniquely tasty—and when imbibed in the course of a few days, it had the desired effect.

AFTER A FEW hours, Quang had made some progress in the piles of paperwork, a job that seemed never done. She sat back in her swivel chair and sighed. Her hands shook a little, but the thought of the Gold Tea gave her patience.

Her deputy Liu Hui was still in Urumqi, working on inventory and shipping. Her soldier, Zhang Wei, was at the Shanghai warehouses, checking up. On the desk before her lay documents, many of them lists. Lists of the artifacts to be shipped West, ceramics, jades, sundry items that would bring a good price. For her, the most important list, however, was of the artworks coming in, the paintings, some of the best in Europe and America, some of them China's lost ancient treasures.

Her mind was exhausted, though her spirt of ambition remained thrilled. It was time for a break, time for her mediations. She let her mind wander for a while. Then she stood and walked to the great screen, behind which stood another door. It led to her inner sanctum.

Quang was no mystic. She had no folk religion, and like the Marxist-Leninist-Maoist thought of the Party, she had no gods. Yet there was something in the Chinese soul that needed a center. For some it was the vague idea of the Celestial Heaven, a kind of fate that ruled the world. Maybe that was so. There must be fate. What her race had always needed, meanwhile, was a personage too, a Yellow Emperor, indeed a Mao. She instead had Empress Cixi.

Perhaps those visitations were a ghost. There were no apparitions, but they were very real. The manifestation was more than simply her knowledge of Empress Cixi's life, written in the empress's famous diary. It was also more than Cixi's stature as a ruler of China, the last Dowager Empress, on that throne for forty-seven years. The empress had a husband, son, nephew, and grandnephew all of whom became the emperor, but with a willful presence, nevertheless, Cixi had ruled over it all. More than all these, Empress Cixi was still present, at this hour, at least to Quang.

Empress Cixi was also a poet, a painter, using the brush. 'Qishu,' the 'wondrous brush.' That brush is what Quang, with her wide-ranging plans, figuratively held in her own hands, and it would be wondrous indeed.

Behind the screen, she opened the door, entering a darkened chamber. She flipped a switch. A soft light filled the room, which had a window darkened by shades. She lit an incense candle. To her left was a low, soft divan, which allowed her to repose in any way that suited her. A black rug with bold red and gold Chinese script lay under a small table. The walls were festooned with artworks. Some were permanent, others alternated as she pleased.

Quang opened the doors of a cabinet which held her diary and a small wooden box lined with silk, from which she took out the oracle stone. She held four thousand years in her hand—maybe the first Chinese writing. She made tea in an ancient cup and brought it with the diary and stone over to a small table in front of the divan. Once she arranged everything just so, she began to relax and focus her thoughts. On one wall was the first historic painting she ever obtained, a masterpiece on silk from the Tang Dynasty. While in Urumqi, she wanted to bring the American cache, the so-called Gardner Collection, here to her private sanctum. As a group, they held a significance for Quang.

The artifacts were owned by a Miss Gardner, a kind of American dowager, a woman whom Quang felt was her match, even her rival. Gardner was a wealthy American collector. She was part of the buying spree in China in those chaotic days at the turn of the century. Long after Gardner's death, some of her collection was stolen, and it had already been more than thirty years since that happened.

As a student in the United States, Quang visited the Gardner Museum in Boston, which was the woman's mansion and home. She saw the empty spaces of the lost items, stolen in 1990, and now famously called the "art heist of the century." An idea crystalized in her mind. Over the years, with her wealth, her cunning, and her art market connections, Quang scoured Europe for the artworks. She first located the one Chinese artifact among the Gardner cache, a Shang Dynasty bronze cup. Once she obtained the cup, the sellers offered more. She bought a painting or two. She continued until she had all thirteen of the stolen artworks. Money was no problem. In time it all become hers. Not everything to her taste, but a great symbol, a Western icon now in China's possession.

Of the paintings, she liked the Vermeer best. In Chinese art, it was the subtlety, what was left out, that conveyed the interior of the artist, even the ways of nature itself. The Vermeer had this, with its large open room, leaving a great deal of empty space, placing the figure in a corner, space and light doing much of the work. Just like one of the Wang Masters.

As she recalled this earlier quest, Quang looked about her inner room. Someday she might have all of the Gardner cache sent from Urumqi to her inner office, including the Shang Dynasty cup. Then should could have the cup at her side. She could drink her Gold Tea from the cup, as did royalty three thousand years in the past, evoking a hundred royal ghosts. For now, though, the infamous Gardner artworks were at least safely in China and that was enough.

Empress Cixi would be proud.

The Gold Tea was working. Her reverie was at a peak. Such mediations, like flights into a nether world, never helped Quang escape from the immediate pressures of her business. But they were always there as a respite, a haunting interlude. The room, and the Gold Tea, always sent her mind back.

She looked at the wall and remembered. She'd had her Harvard certificate framed, and there it hung. That was the time of China's second great "open door policy." China and the U.S. had been exchanging olive branches since the late 1970s, and a decade later, Quang was among the elite students sent to elite American schools. She went to Cambridge, Massachusetts. She studied at Harvard's Fogg Museum. The museum, back in the late 1800s, was America's first center of collecting Chinese art.

She was young and rebellious back then, despite her attendance at Party high schools and all the rest. And at Harvard, a veritable Sodom by Chinese standards, she smoked cigarettes, read Nietzsche, de Beauvoir, and Foucault, and bathed in illicit love.

Now she mused to herself that many people had family secrets, but probably only one. She had two, both going back years, but only one of them remained at the forefront of her mind. The other she had long buried. And though she could still see his face, she had managed to erase his name from her mind, as if they were oil and water, never to mix, though it took years to arrive at that satisfying place.

Yes, that face. He was a handsome young exchange student from Beijing who was now one of Shanghai's real estate moguls. Their Harvard fling, as the Americans say, recurred back in China, but ended in an alienation: her lost pregnancy, his courting another, then his marriage into a rising Shanghai family, encumbered with its elite status in the Party. It was a tumultuous political time as well. They went separate ways, though he had grudgingly assisted her in setting up a business; she would not agree if anyone called it blackmail. He owed her, and in China's new economy, there was room for both of them to rise in the increasingly private-sector ranks of Chinese society. She had gone utterly her own way, not looking back, compartmentalizing that part of her past from her future. After all, it was no longer love she sought, but wealth, because in China you could buy freedom and privilege.

She needed both to carry out her ambition. In America, she had gained the knowledge of Western condescension to China. As a carefree student, she didn't care. She almost agreed. But it did not take long for her Chinese blood to boil. New England had perpetuated the opening of China. She rambled the galleries and stacks of the Fogg Museum. She saw what was taken from the Middle Kingdom. She felt, finally, that the West was vile. It had not controlled its gorged appetite for Chinese treasures. Her ambition was to reverse that.

Quang reached for the oracle stone and held it erect in her hands. Her eyes closed, she concentrated, then let it fall gently to one side or another. Eyes open, the lines she saw first were the message to her from Empress Cixi. "You are to be me." That message came often. "You are to restore." It all made sense to Quang.

It was time to pick up her diary, where she began to write. She was putting down thoughts from her elevated frame of mind, above the mists. The thoughts came slowly, then swiftly . . . after a time the pen stilled.

She loved the naturalness of it all. Yet these were modern times. She often worked at her desk, with its computer and the Internet. Even there, she would jot in her diary, often leaving it in a drawer, when it should always be put back in the cabinet in the secret room. Through the computer, she spoke to the world. She wrote an anonymous blog called "The Ghost of Empress Cixi." She reminded her thousands of readers of what happened before: the life of Cixi and the loss of the art treasures from the Imperial Palace. And yet no one knew where or who Quang was.

Now she sat back on the divan, her meditation over. She looked at the art on her walls, especially the two Western paintings. They were copies, paintings done after the originals. They were both portraits of Empress Cixi.

During the ancient Tang Dynasty, the splendors of court life had become a common topic for court painters. They produced full length portraits of emperors and empresses sitting on thrones like cutouts pasted in place, excessively colorful and in a flat abstract format. In contrast, the two paintings of Empress Cixi on her wall reflected the style of two European artists ensconced in the Qing court. They were realistic works, using light and shadow—though the Empress refused to have the shadow side or her face dark, as European chiaroscuro often did.

Quang's portraits of the empress were actually replicas, but quite well done. After the tortuous journeys of the originals—neglected in storage in Taiwan and later grasped by the hands of European collectors—they both ended up as possessions of the Freer Museum in America. Quang believed that one day she would have both originals. She would bring Dowager Empress Cixi back to her homeland.

SHE LEFT HER inner room, emerged from behind the screen, and went to her desk, getting back to work, plotting ways to outsmart her rival, Omni Art Global, Madame Soong Wei, who was flaunting her privilege as the wife of the former top leader of China.

A new man now ruled the country, her uncle, Ren Jinuah, supreme chairman of China. No one believed her yet, not even her uncle. For years now, she had worked out the genealogy, how her very own blood had gone back to the royal household of Empress Cixi. In the lineage, too, was a darker secret, a family secret much closer to home—much closer to the current ruler in Beijing.

London

UNDER A MOIST gray London sky, Peale and How set off for their appointment with Arthur Moore, a man of colorful background. Before joining MI6—British foreign intelligence—he apprenticed at the Asian department of the British Museum and worked on the Victoria and Albert Museum's Chinese collection. He still consulted for Christie's Auction House on Chinese art. To Peale and Ho's thinking, he fit the image of the unique British mix of art and espionage. But they were more curious about what leads Washington believed he could give them.

Puffing his pipe, Moore met them at the back entrance of his Georgian row house—as he had requested—and they took up their conversation in his living room. Its picture window looked over the Themes River and upriver towered a green-glass modern structure, like a layered cake, that housed the Secret Intelligence Services. Moor showed them the view. "MI6 used to work out of some old brick Victorians at Cambridge Circus, now look at it," he said.

He led them to chairs around a coffee table. Once all were seated, he got to the point.

"I was briefed by our cousins across the pond," he said. "I may have something for you. The main thing is a contact in Spain. There's also something I've heard of in Vienna. And then there's the big picture, what Washington wants to know about art smuggling from Europe to China."

"It's a big plate, I agree," Peale said. "Any details would be helpful."

"And I was informed that you don't want to work with Europol, which I understand. They watch this sort of thing, art theft, but it leaks. You don't want diplomatic backlash, correct?"

"That's correct," Peale said. "We may go into the China, so no ruffling of diplomatic feathers."

"Ah, yes. And Miss Ho, are you from the mainland?"

"My parents are, but I was born in Chicago."

Moore gave a pleasing nod, then settled back in his chair, gazing for a time at the great window. "So, stolen art going to China is our topic."

"Yes, sir," Ho said.

"With modern China, in terms of transfers of art, I would say the present is again mimicking the past," Moore said. He went down the historic precedents: Napoleon ravaged Italy, put its art in the Louvre. The Nazis tried to confiscate all the great art in France and Italy. The British Empire had its taint as well, the Elgin Marbles being just the tip of the iceberg. And when the Soviet Union fell, the collections of major East German museums were found still crated up from the 1940s in dusty basements of the Hermitage in former Leningrad.

"The lesson seems to be that when empires expand, they have a cultural agenda as well. They confiscate what's best in the world, and then try to transplant their own cultures on foreign soil. That's a bit simplistic, but you get my point. Now it seems China is in the same pursuit."

Ho shifted in her chair politely enough and said, "We've been told that you may know something about the stolen Vermeer painting, and that would be a great start."

Peale sat back, his arms akimbo, his legs crossed. He decided to concede to Ho the role of liaison with the MI6 storyteller—at least until he had his own pointed questions.

"Yes, of course," Moore said, "but before we get into details, I'd like to make one more point. Modern China since the communist revolution has tried to erase its entire past as a feudal aberration. The truth, however, is that the past keeps shining through. All of its dynasties, from the earliest Shang to the last one, the Qing, developed the Chinese as a picture people, and I say that thinking of their form of writing and then their invention of ink painting."

"So does that make them a picture people today, I mean under the People's Republic?" Ho said.

"I would say so," Moore said. "Pictures tell a story, and despite what China has become, it continues to tell a very ancient story. During all those dynasties, there were very strong Indian and Tibetan influence from the South, Turkic from the west. Then China's heartland was invaded by the Manchus and the Mongols in the north."

"And behind all this, the great myth of the Yellow Emperor," Ho offered.

"You've got my point exactly. The Chinese need an emperor, and they need a pictorial symbolism to bind all their diverse origins together. Well, I digress, but if you want the bigger picture, that's what is happening with art going to China, and with China representing its artistic tradition across the world. And why is China on this path? Again, history echoes. Halfway through the final Qing Dynasty, Emperor Qianlong gathered up all the art of China's history and brought it to Beijing. It was all there for the taking when Western countries arrived. That was the 'golden age' of China art collecting. The communist leaders, I believe, have not forgotten that. They want it back."

"Especially their historic paintings?" Ho said.

"I think that's true," Moore said. "After all, Confucius himself said, 'I take my recreation in the arts.' Calligraphy and ink painting were personal expression, a sign of nobility. Calligraphy evolved into a distinctive kind of Chinese painting called 'shuimo,' 'water and ink.' The Chinese say, 'In ink there are all the colors.' Even Mao Zedong, the scourge of ancient tradition, went up on a scaffolding in the Great Hall of the People after the Revolution and painted a big calligraphic poem on a traditional landscape mural, just as if he were in an ancient imperial household."

Moore made a few spontaneous motions with his arm. "Yes, all the emperors showed off like this," he said. "A blossom in one stroke, a bamboo shoot by a quick dab of the brush." He said that it was Abstract Expression before its time, the earliest form of Action Painting. Both where modernist innovations in New York in the 1950s.

"Quite different from Western realism," Ho said.

"They read a landscape very differently. There's no linear perspective. It's what we call a bird's eye view, seeing 'far and near' all on the same plane."

"Very different from the stolen Vermeer," Ho said, still playing a friendly verbal tennis with British scholar.

Moore chuckled, his eyes now bright. "And so we return to our subject. My sources in MI6 have confirmed what you say about the stolen Vermeer. Yes, its trail turned up in Spain. I have someone you can visit in Madrid. Yes, probably on its way to China. The name Silk Road Company also comes up. Worth checking out."

"Okay," Peale said. Now we're talking, he thought.

Moore then pointed their attention to something called Omni Art Global, a business branch of the People's Liberation Army. The PLA had now entered China's business sector with its own corporations for real estate, investment, manufacture, arms sales and even womenswear.

"It has become a major player in the international art market, especially in Europe," Moore said. "It's rivaling the great auction houses of the West, outmaneuvering some of the West's top art dealers. Most interesting, a Madame Soong Wei, the wife of a previous general secretary, is head of Omni Art Global. So you see, Party connections, family connections, run deep."

"That would be like the U.S. Defense Department running an art business," Peale said.

Ho said, "And a former First Lady running it for the Defense Department."

"That's about right," Moore said.

"Do you think the Omni group was involved in the Vermeer sale?" Peale asked.

"I don't know, but it's a trail worth following along with these others. Here in Europe, quite a few private collections have been on the move, doubtless with Chinese buyers, some with this Omni group, others with anonymous fronts. Quite a few Chinese students are over here. They come with a warning label, I've been told. Chinese government scouts of sorts."

Peale said, "And I understand there's been some thefts."

"Oh, yes," Moore said. He detailed the break-ins at the Oxford museum, a private London gallery, and a few others. In one case, a rare oracle stone was swiped. "One of the few remnants in the world with the earliest Chinese script."

"I'm curious about the Vienna case," Peale said. "Is there much detail?"

It was a small notable collection of paintings. "It had one very valuable Chinese work, I understand. Quiet a rare one. Known as *Celestial Mountains, Loyal River.* A Song Dynasty masterpiece. An original, 'from the hand of,' said to come from an emperor's inner sanctum."

"That is rare," Ho said. "Not a copy?" That was common with older works.

"Original," Moore said. "There was no shame in copies, but it does set our two art worlds apart, Chinese and Western. To copy in the 'style of Rembrandt,' 'school of Rembrandt,' is far below an original. For long in China, however, copying the 'school of Wang,' say, was no demerit."

That, in turn, had created much debate on authenticity in China's historical paintings.

"Today, China has thousands of these copies, the West, too. But for Beijing's purposes, it's all presented as valuable ancient art. All originals. A masterstroke of Communist Party marketing." Moore abruptly stifled an old man's yawn and said, "I could use a stretch." He rose from his chair, hunching slightly, then stood. "I used to be ramrod straight."

Peale and Ho did likewise. Their minds were full, and they declined another offer of tea.

Moore had padded over to the room's large window, with its view down on the street and over the Thames River. "Uh-huh," he said, pulling the lace curtain slightly aside. "As I might have thought. There's someone down there watching us."

Peale And Ho moved over next to Moore and set their gazes on the street below.

"See that gray car?" Moore said. "There's a Chinese man and woman in the front seats. They pulled up after you arrived, I believe. There's teams of them around London. They watch the collectors, the experts. They're less conspicuous at the museums, of course. Crowds everywhere."

"And they're watching you?" Peale asked.

"They do time to time. I do get a lot of visitors, curators, players with interests like mine." He pivoted slightly and nodded in another direction. "Now over there, do you see that white Peugeot? That's Europol if I'm not mistaken."

"Europol?" Ho said.

"As I mentioned, there's been some art thefts around London, so we've got some cat and mouse going on, I believe."

"Geeze," Peale said, "it's getting pretty crowded around here." Not what he had expected.

"Nothing to worry about."

"How would they know to follow us?" Ho asked. At that moment, the woman in the car got out, went to the trunk in the back, then after a minute returned to the front and got back inside. Ho was no clothes horse, but she noticed the cut of the woman's dress, the sleeves on the slim blouse, and the color.

"They probably don't," said Moore. "They're on their circuit. After a while, they'll leave. They go around, and Europol goes around watching them. They'll leave in a while, then we'll call a taxi and you can go. Just be yourselves. After this, go to those museums I've mentioned. Play the tourist-scholar role you've been assigned."

They sat down again, and Peale had one more topic he wanted to cover. He explained to Moore a theory that had been floated around the state department's cultural division. "The theory is that

China has a long term plan to buy up Western art, very long-term. Something like China becoming the 'museum of the world,' where you'd have to go to Beijing to see the *Mona Lisa* or Gainsborough's *Blue Boy*, for instance. What do you think?"

"China is thinking very long term," Moore agreed. "It's in all the news. First China 2025, then China 2049."

Ho said, "Even the Politburo mentions the Yellow Emperor time to time."

"Back to a mythical age," Moore said. "You can't get more long term than that."

It was time to finish up. Moore gave them the contact in Spain, a man named Rico Molina, a reliable source in Moore's ill-defined intelligence network.

"I will inform him of your visit," Moore said. "He will give you what he knows about the Vermeer and the black market in that part of the world. I suspect he may know more about the Austrian sale."

BY NOW, THE two suspicious cars down on the street had left. Peale and Ho exited by the back entrance, got a taxi, and planned to spend the rest of the day in London. The next morning they would head for Spain. For now it was off to the British Museum, with its venerable collection of Asian art. The taxi dropped them in London's vast museum sector, where they'd also get a feel for the Chinese presence in England's capital city. Walking about, they swiveled their heads like sightseers.

"Bolo," Peale said. It meant "be on the lookout." He wanted to see if it made Ho laugh. Well, alas, her Madonna face retained its Olympian calm, but at least their rapport had been loosening up.

There was nothing new about fog in England, but there certainly was about Chinese. Tourists from the East were everywhere. Much as in Washington, there were busloads. However, when Peale and

Ho emerged from the British Museum nearly two hours later, the scene outdoors had bulked up considerably.

Across from the museum complex was a park with a fountain, and on the circling road a great line of tourist buses were jostling to park, pull away. It was a traffic jam. Large groups of Chinese were milling around, loading or waiting. Not twenty feet from the tourists, in the park, two different groups of protestors were shouting at the milling crowds.

It took Peale and Ho a long instant to figure out what was going on. The protest signs soon told them. One group, which was made up of what looked like working class Brits, some wives and even two strollers with infants, were shouting "China go home." The signs said the same. Another read "Jobs for England" and another had a picture of China's leader, Ren Jinuah, with a red circle and crossbar over his face.

"Let's go over," Ho said, moving before Peale could respond.

"Hold on . . ." he said to no effect, so he followed in her steps.

Amid the throng, some Chinese tourists were yelling back at protestors holding up a big sign saying "Free Tibet." A young woman, a kind of London hipster, was raising it up and down. Other young people, including what looked like young Tibetans, bright scarves giving the clue, were jostling similar signs. As Peale and Ho got close in, the melee began.

Some of the men among the knots of tourists began to grab at the signs. To Peale, they looked like trained operatives, probably Chinese government staff traveling with the European tour. Two of them had a hold of the Tibet sign. They began tearing apart its flimsy cardboard. A woman began to hit them with a smaller sign. More Chinese joined the ruckus. The bus drivers had panicked and were running around, telling the tourists to get in the buses, or at least leave the area.

A fight had broken out at the other protest group over the sign that displayed the image of China's leader. Unfortunately for the aggressing tourists, they'd picked a fight with some John Bulls, blue collar Englishmen who'd seen a few pub or football brawls in their time. The push turned to punches.

As one Chinese man lunged into the scrum, he jostled aside a stroller, and with its infant, it began to roll toward the fountain. Ho was off her mark, and reached it before anything untoward happened. Now she didn't like the guy, tourist or whatever, so she went over, grabbed him by the collar, and kicked him behind the knee, an easy move to bring someone down. It did not stop the show. The rumble continued, with the bus drivers, and now two Bobbies in black and white, separating the groups. The police tried to direct the crowd, which was meandering like a Chinese dragon in a parade.

Peale had to drag Ho away. "Nice undercover work," he said. "Are you trying to screw things up? That's none of our business." Of course, saving babies was good, but she was getting too wound up.

"Just a nice day at the museum," she said.

That was a bit cavalier for Peale.

As the crowd moved away, a man and a woman who looked vaguely familiar—the woman, her dress, color and blouse—stood their ground. They were glaring at Peale and Ho. The man held a camera, and he began to take pictures of them. Ho was wound up. She was not in the mood for the uninvited attention. "Wait here," she said.

"Don't—" But Peale watched her stride briskly over to the two.

In commanding Chinese she said, "It's not polite to take other people in your pictures." She raised a hand, "You must always ask."

"This is free country," the man said.

Words straight out of the handbook, Ho mused. "Give me that," she said.

Oh boy, Peale thought, looking around nervously.

She reached for the camera, taking it in her hand. To her surprise, the man made a martial arts move. She pushed his arm outward, pulled him forward, and gave him a knee punch—second in a day and sufficient to bring him to a crouch. Then she put his arm in a painful lock.

"Now give it to me," Ho said, grasping up the camera. The strap gagged the man's neck, but she held on, found the camera's slot for the tiny hard disc, and removed it. She let the camera fall back. "You can take more photos. You won't need these." The whole thing had blended into the chaos, and no one seemed to notice. The man swore at her, picked up and left, scowling over his shoulder.

On her return, Peale said, "You're not going to listen to reason are you." He was beginning to wonder who was in charge, since that had not been spelled out explicitly. Obviously, their little team had a power vacuum, or was it the eye of a hurricane. As he was finishing his reprimand, he caught a glimpse of the white Peugeot. Then he saw two men in dark police uniforms approaching them. "Oh God, what's this."

Ho said, "Looks like Europol."

That was exactly how they introduced themselves, friendly enough. "We have been alerted by the FBI of your visit to London. Could we be of any assistance?"

Peale and Ho put on Stoical expressions, but both were thinking, *FBI! Whose been leaking from Washington?*

Peale alone was thinking, *Hargrave?*—the name Castelli had mentioned. Peale took the initiative and said, "Well, thank you for checking in. We're actually doing fine." He shot a glance at Ho, then said, "You can report that back—to whomever." Probably to Hargrave, he presumed.

The lead man gave a small salute from his cap, and they walked off.

"Damn, what's going on?" Peale said. "I'm going to call Castelli before this gets any more complicated."

Ho had her theories, but kept them to herself.

Europe

PEALE'S CALL TO Washington was not reassuring. Castelli took the information and suggested that, indeed, the FBI apparently was trying to keep a hand in this. "Maybe even scuttle it, keep it to themselves," he said. "Some of them are thick with Europol."

Both Castelli and Peale had worked with the FBI and held up the agency in mild awe. They also knew how turf minded it could be—especially with a decades-old case that had grown cold and tarnished reputations.

"Someone's leaked," Castelli said. "Probably this Hargrave fellow. He worked with Europol back in the day. I was hoping this inter-agency crap wouldn't come up. I'll look into it and keep you informed. You're good. We're cleared at the top. Just keep your eyes on the prize."

Which Peale and Ho tried to do, strangely creating the flicker of an us-against-them bond between them. The next morning they flew into Madrid. During the flight, they agreed that a trip to Vienna might turn up more. From the airport they taxied downtown. The city's French and Baroque architecture contrasted with its steel and glass humdrum business districts and neighborhoods of red tiled roofs. Their contact was in the Huertes Quarter, not far from the city center. Tucked between something baroque on one side, and a four-story block of offices on the other, they found the address. It was a low-roofed storefront bearing the sign Madrid Exchange.

Peale was a little surprised. Their liaison was Rico de Molina by name, but Chinese by race. "My parents are from Hong Kong, a trading family," he said. "I sometimes use my wife's family name. Good for business, yes?"

Inside, the shop and office showed nothing of the owner's art interest. A spare square room. Files on the wall. A cluttered desk. Wooden furniture and some molding with Spanish flourishes. After pleasantries, they commenced their conclave.

"The economy is very poor—but there's always a bright side," Rico explained with a furtive look. "You have an active black market. Customs are very lax now. Old Franco's time very strict, but now a smuggler's paradise, no? We have a Chinatown with many helpful connections, you know, with China."

Peale said, "Our mutual friends tell me you've heard something about a particular painting, a Vermeer painting, on the market here. Seems to have headed for China. There's also been a sale of art in Vienna, China related."

Rico invited them to sit down. "Here is what I know." In his rounded English, he spoke of his own networks in Spain. He had heard of the Vienna sale, since it had been shopped around, and he was not surprised if it found a Chinese buyer. He was more specific on the Vermeer painting, having heard that someone had been trying to sell it back to the Americans, but were brushed off.

"So, yes," Rico said, "what I've heard is that the Vermeer found a Chinese buyer." The sale price was high, and that's why the news was on the grapevine.

"Where did it go from here?" Ho asked.

"I would imagine through Eastern Europe. That's the pipeline. Kind of a straight shot. Easy customs. Eastern Europe to Central Asia, then you're into China."

"By what means?"

"Airplane. Customs is very casual, especially with a little exchange of money." Rico's eyes seemed to twinkle.

Peale said, "In Madrid, have you ever heard of the Silk Road Company in terms of art smuggling?"

"That doesn't sound familiar, but I'd have to check. There are two Silk Road Restaurants in Chinatown, now that you mention it. If you want to eat out, in my opinion, the best Chinese restaurant is the Empress Cixi."

Ho said, "You mean Cixi, the last Dowager Empress?"

"That's right," Rico said. "There's even a ghost story, at least among the mainland Chinese over here. 'The Ghost of Empress Cixi.' Come to think of it, some of the art traders, if I recall, sometimes say 'Empress Cixi wants her art back.'"

Ho knew that at the end of Cixi's reign hordes of art was plundered from Beijing. So did Peale, who now looked puzzled.

"Sort of a joke, I guess," Rico said. "You hear it every once in a while, mostly 'ghost of Cixi.' Some Chinese are superstitious, you know. Uh, let me look up if there's a Silk Road in Madrid." Rico went to a bookshelf, pulled out a thick phone directory, and flipped the pages. "There is a Silk Road Company."

Peale looked at Ho, who shrugged. "We could have a look," he said.

Ho asked for the address.

"Not too far," Rico said. "I can take you over. Taxi is quick."

From the shop entrance, they walked a few blocks to a main road at a square with a few trees and a statue. Their taxi wove around it and caught a fast moving avenue. A mile later they were at the address.

"Wait here," Peale said. "I'll take a look." The two-story stone building, a narrow slice of frontage amid brick residential flats, had a brass plaque: Silk Road Co. Underneath was a large Chinese calligraphic character. Peale rang a buzzer. A minute passed. He tried again. Nobody answered, so he returned to the cab and said to Ho, "Come see this."

At the brass sign, Ho said, "A Chinese character. Fenghuang Zu. That's Chinese for Phoenix Group."

That was new, another lead perhaps. Ho and Peale stood there for a minute, looking into the windows. Nothing could be seen in the dimness behind the glass.

"I say we've found something," Peale said. "Silk Road is somehow the Phoenix Group. Which happens to be written in Chinese." He was already thinking of Vienna, the Shönberg collection, its own kind of red flag, as Moore said back in London. "Hopefully more in Vienna," Peale said.

Peale paused for a moment, thinking that he'd better probe one more thing. "Rico, is Europol poking around on this art stuff, the Vermeer in particular?"

"Oh yes, they and the European art police. They're not happy about some of these things. I mean so many dead ends. In my business, of course, I keep an eye out. We avoid getting on their radar." Again, that furtive look crossed his face.

Back at Rico's office, they thanked him and slipped him some euros. They said they'd stay in touch if necessary. Their hotel was close to the great circle with fountains and a statue, a point of Spanish pride, the Plaza de Colón. A marble statue of Christopher Columbus, arms outstretched, towered over the plaza.

During their downtime, and as they navigated the mismatch in time zones, Peale used his SAT phone to get through to Washington. He passed on to Castelli their clues so far: Silk Road Company and Phoenix Group, both out of China. He also conveyed the information on Empress Cixi, or Dowager Empress Cixi, for what it was worth.

"Yes, Empress Cixi, spelled C-I-X-I," he said to Castelli. "Your people should be able to find how it's spelled in Chinese." Just as they should for Silk Road and Phoenix Group.

Then Peale voiced his concerns again about the FBI's agenda, and whether that was going to gum up the works. "I mean, no objections to them doing their job, but the whole idea here is to get around all that."

"Yeah, yeah," Castelli said. "The guy I mentioned, Hargrave, is lobbying hard to get in on this. For now we're compartmented off from that, but it's hard to put a damper on what they do with Europol. We have the ear of the higher ups, so proceed as planned. I'll worry about that back here." For long, the FBI had solo agents in the main U.S. embassies in foreign countries—including the one in Beijing—but they were limited to liaison roles: Being in embassies, they finally came under the state department. But still . . .

Somewhat reassured, Peale then explained the trail to Vienna and asked for flights to be booked for them the following day. The next morning it was a go. Though uncertain of their time abroad, both had packed light.

Peale had stowed his trousers, two shades of gray. They kept a reasonable crease—in case he had tea with Queen. He had long sleeve button shirts, synthetic thermal underwear, and dark leather shoes. They had a shine, but also metal shanks and thick gripping soles. He'd considered taking his brown leather fight jacket, then chose a leather jacket more in the cut of a blazer. It was a wardrobe for diplomacy and for action if need. Something between tourist and professor—just right.

"Nice duds," Ho said in the hotel lobby, where they checked out. "A lady's reputation rests on her companion's dress."

Peale looked her up and down. "Not bad yourself." Her travel gear had leaned toward dark cotton slacks and khaki blouses. Her shoes looked like dress, but were a runner's footwear. Ho hoisted her black travel case and said, "Let's go."

At the airport, as elsewhere in Europe, large groups of Chinese were coming and going. "I wonder how many have Western art treasures in their suitcases," Peale said.

WITH ONLY THEIR carry-on, Peale and Ho were quickly through the Vienna airport, similar to others in modern Europe—a geometric glass and steel structure in the International Style, efficient and impersonal. A taxi carried them into a section of the city that was far more baroque than even old-world Madrid. They were refreshed by the cool air of the late Vienna spring, lifting some of their weariness from odd travel hours—but especially from waiting in airports. It had been less than two weeks since they hatched the plot at the Chinese Restaurant in Northern Virginia.

Checked into the hotel and brushed up, they set out to meet a man named Tobias Muller, someone Castelli had tracked down. He was a colleague of Count Shönberg and an art dealer. Castelli had made the appointment. Muller had a very nice art gallery near an ornate plaza in Vienna. When they arrived and entered, a fresh-faced young woman greeted them. She seemed unaware of the arrangement.

"He's not here today," she said.

"Do you know where we can find him?" Peale asked.

"He may be home. Um, I think he said he was visiting an associate out of town, but I'm not sure."

"Do you have a home address?"

She looked worried but gave a contrived smile. "I'm sorry, but I don't think I can provide that without his permission."

Peale was stymied, not wanting to be too forceful and close off a second chance to find Muller at his business address. "Well, thank you." He did not offer a business card, not having one, and Ho played along with a gracious smile. They walked away and around the corner shared their suspicions.

"He's avoiding us," Ho said. "Someone talked to him."

"Leak from Washington," Peale said. "That damn FBI thing, probably."

They decided to walk the area to see how they might monitor the place and then found their hotel. The rest of the day, which included a tag-team observation from street corners or cafes, passed in frustration. At one point, Ho offered to get Peale some coffee, asking what he wanted with it. He said, "A cup would be nice." This managed to elicit almost a laugh on her Stoic face, which he was growing fond of, in an avuncular sort of way.

They continued in the morning, keeping in touch with their SAT phones. Eventually, over a morning coffee and crisp Austrian croissant, Ho spotted Muller arriving at the gallery. Quick to her phone she said, "He's here."

Peale walked the four blocks at a brisk pace, met up with Ho and they approached the gallery door. The sign said closed, but a turn of knob let them in. Muller was behind a counter, his back turned and he swung around, surprise on his face.

"Herr Muller?" Peale asked, revealing that he was probably an American.

"And who are you?" Muller said in heavily accented English, somewhat ingenuously. "I'm sorry we are closed."

Muller was a short, dapper, engaging figure. Peale sized him up, picturing him as a cog in the well-oiled machine of the European art market. Most important, as a confidant of Count Shönberg, Muller had the man's inside story.

"We had an appointment yesterday, and I was hoping we could pick up where that left off."

Muller stared at them. Neither Peale nor Ho could read his mind, but sensed that he felt cornered and was challenged to come up with excuses—or throw them out.

"It's very important that we speak to you," Ho said. "We need your help."

The man stayed quiet for a while, moved a few things around on the counter as his shoulders seemed to slump. He looked up and said, "I was hoping to not get involved."

Peale wondered why, so he asked, "Is there some trouble surrounding the Count Shönberg situation? We want to be sensitive to that." Ho was nodding.

"Come in," Muller said. "It's not that bad, I suppose."

Given the fact that an art spook like Moore in London had heard about the Shönberg sale, Peale and Ho surmised that there must be buzz in Austrian circles as well. As they would soon learn, art dealers in Austria were in a kind of cautious lock down because of some high profile art thefts and the resulting media headlines. In other cases, taxes were owed, and tax authorities had become far more vigilant.

"Europol?' Peale asked.

"Not directly for me, but some stirring up."

Pealed shot Ho a look and they both thought *FBI*!

In a reassuring manner, Peale tried to explain that they had no government capacity. They were working as independent investigators. Not insurance. Not taxes. And finally, with concerns far from Vienna.

"Yes, yes," Muller said. "A Mr. Castelli had assured me of that."

Castelli had represented them as a research firm doing confidential work for clients. Muller obviously had second thoughts after Castelli got through, Peale presumed. And he probably hoped that if he was gone on the appointment day, that would be the end of it.

"Please sit down," Muller said. "Perhaps I can help, but I'm not sure just how." The Austrian art dealer seemed a bit nervous. "I must say, the call from Mr. Castelli was a surprise." Now he wished he'd wriggled out of that from the start.

Peale concealed his impatience. He needed to play this persuasively. "But you had agreed to meet us."

"Reluctantly," Muller said with retreat in his eyes. "Isn't there some other way—"

"Herr Muller, this is the best way," Ho said, her face strangely alight.

Peale noticed the charm offensive. So far, this was not her usual modus operandi.

Muller sighed and looked around. Then he began, "The count was very proud of his collection. To his knowledge, the works had never been stolen by past royalty. No taint during the Nazi confiscations of art. It was 'pure,' long family ownership." But times had changed, he went on. "The children wanted the money. It was a quick sale, no publicity." He smiled. "Probably no taxes. He sold the collection, then suddenly passed away. Last time I saw him, he was in good health. Anyway, the Chinese got his collection free and clear."

"Chinese?" Peale asked.

"Yes, a Swiss and a Chinese woman, agents for Silk Road Company." They were sitting down by Muller's desk, and he reached into a drawer to take out some papers. "I have a list of the Shönberg collection. Classics from Europe, but this one is of particular interest." He pointed to the single Chinese artwork on the list. "It's quite rare, quite valuable, I would think."

Ho knew the work by name. Peale was still learning.

Ho said, "*Celestial Mountains, Loyal River.* Eleventh century, Song Dynasty. Master Guo Xi. Famous court painter, early theorist."

At this point, Muller shuffled through the stack. "There's some other things here. The count's wife gave me these." He held out a flimsy sheet of paper, a kind of full-sized receipt of some kind. Along with that, he passed over a business card that said Silk Road Co. printed in black, then with a golden Chinese character below.

"May I see that?" Ho said. "This is the same as in Madrid. This gold calligraphy. Phoenix Group."

"And there's this shipping document," Muller said, pointing at the large receipt. "I think that's what it is."

Peale looked at what seemed to be a bill of lading.

Muller said, "It looks like they want someone to pay an outstanding bill. Not a whole lot, a hundred American dollars or so."

"And his wife found this?" Peale asked.

"She's been distraught recently, so I think she's just piled a whole lot of things together. She gave it to me in case there was anything important."

Peale could see that the outstanding bill listed the number of boxes, weight, date, and an overdue fee. It said Vienna, then some other locations. Otherwise, it was in German, so he asked Muller to interpret.

"The route, it says here," Muller pointed, "starts in Vienna, then Budapest, Hungry, and then Urumqi, China."

"Son of a gun, Urumqi," Peale said. He looked at Ho. He knew it from his time in Afghanistan. It was a rising industrial town, developing commerce with Central Asia and Eastern Europe. In fact, they used to say its middle name had always been "business" since it was an ancient stop on the Silk Road. Peale thought for a few moments. Did the Shönberg Collection go to Urumqi, the far reaches of western China?

"And I wonder . . ." Peale and Ho said at the same time. They paused a beat, and Ho said, "I wonder if the Vermeer followed this route. And the names, Silk Road Company, Phoenix Group, Urumqi . . ." She trailed off, and they said no more.

Peale asked, "Have you heard the name Omni Art Global, a Chinese firm?"

Muller cleared his throat and explained that Chinese buyers in his part of the world were both above the surface and below. "Omni Art Global is fairly prominent above, public trading. Active at auctions, I've heard. It's noticed in Europe because, oddly enough, it's part of China's PLA, their military. That's why it seems to have so much money. Of course you never know. There are quite a few Chinese buyers, some with agents in France, England, and obviously Switzerland, where you have the banks. Then again, a lot of it's nameless. Auction purchases are often anonymous."

He explained that for shipping luxury goods, like fine art, in and out of countries, there's always a desire to skirt customs. For a place like China, the best way is to hop through small countries.

"Places like Georgia, which does a lot of trade with China," he said. After a nervous paused, he said, "I would be grateful if you don't get me involved beyond this. Well, I'm in business, you know."

"Just between us," Peale said.

Ho crossed her heart, which puzzled Muller, but they all parted amicably.

On the way to the hotel Peale said, "We'll give this to Castelli right away. He can put the intelligence shop on it. See if there's any logic to this." At the thought of Washington, he added, "I don't know, I hate this kind of confusion."

"With the FBI?"

"That and everything else."

"So China's a no-go?"

"Remains to be seen."

Don't chicken out on my now, she thought.

THEN THE CONFUSION only got worse. In their hotel lobby they were greeted by two men in dark uniforms marking them unmistakably as agents of Europol. News travels fast in such circles, Peale knew; an all-points bulletin system linked Europol, the FBI, and the national police across the European Union.

"This is getting to be a pain in the neck," he whispered to Ho. They kept their poker faces as the encounter began.

The men approached, and the lead officer said in accented English, "Is it Mr. Peale?"

"That would be me. What's up?"

The informality seemingly ruffled the officer. "Our friends in the United States asked that we assist you."

"Do you mean the FBI?"

"We work with all law enforcement," he said, evasively. "Is there something in Vienna we can help you with?"

"No, not in particular. If you are talking to the FBI in Washington, they'll speak for us, as you may already know." He wasn't going to play the state department card. And he was trying to stay away from specifics. Hopefully, the two cops were not aware of their visit to Muller. Nor was he going to flip out his passport as if he had to explain himself. "We're looking into a few things, that's all."

"Such as?" the Austrian cop said.

"As I said, you can check with Washington. We're also enjoying a trip to Europe. Beautiful country, Austria."

The officer looked askance at Ho, then back at Peale. He took out a business card and handed it over. "If you do need anything, let us know. And, if you find anything interesting, likewise."

Peale took it—part of his growing collection—and said, "I'll definitely keep that in mind." The officers must have been given his name by someone in Washington, and then did a computerized hotel search. He didn't know if this was intimidation, or if someone—the FBI's Hargrave came to mind—wanted to know what they were up to.

"We're flying out tomorrow, so we're good."

The officers left, and Peale and Ho headed for the elevator—time to put a call into Castelli. They hunkered down in Peale's room. The call reached Castelli in his late morning hours.

Peale explained and said, "Look, Joe, this is getting bothersome. Can't you reign in the FBI for a little while? I mean, can't State put the kibosh on this?"

"Unfortunately, not easily," Castelli said. "As you know, they've built up this obsession with the Gardner heist. With the slightest hint, they go bananas. Obviously, Hargrave is talking to his European contacts. I suspect he's trying to shut us down. How he'd do that I can't imagine. Look, not worth worrying about. What's happening there?"

Peale conveyed everything they had found. It was an assemblage of pieces. They were lining up, it seemed, pointing to Urumqi, a location that perhaps was another piece of the puzzle.

"So it's decision time," Castelli said. Either you come on back and we sort this out, or you head for China. It's essentially up to you."

The call was on speaker phone, so Ho was listening in, getting anxious.

Peale said, "I'm inclined to return, get this thing off our back. Evaluate what we've found." There were two ways to resolve an interagency wrangle, confront it or ignore it, Peale had learned from experience. He was up for a little confrontation.

At Peale's words, Ho gave out a mild note of disgust. "I disagree," she said quickly. "I say we head for China. I mean, that's way out of their jurisdiction."

Her contrary assertion irked Peale and he eyed Ho with a glare. Before he could follow up, Castelli said, "You two work it out. Either is good." He was actually hoping they'd forge ahead into China. Even so, he could see the wisdom of untangling things in Washington first—it might help matters in the long run.

"We'll get back to you," Peale said. "Over and out."

The connection went dead and he gave Ho a dead-eyed stare. He had recoiled at her lunge into the London protest. This, however, was their first strong disagreement on a fundamental issue and, of course, it resurrected the topic—never quite resolved—as to who was in charge.

"At this juncture, I'm inclined to pull rank," Peale said. "I'm not going to head into an interagency food fight. It never comes out well."

"I disagree. We've got a lead in China. We should follow it."

"Back in Washington—"

"Back in Washington, the FBI's trying to shut this down, don't you see? Okay, so the FBI and their Europol friends will forever feel burned about the Gardner fiasco. If we get to the table with them, I mean, they're going to try to prevail. Take the thing over."

"Well, so what? They take it over, maybe they can do the job."

"Look, they can't do what we can do in China. That's where we pick up the trail. If we give them our information, then we're out to pasture. Don't you see?"

Putting it that way, Ho had challenged Peale to claim ownership of the task at hand. The ownership was in fact what motivated them both from that start: solve the puzzle, come back with the goods. Peale was no coward, but he hated bureaucratic infighting; he'd had enough for a lifetime. She had a compelling point—they had indeed had something to go on and, unlike the feds, they had the Chinese advantage, namely Ho's language skills and a great unknown in a place called Urumqi.

Peale checked his watch. "Let's get something to eat," he said.

They went downstairs to the street and walked on in silence. Peale could sense her steaming a half step behind. They found an eatery, ordered, and took a table, not making eye contact for a while.

"Okay, let's do China," Peale said. "Let the chips fall where they may."

"That's the right decision."

"Oh, the loneliness of command," he said.

Ho actually laughed at the intended humor, perhaps a first, Peale noticed.

"Just don't rub it in," he said, suggesting that she'd not yet won their tennis match. "I'll call Castelli."

They were soon back on the line. Castelli welcomed their decision and said it would be another few hours before things were worked out on his end. "Go have lunch, or whatever."

Peale and Ho had just done that, so they went back to the hotel. They had to stick together for Castelli's reply. So they killed time in the hotel bar, stewing a bit over their disagreement, flipping through tourist reading material, some Austrian newspapers and magazines, and avoiding small talk. They took a walk to another eatery with outdoor seating, but were only up for coffee.

"Cream?" Ho asked, this time not giving Peale an opening for his joke.

"I take it black." She hadn't yet noticed his actual tastes. "Nice city, Vienna," he said, stating the obvious.

The evening approached and Castelli finally rang through. "Urumqi is a go," he said. "This took a while. We ran all those names, Phoenix, Silk Road, Omni Art Global, Urumqi. There is a

Phoenix Group in Urumqi. There's also an Omni Art Global. Don't know about Silk Road, but then again, the name is—"

"Like restaurants," Peale said.

"Restaurants?" Castelli said.

"A common name."

"Sure, I got it." Castelli wasn't going to go into the soap opera back in Washington, where the FBI's Hargrave was growing vocal over turf violations. Castelli was their firewall on that. Importantly, he reported that his assistant was looking into travel arrangements at that very moment.

"We'll take what we can get," Peale said.

"And you've got those UNESCO credentials we gave you?" Castelli asked.

They did, part of their package from the start.

Castelli said he would send over the air ticket information as soon as it was in hand. Then he paused. "There's one other thing you should know."

"Okay," Peale said.

"There's been a couple of terrorist bombings out there in western China, a bit unclear at this point. Apparently some al-Qaeda, ISIS-type incidents. They infiltrate the big Uyghur population in that part of China, sometimes causing a little trouble."

"Right," Peale said.

"I don't think it's anything to worry about." Castelli was being somewhat casual with the heads up. He knew that Peale had done a tour in Afghanistan, and Ho was no newcomer either.

"Right, no worries," Peale said. He'd seen enough bombings in Afghanistan, even felt one, the reason he'd retired from Navy Intelligence. Oddly, at the moment, he was unfazed.

"Keep your eyes on the prize," Castelli said. "Look out for bombs."

8

Urumqi, China

VIENNA HAD A precarious rapport with Asia. Centuries earlier the city was almost gobbled up by the Ottoman Empire. It still looked east, but to get to China, it would take a hop to Tblisi, capital of the former Soviet country of Georgia. Then China Southern Airlines would carry them into China's main western city—from Tblisi to Urumqi, two thousand two hundred miles.

"Just sit back, think D.C. to Los Angeles," Ho said. "Our shortest possible route."

The flight promised some good scenery. Roughly it would follow the west-to-east Tien Shan Mountains. At a cut in the range, Urumqi was a stop on the old Silk Road, which had been carved through desert oases that skirted the mountains. To the north, the prairieland of the Great Steppe stretched along the border of China and Russia, the ancient highway of nomadic armies.

Peale whispered, "This is the pilot. We're now entering Marco Polo territory."

Nerves were a bit frayed by now, and Ho caught his mood. They'd just breached the Bamboo Curtain; what was wrong with a little lightening up? "Oh, look," she said, leaning across to peer out his window. "Isn't that Genghis Khan?"

At the Urumqi airport, they had a straight path through. Elsewhere, they saw milling crowds, a sea of tired, distraught faces. Luggage all around.

What's this? Peale wondered. They passed a European couple with backpacks, some of the scruffy, year-round trekkers seen in such far-off places. Peale glided over to the two and said, "English?"

"Oh, yes." A Scandinavia lilt.

"What are all the crowds?"

"Some trouble in Khorgos, the border."

Peale asked for more details. The young man was quite informed. Khorgos was the big border city between China and Kazakhstan—a major spot for China's Belt and Road. New highways, train tracks, buildings. Khorgos was the straightest shot out of China, just four hundred miles.

"A terrorist attack there," the young man said. "They stopped flights and trains going there." Fortunately, he was heading to Shanghai by train.

"Thanks," Peale said. "Have a safe trip."

He turned back to Ho. "We'll pick up a newspaper, see what happened." After all, Castelli had forewarned about the troubled border. Peale glanced up to look for the time zone clocks that usually adorned international airports, a guide to global travel. There was only one, at a far wall, and it seemed to give a time that was a few hours ahead of what he'd expected. Momentarily confused, he was in no mood to do the time calculations. He'd stick to the watch on his wrist, which showed Europe time, five hours ahead of Washington, which was supposed to put them eleven hours ahead in Urumqi. They taxied into the city and went over their cover story again. They had passports, visas, and UNESCO credentials. Enough cash for a start. Also a small digital camera and two SAT phones with secure satellite links.

Of late, Beijing and UNESCO—the United Nations Educational, Scientific and Cultural Organization—were adding many new features to Urumqi, a sparkle to its industrial heart. As Silk Road territory, this was a cultural melting pot. The UNESCO-Xinjiang Silk Road Museum had opened and ethnic color was being celebrated.

Peale and Ho began to think like one of the many "citizen emissaries" visiting Urumqi, lovers of Chinese history and art. There was the museum and the historic sites not far outside the city. For the past month, the Silk Road Museum was featuring a rare exhibit of Tang art—superlative finds flown in from Beijing—the earliest block printed scrolls, rare porcelain and jade, highpoints of the eighth-century Tang Dynasty.

To Western eyes, Urumqi looked like a mid-sized American city rebuilt from the 1980s. There were brick and stone facades, green plate glass, wide avenues, and bus stops. Adding to this were Soviet-like high-rise housing blocks, street-side Chinatown shops with red neon, and pointed Islamic arches and minarets incorporated into modern buildings, including a few authorized mosques. Red flags adorned the streets, snapping in the desert breeze.

And most of all, there were China's closed circuit television cameras, the CCTV, which was going to be a challenge. Peale had read that two hundred million were in operation, and one day there would be two for every Chinese citizen. You just had to go with the flow, Castelli had advised him. Try to stay where lots of Westerners are out and about, which fortunately, seemed fairly common in Urumqi at the moment.

After checking into a hotel, they called to meet with a minor diplomat in Urumqi, Brad Pinsky. He was a U.S. Trade rep, UNESCO liaison, and a watchful eye in China's far northwest. They met at the edge of People's Square, across from the obelisk.

Pinsky said, "We wear a few hats. I'm a cultural attaché as well." He didn't mention that one of his jobs was to keep an eye on China's treatment of the Uyghur Muslim minority in Xinjiang. A million Uyghurs had had been put into reeducation camps in the province's obscure southern desert.

"First things first," Pinsky said. Peale and Ho had declared their cash at customs, as required, but they'd need more for the operation. Pinsky handed them a thick envelope of mixed currency.

Peale stashed it inside his coat, then asked about the Khorgos hubbub.

"They've closed down travel to Khorgos," Pinsky said. "Mainly a big truck route with Central Asia. This happens now and again. Back to normal in a week or two." Pinsky added matter of factly, "By the way, a few bombs went off here in Urumqi lately. That's settled down."

"That we didn't hear," Peale said.

"Do you know about the time out here," Pinsky asked. "The double time?"

"No . . . what about it?" Peale asked. He recalled his confusion over the airport clock.

"There are two times in Urumqi, official and unofficial. Only place in the world." China used to go by normal world time, by time zones, but that changed in the 1970s. Party leader Deng Xiaoping put all of China on Beijing time. "It's just as if, one day, the American president tells everyone in the country to set their clocks to Washington time, forever."

"I see," Peale said. That was why the airport clock was three hours fast.

"Good rule is just follow the sun, follow the people," Pinsky said. "When they get up, go to work, close the shops, or fill the freeways. It will look strange on your world-time watch, like they're getting up at ten or eleven in the morning." Pinsky kept his watch on world time, but didn't talk about it out loud. "If you're heard bragging that it's ten o'clock in the morning, but it's really noon Beijing time, they might think you're a Uyghur nationalist."

"So if I want to call the general secretary in Beijing, I'm on his time, right?" Peale said. "Wouldn't want to wake him up."

"Not good," Ho agreed.

Pinsky suggested they first visit the Silk Road Museum and get into the UNESCO mix. Mercifully, he didn't get into the times on the museum schedule.

"Lead the way," Peale said. "We'll get to details later."

"Out here it's pretty informal," Pinsky said. "The UNESCO sites and all the tourists, many of them domestic Chinese. But looks can be deceiving. Don't be surprised if someone is watching. It's what they do."

"National police? Provincial?"

"Both, and some PLA. The army's branched out in recent years. Sells art, buys art, watches travelers interested in art. The good thing is that they're focused on the Uyghurs. Not good for the Uyghurs, of course. Good for us Westerners. They're stretched thin, so we're a low priority."

The museum stood on the People's Square, with its large state obelisk. There was also the Communist Party building, a stern façade in weathered gray stone. "I'll take you to the Grand Bazaar later, for lunch. We can talk business there."

As they crossed the paved square, past its lines of trees, Peale saw a disturbed area on its edge, like a construction site with yellow tape, a few PLA guards, and areas that seemed blackened by smoke.

Pinsky said, "That's one of the two terrorist bombings last week. First sirens, lots of PLA jeeps, green uniforms all over. Then it tapered off. You'll see the other one later."

Inside the museum, the halls were set with government symbols, but also showcases of minority cultures, of which thirteen major ones co-existed in Xinjiang. "A lot of Indian, Buddhist, Mongol, even Persian, cultural influences," Pinsky said. "The only really indigenous art was in jade. China's jade deposits are in nearby mountains."

They entered a room of Tang Dynasty exhibits.

After a time, Ho said, "Quite impressive. Some primary works." She assumed the security was not lax around these priceless offerings, shipped in from Beijing. As with Peale, it was the prints and paintings that spoke to her, not the ceramics, the silk headdresses, or the jade jewelry.

They continued to look around, and Pinsky lowered his voice. "This is part of the 'Hanization' of Xinjiang. Beijing's dream, but often an ethnic minority's nightmare. In the rest of the museum, you'll see why. The Han were late comers out west. Buddhism from India, Turkic, and Mongol influences were first. This is a very foreign population, so they keep spreading the Han umbrella."

"Reeducation," Ho said. She knew that the Han ethnic group, the largest in the world, took its eponymous name from that later dynasty, even calling Chinese writing Han script.

"Han education, Party education," Pinsky said. "This urbanized half of Xinjiang is nearly all Han. The south half, the desert, nearly all Uyghur. And you'll notice how much space the museum gives to the Qing Dynasty, the second time China conquered, well, 'unified' we should say, this area."

As soon as they arrived in Urumqi, Peale had assessed how well he and Ho would blend in. A lot of the Turkic population was fair skinned and dark browed, and by his looks Peale could have been one of them. The population also had many Hui Chinese, a group that historically was Muslim. These Chinese women wore the obligatory head scarf. Ho had one handy, if she ever wanted to look like a Hui.

Peale asked, "How do the politics work out here."

"There's an old Chinese saying, 'The mountains are high. The emperor is far away,'" Pinsky said. "This is still a faraway place. An autonomous region, one of a few, like Tibet or Inner Mongolia. There's some leeway here for provincial leaders, Party leaders, even the PLA, to do business as usual. Beijing is far away."

Nevertheless, the Politburo in Beijing set the wider policies, such as border security and investment in national projects, he explained. The provinces had some say, at least every five years. That's when the 2,300 provincial Party leaders traveled to the People's Congress in Beijing. They elected the rest of the pyramid, with the General Secretary on top. And that personage, as they all knew, was Ren Jinuah.

Pinsky looked at his watch. "They have a UNESCO cultural lecture today. Any interest?"

Peale and Ho glanced at each other. She shrugged, and Peale passed on their sentiments, which were getting more in sync all the time. "Maybe we'll pass," he said.

Around the museum, where a crowd was heading for the lecture, they saw what looked like Chinese college students, a European tourist group, and a few backpacking trekkers. Sauntering through the halls, Peale stopped at a UNESCO sign on the wall, in Chinese and English: The museum aimed to "build peace in the minds of men and women" by offering "a broad overview of Chinese civilization along the Silk Roads and local ethnic cultures."

Despite that conciliatory thought, Peale turned to ask Pinsky about the police situation in Xinjian Province.

"Oh that," Pinsky said with a chuckle. "The local police have different personalities in different parts of the country. I'd say pretty lax out here. Beijing's got two long arms, the Ministry of Public Security and Ministry of State Security. They each have police of their own. Public security is strong around the borders out here, state security goes after the terrorists."

"And the spies and provocateurs," Ho said.

"That's state security, for sure," Pinsky said. "They frown on 'counterrevolutionary activity.'" Peale and Ho shot each other a glance, smiling at Pinsky's sly mocking of orthodoxy ideology. They weren't exactly smuggling in arms for a coup d'état.

Pinsky jerked his head to one side. "Come over here." He led them to a map of China. "UNESCO's obligated to give an official history, you know, focusing on a few great dynasties, the Han, Tang, Song and Ming. It's far more complicated, of course."

Peale and Ho exchanged glances again. "Okay, we're listening," Peale said.

Pinsky was in his element. He'd given this talk often, to American trade groups, occasional VIPs.

"Yes, it's all true, that the China heartland began between the two great rivers, the Yellow in the north, and Yangtze in the south, waters coming down from the mountains in the west, leading to the East China Sea. In the west, the watershed of the Tien Shan Mountains fed the string of oases. Before the Han race spread out, like here in the deserts, you had Turkic races, and in the Great Steppe you had Mongols and Manchus, both of mysterious origins." Pinsky covered a few more thousand years, up to the Qing, the last dynasty, the conqueror of the western regions.

"Again, my point is that, despite all this mixing, the official message today is that China stems from the Han. Today it's supposed to be ninety-two percent Han. Even with fifty-five official minorities."

"And don't forget the Yellow Emperor," Ho said.

"Never forget that," Pinsky said. "And get this. One of the official Party anthropologists says the skull of Chang Man, which was found a few years back, proves that the Han originated separate from Africa."

"The polygenism theory," Ho said. "Two separate human origins. Hey, I feel pretty good about that idea."

"Yes, we know you're special," Peale said, glancing around the exhibit.

"In my heart, I know I'm Han," Ho said. "But I'm also in touch with my inner Manchu."

Funny, Peale mused to himself. He thought that was her inner Mongol. The Mongols were aggressive nomads, while the Manchu were settled farmers and a bit more refined.

"It's all there in the new textbooks," Pinsky said. "You may not find it in the earlier 'Thought of Chairman Mao,' but you see traces now in the 'Thought of Deng Xiaoping,' the thought of whoever's general secretary, even our current one. 'The Thought of Ren Jinuah.'"

"In a perverse way, it's quite brilliant," Peale said. "He who writes the history—"

"Rules the nation," Ho said.

They paused at the thought. It was enough historical thinking for a while.

Peale said, "So to return to the point, this is also about China's art history. Ergo, today's art market. Ergo, our search for the Vermeer painting, last seen, reportedly, on its way to China."

"Here in Urumqi, maybe," Ho said.

OUTSIDE, PINSKY SAID, "Since you've come all this way, you should have some Uyghur cuisine." They crossed the square and headed for the Central Bazaar, with its tall minaret-like tower.

Pedestrians were everywhere, as were bicycles and men in Turkic skull caps and children with sticky faces from eating dates. Women wore colorful Uyghur head scarves. Ho decided to take hers out and wear it.

As they walked into the district, Peale and Ho saw a repeat of the earlier scene. A scorched building with yellow tape. Two PLA soldiers in green lingered by.

"This was the second?" Peale asked.

"Fifteen minutes later," Pinsky said. "Interesting, too. It's a trade office, Omni Art Global."

Peale and Ho looked at each other. That raised a red flag. Things were getting curiouser and curiouser. Peale had said earlier that this job was taking them down a rabbit hole.

Pinsky noticed their double take, and explained what he knew about Omni. "It's a big company out of Beijing, dealing in regional artifacts. Don't get the Uyghurs wrong, though. I mean the bombs. If there's a politics for the Uyghurs, its nationalism, electoral politics, all non-violent. The bombers are bad guys, cells of Islamic State, al-Qaeda, who inserted themselves among the Uyghurs."

As they reached the restaurant and began to enter, Peale looked over his shoulder, said, "I notice that we may have some company. PLA?" He was eyeing two men in blue uniforms and ball caps, not the traditional gray-green.

"You can't tell," Pinsky said. "They seem to rely more on the CCTV cameras, otherwise you'd have uniforms following every other citizen. Just think like a cultural tourist with UNESCO. They'll get the vibe."

Peale and Ho exchanged a glance. Peale shrugged and tried to exude the vibe.

The restaurant was half full. They sat and were served black tea and pieces of flat bread.

"We'll do half and half, pure Uyghur and some Chinese mix," Pinsky said.

Ho could read some of the offerings. Uyghur food traditionally did not include green vegetables, rare in arid Central Asia. It was mostly rice, soft noodles, meat, and dried fruit.

"Okay," said Pinsky after ordering, "the Uyghur and Chinese. You'll see the difference."

When the two steaming platters arrived, they could.

"China's contribution to civilization," Ho said. "Stir fried and chopsticks."

The Chinese platter was exactly that. The Uyghur dishes of rice and meat were known by their bits of dried apricot and raisins, and the tang of spice.

"The interesting thing is the tea," Pinsky said. "Central Asia, with its climate extremes, does not grow tea, historically. It was carried on caravans, mostly from South China. Now, you have tea farms out here. They use green houses. The soil is supposed to add something special."

"Huh," said Peale. The tea did taste a bit sweeter than usual. He put down his cup and asked, "So what can you tell us?"

"Okay, I was given your information, the names you found. There is something in Urumqi called Phoenix Group, a business. It owns Silk Road Company, which in turn has a tea farm outside of town. If you're game for some detective work, you might go there, knock on some doors."

"Just like that," Ho said.

Pinsky said, "A lot of Westerners do business out here, so you won't stick out. It's in a neighborhood with high-tech factories. China's big cell phone company produces there, ships to the European market. The French have a complex, too. Cell phones, computer boards. Cheap labor, diligent labor, and the shortest shipping route to Europe."

Pinsky had explained that he was at the end of nearly two weeks in Urumqi, had to get back to Shanghai. "Now I've got to catch the bullet train back to Lanzhou."

They went out of the restaurant, found a large street on People's Square, and hailed a taxi. "You're on your own now. You'll do fine."

IN HIS LIMITED Mandarin, Pinsky told the taxi driver the address in the northern industrial sector.

"English okay," the driver said. "Some English I have."

Peale and Ho got in. The taxi wove through the back streets of Urumqi, caught a small highway on the periphery, and soon it was carrying Peale and Ho into a hodgepodge of industrial parks, the rundown ones mixed with the sparkling new. Smokestacks rose in a distant area. Small red flags were everywhere.

"I have an idea," Ho said. "Let's check out the tea farm first. I've got a feeling . . ."

"I know, a woman's intuition. Fine by me."

Ho said to the taxi driver, "You know the tea farm?"

"Tea farm, many tea farm, yes," he replied. He pulled over on the road. His eyes went wide. "You want tea farm?"

There were more than one, according to Pinsky, so Ho held out her map and pointed to where he had described.

The taxi driver nodded his head vigorously. "Big tea farm, yes."

Taking a new direction, the driver veered out of the industrial maze, following quiet backstreets past large and small factory buildings, and then onto the congested main roads, where trucks and imported German cars jostled for passage. When they reached the city's edge, steep cliffs began to tumble down from the snow-capped Tien Shan Mountains. Next came the oases between the ridges, now green, soon to brown in the summer heat. As Peale and Ho surveyed all around, they saw two panel vans coming their way from the opposite side. The highway was narrow so the taxi slowed a bit and hugged its side of the road.

As they passed the two vans, Peale and Ho paid attention.

"Did you see that?" Peale said. "A PLA guy was driving the first one." He'd noticed the green uniform. They both saw that the second van said Phoenix Group on the driver's door.

"Tea farm coming," their taxi man said.

They reached a small unmarked turnoff with a narrow well-paved road. Up ahead was a low-lying complex, a steep mountain rising up behind it, a watershed for growing tea. The road led to a gate. The sign read Authorized Personnel Only. The tall chain-link fence created a very large, squarish compound, several blocks in dimension. They could see a building with two cars at the front. Row upon row of greenhouses were beyond.

Peale and Ho got out of the cab but asked him to wait. There was a buzzer at the fence. They buzzed, waited, buzzed again. Ho was to say they were travelers in town with UNESCO, and were interested in tea farming. Still nothing.

Peale wondered aloud if there was another way to get in. "You have to break some eggs to make an omelet."

"We can break things later," Ho replied. "Let's try that other address. Phoenix Group."

Back in the taxi, they returned to the highway, through the industrial stretch, and into an oddly mixed industrial park. As they approached the new address, they asked the taxi driver to pull over. They wanted to walk up to the building. A road with plenty of taxis was nearby, they noticed, so Ho paid up and thanked the driver.

"I can read the streets signs," Ho said. "Follow me." As they walked, she spotted a car that had come in after the taxi and was now idling across the street, its windows of darkened glass. "I think we may have visitors," she said. Peale had also picked it out.

At the address, the building had a small sign in Chinese calligraphy that said Phoenix Group. One of the panel vans they saw was parked on the side, "We've got our story down, so let's check this out," Peale said. "You take the lead." She had the language.

"Say please," Ho quipped.

As their time in China extended, this kind of leadership issue was going to come up in practice, and Peale began to wonder how it would unfold. He felt his limitations, not speaking the language and not catching the cultural nuances. As the plot thickened, he would see where it all went. At least he didn't want to feel useless.

They approached the building, went under the entrance overhang, and Ho pushed the doorbell. There was a camera above the door. A minute or so passed.

"Yes," came a Chinese voice.

Ho responded in kind. "We are visitors interested in art sales. My apologies, but we don't have an appointment. May we speak to the manager?"

The intercom clicked, and then there was a long pause. A few minutes later came the sound of door locks, and a man in a PLA uniform appeared.

"I'm sorry, we are not accepting visitors," he said. He was looking at them up and down. "You must arrange that through the main office."

"My apologies again," Ho said. "We are only interested in art sales. Do you have a catalog we can take with us?"

"No catalog," the man said. "Only tea. You must contact the office."

She started to ask, "Where is the office," when the man shut the door. Peale and Ho stood for a while, then acquiesced to the dead end. From the two locations, they'd at least drawn two impressions. Peale wasn't sure if their impression were the same, however. He was feeling oddly constrained to take any action, so unfamiliar were the Chinese surroundings. Ho seemed to be a fish in familiar water.

THEY BEGAN TO walk back through the neighborhood, toward the main road in search of a taxi. It was a booming entrepreneurial trade in Urumqi, usually with desiccated vehicles and part of that storied gray market. That's when they saw two men coming toward them, again in blue uniforms with ball caps. They came right up, and said, "May we see your passports."

Ho asked, "Who are we speaking too, city police?"

"Public security," the man said.

National police, Ho thought quickly. "We're on travel visas for the UNESCO events. Is there a problem?"

The man in the lead did not answer. Ho decided to comply and Peale followed her moves. The man looked over their documents, glancing at their faces. Peale brought out his UNESCO pass for good measure.

The man spoke sharply to him. "What did he say?" Peale asked Ho.

"'Not you, round eye.' They're interested in me." Peale didn't know if she was joking or not.

The two men told them to come to their car, gesturing. It was the same navy blue Volkswagen sedan they'd fingered earlier.

"They want us to come to the station," Ho said. Peale was inclined to resist. She moved beside him, close to his ear. "I'll handle this," she said.

Once in the back seat, the car left the north district, retracing a circuit the taxi had taken them on. Then it headed into the downtown traffic. It parked at an austere one story building, which wore its status lightly. A dull brass plaque was on the outer wall, a red flag on either side. It also had a small gold and blue insignia. That was public security, not state security, the latter being spy-catchers. They were escorted inside and then to a mean little room with a stained cement floor.

"We should call the embassy," Peale said, though it was a little late for that.

"Let me handle this," Ho said again.

A man in a suit and spectacles came in, holding the passports. He handed them back to Peale and Ho.

"Will you be in Urumqi for long?" the man said, seating himself.

"A few days," said Ho. "The UNESCO events, some sightseeing."

"And your passports are in order?" he asked.

"You have them, yes." She took out her own UNESCO credential.

"Are you interested in tea farming?" the man said.

Ho said it was fascinating.

Peale tried to assess the mood in the conversation, but it seemed impenetrable. Instead he wondering whether they were picked up on those damn CCTV cameras, or maybe it was just bad luck.

The door opened and another man came in. He set down some cards and a little box on the table.

"This is just routine," the first official said. "For your safety. We would like your fingerprints."

Ho translated for Peale. "This is absurd," he said under his breath. Ho stayed calm as the man laid out the two cards marked with five squares, and then an ink pad. A few scenarios ran through Peale's mind, and he leaned toward the more harmless one. With the bombings, the brass in the head office was probably cracking the whip. The street police wanted to look busy, so they'd turned into martinets, harassing even tourists. After all, Pinsky said it was pretty lax out here. Peale was taking his word for it. Hopefully this was all police bluster just for show.

The official was saying, "We must insist. For your safety."

Ho decided it was best to go along with the finger printing. "Then we're done?" she said. The official nodded yes. She offered her hand and its digits were printed. She gestured Peale to do the same. Once completed, the policeman with the kit handed them both a damp paper towel to clean their hands.

Through it all, Peale listened to the Chinese conversation. Ho had gone into a long discourse. The official stared, nodded on occasion. Then she reached into her purse, counted out what amounted to a couple hundred dollars, and handed it to over.

The official nodded, but still seemed insistent. Ho insisted in return. The man sat back in his chair, then stood and gave what sounded like an order before he turned and left the room.

"What happened?" Pealed asked. He sensed that the security police were particularly interested in her and her passport. Maybe some chauvinism in play, or maybe they suspected she was a Hui, a Muslim Chinese. He would later learn that sometimes a Chinese woman with a Western man was a cultural trigger in the back streets of China.

"Standard practice," she said, referring to the cash transfer. "Our donation to Urumqi's cultural blossoming. It softens the blow. I'll tell you more outside."

They were collected by one of the men who brought them in. He pointed, and they followed him out to the lobby, where he pushed open the glass door. He said something, and Ho replied, polite in her tone.

"Damnit," she said, once they were alone. "Bloody hell." Her mind was racing, thinking back to her other times in China.

"So what was that?" Peale asked.

"They want us to stay in our hotel, where they can reach us. Some follow-up."

"On what?"

"Maybe it's nothing, just an empty threat. But I don't think we should stay around to find out." They'd bought some time and now they had to use it.

9

Urumqi, China

THEY RETURNED TO the hotel. Now it was Peale's turn to become insistent. What was up? Ho told him not to worry. They had traveled light, could pack quickly.

"Change of plans," she said. "Trust me on this." She was thinking of herself, but also of Peale, who was now being draw unwittingly into her past exploits, but only maybe.

Peale was accustomed to taking orders, but usually he did so with comprehension. On the other hand, to him this was still mostly impenetrable China. Ho was their Chinese way through it all. At the least, they had gathered up some worthwhile information.

At the hotel they packed, called a taxi, and headed to the airport. "We'll check in early," she said. "Then turnaround and drive out of here."

"Foreigners can't drive in China."

"Don't worry, I know what to do."

First they had to leave their bread-crumb trail to the airport, evidence of a departure. Then at the airport terminal lanes, Ho hailed another cab. After a while on the road, they found themselves at a tourism office, its title on a placard with several languages, a picture of a globe, and a red emblem in the shape of Xinjiang province.

As she got them tickets, Peale persisted. "Don't you have some more explaining to do, Miss Ho?"

She directed him over to a bench away from other tourists waiting for the bus and sat him down. She said, "Okay, look. I hoped this wouldn't happen, but you never know. I'm a known quantity in China. Past work. You don't need to know. Somehow they flagged me. Well, not me, but the other me."

"Other you?"

"Sometimes in this job you have 'another you.' Maybe two or three others. Very long story." And there were the U.S. State Secrets Act documents she had signed in the past, quite a few in fact. They said she could not divulge her past covert activity, even to a fellow agent.

Peale would have been satisfied with a short version of her story, but for now he worried about the other SAT phone, whether Ho had a second track going back to Washington. "That SAT phone of yours. Are you doing your own thing?"

"Absolutely not. Like I said—"

"You've been in trouble here before?"

"Look, it's not trouble. Way back I was here with an exchange student group, then some translator jobs, business groups, once some museum curators." She'd used many different guises. She didn't know if the finger prints would turn up anything. She'd certainly had times in the past when she'd left them on a water glass in a restaurant here, a door knob there. Scrutiny of the passport could also raise a red flag.

"Spying around?"

"Checking out the situation."

"But you're not on that SAT phone?"

"Simply no way!" She gave a frustrated sigh.

"Okay, no problem." He believed her, of course, and felt a bit foolish for a moment.

The taxi took them to a tourist depot by a truck route and a small park on the western edge of downtown, halfway back from the airport. It was milling with holidayers looking around the shops. Others wandered the grounds. Everyone was waiting for the bus. In the midst of all this, Ho said, "Follow me." They paced toward the truck stop. Dozens of trucks, large and small, hackneyed and new, were stained with dust. Most were waiting in line to gas up. Others pulled over for a rest. There was also an assortment of taxis, motley freelancers every one of them.

Ho said, "I'm going to hitch a ride. Wait here." Fifteen minutes later, she was back. "See that car, kind of a beat-up minivan, green-ish? That's our ride."

"Ride to where?" Peale asked.

"Out of China."

As Peale Would soon learn, Ho had already brushed up on the Xinjiang Province road maps. The straightest route out of China was through Khorgos, four hundred miles, but as they had learned, that was closed down.

"Okay, I've talked to the taxi guy. No problem going north to the next big stop, a city called Karamay. That's a big tourist route. It goes over the mountains to a lake resort, Ulungur Lake, a big national park. The Aspen of Xinjiang."

"Damn, we forgot our skis," Peale said. It was humor under stress, and he hoped it worked with Ho after their little spat.

"More like camels," she said. "Any route is mostly desert." She explained more. Northward took them to Karamay City, about two hundred fifty miles. That was five hours before sunset. Then she said they'd think it over. The could cut west and try to hit the Kazakh border at a town called Tacheng City. It was a big border crossing complex.

"Bigger is better sometimes," she said.

"And the alternative?"

"If Tacheng looks iffy, we keep going north. Then east toward Kazakhstan, a crossing called Jimunai Port. Farther, but probably easier of the two."

"Easier?"

"Less uptight," she said. "Either way, we're going to make some donations." She patted where all the currency packs were stowed away. "Forgot my American Express."

"How far we talking about?" Peale was an Afghanistan vet and no stranger to desert stretches.

"From here, about four hundred miles to Tacheng. More than seven hundred to Jimunai. For the first, just think a desert drive from D.C. to Boston."

"For the next?"

"Say, less than Albuquerque to L.A., at least an hour less."

"Look at the bright side," Peale said. "Both are beautiful desert drives." He awaited Ho's response to that, which came after a pause.

"I can't guarantee palm-shaded waterholes. Those exotic bazaars with belly dancers will have to wait."

"Those were the days," Peale said. Yes, he assured himself, she does have a sense of humor under that reserve. Humor under fire. It always helped, and it was the only antidote to nerve-wracking circumstances in the field, at least for him.

The day was getting late. In either choice of the route, they'd be crossing into Kazakhstan in the dark of night. They needed to use the daylight to their best advantage. Having gotten into the taxi, Ho in the front, Peale in the back, they headed north. The driver was middle-aged man who wore a squared cap and a five-o'clock shadow. The road followed the oases along the mountain. Eventually they passed by the Phoenix Group/Silk Road Co. turnoff.

"*Reddam*," Peale said with a flourish, looking at Ho. "Latin for 'I shall return.'"

"If anybody, its 'we shall,'" Ho said.

The road curved northward. The green around Urumqi gave way to Xinjian's lunar landscape. Ridges carved up the sanded areas, which were flat as a dinner plate. Hues of gray, rust red, black and brown tinted the soils. Their heads grew a little light in the accumulating heat of the day. There was nothing left to do but sit like melting waxworks—or talk.

Adopting a Cowboy twang, Peale said, "There's jade in them thar hills."

Ho said, "For my cultural contribution, I have a Chinese proverb."

"And that is?"

"*Du wanjuanshu bu ru xíng wanlǐlu.* Mandarin for 'Reading a thousand books is not as good as traveling a thousand miles.'"

"Don't remind me, I mean, the thousand books," he said. "It makes my head ache."

About two hours in, mostly quiet with a little dozing, he said, "By the way, since you're saving my life and—"

"Don't jump to conclusions."

"Well, let me ask you something anyway."

"As long as it's not my weight," she said.

After so much thinking about the Han, this Han, that Han, Peale asked, "How do you deal with the whole racism thing? I mean, the American railroads, 'Chinamen' labor, the Exclusion Act and all that. Not a pretty picture." That was the troubled history of early Chinese migration to the United States.

"There's some kind of racism all over the world, but it doesn't control my life."

"Not even a little?"

"For me the past is fascinating, but it's not the now. It's not necessarily the future."

"Be here now," Peale said.

"Ah, so you're a pop philosopher, too."

"I try."

Ho said, "Okay, I guess what's really Chinese about me, besides the chopsticks, is this. It's very old. Very Confucian in fact. You have parents. But you also have a country, a kind of parent, and for me that's the good old US of A. It makes you who you are, whether you were born there or live and die there. My mother and father told me this. They also said, 'When you visit someone's home, you don't rearrange the furniture.' And I've been persuaded."

Peale said, "So, Chinese-American."

Ho wanted to say it could be worse, she could be a Uyghur in China—but instead she said, "No, American-Chinese."

"Much clearer," Peale said.

The desert stretched to every horizon. At times a long line of covered trucks would pass by in the other lane. The hot wind would rock the jeep and raise dust. Far off they both noticed a dark cloud. It hung over a mesa, and stranger still was the rumble of distant thunder. Some of the tall protruding rocks cast knife-like shadows.

Peale was still curious, so he said, "Okay, so we've got the Secrets Act, but what can you tell me about yourself before this government business?"

Ho sat quietly for a while. She'd prefer to talk about the weather, but the lull was like a vacuum, sucking out her memories. And it wouldn't be remiss to tell her partner a few things. She started with her upbringing in Chicago, a bright Asian kid who got into the University of Chicago with a humanities major.

"So around the campus there was this Chinese student organization, exchange students from the mainland, and some off-campus activists. I kind of got sucked in, you know, youthful idealism. Make a difference. The group mainly did protests. If a professor was teaching about human rights problems in China, they'd hold a protest. Same thing with any China issue, and there were quite a few in the Midwest, you know, trade type issues. Tibet issues a lot. So the leaders of this group were always, you know, protesting discrimination, anti-Chinese stuff, a pressure group. After a while, I didn't like it, especially the guys who were running this from off-campus. One guy had an ego of Himalayan proportions. So I quit, but they kept badgering me with a guilt trip. Anyway, I had to choose sides. An existential dilemma as you philosophers say. So I decided to get away, quit university in my junior year. Signed up for the Marines."

"Quite a story," Peale said. He himself had just slid into the Navy on the back of his own Navy family. It was what the family did. "And then what? After you became a counterrevolutionary?"

"You forgot to add 'capitalist running dog.'" She said it with a small laugh, having used Mao Zedong's favorite slur for Chinese turncoats. "Anyhow, I was a talented kid, bilingual, so I was sent over to Marine intelligence for training. Eventually I was put in the field. I got to travel, see the world. As you know, we Asians all look alike. But sarcasm aside, I really liked it."

"But your parents didn't, right?"

"Not quitting university, no. What they really didn't like was that student group. I think they knew something mainland was going on. I learned my lesson, I suppose. Don't believe everything a

Chinese tells you. It was the U.S. or China, so I chose McDonalds and the suburbs."

"Good choice," Peale said.

The jeep interior had grown hot as a Turkish bath. Off and on now, they wiped away trickles of sweat. It was trailing down Peale's back. Oddly, he saw snow on distant mountains. A mild wind came from the northwest, sucked in as the desert heat rose, creating a vacuum.

They had just ridden the spine of a miles-long ridge, and were no descending. A shamble of houses was up ahead. There were also a few cars, and a few donkey carts, and getting closer they could see a store and a gas station sign. The taxi driver spoke, and Ho translated. "We'll stop for fuel and food."

"Camel jerky," Peale said.

"Dried fruit and bottles of water. The desert's guilty pleasure."

After that, they continued on. Where clay mountainsides stood, they were furrowed by rain like veins in a giant leaf. Between these the stretches of sand expanded. What the landscape lacked in vegetation or rubble it made up for in sheer magnitude. Spiky monoliths of harsh red rock rose here and there. The lunar landscape had turned Martian. The road soon went draftsman straight, a line that become a wavy mirage in the hazy distance. On and on and on.

Peale had begun to doze when the driver said, "City ahead."

A square white sign was anchored on a post by the road. It bore black and red script in both Chinese and Uyghur and then a number, apparently a mile marker. The road began to wind, rising up and down on undulating hills. As they came down over one horizon, they saw an open area roughed up by tire treads, a kind of crossroads. Signs were here and there and also rotting posts in the ground. A rusting hulk of a car tilted like a grave marker in a field.

"Crossroad," the driver said.

Ho was handling her map. "Here's where we decide," she said. "The lake is over the mountain, so here we can either try the shorter way, west to Tacheng City, or go that way, more north, and try Jimunai Port."

As the driver slowed, Peale said, "What's that ahead?" Two trails of dust were rising from one of the branch roads. They could see better now. Two green covered jeeps appeared. PLA vehicles.

"Uh, uh, look," the driver said, frowning nervously. "I think we stop. I think is okay." The PLA jeeps often showed up on the roads, doing inspections or breaking up traffic jams. They drove routes between PLA outposts, often garnering bribes.

"I think we not worry," the driver said.

Except that the PLA jeeps were speeding toward the nexus in the road.

"Okay, we play it by ear," Peale said. "Documents at the ready."

By the time the taxi slowed down, the two jeeps had parked across its lane of the road. Six men in green with red trim were standing around their vehicles. Five wore PLA ball caps, another wore a peaked cap, maybe a lieutenant, the lowest rank. One soldier in a ball cap was on the road, his flat palm out. The taxi pulled to the side and the engine died.

"Okay, Miss Translator, diplomat extraordinaire, do your stuff," Peale said.

As Ho had mentioned earlier, these types of shakedowns had a pattern, if that's what this was. "They say there's a road tax." She readied a packet of bills in the pocket of her gray jeans. In the heat, she'd stripped down to her khaki blouse, a little provocative in a country where women covered up. She pulled out her colorful head scarf and put it on.

The soldier with the hand up marched to the Jeep, waved for them to get out, and spoke some words. The driver understood, as did Ho. Peale followed their moves, sometimes whispering, "What did he say." Ho was translating under her breath.

The soldier said, "Over here."

As Peale's party did as it was told, the other soldiers moved up, two with rifles slung on their shoulders.

"They're just kids," Peale said. Chinese often looked younger than they were, but he was certain these six guys were nineteen or twenty years old. They had no marks of life on them. Their swagger was immature, and a mischievous look was around their eyes. Peale was no snake charmer, so he waited.

"They start them young," Ho said.

The man asked for documents. As these were being exchanged, the other five men casually gathered around to watch. A cagey looking one had sidled up to Ho, looking her up and down. Closer still his hand squeezed her butt. Ho stiffened. Self-control, she told herself.

Then the man's hand came up and fondled her breast, a grin showing his white teeth. Before Peale could intervene, Ho's arm came up, grabbed the man's wrist, her other arm spinning him sideways, pulling his arm up behind his back. Then she pivoted on her left foot, swinging her right foot into the back of his knee. He yelped, swore, and crumpled to the ground. The other men stepped forward. Two of them brought up their rifles, pointing the barrels.

Then suddenly the soldier with the peaked hat spoke in anger. He stepped over to the man on the ground and kicked him, letting out a stream disapprovals.

A good sign, Ho immediately realized, whispering to Peale, "Play it cool."

For a time, the man in the peaked hat kept up his harangue. The soldier on the ground was dusting himself off and, strangely, the other men were laughing. The man in the peaked hat came forward. He could see Ho was Chinese, so he spoke.

"A misunderstanding, Miss Lady," he said in English with a muted smile. "He's out in the desert too long." The men laughed again. Peale watched, thinking it was almost like a group of college kids. Now the guns were slung back on their shoulders and the group continued to linger.

From this point, it was all Chinese. Ho had begun a kind of curt conversation with the man in the hat, obviously the leader of the patrol, or whatever it was. Slowly, the conversation mellowed, almost as if it was two travelers having met and engaging in friendly small talk. As Ho spoke, she reached in her pocket, brought out the sheaf of bills. With both hands, she handed them to the man with a slight bow.

More talk followed and then Ho said, "Julian come over here." Speaking in Chinese, then English, back and forth she said, "Julian this is Lieutenant Huang-li, head of unit. Lieutenant, this is Julian Peale, a well-known scholar of Chinese art and history. A well-known advisor for UNESCO." And so it went back and forth. Peale gave a slight nod, then Lt. Huang-li put out his hand. He gave a firm shake. Peale marveled again at his youth. In fact, they were all a bunch of kids, kind of like a play army.

The scene suddenly went casual. A few of the soldiers sat back on the jeeps, as if watching the show. One pulled out a bottle of water and took a swing. Another reached for it, then took his own.

Ho eventually turned back to Peale, smiled and said, "The lieutenant would like to welcome us to his province. He knows we're traveling to Kazakhstan, so he's recommended the best crossing for us." She gave him a look, sort of a wink. "They want to make a good impression on travelers. Travelers are good business. So they're asking how they can help."

Some of the soldiers on the jeep were bantering, a few laughs.

"I'll explain in full later," she said.

By now the lieutenant was speaking again, gesturing up this road, then at the other.

"Though it's farther, he recommends the Jimunai Port," Ho said. "He says his uncle works there. It's a friendly place to get through. They're headed that way."

"An escort? Can we trust them?"

She smiled at the lieutenant, who waited patiently. "I think it's a good bet. A bit farther. He said that way"—she pointed at the other road—"is shorter over to Tacheng City, but has a bunch of tight asses."

"He said that?"

"To that effect, a Chinese version. Also said they're getting a lot of opium stops this season, so they're poking a lot, you known backpackers, strip searching. I told him that they don't have to strip search me because all the opium's in the truck. That made him laugh."

"Charming. Reverse psychology. So we go his way?"

She turned to the lieutenant and said they'd take his advice. He seemed pleased. Suddenly he said, turning to Peale and smiling, "Like Americans, yes. Rock and roll."

Two of the soldiers said, "Yah Bee Gees. Stay alive. Stay alive. Hu, hu, hu hu." In the other jeep, the one who was scolded sat mute. Peale noticed, hoping he was not more trouble down the road. He couldn't wait to hear Ho's full debriefing.

The lieutenant turned, issuing some words that sounded like orders. Then he waved his hand and the five men all jumped back in their jeeps.

Ho said, "One of them continues on patrol, the other is heading our way out. That's the lieutenant's jeep. We can't turn down an escort, right?" Then she whispered reassuringly, "The hands-y one is on the patrol."

"Good thinking," Peale said. "Anyway, our circle of admirers has widened." That apparently included the taxi driver. The man had stayed agreeable through the entire episode, smiling, following everyone's orders, and probably thinking of the substantial fee he'd bring home to his wife and kids.

"Taxi will follow jeep, make caravan," the driver said.

The road was now rising again, a vast blanket of soft hills, craters of sand, small cliffs jutting up from the erosion, jagged pinnacles cropping up like sentries watching the road. The colors changed with the setting sun, turning reddish with purplish shadows. Glints of light shone off mica particles in the sand. They were racing the sun, but would still have to negotiate the Kazakh border in the dark. They didn't know if that helped or hurt.

As they drove on, Ho explained what happened back at the PLA stop. Slightly amused, she told the back story. "These are a bunch of kids who grew up together in Urumqi. Like a lot of kids, they joined the PLA. But it's kind of like a reserve. They have other jobs and play soldier a few times a week, or maybe for a given period. The lieutenant said, 'We're county boys. The hell with Beijing.' His jeep was going back to Jimunai Port, where his uncle runs one of the border gates."

"Our VIP ticket through," Peale said. "In my case, a senior's pass."

"Don't be so hard on yourself. Anyway, these guys like Americans, which of course they certainly should."

"We're a likable bunch," said Peale. "The Bee Gees are Australian though."

"You can see it in their faces," Ho went on. "A few are Chinese, one looks Turkic, probably a couple from Uyghur backgrounds. A little United Nations."

"All buddies from back in Urumqi days."

"Looks like it. You're military, so you must know what the PLA is like these days."

Indeed he should, Peale agreed. Back in Mao's time, his entire national following was the People's Liberation Army. Once they pushed out the Nationalists, Mao deployed them as a civilian workforce. The Soviet came in by droves—advisors, engineers, the works—and in the 1950s all those young PLA soldiers were the labor building the new state. By the 1960s, Moscow and Beijing were at odds, and the Soviets pulled out everything, manpower, knowhow, and money.

The wars in Korea and Vietnam again hardened up the PLA, but besides that, China had no wars. The Army became a bloated system, another part of the collective socialist state. They needed a job to do, so when the economic liberalization came, the modernizers mass deployed the underused soldiers into the countryside for skilled and unskilled labor.

That had scaled back the PLA fighting force, shedding the fat while hardening its core. It was a more efficient tool for trouble spots. Then later, as Tiananmen Square illustrated, the Chinese army was divided. Some commanders refused to send troops into Tiananmen, so outside regiments were deployed. Purges in the military followed, then a further stiffening of the PLA backbone. Even so, China had changed, and men at the top caught the winds of reform. Like any military, they adapted by becoming doves, hawks, or opportunists.

Now, as Peale and Ho just experienced, there was a kind of Chamber of Commerce version of the PLA. It was a career track for young men and even women. They were signed up, trained, and deployed to do the routine work of solving traffic jams, helping with construction projects, driving around showing the flag, and on the sly, hiring out their trucks to move things. Even helping wayward travelers, like Peale and Ho.

"Kids are the same everywhere," Ho said. "The lieutenant gave me his card, phone number and everything." She took the card from her chest pocket. "A good politician in the making. Join the PLA. Be an entrepreneur. Have a good life. The new China."

"Make allies where you can," Peale said.

With a wave, one of the fresh-faced soldiers said, "See you again sometime." Ho waved back.

The Kazakhstan crossing was slow and bureaucratic, but the young lieutenant delivered as promised. The taxi driver from Urumqi was licensed to cross. The night was now dark and the stars were out, with gray wisps of cloud catching some moonlight. The arid desert smell was all around. They taxied off to the nearest Kazakh city, which was too small, so it was on to the next, and better luck. Peale and Ho found a hotel. In the morning it was again city by city, until there was one large enough to have an airport. They'd cleaned up at the hotel, but still felt damp with sweat, tired, and feared that they stank of intrigue.

They'd not come up with much, but it was a start.

"Don't worry, HUMINT is like this in China," Ho said from experience. "We'll be back. We just need some more ammunition."

PART TWO

10

Beijing

GIVEN WHAT WAS at stake, General Secretary Ren Jinuah was feeling calm. He was finishing his morning walk around the central government compound, the Zhongnanhai. As a former imperial garden, it was festooned with arboreal delights and curving lakes.

His morning thoughts varied little, though each day ahead would bring countless diversions. This was the time he reserved to wallow in his singular political vision, the "Peaceful Rise" of China. It was one of his newest slogans, and it looked beautiful in its calligraphic form. Ever since the unfortunate "incident" called Tiananmen Square, the world had tried to circulate a contrary slogan, the "China threat" slander. He was reversing that.

True, China would lead the world in hard power, through money and armies, but it would be wrapped in soft power, *ruan shili*, as well. True also, the slogan "Ruan Shili" had emerged at an earlier Party Congress, before he became general secretary, but he was taking it further. Much further.

Chairman Ren strolled back along the lake and down a path, returning to the government compound. He could see the black limousines arriving, the other eight members of the nine-man Politburo Standing Committee. From different parts of Beijing, they were carried through Beijing's morning traffic. With their special license plates, the traffic police, in light blue shirts, or the public security police in green uniform, gave them right of way. Then around the great asphalt Tiananmen Square, by the looming red Tiananmen Gate, they caught a glimpse of the Mausoleum of Mao. Then it was into the Zhongnanhai, the Politburo's perfect island of power.

Earlier that morning, he'd read a paper from the Party ideologists. They worked on making Chinese Marxism cutting edge, keeping it orthodox yet responding to new dialectical conflicts in the late stages of capitalism. They were now focusing on culture, adopting the work of Gramsci, founder of Italy's Communist Party: capitalists ruled not only by controlling the "means of production," but more so by dominating culture. Ren was taken by his ideologists' prescription: Revolutionary China must shatter the hegemony of Western culture, a necessity in the dialectic of history.

Their examples caught Ren's attention: the "objective conditions" were thus—the West dominated with blue jeans and cell phones, now on par with China's chop sticks, stir fried, and the blue-and-white Ming dishware. The point was to go further—give universal play to China's art; a scroll in every house, ink calligraphy as interior design, a red calligraphic stamp on every document. In time, moreover, Beijing's hegemony would force Taiwan, with its portion of the imperial art collection, to join the mainland.

Such bold ideas were as refreshing to Ren as the morning air.

For late spring, the north winds brought some chilly days to Beijing, but at least the frozen pall of winter had passed. This part of the city looked as it had for two centuries. Around the old Palace grounds, the countless ancient red roofs—stacked in twos or threes—curved upward at the edges. The design had been set a millennia ago to let sun in the windows. On this morning, Ren observed, the tiled roofs all had a dull red sparkle seen through the haze of city smog.

Back inside the compound, he paced across rooms that also showed the signs of tradition. Draped red flags marked corners of larger spaces. A few brass-colored hammer-and-sickles decorated central areas. Potted plants offered accents here and there. The building had the aura of a miniature People's Hall, the monumental gathering place of the Party congresses, also on Tiananmen Square.

Soon the other eight Politburo Standing Committee members gathered in the elegant conference room. It was rare, if ever, that the room saw the thrust and parry of floor debate. On this day, Ren had only a few words for his colleagues. The general secretary was deemed "first among equals," but everyone knew how it really worked: China always had a chairman, indeed an emperor.

"Thank you for coming," Ren said. "I have something to show you this morning. I apologize for taking you away from your many important duties."

As usual, he waxed eloquent. He often gave small speeches. His eight Politburo colleagues all listened attentively, though he did not always know what was in their minds.

"I want to begin by reminding us all that we represent the Party, the blood and soul of China." He praised the nation's Constitution, the operating principle of the People's Republic of China since 1949. Of particular note was one clause, which he would cite again. "Thanks to our Constitution, we have a working government, an example to the world. Yet we should never forget that one wise phrase, that the Party has a 'leading role.'"

Indeed, as everyone knew, the Party was the ghost in the machine. Lacking any kind of legal status, the Party was nevertheless the source of power, essentially unreachable—except through the ways of the Politburo.

At this reminder, the eight men felt the pride of how they had risen. They also recalled how their discourse had changed since the time of Mao, a time of hurled accusations. If a group was lukewarm to the leader, it was a "faction," but if it was a rival, it was denigrated as a "clique." The terms still surfaced, if carefully, so imbedded were they in the revolutionary tradition. Now they were also thinking, What was Ren up to today? As he finished his remarks, Ren caught the glance of one member of the so-called Xinfeng Clique, his rival faction. This instant of recognition happened often, this sparkle, or maybe it was a glint of resistance, in the man's narrow eyes. Ren wondered where the man really stood, and kept that thought in his mind.

"Let us now take a trip to the imperial grounds," Ren said.

They all began to disperse to the front. Limousines were waiting. The drive was short, out the parkland, up to the Tiananmen Gate—bearing the giant image of Mao at its center—through a side entrance. The wheels of the limos hummed swiftly over the inner cobblestones. They arrived at the Palace Museum, tucked into a vast forecourt of the Forbidden City.

As they went inside, guards straightened their backs. Then Chairman Ren, standing before a wall filled with paintings from the Han, Tang, Song, and Ming Dynasties, began to speak again.

Given the venue, it was obvious to the other men that Chairman Ren was not going to talk about his great "Belt and Road Initiative," his visionary plan to build shipping and commercial routes to countries and continents. Some of them had quibbled with him about the name of the initiative, since the calligraphic name was always important. Some had suggested "The New Silk Road Initiative," but that was too evocative of the past. The project needed a modern, industrial, and yet poetic name, and so it was. This project was what many Politburo members had been investing time in, for it was essential to China's future. Its goal was to bring in the natural resources China needed, sending out the manufactured goods that its factories produced.

But today's message was different. With the historic artworks as his backdrop, Ren, in dark suit and red tie, began his little talk, another piece added to the "Thought of Ren Jinuah."

"In these times, a time of great pressure on all of us, the esteemed Standing Committee, we must remember our ancient history, our legacy, our art." As he spoke, he gestured at the artworks, shuffling one to another, as if he was a great art curator for the nation. "From these works we still draw lessons. Perseverance, subtlety, and most of all, civilization, the oldest in the world." As to the oldest, he was taking liberties with history, but that was the point of being a visionary chairman.

The cadre knew Ren's general themes very well. But this particular talk seemed to be a sign, a crystallization of Ren's thought. Perhaps it was a new element of orthodoxy. That had happened many time before, just like the "The Thought of" markers from Mao Zedong to Deng Xiaoping, both of whom opportunistically revised political doctrine.

"Behind all we do, this must be our thinking," Ren Jinuah concluded. "This is our soft power. The 'Peaceful Rise' of China. The 'Celestial Face of China.'"

It was well received on the face of it. The short ceremony ended, and given their busy schedules the top Party members again passed greetings, exchanged brief words, and headed back to the limousines. Before that, Ren scanned the group, caught the eye of two of its members, nodded slightly, and they nodded back. They would meet in the afternoon—privately.

SEVERAL HOURS LATER, Ren Jinuah returned to his office, preparing for the next appointment. He came back into the building by the normal process—through the foyer and then an inner room with tall ceilings. The guards in green uniforms snapped to attention. He went into his private bathroom for a moment to freshen up. In the mirror, his dark hair shone, as if in a waxworks. Everyone in the Politburo, all twenty-five, dyed their hair. Having passed his mid-sixties, Ren also had gray temples to hide.

For all its park-like ambiance, the Zhongnanhai offices, which foreigners called China's "White House," had retained an aura much like that of the People's Hall, with its Soviet design. He often thought of that hall, especially now that the Party vote was to come in the autumn. A day earlier, he had dropped by the great auditorium. The springtime cleaning crews, a veritable army, were putting on the annual polish-up, a dust-free gleam. The great Hall, which sat ten thousand, had a stage framed by ten towering red banners. A brass-colored hammer and sickle hung at its center.

If all went as planned, Chairman Ren would be leading the nine members of the Standing Committee of the Politburo onto that stage—meaning he would be at the head of the line. He would have a third term, and possibly tenure for life. The ceremony took only five minutes. Yet every five years, it shaped history.

It was all thoroughly modern, as was China. Even so, its top leader could take on the aura of a folk hero, evoking images of Chinese sages of the past and showing that, while expert in Marxist-Leninist doctrine, China's leader could also be a wellspring of ancient knowledge. Ren Jinuah believed that he carried that aura. The "Ren" bloodline had not only been warriors in the ancient Qin Dynasty, but earlier still, a chief disciple of Confucius.

More than once he told the story of such a personage, the hermit Ren Tang of the ancient Eastern Han Dynasty. One day, a powerful governor visited the hermit who, breaking protocol, did not bow and scrape. Instead the hermit acted out an appeal. First he pulled a patch of weeds from the ground. Then he brought over a bowl of clean water. Only then did he bow.

The message was clear: the potentate was to treat corruption like weeds, to be wrenched out, and his own rule to be as clear as the water. The story went down well, even if the Party, as everyone inside it knew, was still a field of weeds, clear water a rarity. For Chairman Ren, the story also suggested that China had not changed in two thousand years.

Those ancient truths could be appreciated, even if all the feudal pomp of imperial dynasties had been cleared away. The spirit of the new was seen in the redesign of some Party buildings, and in the modern attire of the cadre. Nobody wore Maoist uniforms anymore, at least around the capital. Still, the proletarian look had its place. The green uniform, actually styled after the nationalist Sun Yat-sen smock, with its small vertical collar, was worn at official events and private Party meetings. Otherwise, modern business suits had pushed aside much of that. In dark suit and crisp white shirt, Ren Jinuah was the epitome of China Inc.

A light knock came on Ren's office door. His secretary peered in, said, "Good afternoon Mr. Chairman." Saying "Chairman" was an informal honor. It was not used in public. That had been the title of the founder, Chairman Mao, and saying it in public, to a current general secretary, evoked mixed feelings at its presumptiveness.

"They have arrived," she said.

"Show them in."

Ren stood as his two visitors entered, both members of Ren's four-member faction in the Politburo Standing Committee of nine.

Each was the head of one of China's main "Leading Groups," all such groups with specific roles, from the state-owned business and national industry to security and the army. These two men ran the Leading Group for Propaganda and Ideological Work, which handled China's cultural affairs, the other the Leading Group for Public Security, the all-seeing eye of the Party.

On their agenda this day was the "women problem."

The secretary served the three men tea, and they settled in. They had known each other for a long time. Sometimes they were mutually wary, other times their interests aligned like planets around Beijing, the sun. Recently the alignment was as strong as ever.

"We have a small problem," said Ming Zhou, head of the Propaganda and Ideological Work.

"How small?" Ren Jinuah said. "I've got many big one's on my desk right now."

"Very small, but very inconvenient. It could become larger."

"This is about my niece. Am I right?"

The other minister, Hua Yang, head of public security, said, "I'm afraid so. And about Madame Soong Wei." The women problem.

The two men had helped Chairmen Ren in his rise, and indeed they had risen with him, all of them at first provincial leaders, moved about and vetted for their Party stamina, then finally to the top. They had weathered the storm and found China at the apex of world affairs. The great economic crisis of a decade earlier had weakened the West. China had been tight with its money, and now it was the world's lender. With that solvency, China pivoted to expanding its cultural influence, and the three men were its pilots.

They were also students of history, and in this respect, their motives were driven by the "Century of Humiliation," when Western traders and armies had arrived, taking advantage of China's first "open door" experiment, selling its people opium and buying up its art treasures. It was a century, ending with Mao's revolution, when China seemed to bow to the West. Now that would be, if not re-venged, at least reversed.

Ren shifted in his chair. With the mention of his niece, the three men were entering family territory, always a delicate matter in the stratosphere of the Politburo. Ren looked at his two compatriots. They were men he could trust. They were part of the four Politburo votes his faction could deliver.

"Let's discuss Madame Soon Wei first," he said. "Where does she stand with the Yellow Faction?"

For him to gain his third term, Ren needed one or two more votes, and those had to come from the Yellow Faction in the Politburo, for the only other faction, the Xinfeng Clique, was ob-stinate. Ren was not too sure about that. One Xinfeng member had often met his gaze with a knowing look. The thought stayed in the back of his mind.

Now Hua Yang, the public security minister, addressed Ren. He had heavily hooded eyes and a wide nose. His dark eyebrows rose and fell as he spoke. Ren considered him his shrewdest counselor. "We are still opposed by the three votes of the Xinfeng Clique," Hua Yang said. That Politburo faction was a holdover from a previous regime. A few attempts had been made on Ren Jinuah's life, and this faction was always suspect. "As you know," Hua Yang said, "the Yellow Faction is the key, if we can get one of their two votes."

The Politburo math was fairly simple, except for the current matter, the women problem, a rivalry between two dragon ladies.

"The Yellow faction is still strongly tied to the family of Madame Soong Wei," said Ming Zhou, the cultural minister. Although Soong had no official position, she held sway over those Politburo members, loyalists of her late husband, a former general secretary. She was also head of Omni Art Global, a wing of the PLA, and an important thrust of the soft power initiative. "We need her to go our way, and that will surely swing the votes we need."

Winning over Madame Soong, in Ren's mind, could be done, but as to the other woman problem, his niece, he was still at a loss. She was Quang Daiyu. She had secrets that could undermine his rise. And unfortunately, she was in competition with Soong Wei of Omni Art Global. As early as possible, he needed a solution. Quang Daiyu could be an obstacle to his smooth rise to a third term. She had a special place in the family, tangled in old family politics. And she had secrets about the family, stories of the past that she could hold over Ren Jinuah's head.

Ming Zhou said, "The good news is that Madame Soong Wei is very pleased with her increased role in the national strategy, the cultural-business strategy. But as you know, she has a problem with your niece."

"Yes, yes," Ren Jinuah said, sipping his tea. "Two jealous ladies. Two power hungry ladies. It's been the long story of China. As I told you before, I will take care of the niece." It was not easy, not easy at all. This was no time to rock that boat.

"May I recommend a measure," Ming Zhou said.

"Please."

Ming Zhou summarized the stakes, and the measures already taken. "I have confidence that Madame Soong Wei will support us, but to make sure, we have taken steps favorable to her, and I recommend a few more. Already, she has been given a secure red phone to our ministry." He then noted that Soong Wei's Omni Art Global had been facing stiff competition, both in the Western markets, and here at home. "We have tried to help by using our intelligence service to bring her better information. The Western traders, of course, are clever. They know what rock to look under for the best deals on the world art market. Our intelligence is helping her."

"And further steps?" Ren said.

"A full financial backing, more than present." At this point in his report, Ming Zhou cleared his throat and sipped the tea, anticipating a potentially awkward moment ahead. "As to your niece, Chairman, Madame Soong Wei does not like her. She does not like her running her business, her so-called Phoenix Group and Silk Road Company."

"And what *about* her business," Ren Jinuah interrupted. "China is in business. All kinds of business."

There was state business, private business, and illicit business, so much of the latter that it was no longer worth the trouble to stamp it out, or even exert more than a modicum of control. In truth, the anti-corruption campaigns had become brash political tools, used to bring down significant rivals to Beijing. Ren Jinuah recalled what he told the Standing Committee on this: "Go after the big, not the small."

Now it was Security Minister Hua Yang's turn. "Yes, about her business, the Phoenix Group-Silk Road company," he said. "As you instructed, we have not interfered. Yes, we have watched. And we have provided a degree of security. She has a staff, a reliable group, and she has very easy clearance. Travel, banking, other small things."

Hua Yang steadied himself, firmly under the glare of Ren Jinuah. "It is not always easy to manage these things in the provinces. Sometimes our security, our PLA workers, can be a little clumsy. However, there is no problem, no worries. It has worked better in Shanghai. Out in Urumqi, well, we've had a few misunderstandings, some mix ups with the security, the PLA. It's all very tense with the terrorists. We've told them that the Phoenix-Silk Road company, its facilities, have free passage, and—"

"Yes, I get the picture," Ren Jinuah said, a little impatient. Bigger things were on his mind. "Please, take care of this, as you have. No bad feelings, nothing to anger my niece."

At that moment Cultural Minster Ming Zhou interjected, moving back to the larger perspective. "In our soft-power initiative," he said, "we have increased our budget, as you know. I recommend that we bring Madame Soong Wei and her Omni Art Global under its umbrella. This will be a sign that her work is important, noticed by the Standing Committee. She has great plans, business plans, in dominating the art markets in Europe and the United States."

Already they knew that she, like many of China's state corporations, supported the "Celestial Face of China" exhibition tour. She also put in a good word when China had negotiated the opening of a special annex in the Freer Museum of Asian Art.

"She has supported the effort of our curators abroad, still working diligently to look for lost China art," Ming Zhou said. "Again, I recommend an increase in her funding."

A cautious man, Ren still viewed Madame Soong Wei and the Yellow Faction as wild cards. But he believed the measure was wise. It would not break the budget.

"Then let it be done," he said. "Is there anything else?"

"That is all for now, Mr. Chairman," the cultural minister said.

Ming Zhou handed Ren Jinuah the necessary documents to be signed and passed on to the Ministry of Finance. Ren added a note, "To be expedited."

As they rose, Hua Yang remembered they'd forgotten to tell Chairman Ren one other thing. "Excuse me, Mr. Chairman, there is something more. Good news, I believe." Hua had their full attention. "As always, we recorded and will be transcribing your remarks at the Palace Museum this morning. I believe they were particularly significant. With your permission, I would like to distribute them privately to all twenty-five members of the Politburo." This would again be an edition of the "Thought of Ren Jinuah."

"An excellent idea," Ming Zhou said.

"Yes, that is commendable," Ren said.

The two men thanked him, offered slight bows, and left the supreme leader's office.

Ren Jinuah lingered at his desk for a while, then meandered over to his large window. It looked over the beautiful garden-like grounds. He tried to clear his mind of the bigger problems that demanded his time and attention. There were the trade talks, the question of energy for China, the UN pressures on environmental problems, keeping the PLA sufficiently in Party control.

And now family issues might boil over and stain his image. As was the custom in China, little was known to wider circles about the families, even the ancestries, of many top leaders. There were the high points, of course. A leader may have served in the time of Mao Zedong, the time of Deng Xiaoping. Others at the top had notable provincial accomplishments. In any case, the old guard was gone, or going, and new material had to be tapped.

Within this upper circle, Ren Jinuah had developed his supporters. Otherwise, his family history was a black box. He protected it with his life. Unfortunately, his niece knew what no one else did. He would have to keep her happy. He would have to, at least until an alternative came along. For she had her way, like so many dragon ladies in China's history.

It was perhaps time for a meeting with his niece.

11

Washington D.C.

A WEEK LATER, the head of the CIA's China desk in Washington knocked on the door of his boss, deputy director Lucy Anderson. She was busy at her computer alongside a steaming cup of coffee.

"Come in," she said distractedly, knowing it was Flynn.

George Flynn glided in and handed her a copy of the transcription. "Hot off the presses," he said. "We've picked this up through intelligence, and you might find it interesting. More 'Thought of Ren Jinuah.'" The CIA had gotten hold of the transcript of Ren's talk at the Palace Museum.

Anderson pulled a strand of flaxen hair behind her ear and scanned the sheet. "Very interesting."

"I've got nothing against HUMNINT, but electronic hacking still gets a lot of the goods," Flynn said.

Reading through, Anderson said, "He's very big on this soft power thing, especially with the art." She was also thinking, All Ren Jinuah needed now was that third term, then chairman for life.

"Beijing is very good at this," Flynn said.

"At what?"

"Borrowing from the West. First Marxism-Leninism. Now 'soft power.' That's an idea from a Harvard academic, *Foreign Policy*, 1990. Everyone knows the definition by now, 'getting others to want the outcomes that you want. Co-opting people rather than coercing them.'"

"I'll take this with me today," Anderson said of the Ren transcript. In a few hours, there was a meeting at the Department of State to discuss what two agents, whom Anderson had never met, had brought back from Europe and China.

THE MORNING HAD begun cloudy in Washington. Under those gray skies, across town, the "thought" of the supreme leader Ren was being considered at the Embassy of China. The embassy was nestled back in a sheltered neighborhood, high up in residential District of Columbia. The curatorial staff of five Chinese nationals, in America on special visas, had arrived at the Embassy to begin the day's work down at the Freer Museum of Asian Art. On some days, only two or three took the embassy bus to the Freer, the others staying behind. There was other work to do in the embassy basement. And so it went day by day.

Today all five were en route, but before they got underway, they were detained for a short while by the deputy ambassador, their charge. He had some new inspiration from Beijing. After he summarized, he said, "I hope this will help you in your mission. Very few are privy to the 'Thought of Ren Jinuah,' now at least. Someday I hope it will be known by many."

The five curators, having been sent to America on a cultural exchange with the Freer Museum, were happy to hear their work was so important—risky work, but work that needed to be done to right the wrongs of the past. It was an exciting time for another reason.

The great "Celestial Face of China" exhibition was ending its two-week stay in Washington. It had already been to Los Angeles over the winter, and then Chicago in early spring.

After the pep talk, the five Chinese curators followed their team leader out to the driveway. The day ahead would continue the delicate work that had begun several weeks before. They climbed into the passenger van. It headed down Massachusetts Avenue, along the lengthy Mall drive. As the van turned the corner, the group could see the giant "Celestial Face of China" banners on the National Gallery. Soon they entered by the back of the Freer Museum, their pride palpable, as if filling the museum interior. They were ready to get back to work.

AS THE VAN left the Embassy of China, Grace Ho was taxiing her way into D.C. from Northern Virginia, across the Potomac. Peale was also heading in, driving over from Annapolis. With the China escape less than a week behind them, he was ready for some air conditioned bureaucracy, but reluctant to come face-to-face with the FBI, the source of some consternation when they were in Europe. For the first time also, he would darken the halls of the state department. He needed a plan.

To that end, he had spent the past two days mulling how to handle this. Keep his own counsel, or do a "winning hearts and minds" to try to calm the waters? A little reading gave him an idea—and the content for a little speech he might give. In the past year, the head of the FBI had spoken quite openly of China as the leading threat to the U.S. economy and security. This was not talk about "soft power"—art and culture—but the stealthy power of espionage. Peale had worked with the FBI before. He wanted to show his respect and his knowledge of their important work on China. On that platter, he would also serve up why Ho and himself should continue as a solo investigation, with an emphasis on solo.

For a start, of the FBI's five thousand active counterintelligence cases, half of them involved Chinese activities on Western soil. Some involved Communist Party pressure on families back in China to manipulate their family members abroad. The two most nefarious mechanism, the FBI believed, were Beijing's "Thousand Talents" program and the so-called "Fox Hunt." In the first, the Party, acted like a grant-giving foundation, while actually buying Western trade secrets. As to Fox Hunt, it was ostensibly China's open-armed co-operation with Western police agencies to curb international crime. Actually, Beijing used it to blackmail or coerce Chinese abroad to do its bidding.

The day had arrived, and Peale drove the crosstown route to the meeting. He had his short monologue at the ready—and he'd judge the atmosphere at the state department meeting before he decided what to do with his encomium to the FBI. The roads took him past the Freer Museum on the Mall. He arrived at the gray building of the state department in Foggy Bottom about the same time as Ho, except he had to navigate the secure gate at its basement garage. They met in a third floor lobby, where they were greeted by Castelli and two people in dark attire, Deputy Secretary Lucy Anderson of the CIA, and special agent John Hargrave of the FBI.

Peale knew it would be awkward with Hargrave. Castelli introduced him to the dark-haired man with graying temples in a well-tailored suit.

"So you're Peale," Hargrave said. "We hope you'll consider a career with the FBI." The humor was hard to separate from the sarcasm. The Federal Bureau of Investigation had been looking for the Gardner Collection for over thirty years; three decades of special agent deployments, leads, dead ends, resources, follow ups, and now Hargrave had been told that this pair in the lobby had probably tracked it down.

Peale was on his toes for this eventuality. "I had the pleasure of working closely with the feds in New York City, and I can't think of a more harmonious relationship." This could be taken two ways, at worst a tit for tat, so Castelli intervened.

"Those were the days," Castelli said, putting his hand on Peale's shoulder. "That stubble's coming in nicely." Peale was unconsciously scratching the week of beard growing on his face, begun in the last days of Urumqi. "Keep it growing, maybe a mustache and goatee, something like that." Castelli had been thinking ahead; Peale might need a new passport photo, different from his last one.

That chilly moment thawed quickly, and everyone put aside their status on the federal government G-scale, or their departmental ranks, and the group ambled as equals into a small conference room. The sun had dispersed the clouds. It glinted through the venetian blinds, casting bright stripes across the carpet floor. The man from State, Carl Schmidt, had requested the meeting. He came in soon after, greeted everyone, and said, "Okay, let's get started. We've got a lot to pull together."

Anderson said, "Before we begin, I'd like to hand everyone this transcript. A new edition of Ren Jinuah's thought. Just in." The copies went around, one for each.

Schmidt said, "I've also got something to say before we start. It's good that we have this meeting, and in particular I'm thinking of Agent Hargrave and Joe Castelli's team. We all know how inter-department turf works, and none of us are naïve about that. My role is to referee this sort of thing. The administration has given me a final word on this. I've asked Agent Hargrave to join us at this meeting, but we've already talked some things over. This Gardner thing is the FBI's baby, and I realize that. But now we're looking overseas, so we've come to an understanding that will keep them in the loop, but give Castelli's team room to move." He didn't go into the late unpleasantness with Europol, nor did he mention that Hargrave had wanted to shut down Castelli's operation, garner its information, and take the lead. Everyone knew that through the grapevine, and as to grapevines, Washington was a vineyard par excellence.

Unshaven and feeling it, Peale cleared his throat and said, "Secretary Schmidt, may I speak to that topic for a moment?"

There was a stunned silence as all eyes were on Peale, who seemed to have spoken out of order. Ho's eyes drilled into him. She was not given a heads up, so what was her partner thinking?

"Speak away," Schmidt said.

Now Peale had the floor. He was a bit slow off the mark, but gained speed. He opened with a note of appreciation for the state department and FBI, both working in serious waters abroad, and how they had arrived at some guidelines in that matter. Then the meat of his little speech—acknowledging the pressing things the FBI had undertaken in American interests abroad, and accordingly, how the art heist, perhaps, paled by comparison. Hence the value of independent investigators filling that small gap with precision tools, leeway abroad and ability to cross the Chinese language barrier. The pitch was short, a kind of velvet argument, and now Peale had it off his chest—and into the minds of the stake holders.

Schmidt said, "Well, I would say that's a perfect cap to what Agent Hargrave and I had chewed over." He looked at Hargrave, who remained poker-faced.

"I appreciate Mr. Peale's perspective," Hargrave finally said.

"So that's settled, let's get started," Schmidt said. He put his gaze firmly on Castelli.

Peale had somewhat stolen Castelli's thunder, but as supervisor of the team, the former New York cop stayed with his planned introduction. "By now you know Julian and Grace, two of my best independent operatives. Birds of a feather, you might say. A little tour through Kazakhstan at the end, but that went so well it was like a paid vacation." Only the CIA's Anderson smiled.

Schmidt said, "Okay, team report."

Ho and Peale glanced at each other, not sure who was in charge, much like their days abroad. Ho quickly deferred to Peale, saying "Mr. Peale can summarize." His second time up to bat in as many minutes.

He briefly summarized their experience, concluding with, "So there are a lot of connections, but despite what we found in Europe and in Urumqi, it's still fairly circumstantial, at least the whereabouts of the Vermeer, and so the whole collection for now."

The FBI's Hargrave wanted to jump in. Indeed, he had a list of things, but twice now he had agreed to hold his fire. There was no use at this point.

Schmidt said, "Julian, give us the broader picture. What's going on over there with the art trade, the geopolitical dimensions, China in particular?"

Peale tried not to lean his elbows on the large table. He tended to do so despite himself, focused on what he was saying. "As I think you may have gathered from your own intelligence work, China seems to be on a cultural offensive. While I'm sure there are links in Beijing, probably Shanghai and elsewhere, it's safe to say that a lot of the commerce is probably coming and going in Urumqi, closest to Europe."

Peale looked at FBI agent Hargrave and said, "To track down the Vermeer painting and all the rest perhaps, it's going to take some more footwork in China, I think."

Hargrave said, "That's why we have liaison agents abroad, specialists. We should bring in Europol, make this a—"

Schmidt expected this, so was quick to interrupt. "No, we have to keep this close to the vest, a soft footprint. The last thing we want is too many fingers in this, something blowing up on the diplomatic front. We'll keep pushing, but with the bigger matters of U.S.-China relations in mind. Very delicate right now."

Hargrave looked a bit deflated, but he had agreed to be a team player, so he sat back to listen if still grudgingly. With effort, he was managing to say nothing.

Schmidt wasn't finished. "As we all know, the administration is under a lot of domestic pressure. The Chamber of Commerce, manufacturing, the free-traders, globalists, Google, Amazon, Apple, you name it. They're saying, 'Be nice to China.' Cheap labor, a billion consumers, a gold mine. They've all put on rose-tinted glasses."

Peale was thinking, Yeah, right.

At times like this, when politics and cold-eyed policy clashed, Ho was inclined to sift through the many past tangles between the U.S. and China, particularly the opening one—and it was a bit personal. In the 1800s, tens of thousands of Chinese came to the West Coast during the Gold Rush. They'd heard about "Gold Mountain," but ended up building the railroads. Fear of Chinese swamping the population had led, finally, to the 1882 Exclusion Act. Two generations later, Ho's parents were in the next wave of migrants allowed to come over.

Peale resumed talking and apprised everybody of the pieces of the puzzle: the activity in Spain, the hints around the sale of a Vienna collection, and most important, the names Phoenix Group, Silk Road Company, Omni Art Global, even the name Soong Wei, a big player with Omni Art, with family ties in the Politburo. The companies were active in Europe and Urumqi, and presumably in Beijing and Shanghai—to what extent, still to be determined. And, of course, all of this was against the backdrop of China's General Secretary Ren being big on "soft power" and seeking a third term, perhaps tenure for life.

"Lucy, I think you have the most to tell us, some findings from the surveillance pickups," Schmidt said, turning to her. "And this paper you've given us."

"There's quite a lot," Anderson said. "Not a lot of correlation yet, but definitely some red flags. As you can see, we've just gotten a transcript from General Secretary Ren's 'thought,' as it were. It's about a cultural push, which he calls 'Peaceful Rise' of China. There's more use of the term 'Celestial Face of China,' like the art exhibition that just came through."

"Leave it to the Chinese to come up with a name like that," the FBI man said.

"Well," Anderson said, "calligraphy uses a lot of big words like that. Anyway, this is something new. We've not seen these two used together before. It tells us there's a new focus on the art market, retrieving lost art, sending out China's image." She pulled out a different document, a thick sheaf of papers. It too was a transcript like-report.

"Okay, in their early reports, Julian and Grace passed on this idea of the Ghost of Empress Cixi. By the way, my compliments, being alert to these kinds of oddball things."

Ho said, "It did strike us as something."

"It is something, a kind of world in the mind of someone on the Internet calling herself, or himself, 'The Ghost of Empress Cixi.'"

"Where on the internet, secure, government?" Schmidt said. He knew online censorship was strict in China.

"As you know, the Internet in China's mainland is blocked. We sometimes get through that, but not always. What I have here is quite public, information that's gone out of China," Anderson said. "Despite the blockage, with a little work we've tracked down its IP addresses, one in Urumqi, western China, and one in Shanghai."

"Very interesting," Peale said.

"That's the technical part. Job well done by our teams, getting around all those anonymous servers. Then, another heads up. The blog, whatever you call it, is a strange combination of history, a lot on the 'Century of Humiliation,' and a kind of diary, apparently a woman, talking like she's the Empress Cixi. She's talking about a lot of the things we've been looking at, things in the Gardner Collection, then a lot about art taken from the Qing Dynasty—did I pronounce that correctly?—all kinds of things about art stolen from China, well, etc. etc. It's a bit eccentric, but where there's smoke, there may be fire."

"And we have no real name attached to this?" Schmidt said.

"Nothing hard," Anderson said. "The woman, this Empress Cixi ghost, very often suggests she has some family status in China, of course not royalty, but you know what they say in China . . . to understand the politics, follow the family."

After a breath, she continued. "We tried to get physical addresses for the IPs, and if we could, we'd try to find out who owns, rents, occupies those addresses. No luck. We cooked up something else, a bit thin, but what do you think: the blogger does mention some names, mostly in the news, Chinese officials, nothing specific. However, there are strange allusions, something about 'Black Jade knows,' an occasional mention of someone named Quang, 'Quang knows' it also says. We put it together. That would be, I presume, a Miss Black Jade Quang, or translated Quang Daiyu."

"So?" Castelli said.

"So, that's the name of General Secretary Ren Jinuah's niece. That tidbit is surprising enough, since Ren's family background, past and present, is such a puzzle to intelligence and to Sinologists. We put out the name, scrubbed every kind of data we could, and lo and behold, there is some data on the Internet associating Quang Daiyu with Silk Road Company in Shanghai. In another case, that name is the same as a Chinese exchange student at Harvard, back around 1988. Specifically, she was at the Fogg Museum on Asian Art."

Hargrove said, "We've got agents in Boston, so—"

"Yes, I understand," Anderson said. "The CIA can't do domestic surveillance. It can do research, however. And it can hand that over to deputized agents." She was thinking of Peale and Ho who, after all, we're not really working for any agency in particular.

Ho decided she would complement Peale later on his "nice little speech," but for the moment she was eager to jump in and show she was up on things. She also wanted to put them back in a historical context, out beyond jurisdictional squabbles. "The Fogg is one of the museums, like the Freer, that gathered a lot of China's art in the 'golden age' of art collecting. What do your analysts make of this?"

Anderson said, "Just the facts ma'am. Nothing 'aha' at the moment."

Schmidt, no computer whiz by any means, was thinking of all the crazy bloggers on the planet, a room of mirrors if there ever was one. "How does this name, this data, help us with the Vermeer, the bigger picture we're trying to gather?"

"I don't know," said Anderson, speaking for all the powers of the CIA.

"Sounds like it will need some footwork," Castelli said. That was his forte, but not with his own feet anymore. "Why don't we send Peale and Ho up to the Fogg Museum, see what they can find. That's a lot closer than Shanghai."

Schmidt looked at Hargrave, seeking a reaction. The face was stone-like. "No comment," he said. At least he didn't say that the FBI had agents a few miles from Harvard. And meanwhile, if this was starting to look more and more like an overseas China intrigue, well, the FBI was neither in that game nor part of the diplomatic corps.

Out of the group, Castelli offered the most concrete step—more work by Peale and Ho. "They'll do the FBI proud." He might have best held his tongue, but no matter.

"Then, good, get your people back on the road," Schmidt agreed. "If they've got to go back to China, that too."

Everything that could be said was already said, but Castelli still had more. He looked at Peale and Ho. "You two ever been to Boston?" They were embarrassed to admit that in fact, they had not, so Peale, looking at Ho, said, "Sounds good."

"What about Shanghai?" Castelli said. Peale looked at Ho, waiting for her to fess up, revealing her secret life, perhaps as a Shanghai spy.

She thought quickly. "I'd love to go to Shanghai, and Boston, too."

"We've already got a new identity for you two. You'll like it. For now please start to pack," Castelli said.

ACROSS TOWN AT the Freer Museum, the five Chinese nationals had been hard at their curatorial and conservation work through the morning. They were due for a short break, some fresh air. In a cabinet, they locked up the portfolio-like briefcases they brought each day, then went upstairs to the Freer Museum's main floor, through the lobby, and then out the glass doors.

Outside, the Washington Mall was filing up with the signs of tourism as summer approached. Far across the vast lawn of the Mall, the "Celestial Face of China" banners still fluttered in the breeze, but now they were being taken down by workmen on scaffolds. Amid the joggers, dog-walkers, and government employees, formally dressed by contrast, were also the lumbering tourist buses, CHINA TOURS emblazoned on their sides.

What they probably didn't know, despite the Mall's monumentality, was that the modest Freer was the first museum there, opened in the 1920s. It bore the name of Charles Freer, an up-by-the-bootstraps American, who in Detroit made his fortune building rail cars for the booming railroad industry in the late 1800s. In the West, the trains ran on a railroad largely built by Chinese immigrant labor. During his travels to China, Freer became one of many taking advantage of the "golden age" of the West's collection of Chinese art. In cooperation with the U.S. government, he funded the building of the Freer Museum, a permanent home for his Chinese objects d'art.

Now the Freer had become one more focal point for a new cultural exchange between the U.S. and China. The new basement wing—funded by Beijing—had been an important diplomatic gesture by the United States. Elsewhere in the United States, China had also sent investigators to review American collections, looking for obvious items known to have been pilfered back when the British, Americans, French, and Germans stomped through the Qing Dynasty with near impunity.

The Freer Museum, also driven by guilt and by diplomatic necessity, had upped the ante by opening the new Chinese wing, allowing the visiting curators to inspect their collections, making lists, testing authenticity, and examining closely the provenance of works. It was ostensibly for on-site preservation work, but as if interrogators, the Chinese often asked whether an artwork was purchased, or was it stolen?

Out on the Mall, the tourists from China were in large clumps around the Mall, animated and talkative, moving down one cross street after another. They headed for the Natural History Museum, the National Gallery and, of course, the Air and Space Museum, the most visited of all showcases in the United States. The five Chinese curators, taking in some sun, felt they were hardly noticeable, which was very good.

"We shall return to our work now," the team leader said. They spirited themselves back into the main building, eager to complete their tasks in their rooms below.

"A very nice day," one young lady on the China team said to a Freer Museum staff member as they re-entered the museum. That was about the extent of her English. "Thank you. . . . nice day, thank you," others said as they filed in, going back down to the Middle Kingdom Research Center, which was underground. The center had a half-story above with a sky-light, surrounded by a new garden, compliments of Chinese corporations.

In their work areas, all five knew their given roles. Works had been retrieved from the Freer Museum archives and brought into the sterile room. The team worked on preservation with new chemical treatments developed to clean the works on paper and silk. The paints and inks were tested for age and authenticity. Sequestered from the everyday doings of the Freer next door, they also took high resolution photos of the works.

On days when not all five went to the Freer, the remaining number repaired to a laboratory in the embassy basement. Stocked with a specially aged paper and silk, this team replicated the original treasures in the Freer. Experts in their craft, they made copies of the originals. Then, on given days, the team members, bearing their large, flat satchels, brought the forgeries to the Freer. Behind closed doors they exchanged them for the originals. The venerable works, presumed to be stolen property in principle, were spirited back to the embassy. Then they were headed for China—a new kind of industrial theft of a very refined sort.

"How was the work today," a staffer at the Freer said to the group of five as they left at closing time. "It's been a long day."

The leader of the Chinese team, smiled, rolled her narrow eyes. "Very long, yes. So tired. Two of us take break tomorrow, see you next day."

12

Boston

PEALE AND HO took an evening shuttle out of National Airport. They were in Boston in less than two hours, then taxing into Cambridge, the great academic bastion of New England. On the flight, they leafed through *Boston Culture*, a travel guide. It had a section on the early New England trade with Asia, explaining how the two big Asian collections of the city, the Fogg Museum of Harvard and the Boston Museum of Fine Art, came to be.

It began with a privateer in 1785, sailing an old ship from the American Revolution, the Grand Turk. It reached Canton, a round-trip voyage of more than two years and over three thousand miles, but it paid off: the ship brought back porcelain, silks, jewelry, art-works, and dishware. Its port was Salem, where the motto had become, "To the Farther Ports of the Rich East." Indeed, Salem boasted the nation's first millionaire.

"They went to do good and did very well," Peale said.

Eventually, the guidebook explained, the Boston Brahmins met the Chinese Mandarins. By the mid-1800s, Boston's educated class, from scholars to poets, had an eye on Asia, China in particular. That had led Harvard to open in 1895 the Fogg Museum at the north edge of Harvard Yard in a Beaux-Arts building. That was torn down later and the collection moved to a new Georgian Revival building in 1927. On top of that structure, all the modern space-age additions were heaped. Now the entire complex, the Harvard Art Museums, looked like a sky-lit science center fronted by a block-long Georgian façade of red brick.

The Fogg collection was the first of Asian art in the United States, a pioneering research center that also trained the early curators who ran the first big American museums. And as with the Fogg, many of the museums were built from donations by turn-of-the-century tycoons, parties to the "golden age" of collecting art from China.

Before Peale and Ho arrived, the Department of State, which had been working with the Fogg on some of the China issues, called through. Given the odd nature of the request, they'd meet with a post-doc student. She was Lynn Cheng, a first generation Chinese-American, born to parents from Hong Kong, who would help them out.

Peale and Ho stayed at one of the trendy hotels off Harvard Yard. In the morning, under a luminous blue New England sky, they made their way to the old Harvard Yard gate facing the Fogg. Miss Cheng waved them over. Her hair was bobbed and she wore a pair of old-fashioned round spectacles, though her trim blue dress was very couture. Peale listened as Ho and Cheng conversed in Chinese, nodding in small bows. They used some English words, giving Peale hints of the bonhomie.

"I'm Julian Peale," he said, extending his hand.

Shaking it, Cheng said, "Very nice to meet you. I thought we would meet here so I can take you directly to the archive. Otherwise, it's a maze in there, easy to get lost."

She led them through the main Georgian door. Next, they went down a long hall of dark oak paneling, done up with plaques and paintings. At an elevator, they went down two floors.

Cheng said, "You know, we get a lot of special inquiries. Right now, a lot of the curators are digitizing all the art collections. A big grant so a big priority. So, you get only me, but I think I've found what you're looking for. It's still in paper documents way off in the corner."

Peale said, "This is from the late eighties, so I'm surprised you've saved them."

"Harvard keeps everything. You know the joke, today's PhD dissertations must write 'more and more about less and less.' So even obscure stuff, like exchange student research. Someday it might be a dissertation, you know. 'Chinese students studying Chinese art in America during and after Tiananmen Square, 1989.'"

Peale, just beginning his dissertation, understood her allusion. He was a big picture kind of guy, but for a dissertation, that was no longer allowed. "I know what you mean," he said.

She led them to a room with study desk and stacks. These were rows of ceiling-high metal book shelves on wheels. A crank on each one pushed them together or apart as a space saver.

"Wait here," she said, motioning to a table. The room was empty and silent. They heard Cheng turning the cranks. "Here we go."

On return, Cheng put down a box and from it removed a stack of files, brown accordion type envelopes with string binding them shut. Peale smelled the must of old paper, a reminder that he was back in a library.

"According to the Index, some of the student papers were kept.

I guess back then the exchanges with China were considered ground breaking. So, 'keep the records,' I suppose."

"Plus, someone could write 'more and more about less and less,'" Peale said.

"You've got it."

Two of the folders were marked "1985-1995." In the back of the first one, she found a list of Chinese art history students. On the list, 1985-1990, was the name Quang Daiyu. "Here she is. Maybe some of her papers have been kept."

A lot of the documents were written in Chinese, though most were in English. They looked like essays, term papers, some even thicker like a master's thesis. Ho and Cheng did the sorting.

Eventually, Ho said, "Ah ha!"

A sheaf of papers, held by a binder clip, held several pages in Chinese, but also what looked like a major paper in English. She pulled it out and read the title, "On the Pillaging of China: Art Collecting during the Qing Dynasty."

Cheng said, "Great," then told them she'd be back around the front lobby if they needed her.

"We'll probably need you to make some photocopies," said Ho. They thanked her and then pulled out the thick document, a thesis paper, and began to read page by page.

According to the preface, the Quang thesis promised a new interpretation of Western art collecting during the Qing Dynasty, 1644-1912, and gave a quick overview, especially on how Qing was a Machu dynasty, having displaced the Ming. There were two preeminent Qing personages that the thesis found worthy of elaboration, Emperor Qianlong, who gathered all of China's art in Beijing, and Dowager Empress Cixi, the last Qing Dynasty ruler. Under Qianlong, Beijing had become a virtual storehouse of China's treasures, and under Cixi the Westerners came, buying art and importing opium.

Among those Western collectors was a wealthy matron from Boston, the famous Isabell Steward Gardner.

"She mentions Gardner right from the start," Ho said.

They read further. Back at the end of the Qing Dynasty, it was the young Dowager Empress Cixi's fate to have been regent of the final line of children-emperors-to-be. By will, guile, and some treachery, Cixi kept her supreme power over the hereditary situation for forty-seven years. That period opened with the First Opium war—a second one came later—and then the Taiping Rebellion by the Southern peasants, followed by the Boxer Rebellion, when northern peoples launched an anti-Western civil war.

"The poor woman couldn't get a break," Ho said.

"Poor woman indeed," Peale said, scratching his short whiskers.

By the time of the Boxer rebels, with whom Empress Cixi had sided, the U.S. and European powers all had Beijing legations, or small fortified residential and business areas. After the Boxers attacked, the Westerners brought in troops. Empress Cixi fled to a summer palace. For a year, the Westerners occupied Beijing, and little by little, the Imperial art collection was pillaged. On the Western withdrawal, Empress Cixi returned, now constrained by treaty obligations. She lived out the last years of her rule, dying in 1908, overseeing a royal court with a grandnephew fading into obscurity. The last remnant of the royal line had withered away.

Interestingly, the paper was appended with a "concluding essay," which discussed the June Fourth Incident, the euphemism for the Tiananmen Square protests in spring 1989, and the military crackdown that followed. Quang tied that turmoil to the struggles of Chinese in her age group to find their personal identities. She also expressed the notion that it was China's ancient legacy of civilizing art that was, similar to European existentialism, the place that a modern citizen of China could find repose, an identity, in the shifting political sands.

"So clearly Quang is obsessed with four things," Ho said. "First, the Beijing treasure. Second, Empress Cixi, and third the Tiananmen Square incident, which happened when she was over here. Then finally, she's obsessed with Isabelle Stuart Gardner. She sees her as one of the pillagers. Look here." She pointed to lines in the text. "She even says that 'Brahmin Gardner acted like she was a Mandarin.'"

"Intelligent but confused thoughts for a woman at that young age," said Peale. "I also notice she's focused a lot on the Shang Dynasty cup that Gardner had in her Boston museum. One of the items lost in the Gardner heist."

Quang had apparently visited the Gardner Museum, since her papers mentioned its two "Chinese Rooms" and other details.

"So she doesn't like Gardner, obviously," Ho said. "But she idolizes Empress Cixi. One a female role model, the other an anti-role model."

"It looks like there's some psychology going on here," Peale said. "Dowager psychology. This could be what motivates Quang."

Besides the thesis, there were other papers written in Chinese, a few personal traces of her life in Boston as well. Looking through, Ho found a page torn from what looked like a Harvard Year Book. In its lower left, there was a photo of two Chinese students, both smiling and looking young and carefree. The young woman had a serene face. The caption read, "Quang Daiyu and Tian Fengshan of the Middle Kingdom."

"Here's something maybe," Ho said. "Tian Fengshan. I wonder who this guy is."

Cheng returned and asked if they had anything they wanted copied.

"All of this if possible," Peale said, handing her the thesis and a few other papers. The yearbook picture had slipped out and fallen on the chair.

Cheng took the material and said, "It's too bad you don't have time to see all the China stuff at the MFA. It's mostly crafts. Anyway, back in those days the objects, the jades, bronzes, statues, porcelain had the most cache. They were also easy to transport, hardier to put in boxes, like that. The paper and silk were pretty fragile." She gave a small laugh. "In Boston, curators just get weary at all the cups, the dishware. They sometimes call it 'crockery,' not fine art."

"We noticed that at the Freer Museum in Washington," Ho said. "We've both done research there."

"Oh, wow, the Freer." Cheng paused, as if an awkward thought had crossed her mind. She said in a lowered voice. "You know, we've heard about those Chinese curators running a branch of the Freer Museum now. Investigating provenance. We've also had some Chinese nationals over here, doing the same. What's that about?"

"In a word, politics," Peale said. "Diplomacy with China is at a highpoint right now. At the Freer, being in Washington, they allowed the opening of an annex. Then came the investigators. It's part of the U.S.-China good-will agenda. Even a few of the Freer Museum people, as best I know, are little irked by it."

Cheng noticed the yearbook page on the chair. She picked it up, said, "Do you want this copied, too."

"Oh, there it is," Ho said. "Yes that, too."

Cheng looked at it. "Wow, that's Tian Fengshan." He was the Harvard student pictured alongside Quang.

"Do you know him?" Peale asked.

"He's a fairly big name. One of the billionaires in Shanghai. I think he built some of the skyline there. Anyway, we have a Tian Fengshan collection here, and there's one at the MFA also. They're called that because he paid for them—like advertising. Actually they're very small. There are some at other museums as well, like the Asian Art Museum in San Francisco. You know, the art is not great, more of the same. But they get their name in a museum."

"So this Tian fellow is in Shanghai," Peale said. "Just shows I don't read the *Asian Wall Street Journal*." He took the page from Cheng, looked more closely, and casually turned it over, curious at the yearbook pictures on the other side. "Huh, there's some writing in the margin here. Chinese."

Ho quickly retrieved it from his hand, and Cheng leaned into see as well. A column of handwritten Chinese script ran vertically down a white margin.

"What does it say?" Peale asked, noticing that Cheng had put her hand to her mouth and was blushing.

Ho said, "A love note apparently." She roughly translated. "'To my Black Jade. A promise. May we continue our pleasures back in Shanghai.'" She paused and said, "The next could be translated as either 'slave' or 'servant.' 'Your loving slave Fengshan.'"

"So they were love birds," Peale said.

"And maybe Quang Daiyu is still in Shanghai."

13

Beijing

REN JINUAH HAD called a special session for the cream of the Politburo, eight cadre and himself, the elite Standing Committee. He was eager, once again, to clarify the vision for what he hoped to be his role as supreme leader, once the vote was taken in the fall. The group, somewhat solemn this morning, gathered in the Great Conference Room within Zhongnanhai by the lakes in the shadow of the Imperial Palace grounds.

Once all were seated and served with tea, Ren Jinuah came in a side door.

"Gentlemen," he said, "thank you for letting me take you away from important duties today. We have important decisions to make over the next year. It is my role, as head of the Party, to continue to clarify our vision. China is booming. It's easy to lose, as our Western friends would say, 'the forest for the trees.'"

Some of the eight cadre smiled, exchanging glances, and chuckling softly. They each represented one of the three main factions in the twenty-five member Politburo. There was Ren's faction, then the older "liberal" Xinfeng faction. The third was the Yellow Faction, a kind of swing vote. Except for Ren Jinuah's own faction members, others in the Standing Committee still had doubts about his growing power. Here at the hub of decision making, feelings could be intense. Listening to Ren, the three members of the Xinfeng retained their cool. The two in the Yellow Faction, undecided, maintained a friendly but reserved countenance. Ren was reading the faces as he spoke.

Earlier, the Yellow faction had met with Madame Soong Wei, their venerable advisor. Ren's Faction had also met with her. After this formal session inside Zhongnanhai's conference room was over, Madame Soong Wei would try to meet with Chairman Ren privately, as the two factions had agreed.

"As you know," Ren Jinuah continued, "we have made great strides on the international stage." Like a promotion brochure for China, he listed the accomplishment—economic, military, and then the ambitious Belt and Road. Nothing was left out. "Today it is time to take stock of our soft power initiative, the 'Celestial Face of China.'"

There was mild applause.

"For this, we must thank the head of our new Leading Group for Propaganda and Ideological Work." Ren Jinuah paused and nodded at Ming Zhou, often called the "Minister of Culture," so broad was his portfolio and authority. "Thanks to great efforts by the cadre, the 'Plan for Cultural Development' has wings like the phoenix, breath like the dragon."

More applause. There were past victories, of course. The Beijing Olympics in 2008. The World Expo in Shanghai in 2010 and 2018, the growth of Confucius Institutes abroad, and the spread of the Chinese language.

"Our adversaries are many, and while we must be proud and at peace at one level, we must be clever, cleverer than our adversaries at many other levels," Ren said. "Our students, a million fold, a third of them in America, serve as our ambassadors. This is well and good. Now that our economy has grown, our people have great confidence in the Party. We have shown that a 'socialist market economy,' a centralized system, is the best model for the world. It is time to take a further step. Our culture, far different from the West, has been built on our language. Our great contribution to humanity. It is unique as a form of image, a pictograph, far superior and far more beautiful than an alphabetical system."

Behind all the colorful details, something else was brewing, and the cadre could feel it. There were some slight murmurs, a rustling of bodies and limbs through the otherwise stoic assemblage. Ren Jinuah was in the midst of a dramatic pause.

Then he said, "As you know, we currently have the 'Celestial Face of China' art exhibition traveling the world, just finishing now in America as we speak. It will then return to China, a great celebration in the city of Wuhan." Except for the Politburo, few knew that Wuhan was the city of Ren Jinuah's birth. "Then it goes to Europe, another triumph."

Ren went on. "As a final act, I have officially approved the erection in Beijing of the China Global Art Museum. It is to be the largest museum of Western and Chinese art in the world. When completed, it will display more masterpieces from the West than even the Louvre in Paris, the National Galleries in London and Washington. This will set right and reverse a historic wrong. Now the West will come to us, not to steal, but to admire."

At that point, Ren Jinuah demurred from specifics. He was setting the tone. Today, he explained, the plan was being distributed to all the Leading Groups. Each was to consider their contribution.

Importantly, by raising the topic, he had justification for even more revenue. As if new slogans for the nation, he again pronounced the "Peaceful Rise" of China, the "Celestial Face of China," even the "Plan for Cultural Development" of China, all of them with great calligraphic images, like the emblems of his chairmanship. At such sessions, however, haggling over such policies—namely, the new "thought" of the supreme leader—was not appropriate.

Ren Jinuah continued his peroration, reminding the cadre that for thousands of years China had ruled as a kingdom to which the outer realms paid tribute. "This has been called the tributary system," he said. "We envision this once again. China as the center of civilization, the family of nations paying tribute, not in gold or silver, but in respect and honor. This is our grand strategy and the global museum will be the symbol."

The cadre had to admit, it was a bold, even breathtaking speech. They also knew that Beijing, Shanghai, and other cities already bristled with museums. The Palace Museum, with its ancient art, and the National Art Museum, a behemoth, were just a few blocks away, filled with ancient and contemporary art. How was this new venture to be different? How would it stand out from the crowd? What was clear was that whatever the plan, it would have Ren's name attached.

The session was over. Chairman Ren came down among his cadre. They exchanged greetings, lingered over small conversations. All shook Ren Jinuah's hand, with a slight bow, as they left. Over in the corner, the cultural minister and the security minister—both firmly in Ren Jinuah's faction—waited. Their request for a confidential meeting had been granted. After the room was empty, Ren Jinuah led them to his private office.

"CHAIRMAN, WE THANK you for this time to talk," Ming Zhou said. "We are following up on our earlier reports to you."

Combined, the culture and security department were an odd

mix, but potentially powerful. Culture communicated China's image to the world—all media, all grand events. Security ran China's domestic policing networks, its monitoring of the population and the borders. Creating China's image on the world stage had an overt and a covert element.

"All is going reasonably well," Ming Zhou said. "The 'Celestial Face of China' exhibit is receiving 'rave reviews,' as the Western press calls it. We are particularly pleased with the progress our investigative curators are making at museums in America and Europe. We get good reports about the curator team at the Freer Museum in Washington. They are identifying many works stolen from China. The Freer is a good example of how, by telling our story, the Westerners feel the mark of guilt. They are meekly walking in step with our plans."

Then Hua Yang said, "Despite all this good news, we continue to have that small problem. Again, we seek your advice, Chairman—"

"As to who will be leader of the China Global Art Museum," Ren said, finishing the man's sentence. It was no secret that a decision had to be made.

"Well, yes," Hua Yang said. "This involves the art accumulation. In cooperation with the PLA and our security department, Omni Art Global is making great headway despite its many rivals."

The updates from Omni were reporting many new purchases of Western masterpieces and its success at placing replicated Chinese works—that is, modern items that looked antique—in many Western collections.

Ren Jinuah sensed what they really want to talk about. "I thought you had worked out the conflict with Madame Soong Wei and my niece. This must be resolved before October." That was when he needed the vote from Madam Soong Wei's faction.

"I'm afraid Madame Soong Wei has lost patience with your

niece," said the cultural minister. "Omni Art Global is using all the security tools we have, but is worried that your niece's projects are ruining its reputation, undercutting her business."

Ren Jinuah sighed. Handling the armed border disputes with India, corruption in a province, Moscow, or the conflict with the United States over technology transfers, was fairly routine, often with conventional solutions. But resolving the conflict between these two well-connected women was another matter.

It had all begun badly, in fact. As the idea of Omni Art Global first emerged, some years back, his niece Quang Daiyu had come to Ren and insisted that she be its leader, not Madame Soong Wei. "But this cannot happen," Ren told her. "Do you realize the political stakes? Please understand." It had not gone well, and Quang went off on her own to set up her own system, the Phoenix Group-Silk Road Company. Then when she heard that Madame Soong Wei might also be the leader of the new China Global Art Museum in Beijing, she came back, wanting Ren Jinuah to appoint her to that position.

Such a niece, Ren Jinuah thought. His mind had drifted, coming back when he was spoken to.

"May I suggest, Mr. Chairman, that you try to resolve this with Madame Soong Wei today," said Hua Yang. "She has arrived in Zhongnanhai, and begs your forbearance, at least for a half an hour."

"Alright," Ren Jinuah said. "Send her to my office."

AN AIDE TO the chairman knocked, announced the visitor, and Madame Soong Wei paraded in. Her raven black hair was tied back, emphasizing her stern face with its wide set eyes, the irises black, but still seeming a dark green jade. She wore a conservative beige business dress, a small broach and a gold watch, far from her days in the green Maoist uniform.

Ren Jinuah was standing. He greeted her and offered a seat across from his desk.

"This is about Quang, my niece," Ren Jinuah said, positioning himself for what was to come.

"It's always about your niece," Madame Soong Wei said. Party members are supposed to control their errant kin—Madame Soong Wei thought this, but did not say it out loud to his face. "There is plenty of room for both of us to do our work in the Cultural Initiative." This was a conciliatory word. "I have to say, though, Quang is making things difficult. Hers is a side project, Omni Art Global is the backbone. It's the dragon, not the firefly."

As Ren Jinuah listened, the problem became plain enough. Quang was poaching on Madame Soong Wei's turf. She was reaching art dealers in Europe before, and even while, Omni Art Global was working out quiet deals over there. One case in Austria, a major private art trove—the Shönberg Collection—had become a major bone of contention between them.

"And she is using the PLA, the rogue PLA I should say," said the Madame. "When it comes to trade in art, Omni Art Global is the PLA. That has been the arrangement from the start." She thought to herself, If my husband were still general secretary, none of this crossing of lines could have ever taken place.

Ren Jinuah divined her thoughts. "Your late husband was a great mentor to me. Honestly, Madame Soong Wei, I take your side in this. My niece, well, it's complicated. She is very independent."

"And she's dealing in stolen property. There's a difference. The Party has an official restitution plan, restitution of what rightfully belongs to China. She is not part of that. Her companies cover for her smuggling. She flies all over China. And I know she has other secret warehouses."

At this point, however, she was not going to mention the Party's anti-corruption campaign, since Omni had always operated fast and loose. So-called "corruption" was always a sensitive topic. Party members did not investigate themselves for how they conducted business. They only probed rivals, typically lower in the Party. In this sense, Soong Wei was virtually immune from suspicion, so high in the Party was her status. Regardless, it was not a topic she liked to emphasize too much.

Chairman Ren sensed what was really going on between Soong Wei and Quang. It was a kind of generational clash, perhaps deeper than he had imagined. Just then, Madame Soong Wei, as if reading his mind, voiced what really was her deepest complaint.

"She has a Western seed," Soong said. In other words, she had been to America in her youth. To old school cadre like Soong Wei, allowing entrepreneurs like Quang to operate under Party auspices was a grave political error.

The chairman became expressive and raised a hand, if gently. "Many of our best young Party members studied abroad. To China's benefit, many are successful entrepreneurs. At home we train them, shape them. 'Jade must be polished to become a gem.'"

The old proverb did not impress Soong. "She can't be trusted," she said, adding her own adage, "'The seeds blossom into mischief.' She is of that generation, not our generation. We would never waver from the Party. She is like a bee, going to the nectar, not loyal to the hive."

Ren could not help but sigh. It was hard enough rearing his own children.

Madame Soong Wei said, "You must take some action."

Ren Jinuah put his hands together and shifted in his chair. "I agree, something must be done. You realize this is family, of course, and any actions could have other repercussions. I have been considering a few options, the first simply to ask Quang to curtail her activity. If you give me time, I will look into that."

Ren Jinuah was balancing his conflicted feelings, calm on the surface, but slightly enraged inside. It got this way when one top Party family questioned the integrity of another top Party family. He had power over Madame Soong Wei. He could even try to remove her from her position. On balance, however, the vote of her Yellow Faction was much more important for his future. The family secrets that Quang held might be dealt with more efficiently, and far more quietly.

"I see your concerns, Madame Soong Wei, and I promise I will look into this," he said. "In the meantime, I understand Omni Art Global has prospered. We have had your unwavering support for 'Celestial Face of China.' You have backed our broader cultural agenda." He was giving far too much credit to Soong Wei, but it moved her disposition in the right direction.

She seemed to relax, having expressed her frustration. Time was on her side. "The Party's support has been very helpful, and for that, I thank you personally, Chairman Ren Jinuah. I'm sorry that this other issue has clouded our good working relationships."

"I feel the same way," he said. "I will make your concerns a priority."

She smiled. "And, as the wife of a former general secretary, I know that your priorities must be many." Still, her own were just as important, she thought.

He smiled again, stood, and with a slight bow said, "It is very good that you have come to me directly. This is how it should be handled."

She bowed slightly in return, and gracefully left the room.

Ren Jinuah felt a strange weight, part anger, part helplessness. How was he going to approach his niece? She with the family secrets.

14

Beijing

QUANG DAIYU HAD not been to Beijing for a long while. The trains had certainly gotten faster, the private compartments more comfortable. Though she was raised in Shanghai, there were many relations in the capital city. It was where she had attended some Party school events, and where she began to comprehend all the art of China.

One particular year, she spent much of her time not studying, but wandering the Imperial City and the Beijing art museums, resplendent as they were with the art of dynasties past. Modern art was very big now, an economic powerhouse. That was for others, however. Quang knew the heart of China was in its ancient motifs, even though, true, those same motifs had been used again and again by modern artists, often as a critique of society, and of the past.

She was heading back to Beijing for a meeting with her uncle, General Secretary Ren. He had requested it some time ago, and given his travel and his busy schedule, this Wednesday was the appointed hour. Quang was not a schoolgirl anymore, as when he was the "distant uncle." She was naturally nervous, yet deep down, confident. Now she was a very grown woman with a lot of worldly experience.

At the train station, a limousine was waiting for her. As it maneuvered through the streets, then began turning at Tiananmen Square, she looked across its vast tarmac, covered with hundreds of pedestrians below the great Ming Tiananmen Gate, a dull red now with age. On the gate still hung the great color portrait of Mao, for the Chinese were a picture people, a calligraphic people. Known since the Manchus as the "Gate of Heavenly Peace," it now bore the great Party placards in calligraphic red and gold. The giant text on the left side read "Long Live the People's Republic of China," and on the right, "Long Live the Great Unity of the World's Peoples." As a youth visiting Beijing, she'd been caught up by the grandeur of the words, let alone their monumental size. Now they came off as an embarrassing bit of bravado, though at times the sentiments could still inspire even her, Black Jade, as jaded as she had become.

Through the lake drives, past the well-kept parks, the limo entered the grounds of Zhongnanhai, China's White House, its Downing Street, its Élysée Palaces, as it was patronizingly called by the Westerners. She knew it was more than any of those, and it was her privileged fate to have an audience there.

Down the halls and past the flags, she was soon entering General Secretary Ren's office. He was at his desk. He stood, approached and greeted her, a smiling benign uncle in this incarnation.

"Thank you for this audience," Quang said with a slight bow.

Chairman Ren dismissed the deputy who had shown Quang in. "Please have a seat," he gestured. They ambled over to the imperial desk. "I hope your trip was not tiring."

"I always enjoy returning to Beijing," Quang said.

Normally, they might have talked about family, asked how one relative or another was doing, the matter of everyone's health. Instead, they avoided such familial quagmires. They got down to brass tacks. This was the other incarnation of her uncle, the ruler of China, and she, one of its countless interested parties. The politics of it all was legendary.

"Niece Quang," Ren said, "You have made a very serious request. Of course, I would expect this. Your many accomplishments, well, you have made them clear enough. Yes, China wants to become the art center of the world. It wants to bring back all its stolen treasures and spread its celestial face across the globe."

Ren sat back in his chair. He gave Quang a stern look. "The position of leading our China Global Art Museum in Beijing is a very high position, and while there are candidates, I'm afraid you are not one of them. This has to be a shared decision of the Politburo."

"Which you control," Quang said.

"It's not so simple," Ren said, "though I'm flattered that you think so."

"Why then is Madam Soong Wei a candidate, and a leading candidate?" she asked.

Ren smiled and sighed. "Niece Quang, she is from a very old family. Her husband once sat where it sit now. It is expected. She is a personage, someone who would represent the interests of the Party and the whole nation very well."

Quang wanted to say that Soong was an old witch, but she held her tongue. Instead she said, "My collection of art, my networks, my connections, are very great, Uncle Ren. I have the knowledge to run the global museum. I have a love of the art, many ideas about what it will do to enlarge the confidence of our nation." Plus, she thought, I have the family secrets.

"Yes, yes," Ren said. "There will be many important offices in the new strategy, the museum being the hub. Conferences, tours, more collecting and curating. There will be many prestigious positions open, as I've mentioned to you in the past."

"Uncle Ren, I appeal to you, what I wish for—"

"Niece, you must not be so persistent. The top is not open to you. I think that is final." He sat for a while, watching her expression, and felt that he must raise the issue before she did. "I know what you are thinking, Niece Quang. You are thinking that you know about a family line, one that involves your uncle, one that involves you. As I have said before, this is wishful thinking. It's fantasy."

As before, Ren's approach to the whole topic was to be unyielding on the surface and force her into self-doubt. Such a genealogy, which she had found and pieced together, would surely not survive close scrutiny, which is what it would receive if she went public.

Quang averted her eyes in the middle of her uncle's sentences. She could not give into the doubts. That would undermine all that she wanted to believe, all the work she had done for so many years. There was a destiny at work, for hadn't she herself, a baby girl of illegitimate birth, survived, eluding the abortion regime of China's one-child policy? That good fortune, that fate alone, endowed the genealogy with significance. It was true, that genealogy would need to pass the strictest rebuttal. Perhaps even more corroborating evidence would be found. Blood tests could be performed, DNA matches looked for. Perhaps, but only perhaps. There was too much that the Party and its leader controlled, not just the doctors, but the media.

She had prepared herself for his rebuff. Still, she had to have the last word. "I was hoping you would be proud that a member of your family line would take such a glorious position in making China the art center of the world. Family, through all of China's travails, has helped us to survive and prosper. It just seems the right thing to do."

It was, she knew, a time-honored sort of appeal. But in these times, probably even in the past, political calculation always prevailed. Looking at Uncle Ren, she could see a man of thoroughgoing calculation.

"Yes, Niece, China was built on the family, and I, as leader, must think of our people as a family." He held her gaze while calculating her thoughts, which were inscrutable yet also predictable. She wanted to depart his office with something.

"I propose this," he said. "I have talked with Madame Soon Wei, and while she is reluctant, I have prevailed on her to have a meeting with you. You are the two great women of art in China. I think this is a generous offer. You must see her as pre-eminent in this, but as equals in other respects. I think you can find a way to work with her, a way that is very beneficial to your talents." He smiled and said, "And your ambitions."

Quang let out a sharp breath. This she had not expected, and did not particularly welcome. She had run out of ammunition, however. She didn't want to leave with a door slammed behind her, though she still had levers to open it—the family secret, maybe. She was done, and so as firmly as she could, she said, "Yes, I will agree to a meeting with Madame Soong."

Ren swiveled in his chair, reached for paper and pen, and began to write something down.

Quang watched silently.

"Madame Soong is, of course, in Beijing," Ren finally said. "She has a very busy scheduled I've been told." He handed her the paper. "Her staff will be expecting your call. I would recommend, while you are in Beijing, to take a hotel, relax. See some of the old city again. I expect that she could see you any day."

Quang took the paper, feeling her grudge get the best of her. She folded it and put it in her purse. "Thank you for the recommendation, Uncle Ren. It would be good to resolve this"—she rethought her proper words and continued—"make this an agreeable arrangement that is satisfactory to everyone involved."

Ren smiled, satisfied for the time being. "I'm sure you two brilliant ladies can work this out. Madame Soong will inform me of your agreements."

That roiled Quang, but she kept face, a placid look of calm. She stood, bowed slightly and said. "I will be going now." He stood also, and she left the room.

15

Washington D.C.

AT FIVE IN the evening, the team of Chinese curators was packing up at the Freer Museum, progressing out of their basement warren to take the shuttle ride back to the China Embassy, the shuttle that sent them forth each day of their work. Keeping up their cheerful veneer, they gave farewell greetings to staff who were closing up the museum. They exited by the back door, a security entrance, and passed through the garden-like setting. The van was waiting for them on Independence Avenue. They all climbed into the two rows of back seats.

The driver pulled onto Independence Avenue to begin their normal route, northward into the District's Forest Hills enclave. The van continued on Independence to reach Seventeenth Street, on the far side of the Ellipse, the large round park abutting the grounds of the White House. A left turn on Seventeenth took them past several of Washington's famed edifices, the Organization of American States, and farther up, the Eisenhower Executive Office Building, and then past Lafayette Square in front of the White House. In the stop-and-go traffic they eventually crossed K Street, known for its bristling number of lobbying firms. After K, the road widened and the van motored up to Dupont Circle, then turned up Connecticut Avenue, home to many embassies, though China's was back in a particularly remote area.

Now the traffic began to snarl. Many one-way streets crossed Connecticut. The van rushed to catch its green light at Q Street, when from a side street a speeding car cut in, nearly missing a D.C. Metro bus. The massive bus swerved sharply. Its rear hit the embassy van, exploding a window and letting out a long screech of metal on metal, the van bumper tearing off and flying. Bystanders heard screams as the van spun into a parked car with a deafening crunch, and then fell on its side, glass shattering everywhere. The Chinese, all in safety belts except for one, where violently thrown about, and as a side door flew open, some of their satchels scattered on the street.

Within minutes, they heard the sound of arriving ambulances. Pedestrians had gathered and two police cars were on the scene. The police helped the driver and curators out of the van and told them to sit down on the curb. The unbelted woman, dashed against the van interior, was laid down, a man giving his coat as a pillow. Arriving medics with the two ambulances quickly gave her a neck brace. They put her on a stretcher and with sirens wailing sped off to nearby George Washington Hospital. As the others were being escorted to the second ambulance, two of the curators resisted. They tried to get to the overturned van, its radiator now steaming, their faces distraught over the strewn belongings.

"We'll collect those for you," a policeman said as he began to redirect traffic. Another policeman, having assessed the situation, called the China Embassy and the Freer Museum. Only the latter call got through. In twenty minutes, the deputy director of the Freer

Museum was on the scene. The police had secured the personal property of the passengers, and had it stacked on the rear of a police cruiser.

"They're over at George Washington Hospital," the officer in charge told the Freer Museum official. "We've put their belongings over here."

As the Freer official assessed the satchels, well known as the daily carry-all of the Chinese curators, she noticed something odd. The flap on one of the satchels had jarred open. Protruding from it was a Chinese scroll.

"This is not right," she said. She looked deeper, and found that it was an entire artifact. Shocked by the discovery, she looked in two other satchels. They also held artifacts from the Freer Collection. The impossible suddenly crossed her mind. She pulled out her phone to ask the Freer front desk to connect her to the director.

"You won't believe this," she told the director. "They've been taking things from the collection. What should I do?"

The director put her on hold while she got on another line with the head of the Smithsonian, the Freer's formal affiliation to both the complex's security and the top management, which answered to the government. This had to be handled delicately. The satchels would be closed and delivered to the Chinese curators at the hospital, as if nothing had happened. Then, they'd investigate more deeply.

Later, at an impromptu meeting, the Smithsonian director said, "So you think they're stealing stuff. How long has this been going on?" That had to be determine without upsetting relations with the China Embassy. "We should close shop and investigate," he said.

"That will tip off the Embassy," said the Freer Museum deputy.

"Okay, I've got an idea."

This was cleared by the upper ranks, including a desk in the Department of State. The appropriate phone calls were made. The head of Smithsonian facilities was brought in, and said yes, it could be done. By the next morning, a large stream of water was pouring out of a sewer on Jefferson Drive, which fronted the Freer complex. Several construction vehicle had arrived, the street was closed off and yellow tape put up around the museum grounds.

The local press was on the scene.

"We've had a water main break," said the Freer director, now outside to answer questions. "We've got to close the collection down for a few days. They may have to do some digging."

"So the museum's closed?" a reporter asked.

"Yes, for the time being," came the answer.

By the end of the day, the China Embassy had heard the news. It was on all the local news websites and already heard on the D.C. radio stations. The full story was in the print editions the next morning. The headline read, "Water Main Breaks by Mall Museum. Freer Doors Closed as Curators Worry About Damage to Artworks."

Inside, however, the staff was busy inspecting the annex area where the Chinese curators had been at work for the past month. Given the fact of the satchels, they closely examined the collection's originals, those being worked on by the Chinese curators, and indeed, something was not right. As the day drew to a close, their experts had concluded the unimaginable: many of the works in the Freer Collection were copies, expertly done, but clearly high quality forgeries. Politically, now, they had to go upstairs, all the way to the Department of State and the White House.

"Unbelievable," said the president at the briefing.

The state department, the Smithsonian, and the justice department had all sent a representatives with the evidence. National Security Advisor Ronald Frey was also on hand. At first they discussed the obvious response: a protest to the China Embassy, a demand to interview the Chinese curators, and whatever it took to recover the originals from the Freer Museum.

"Is it doable?" the president asked. "Or is that being too blunt, too quick to act?" They all knew how, in moments of diplomatic controversy, China would go into a siege mentality mode and deny everything. As always, they would bristle at the insult.

The Smithsonian director said, "We've just begun to evaluate how much damage has been done. The forgeries are extraordinarily well done. In many cases, we're having a hard time telling the difference."

"I have a better idea," said Frey, the National Security Advisor. "It looks like it will take time to gather conclusive evidence, specifics, which artworks and the like. This could be an important card we can play with the Chinese. Is there a way we can act as if nothing happened? Send condolences to the China Embassy for the accident, explain that their curators can get back to work in a few days? That gives us time to figure this out. Once we have, it's a strong playing card. The Chinese are very concerned about loss of face."

"So you're saying, act as if nothing's happened, gather the irrefutable evidence, and wait for the right time to bring it to China's attention?" the state department deputy said.

"Exactly," said Frey. "A bargaining tool."

"But what about our collection, our valuable artwork?" the Smithsonian head asked. "This is theft of cultural property."

That was a good point, but it did not seem to persuade the others that Washington should raise the alarm. Not yet, at least.

"I think we should keep it under wraps," said the state department official. "After this plays out, we can recover what's been taken. Governments don't get away with obvious thefts, though professional thieves often do."

The president sat for a few moments, thinking it over. "I think in the end, this can work out in the wash," he said. "Okay, we continue as if nothing happened. Develop our case, an irrefutable case. Then we bide our time, use it at an opportune moment."

Two days later, the water main was repaired, and the Freer Museum was back open. Nobody knew what the China embassy was thinking, but on the next morning, four of the five curators returned with their satchels, doing their work. "One of our colleagues had a neck injury, so she is convalescing for a while," the team leader explained.

FOR THE NEXT few days, all went back to normal. The four Chinese curators did not seem shaken and the daily pleasantries were as they always had been. But something in the mood had changed. Then, suddenly, the China Embassy informed the Smithsonian officials that their research project would be suspended temporarily. "The traffic accident has shaken up our staff. We have decided to give them some time to rest."

16

Shanghai

PEALE WAS SEEING Shanghai for the first time through a skein of wispy clouds. The airliner was banking to his side, the view wide. Ho had been here before, he presumed, but that was never their topic. They'd only discussed its storied past, "City above the Sea" to the earliest inhabitants, and "Pearl of the Orient" to Western traders. They were arriving long on motivation but still short on detail—except one. Tian Fengshan, the long ago romancer of Quang Daiyu, was down there somewhere, and perhaps Quang as well.

In lore, Shanghai had been a den of vice and profits; then, after the Maoist revolution, a holdout for the radicals. Now it lived down its reputation as arch rival to Beijing. The average Western visitor would feel they'd landed in just another super-metropolis.

As the high clouds parted, Peale got a better look at the Huangpu River, a seventeen mile tributary dug off the Yangtze. Dug as a port haven, the river made a sudden loop, like a horseshoe. On the east side was Pudong, a bulge of land with glittering skyscrapers, the financial district of Shanghai. On the western side was a curving shoreline, site of the city's historic port, a stretch of Western co-lonial-era buildings called the Bund, and the center city and the government, still populated with historic remnants and landmarks.

"Tian Fengshan's office is in one of those skyscrapers," Ho said. "We're staying on the opposite side, the west, in the sticks." They'd made a hasty hotel reservation, but it was a discrete lodging, allowing them an easy coming and going and a better chance of avoiding the surveillance net thrown over much of the city.

Noticing the financial district's utter flatness, its glass and steel pinnacles, Peale was wondering why the Bund, the port and prom-enade, had arisen on the other side of the river, and then Ho inter-rupted his wayward thoughts.

She tried to point out one of the highest skyscrapers and said, "That one's called the bottle opener." The building's top ended in sleek form, an isosceles trapezoid with an empty center, like the busi-ness end of a bottle opener. "Beijing is traditional, Shanghai is mod-ernist. They say you could fly a small airplane through that hole."

For more than a week, Castelli had busily set up their travel profile, both a back story and new passports. Peale and Ho were representatives of Amity Ltd., a company that invested in cultural exchanges. Their names were John Morgan and Alice Wang. Now with a mustache and goatee, Peale wore coat and tie. Ho fastened her dark locks to another side with a gold hair clip. She wore eyeshadow behind stylish horn-rimmed glasses.

On hearing the nom de guerres, Peale said, "Alice down the rabbit hole."

"I noticed that," Ho said. "Morgan and Wang. Sounds like a—"

"Clothing store." If you added Perlmutter—his former com-manding officer's name—you'd have a law firm, Peale thought. He always like the ring of that name. *Okay, time to focus!*

They would circumvent the U.S. consulate in Shanghai, just in case of reverberations from their brush with the police in Urumqi. According to Castelli, they had a Shanghai "asset" as backup, depending on what they found. Strangely, the NSA experts in Washington could not discover any relevant references to Quang Daiyu or the Phoenix Group in Shanghai. By contrast, Tian Fengshan was in the newspapers. His firm was also a corporate sponsor of the "Celestial Face of China" traveling exhibition. Tian's office was contacted by Castelli's faux company, Amity Ltd.—now with a convincing website—seeking an appointing with Peale and Ho, newly minted as Morgan and Wang; two suave urbanites visiting China for investment and sightseeing.

The airport was ten miles west of the river, so their taxi took them in toward the city to the hotel, The Granger-Shanghai, about half that distance. The city was bisected north-south and east-west by five elevated freeways, the routes by which millions of workers came in and out every day. Shanghai's population was large, nearly twenty-five million, and historically so independent that the "city" had the status of a province.

Peale said, "It's as if New York City was made the fifty-first state of the union." They still had to find their way around. But it seemed very possible to keep a low profile and avoid being followed in such a buzzing megalopolis. They started their orientation at the Bund, where swarms of tourists passed by the old French architecture. Eventually they took an outside table at a small restaurant—and lingered.

"You're looking very artsy today," Ho said, eyeing Peale in his mustache, goatee, and suit and tie.

"I feel like a stuffed shirt," he said. "But for God and country . . ."

The central feature of the old docking area was an eight-story Customs House of 1920s vintage. The Bund reminded Peale of a vast boardwalk, now maintained in a museum-theme-park

ambiance—ground zero for tourism, and so for crowds as well. They
had a day to kill before their morning meeting with Tian Fengshan,
so they decided to amble around Shanghai's west side.

"Slowly make our way back to the hotel," Peale said.

"Sounds like a plan," Ho said.

Beyond the Bund, they could see some of the government buildings that mimicked 1950s Soviet architecture. It all reminded Peale
of that Cold War era. "Times have changed," he said. "Now it's
China versus Russia."

"Mao had a quick falling out with the Russkies," Ho said.
"Called the Soviets 'tottering old women with bound feet.'"

Peale smirked a bit and said, "So meanwhile we were free to just
watch, and then play both sides of the aisle, sometimes Moscow,
sometimes Beijing." He loved this old Cold War strategy stuff.

They first came upon the old Chinese district, the "Old Town,"
with its cobblestone gatehouses, narrow shaded streets and canyons
of three-story facades, many ornate with red-tiled overhangs and curious street-level shops. In Urumqi, women's blouses had no daring
necklines, but in Shanghai, they were creeping, Peale noticed. As
they sauntered, a few curious eyes met his.

Further on in their meandering, they found the older museum
district, which included the ancient Jing'an Temple, the Jade Buddha
Temple, and the great Taoist Temple. These were preserved in a
warren of mostly dreary streets, lined as they were with weathered
commercial buildings, cheap hotels, and residential blocks. There
was still a lot of backstreet charm, yet it was also quite Orwellian,
given the Party's enthusiasm for CCTV cameras, Peale thought. He
couldn't see them, but knew they were there.

As to the charm, their *Fodor's* told them, the city was founded
by a Lord Chunsen as the Kingdom of Chu a few centuries before the birth of Christ. Later, their walk would take them past a

rebuilt temple from his era, the touristy Chunsen Village. For a long time, Shanghai was called the City of Shen, after his other name, Shencheng.

"How many names can a Chinese have?" Peale asked.

"The number is no end," Ho said.

They stayed away from one picturesque section, the old French Concession, venue of the Shanghai Communist Party compound, a forbidding gray marble structure set back in park-like grounds. Old Shanghai had a number of "concessions," compounds of European governments, and the vintage architecture was still around. In between, they took a quick look at the former homes of nationalist leader Sun Yat-sen and of Mao, and then there was the small shrine-like building where Mao founded China's Communist Party in 1921.

For a late lunch, it was hard to find a restaurant without crowds, but they managed a fairly quiet corner. Peale was still curious about Ho's mysterious past in China and thought he'd try another nudge.

"So you've been here before," he said.

She smiled and said, "That's for me to know, and for you to wonder about." He raised his hands in a kind of submission. To divert that conversation, she segued into the story of post-imperial Shanghai. "Most people think of this place as Sodom and Gomorrah on the East China Sea, all those novels and movies."

"Don't forget the pirates and white slavery. If I recall, our hero was always getting shanghaied," Peale said, referring to the kidnapping tales. As Peale expected, Ho was a fount of information, and she was soon in that mode, which he found pleasant enough, given her usual reticence.

"Once the communists took over," she offered, "they chased out the Japanese and even the Nationalists. Shanghai became the most radical city in the People's Republic."

The communists called it the "imperialist prostitute," roughed it up, then took it over. When Mao launched the Cultural Revolution, the cadres here were the most vehement, tearing down its old vestiges, burning blue jeans and high heels. In fact, when Mao was out of the picture, his wife, Madame Mao, led the Gang of Four here. When Mao died in 1976, the gang was ruthlessly dispatched with and, for good measure, erased from the photos of history.

"Didn't the Gang of Four try to mount a military coup against Beijing," Peale recalled.

"Not for long, not with Beijing's army," Ho said. "Anyway, the next regime imposed orthodox Leninism on the country, including Shanghai. Very systematic. No more populist mayhem. By mayhem, I mean the Cultural Revolution, which killed maybe twenty million 'counterrevolutionaries.'"

Ho paused at the thought, letting the sheer number resonate in the air, then continued. "Shanghai got awfully quiet after that," she said. "Eventually, with the economic liberalization, it became a model of state-owned companies, the only place in China. All the profits went to Beijing, of course. Strong PLA presence, especially after Tiananmen Square, protests in the streets, including here. The whole country was locked down. Shanghai was so used to doing its own thing that it developed what's called 'the Shanghai Gang,' members of the Politburo with a local power base here, loyalties to rely on."

"It didn't end there," she went on, as if a tour guide, which in fact had been one of her covers in the city on previous exploits. "Shanghai went super capitalist, as you can see. At that point, Beijing mounted its anti-corruption campaign, took down the mayor of Shanghai and a few of the people who built these skyscrapers."

"And now?" Peale asked.

"Shanghai's been pretty much tamed, I think. A great money maker."

They were soon back on their feet and their walk took them out to a clearing, with a view across the River and the financial district skyline.

"See that spire that looks like Disneyland a hundred years ago?" she pointed. "My favorite is the Oriental Pearl Tower." It was a Soviet-inspired tall columnar structure, interrupted by two large spheres, then a pearl-like orb higher up and a soaring radio tower reaching to fifteen hundred feet. It had an elevator partway up. It was Shanghai's tallest structure until 2007, when the financial buildings, the "super towers," began to go higher. Most of those were built over a breakneck five years.

"I sort of lean toward the Shanghai Tower," Peale said. It was the tallest and obviously so. "Look at it, standing all alone, one hundred-twenty floors, straight up for two thousand feet."

"Typical male," Ho said.

"Anyway, we'll be in the thick of those buildings tomorrow."

THE TIAN FENGSHAN Company had its offices in the Yangtze River tower, a skin of blue-tinted glass and a mere nine hundred feet tall.

They took the elevator to the eighth floor—eight was a lucky number in China, while four was to be avoid—and entered the large reception area. They had figured out the etiquette, which Westerners could easily get wrong. Typically, a business meeting, even with a group, allowed only a discussion between the two principals. Everyone else kept quiet, eyes averted.

In their case, Peale was the principal and Ho his translator. They weren't sure yet whether Tian Fengshan used English, and even if so, whether he preferred Mandarin. Either way, Peale would be the emphatic one, Ho stepping in only if the dynamic required.

"Hard for me to keep my mouth shut," Ho said, a bit ironically, as they left the reception desk for the elevator.

"At some point, he's not going to like us anyway," Peale said. "Then we'll probably have to double team him."

Outside Tian's suite, a staff member took them through a polished wooden door. Tian Fengshan was waiting and already standing. He was in a dark business suit, a tall man with hair clearly dyed black. Above narrow shoulders, his long neck bore a block-like head. Peale thought of carved statuary.

He greeted them with courtesies and led them to chairs around his desk, with a spectacular window view of Old Town Shanghai across the river. He began with, "Please forgive my English. I probably don't have enough practice."

Peale said, "It's very good."

Tian laughed and said, "We'll see how it goes."

He looked tired, but apparently in an exuberant mood about his recent appointment to the board overseeing the prestigious "Celestial Face of China" traveling art exhibit, set to return from the United States, and then to open in Wuhan.

At the Politburo's direct request, Tian had helped recruit many of the millionaires in China to put money into art purchases, the traveling exhibit, and other cultural aspects of the country's growing soft power strategy. He went on about the "Celestial Face of China" exhibit, and how it was giving China a wider theme to ply on the global stage. "It's turning out to be a significant global event. It will continue to be a spur to our economy," Tian said.

"And goodwill among nations," Peale said.

Tian gestured to photos on his office wall, showing the city of Shanghai in different periods. They started with old black-and-whites of low-lying, shambled stretches along the Huangpu River, a few of the European structures standing out. Eventually the photos revealed two color images of the modern Disneyland skyline. "We're very competitive in China, province to province, I don't mind saying that," he said. "Shanghai has changed overnight."

"Three cheers for Shanghai," Ho said, prompting Tian to laugh.

"Many years ago," he said, "I studied in America, at Harvard, so I know many American idioms. There was some risk in that adventure. Back then we were among the first exchange students. It was a very proud moment. But there's also a taint. Once you've been to America, there's a sense, among many older Chinese, of 'a bad seed,' that you've lost something, as if no longer Chinese. That's an old-wives tale."

For an instant Tian also thought of Quang Daiyu, and how badly things had turned out, proof that the bad see could bring bad fortune, a thought he quickly put aside.

"Mr. Tian," Peale said, "We have of course talked to a lot of people who are active in the art trade, cultural exchange. We're in China to try to build more productive contacts."

Tian nodded. So far so good.

"We've been referred to someone named Quang Daiyu, and we're looking for a recommendation."

Tian stiffened, but managed to simulate a puzzled face. "Hmm, I don't think I know her. Shanghai's a big town. Perhaps you can ask your other contacts." A frosty smiled crossed his face. He seemed ready to end the meeting.

"Oh, yes, we've tried that, but no luck," Peale said. "You're sure? It would be great if we could meet her."

"No, no, nothing I'm afraid." He looked at his watch, breaking the etiquette rule.

Peale looked at Ho, and she knew a prod was needed. She took out a photocopy from her bag, and handed it to Tian. A copy of the yearbook page. "You knew her at Harvard," she said.

Tian got a peek, but refused to look further. "What is this?" he insisted. "I think you can leave now."

Peale leaned forward and turned the yearbook page over, revealing the handwriting on the back, signed "Fengshan." He was beginning to think that Tian was being blackmailed, and perhaps by Quang herself. "We just want some information, that's all. We're trying to do some justice here."

"What are you police?" he said, bolting up.

Ho said, "Please sit down, Mr. Tian. There has been some stolen art in the United States. That's all we're interested in. Nothing about you." As she spoke, she brought out additional papers.

Tian's brow furrowed and his eyes narrowed. "That was long ago. How should I know? I'm busy with my company." Talking about it would only bring back unwelcome memories. Still, they flooded in, how they met as students in Boston, how they continued their illicit affair in Shanghai, how Quang's pregnancy was terminated by herbal machinations. And finally, how that had alienated them, turned Quang against her former lover, and he to another woman, bad blood all around. She turned into a dragon lady—a woman who needed no man. She was set in her own bitter course.

Ho handed him the paper and said, "Mr. Tian, we know about your accounts in the Cayman Islands, and in Switzerland. Your funding for the Tall River Project and the kickbacks. All those matters are none of our business. But so that you know we are serious, we know a great deal about your enterprises. Things that might alarm Beijing. So we hope you can help us with some information."

Tian eyed them warily. "So this is how you Americans operate."

"None of us are naïve, Mr. Tian," Ho said. "And how do the Chinese operate? Hey, I'm Chinese to the core. We just need information."

"Can I believe that?" he said.

Ho said, "You have to believe it." She removed a piece of paper from her pocket and read off some numbers and dollar amounts.

Tian's eye flashed again. It was the data from his foreign accounts. He needed to make up his mind quickly. In truth, for him, Americans were okay. He was no nationalist. He was a businessman. Sometimes for the sake of business, you play the game, you trade information.

"Alright," Tian said. "Then it's over, correct?"

"Nobody knows but us," Peale said.

Tian began to explain. Yes, he had known Quang Daiyu long ago, during their student days. They went their separate ways, his face revealing something of the lie he was telling, except that he and Quang had, indeed, gone separate ways. Once Tian was in business, he said, he helped Quang start her own company. After all, she was the niece of a rising Party official in the provinces, set for a position in the Politburo. So Tian briefly helped her get started. This was when the independent sector was booming, the gray market, tens of thousands of businesses. In 2001, in fact, the Party had, for the first time, let entrepreneurs join. Everyone got a cut.

"So I helped her set up Phoenix Group," Tian said. "An innocuous name. There's a hundred Phoenix restaurants in Shanghai. Two of my subcontractors, construction, pipes, are Phoenix something."

"A Chinese commonplace," Ho said. "The phoenix and the dragon."

"That's correct," Tian said. "So, I helped her get investors. Recommendations. She set up more things. Black Jade Tea, Silk Road Trade, some others." He explained how it worked. "During that time, an entrepreneur could join the Party. A kind of window dressing. You could give shares of your company to a provincial official or a PLA official. In the Party, salaries are modest. A cadre requirement. But everyone made money on the side. The gray market. Everywhere. China was in business.

"So Quang built it up," Peale said.

"That's my understanding. After I helped, I kept my distance. You know, especially now. Her uncle's at the top. In America you say 'follow the money.' In recent years, things have tightened. Anti-corruption campaigns. More Party control. We say, 'follow the family.' So I've kept my distance. She's done well on her own. I was no longer needed. That suited me."

"And today?" Peale asked.

"Today, nothing."

"And where can we find her?"

"Phoenix Group has a suite in the old part of the financial district. The Shikumen Building. I'm sure you can find it."

Ho said, "Can you be more specific?"

Tian glowered. "Should be Dongchang Road."

"And her banks? Account numbers," Peale said.

"I know nothing about her banks," he said. "Why should I? Anyway, she uses other names. Its common practice. Why bother with me?"

"Do you recall her bank numbers, accounts?" Peale continued.

He sort of laughed, "Of course not. All I know is that she had favorite numbers."

"And what were those," Ho asked, taking over from Peale.

He chortled again. "She was hung up on Empress Cixi. You may know the name. She always used the empress's dates, birth and death. Some combination. She used them in her banking, other things."

"How did she use the numbers?" Ho said.

"Year, month, day," Tian said. That was the Chinese notation. He gave a small chuckle. "Kind of superstitious, twos by fours, bad luck good luck. Not my thing."

Ho was struck by the twos and fours and the idea of luck, but couldn't put a finger on it. She quickly asked, "Can you tell us any more, like Quang Daiyu dealing art, stolen art, for example?"

"No, honestly, nothing."

The interrogation had entered a particularly uncomfortable territory for anyone in the Party, and that was the realm of personal family relations. Tian was mute. Everyone knew that when political infighting arose in China's upper class, there was a methodology. You begin to investigate the extended family, seek petty corruption, work your way to the center, the top family personages, and then lodge charges for major corruption. Even so, nobody talked in public about top Party members' families. Much was unknown, even if children, uncles, or nephews were up to their necks in sly transactions or bribes.

"We didn't talk about her family," Tian said. "What you don't know can't hurt you." An old American saying. "None of my business."

"Right," Ho said.

Tian said. "This is entirely between us, correct? Quang Daiyu hears nothing?"

"You have our word," Ho said. If they could find her.

A very shrewd woman, Tian thought. She, too, had the Western seed. He could tell. "Then, thank you. Our business is done." He stood and gestured toward the office door.

Back at their hotel, they looked up the Empress Cixi dates. Born on November 28, 1835, died on November 15, 1908. Peale wrote it out numerically. First 18351128 and then 19081115. Ho was thinking two and fours, but no conclusion popped up.

"We'll send these to Castelli, do a bank scrub," he said.

They also looked up the Shikumen Building. In a few minutes, they were out hailing a taxi, looking at a map, and heading for 15040 Dongchang Road.

17

Shanghai

DONGCHANG ROAD WAS easy to find, a diagonal slice through a canyon of tall edifices. The office building was an older structure. It sat amid the long city blocks, glossy high-rises mostly, some muted warehouse-type premises. Many looked like they had been thrown up in a hurry, a Shanghai specialty. The most popular common man's car in China, the Volkswagen Santana, seemed to make up half the traffic. You'd know a government official by the black Mercedes, always with rank on the license plates, from 00001 for the Shanghai provincial Party Secretary, and then numbering up. None were in sight.

As they arrived, a breeze swept down the walled avenue. Inside the front entrance was a lobby. The reception desk was manned. Like any daytime office building, people came and went without checking in. There was a glass display with a hundred names of offices, all in Chinese of course. Ho scanned it. No Quang and no Phoenix Group. Scanning again, she noticed an acronym, SR/PG.

"Maybe this is it," she said. *Silk Road/Phoenix Group*? "Twelfth floor."

After the elevator ride, they found a lobby with lounge chairs and several branching hallways. The largest of them went left into another smaller lobby, turned, and ended at the office. On a small brass plaque, a calligraphic character said PG. The door had a key pad. It was the kind that showed red-lit asterisk for each number punched in. Peale held his breath, pushed the number 1 continually until the screen filled, an eight-asterisk limit. Year, month, day— eight digits. They looked at each other, two minds with one great, or perhaps stupid, idea. Obstacles could be brick walls or Swiss cheese, as Peale liked to say.

"We can come back tonight," Ho said. "Let's check downstairs before we leave." She led the way down and over to the reception desk. For today, they had dressed business-like, no-nonsense. "Excuse me," Ho said to the desk clerk. "We have come to see Miss Quang, the Phoenix Group, but nobody seems to be in."

The conversation was all Greek to Peale, but he'd accustomed himself to the language barrier. He'd also come to trust Ho's instincts.

The clerk did not look up at Ho. He seemed distracted, half asleep in fact. He said nothing, flipped through an information book. "No Quang."

"Is SR/PG Phoenix Group? Silk Road Co?"

The clerk looked up for a brief moment. "She's checking business. We're taking messages."

"Oh, then we'll try back later. She mentioned other 'business?'"

"She gets lots of deliveries," the clerk said.

"A Miss Quang?"

"I don't know lady's name," he said, returning to something on a computer.

When They Returned that night, the tower was still open for business. Ho wore a dark pant suit, carried a large purse, and was equipped: her black balaclava, gloves, two small flashlights, and a small high-quality camera. Peale dressed business casual, and carried a copy of the *Asian Financial Times* under his arm. They had miniature radio-microphone plugs for their ears.

They took the elevator back up and entered the hallway. There were no cameras they could see. It was an older building, less high-tech, so they kept their fingers crossed. Peale took his position in the outer lounge, opened his newspaper, put in his earplug. Ho padded down the hall, pulling on her balaclava and gloves—and hoping for the best. At the door, she tried the guess that they were banking on. She tapped in 18351128. Nothing. She pushed the clear button, began again, this time 19081115. The box hummed and clicked.

"I'm in," she said softly.

Peale wrinkled his newspaper and said, "All clear."

Inside, Ho scanned the obvious features, a simple spacious office with one great Chinese painting on the wall. She took a couple pictures. Down a hall, one door opened onto a living quarter. Back in the main office, behind a great standing screen, with its elaborate artwork, was a second door with a key pad.

"Second door with code," she whispered to Peale.

"All clear," he said.

Ho said a prayer, punched in the remaining half of the number series, Cixi's death, 18351128. Again, the box hummed and clicked. "Second door in," she whispered.

"All clear," Peale said. It seemed too easy, like a dream, but sometimes you found Swiss cheese, not a brick wall.

Inside the inner chamber, Ho discovered a remarkable room filled with great Chinese art, and Western art as well. The first thing she noticed was two large Western-style oil paintings of Empress

Cixi. With no time to look under every rock, she began to take pictures. That done, she opened various cabinets. At the one with a tea pot, she found the little wooden box. Opening it, she found the oracle stone. She took pictures.

Photos were good evidence, but she had nothing concrete, nothing small enough to take without the item being missed. Then her eyes settled on a kind of ornate tray, deep and divided into two. She looked at the labels: one was a branded Black Jade tea, the other Gold Tea. She took a few of each, then brushed her hand over the stacks so they evened up again, as she'd found them. The tea packs stuffed in her pocket, she quietly backed out of the room, only to hear Peale, "Heads up, someone's coming in."

It was Liu Hui, who had just exited the elevator and didn't bother to glance at Peale, who was casually reading his newspaper, and went down the hall. Liu Hui had a large envelope in his hand. At the door, he pressed the codes, entered the dark office, and closed the door behind him. "Sounds like he's in," whispered Peale. He quickly went down the hall to the door. By its edge, he steadied himself, listening, waiting to see what happened next.

Ho had been looking through Quang's main desk, but had scooted behind the screen, where she froze. She listened.

The office, with its windows on the city, was illumined enough to get around. Liu Hui stepped over to the main desk, paused a moment and placed the envelope squarely at its center: materials for Madame Quang that she should see the next morning, when he was going to be tied up, coming over later. Liu Hui stopped, as if putting up a mental radar. He looked around the room, quiet except for some traffic sounds below on the streets. A sixth sense told him to check the inner door, so he began to approach the screen.

Ho was wearing her balaclava and was considering her move, tightening some muscles, relaxing her mind for focus.

When Liu Hui finally stepped behind the screen, she reached out to grab the collar of his suit, pulled him forward for a head butt, then using his disorientation pivoted him to the floor, applying pressures to his neck. Just enough pressure, but not too much. The man was effectively dazed. She acted quickly. From her bag she ripped open a Velcro sleeve, pulled out a tube that contained a hypodermic needle ready for use. She found a fleshy part of Liu Hui's upper body, and injected him with the sodium pentothal, a harmless trip into a few hours of sleep.

Peale had not heard anything through the door. When it began to click and open, he stepped back, ready for a confrontation. Instead Ho's head came out. She signaled him inside. Peale saw the man lying on the floor.

She whispered, "Knocked out, sodium pentothal. We have to move quickly." Ho wanted to take photos of every page of the diary she'd found in the front desk drawer, the papers that were already there, and what had just arrived in the envelope. "Here," she said, "you flip each page, I'll click."

They began the process. For the business papers she leaned back, getting each in a fuller camera frame as Peale responded to her commands. "Next, next, next," she said. Now the diary. Ho was able to fit both pages of the open book in her camera frame. Going through, Peale's hands were quick and steady. As the pages flew buy, she stopped. One page had rows of numbers. She put the camera aside to look closely at a scribbled heading—"Fours by twos," then vertical rows of numbers.

"What?" Peale asked, feeling the press of time.

"Nothing. Keep going."

The pages done, Ho said, "Okay, put everything back in order." Besides the knocked-out man, she decided, some other sign of entry should be left. The diary had been in the top drawer, so she pulled the drawer half open—sure to be noticed. Sometimes, you wanted to make your target worry, leave something noticeable behind, stir the pot and see what happens.

"All done?" Peale said.

"Let's go."

He peaked out into the lobby, gave her a nod, and they were soon at the elevator, looking calm as if they'd just been to a boring business lunch. They were still not sure about security cameras, though Ho had looked closely. Peale regretted not having pulled on his balaclava, but then, a man in a balaclava reading a newspaper?

In the lobby they separated before passing the front desk, Ho walking alone, just another Chinese woman, Peale just another foreigner.

Outside, they looked around a mostly empty high-rise court-yard and took a few deep breaths. Peale motioned to the street. They began a brisk walk, staying on the busiest sidewalks. Thick as thieves, they vanished into the darkness that was swallowing the crowds.

Back at their hotel, they waited for the hour when the U.S. satellite was in optimal position, and then page by page, used the SAT phone's capacity to send up the photos, which were no less than eighty in number. They waited for a confirmation of arrival. That reply signal over, they next put a call into Castelli, no matter what the hour.

A groggy Castelli said, just like in the movies, "This better be important." Peale put the phone on speaker, summarized, and requested that a specialist, maybe at NSA—needing Chinese lan-guage—review the material, hopefully drawing some precise con-clusions. They would stay in earshot of their SAT phone for the next eight to twelve hours for follow up.

"Good job," Castelli said. "Alright, I wasn't that tired anyway.

Nothing good to dream about. You two sit tight and we'll get back with anything pertinent."

PEALE AND HO had separate rooms, but they were killing their time in Peale's, which was more spacious than Ho's. It had a better view of the Shanghai Skyline, glittering the night through.

She said, "I got some tea, forensic samples."

"Forensic for what?"

"Anything and everything about Quang. I felt I needed something concrete, and these were small. Won't be noticed."

Peale had a more pressing thought. "Are you hungry?" he asked. "We can do a room service."

"Well, that's very gentlemanly of you Julian, thank you."

"As compared to sticking that guy with a needle," he said, "I didn't know that was regulation equipment for this job."

"Oh, it's easy to pack, like my mascara. From past experience it can come in handy."

When their room service arrived at the door, it came on a large tray, two dishes of food and a tea pot, hot and steaming, but still only water. Tea bags were at the side. Peale and Ho began to eat their meals, with chopsticks the only option.

"They know a Western customer when they see one," Peale said.

"You underestimate your innate skills, Julian."

"On my shirt already, in seconds." His large hands fumbled with the chopsticks. Then he said, "Why don't we try some of that tea you purloined? Research, you know." The Quang tea operation was supposed to be in a high-quality category, not your ordinary tea.

"Okay, Sherlock, we can do that. Research only." She reached for the packages, saying their names, and Peale, logically thinking of the high end, said, "Let's try the gold."

Ho opened one of the packages and put the appropriate number of pinches of tea right into the steaming pot, where it would sink and emanate its flavors. By the time the water sufficiently cooled, they'd have a brew. The food was good. Neither was a connoisseur or picky—food was fuel—but it did taste a notch above standard Chinese takeout.

"Now some tea," Peale said. He poured a full cup for Ho and himself. The tea was at the temperature where you could sip, tasting of its usual bitterness but also something different with a strange touch of astringent sweetness.

"We didn't put sugar in this did we?" he asked.

About ten minutes later, with a bit of drag in his voice, he asked again, "Who put sugar in our tea?" Now they both laughed, swaying a bit, their eyes taking particular notice of shifting textures in the room. Peale thought he saw a string of red Chinese lanterns through the window, swaying outside in a breeze.

Otherwise, they felt just fine, very good in fact, and sipped some more. After a time, they were pouring more and feeling euphoric, suspended in a kind of slow motion, half sleepy, and half acute to their odd surroundings.

"What is it about Shanghai?" Peale said. "Someone put something in our tea."

"Maybe we're being shanghaied," Ho said, giggling.

This went on for a while. They kept picking up the SAT phone as if that would get Washington to call them, for they were feeling sleepy and in a very nice way. The fact that two of them, a man and woman, were in a hotel room together late at night did not cross their minds, except that they might have to take turns keeping watch. Peale seemed to be drifting off faster, so Ho, tittering at his bewildered look, volunteered to answer the phone if something came. She said later she might be in a similar state as he, so then Peale could be on duty, waiting for the word from Washington.

"I wonder what word that will be," Ho said, as if amused by

the possibilities. "Maybe that we're drunk and shouldn't be while on duty."

Peale snickered at the idea, not accepting the likelihood, but still with enough grip on his mind to speculate that someone had slipped them a mickey. For the moment he didn't mind. Given the nature of their mood, he didn't worry about what might happen next.

Ho then had a kind of hallucination, actually seeing the rows of numbers from the diary page, and she thought, Four is bad luck. "Eight is good luck," she said. Curiosity seized her bleary mind. She go out her camera and with difficulty scanned through the tiny screen with the even tinier photos—until she found the page with the numbers.

"What?" Peale asked.

"The numbers. Four is bad luck. These are rows of four numbers, times two makes eight, good luck. Turning bad luck into good luck. Tian said something like that, didn't he?"

This sounded to Peale like dreaminess. "So what?"

A clarity snapped in Ho's mind, and she said, "Get a paper and write these down."

They labored over the tiny image, copying the rows of numbers. "All of these are four-letter segments of the eight digit dates," Ho said. "I bet she rotates these. Puts one segment of four with another, comes up with eight."

"For her bank numbers."

"That, or her security codes."

"We got inside with the full dates," Peale said.

"I know." She couldn't figure it out. "Anyway, keep that list in your wallet. Who knows, it may be something?"

What they soon knew was the heavy veil of sleep, and within two hours both had dozed off, he in a chair she on the couch. A few hours later, the SAT phone rang and sprang them awake.

Without a hello, Castelli said, "Okay, this is good stuff. At this point we definitely want you back in Urumqi, so you might pack for tomorrow. We have two psychological profilers going over the Quang diary. One is a Chinese woman, so that will be coming. Some of the other sheets are invoices, schedules, bills of lading for works of art, things like that. A good number are coming and going from Urumqi. No mention that we can see of the Gardner Collection, but if you didn't find any hints of that in Shanghai, we're going on the assumption that it might be in Urumqi." Then he added, "So sober up."

How'd he know? Peale wondered.

"More information will be coming," Castelli said. "Stay by the phone, please."

After that was done, Peale and Ho put the dinner tray out in front of the door, and Ho, in a weaving step said how much she enjoyed the party. She would see him in the morning—see if the Chinese food had a hangover.

"Like I said," Peale quipped to her, "someone put something in the tea. Just like those Shanghai movies."

18

Washington D.C.

WORKING ITS WAY slowly through the administrative machinery, the Freer Museum affair had only now reached the White
House. This gave the museum, the FBI, and state department some
time to get a picture of what was happening. The Freer "concession,"
as the skeptics called it, was part of the administration's diplomatic
work with China. Nobody wanted to disrupt, least of all undermine,
high-level diplomacy.

As things stood at this time, President Hughes was a creature of
his past. In the U.S. Senate, he had labored over Russian issues. He
ate and slept with Russia on his mind, a complex situation after the
breakup of the Soviet Union. It was nearly what Churchill had said,
"A riddle wrapped in a mystery inside an enigma." A new Russian
leader had emerged, a short man with thinning hair and shifty Slavic
eyes. Before long, he declared himself leader for life.

The saying back then, Hughes often recalled, was that "Russia
stood on three legs." It was a favorite in national security parlance.

The first leg was a mountain of rubles, the result of Russia's bottomless oil and gas reserves, something that Europe and China needed. Hughes himself had made headlines once when he told a reporter, "Russia is a gas pump pretending to be a nation," and a slight protested by the Russian Embassy followed.

The second leg was its refurbished police state, dropping the term KGB, but keeping the system intact. Finally, from the ground up, the new Russia was run by a Slavic underworld, a mafia incorporated. Beneath all of this, like a foundation of rock, the Russian race, despite its flashes of genius in science and literature, remained its docile self, a people with a czar as always.

Now, President Hughes's advisors were coming to him about China, and he was just beginning to adapt his thinking. The Chinese were different, culturally speaking. For a long time, he accepted his administration's premise that capitalism would liberalize China. Decades on, though, it too was looking like Russia, installing a supreme leader for life—opposite of anything called liberalized.

National Security Advisor Ronald Frey entered the Oval Office. "Good morning, Mr. President," he said, taking his chair across the presidential desk to discuss the China topic. They often sat and casually brain stormed. His advisor was an old China hand, and had plenty to say on the topic. He began to evoke a new use of the "three legs" analogy to describe the Asian adversary of the United States.

"The Chinese are a brilliant people," Frey said. "Inquisitive, creative, and very disciplined when they put their mind to it. They had the earliest naval exploration, dug rivers the size of the Mississippi. They built the Great Wall, led with early astronomy. Anyway, my point is that nevertheless, they have had only one political tradition, or should I say three things in one tradition, for thousands of years."

"This is the three leg theory, am I correct?" the president asked.

"Yes, that would be an appropriate term," Frey said. "To use that image, the first leg is the idea of an emperor under the 'mandate of heaven.' That's different from the Japanese idea of the imperial lineage, because if the will of heaven changes, China's emperor must also be changed. If there's an earthquake, famine, or a great civil strife, the Chinese believe the mandate has been withdrawn."

"Kick out the emperor," President Hughes said.

"That was often the case," said his advisor.

"And the other two?" The president, no slacker in his reading, was admittedly on a China learning curve, one that was slowly arcing from Moscow to Beijing.

"Second is the bureaucrat system, a merit system, the old exam system but one that creates a vast layer of regulation and governance. With this, for example, China has always registered where and who everyone is, where they live, and whether they are allowed to move." He would go into the complex credit system, under which each Chinese citizen was given a credit for good behavior, credits that allowed them to rise in the crowded economic spaces of Chinese society, and even into Party membership.

"And the third?" the president said.

"Yes, there's a third." Frey smiled and said, "That would be the tribute, or tributary system. China believes itself to literally be the center of civilization. All other countries, accepting their ways or not, must be subordinate, pay tribute, as the term suggests."

President Hughes thought he heard this assessment before. Mostly he heard statistics about trade, currency equivalencies, military adventurism against Taiwan, imports, and cultural exchanges to make peace. What his advisor was saying, nevertheless, did help make sense of modern China. A bigger picture. The president had a lot on his agenda to make time for such a vast discussion, but this often happened. In fact, he was expecting more on the China topic within the hour—another appointment in the Oval Office.

Bringing the Freer Museum incident to his attention had been hard. It was about the machinations of Chinese art curators, not missile defense. The state department worked on it. So did the CIA's Lucy Anderson. She strongly suggested to the president that the Freer Museum "international incident," still under wraps, might serve as a lever of some kind.

The idea of a lever always interested President Hughes. Every lever helped, however small, if it was in a position to trip up a geo-political rival. Arriving on time for the appointment, Schmidt from the state department and Anderson from CIA came into the well-lit Oval Office, greeting the president and Frey. They'd brought along the Freer Museum director. Everyone took a seat. The President had just looked over a half page summary.

"So, is this a petty theft or an international crisis?" the president said. "Is there a damage assessment?"

The museum director said, "We can't tell immediately. We don't know how long they've been at this. If we charge in, start checking this and that, well, I don't know the reaction on the China side."

"No, we don't want to let them know that we know," the president said. "Okay, keep me informed. Play nice like nothing's amiss. Keep your eyes open. This may be a card in the hand, but I still have to get some opinions on how to play it."

Despite his word of caution, the Freer Museum director was not exactly happy with such a cavalier, back-seat approach. Theodore Roosevelt himself had gotten the Freer Museum approved by Congress. However, the director could see the wisdom in waiting. You didn't want to bust a superpower like China without a plan B. What grated was the U.S. obeisance in all this. The great "Celestial Face of China" exhibit took over the Mall for a few weeks. There were months of preparation involved, a singular disruption of the

National Gallery, all on orders from the executive branch, driven by the "don't offend China" lobby. His stomach soured.

"I'll be talking with some advisors," the president said. "Thank you for your time. I'm sure this will work to our advantage."

The Freer director was uncertain how, but he was trying to be a team player. Still, he thought the China Embassy's action were outrageous. In his mind's eye he saw the faces of the overly friendly, courteous Chinese curators, with their smiles and deception.

19

Shanghai

QUANG RECEIVED THE disconcerting phone call early in the morning. Liu Hui woke her from sleep, saying there was a break-in at the Shanghai office. He had been drugged, had time to gather his wits, and called her as soon as he looked around the office to see what was taken, if anything.

Quang was furious. She immediately thought of Madame Soong Wei, but would reserve judgment, at least for a while. Her office was a distance away so she called a taxi. She prepared herself, always in sharp business attire. Outside, the taxi was idling, and Quang jumped in the back, gave the address, and they were into the slow morning traffic. The drive took them across the river and into the financial district, curving around the great circular footprints of the financial towers to end at her office building.

The office was in an older district of the Shanghai skyline for a good reason. There was less snooping around. The great skyscraper office complexes had the latest security, from cameras to grounds police. She wanted security, of course. But most of all she wanted the ability to come and go unnoticed, working between her office, her home, and her faceless storage facilities out near the airport.

The taxi arrived at the office, and she told it to wait. Upstairs, she found Liu Hui in the hallway, pacing around, looking groggy and disheveled. A little bruise was on his forehead and stubble on his chin.

"Did you let them in?" she said in a demanding tone.

"No! I arrived and put in the code. It was dark inside. Then someone hit me."

Quang thought, *Would Soong Wei do something like this?* Soong Wei had security police at her beck and call. What would she be looking for? The idea of calumny by her rival flooded her mind.

They entered the office and Quang darted about, checking things. She looked around her desk and elsewhere.

"I brought you papers last night and put them on the desk. Right there," Liu Hui said. "I've looked through the folder, and everything is in place, not touched."

"What about my room?" Quang asked.

"I did not check, Madame Quang. It is private."

That's what she always told her staff. She quickly went over behind the screen, used her code and entered. There was an alien scent in the room. It was more intuitive than physical. Looking around, the art on the walls was untouched, her sitting area undisturbed. She went to the cabinet and opened it. All was normal, except for an intuition of something amiss. She returned to the outer office desk. Its drawer holding her diary was ajar, and she wondered if that was her oversight? She pulled the drawer open. The diary lay there as she had absently-minded left it.

"This is outrageous," she said.

"Yes, Madame, a crime and an insulting one," Liu Hui said. "Could it be one of your competitors, or professional thieves?"

"But nothing is gone. Somebody was snooping." She conceded that, in a worst case, they had gone through her files, or the papers, or looked at the diary. "Turn on the computer. See the last login."

As Liu Hui did so, she paced around. She eyed the dawning day across Shanghai from her window. What she saw was Madame Soong Wei, like the orange sun through the smog, a suspicion that grew stronger.

"The last login to the computer was yesterday at four o'clock," Liu Hui said.

"Good, that was my work." Quang sat at her desk, calculating. What could be the reason? Of course, Quang had several covert locations for storage. She also was very active in acquisitions, shipping, more and more in the gray market, dipping into the black. Was someone trying to mount a corruption case against her, the niece of the general secretary, the ruler of China? That would surely be a trick by Soong Wei, a weasel.

She next thought of Urumqi. Shipments were due to arrive all through the month. Over the previous weeks, she'd had Liu Hui transfer a large share of the artwork at the Urumqi office to the tea farm facility, making more room. For a brief moment, she thought of the Gardner cache and the Vienna collection, both already stored at the tea farm, and assured herself they were secure. With the breach in Shanghai, however, she needed to be certain.

"Liu Hui, have the jet prepared to go to Urumqi. First call and see if anything is amiss. Even if not, you should go. Change the codes, then return quickly."

"Yes, Madame Quang, as soon as possible."

She was going to get to the heart of the matter, then request a meeting with her purported uncle, Ren Jinuah. She did not have a red phone, as did Omni Art Global. She still had a direct phone number. She was Quang Daiyu. Family usually got through. It was time to up her demands.

GENERAL SECRETARY REN Jinuah was not supposed to be bothered with most phone calls. It was a Friday, and even in work-aholic China, everyone looked forward to the weekend.

Whichever day it was, however, his niece always seemed to get around the bureaucracy. She had a reputation. Knowing who she was, the security operators were reluctant to refuse her request. Someday, he had to set a stricter policy. At this moment, he wished he was away from the office. Still, she'd probably travel to Beijing if she didn't get through on the phone. So he took the call.

"Uncle Ren Jinuah, I must complain that Madame Soong Wei has crossed the line. She has burglarized my Shanghai office." Her fulminations, though couched in courteous language, were a torrent.

Ren Jinuah listened, letting the cascade of her emotions die down. No one gave him an ultimatum—that was the privilege of his position. He gave the ultimatums. Now she made the same old threats. Maybe he had to put an end to this.

"Dear Uncle," Quang concluded, "I feel that you are too much under the influence of Madame Soon Wei. This is not fair, this is not the way families do things." She paused to let that linger. "I do not want to make this public, but I will. You do not want the public to know, I assure you."

"Please calm yourself, dear Niece," he said. "This is very unfair. I have so many factions making demands on me, including Omni Art Global. I want to help you, but I can do that only if my position is secure. You know that. You too will be risking that, for yourself, if you act rashly. I assure you I take this seriously. I will be in touch."

Quang had calmed a bit. She was playing with fire, a dragon's fire, she knew. Most of the affection between she and her uncle had burned away by now. She was playing a hard game with him. She knew that if she pushed too hard, she might lose. "Dear Uncle," she said, "I trust that you will take care of your family, your kin. That is our honorable way."

She would wait to see what happened. For now, her focus had to be on making plans, ensuring that her facilities were not tampered with again, and thinking of her next move with Madame Soong Wei.

THE CALL ENDED and Chairman Ren Jinuah's mind was in turmoil. As it churned, he caught a glimpse of a memento on his desk—a small polished stone on which his daughter, at school, had painted their family name. The calligraphy was very elegant. He was proud of her. *Ren*. The name was auspicious, yet in some ways, had led to some of his current troubles—especially with Quang, his niece.

In his family, and among his relatives, genealogy had been a pastime. Given the tumult across China's history, tracing genealogy was more art than science. The Ren name, lost in the mists of history, may have once been a matriarchal line, or a patriarchal line from the small Kingdom of Jining. In any case, the name Ren had resonance. It was a great advantage for Ren Jinuah's rise.

Now, here he was, general secretary, putting that name Ren on a page of history. His supporters, and sometimes his sycophantic rivals, would often remind him of that. "It's a name borne by the wise men of China," some would say to him. Indeed, it was believed that the Yellow Emperor himself had named twelve of his children Ren. An ancient name.

Now in the twenty-first century, a reverence for antiquity had been revived. Antiquity gave China its pride of place, a rationale for its rise once again to supremacy. Mao had labeled Confucius a reactionary, a feudal charlatan, all that was bad from the past. Now the Party was not so sure. It needed role models, new wise men, especially if a general secretary was to become a new emperor.

To his chagrin, this looking back was also creating a little problem—the problem with Niece Quang. She, like the family, had a ken for genealogy, and she found out too much. Ren had appointed one of China's top genealogists to head that department at the Palace Museum in the Forbidden City. Quang, with her wily ways, cajoled information from him. After that, she went on her own, finding out more, looking back even to revolutionary days.

It was a long revolution: the demise of the Qing Dynasty, the Western incursion, the rise of the Nationalist and Communist parties, and then the Japanese Occupation. With the Communist victory, the Cultural Revolution followed. The layers of chaos had confounded so much of China's official family records. Only recently had Party scholars begun to reconstruct a "true" history of prominent family lines, bending, as required, past memories to reflect well on the Party leadership.

The problem was, the probing had turned over too many stones, revealing what was best left hidden in the past. For Ren, that troubling past led to the time of Mao and Deng Xiaoping. Mao had three wives and, it became clear, several concubines. Deng's history was no less amorous. The mystery was, were there any unexpected children, blood heirs of Mao and Deng?

According to what Ren's niece Quang had traced, in the 1890s, there was a secret heir to the Qing Dynasty. When Empress Cixi had poisoned the young heir apparent—over whom she was Dowager Regent—it was presumed that line had come to an end. It was also presumed the "boy Emperor" Puyi, was the next legitimate heir, but that was a ruse, a concoction of the royal household. A true heir still lived, hidden in the chaos, a female heir.

That woman was of royal household blood, and she would later be a concubine to Deng Xiaoping, the successor after Mao. An illegitimate daughter to Deng was thus born, secretly raised in the family of Zheng, a loyal follower. In time she too grew to be beautiful, a carrier of Deng's bloodline. She had many suitors, especially among ascending provincial leaders of the Party. One of them was Ren himself. As a young rising Party official, Ren had a few trysts. One was with the Zheng girl, whose beauty got the best of him. She had other affairs, including with a married man name Quang of Shanghai. Ren found it not only distasteful, but dangerous—because Quang was the husband of Ren's older sister.

By that liaison, the unwed Zhang beauty bore a daughter, a scandal to be hidden away. Mr. Quang's wife—indeed, the sister of Ren Jinuah—was a Party loyalist, and in secrecy she agreed to adopt the child, born in 1972. Her adopted name became Quang. This was Quang Daiyu. On paper, she was Ren's niece, but in reality, she might be his illegitimate daughter. After all, she was born about nine months after his assignations with the Zhang beauty.

Ren forced himself to believe the opposite. At worst a story such as this could become a dark rumor. Especially since Quang Daiyu's real mother, shunted aside in the whole sordid affair, had become an opium addict and her late husband was jailed on corruption charges. They were erased from the scene, airbrushed from the photograph. Yet it was like a seed long buried, now sprouting with threats.

Ren assured himself he was only dealing with a mendacious rumor, not a fact. How could it be true? Yet when he looked at Quang, he was haunted, as if a mirror stared back. She had all the cleverness of a Ren. Whenever such paternal affections arose, he suppressed them. Political ambition easily trimmed them back. Besides, for Quang to make such a claim would make her a laughingstock. How could there be such a thing, a woman in the royal line of Empress Cixi, then the bloodline of both Deng Xiaoping the great reformer and of Ren Jinuah, supreme leader of China? Impossible. Regardless, Niece Quang was to be handled carefully.

For now, he would act as mediator, an age-old tradition in China. He would avoid confrontation. Ren Jinuah would set up a private meeting between Quang and Soong, the two dragon ladies. Maybe that would calm things down.

Wearily, he looked at his calendar, which showed the twelve-months dictated by the West and its Julian calendar. By this reading, it was very late spring, but his mind began to mismatch and follow that other path, the lunar calendar. Those days and months had ancient stories and myths about how the celestial order unfolded: first the days of the Rat, then the Ox, the Tiger, the Rabbit, the Dragon, the Snake, the Horse, the Goat, the Monkey, the Rooster, the Dog, and the Pig. It was all a great fairytale, this idea of auspicious times, and yet Ren's mind went there—to the hours, days, and months, where *feng shui* energy, good luck energy, from the stars held a mysterious control over earthly affairs.

He tried to shake the bizarre thoughts from his mind, wondering why they even came. Despite himself, Ren knew that at this time of the year, he was under the Snake, passing into the Horse, awaiting his fate—the Politburo vote taking place under the Dog. Quang was born in the year of the Rat; she was crossing his path in the month of the Snake rising. *Utter foolishness!* It was grotesque. *What is my mind doing?* For years he excelled in exams at the Party schools. He won awards for his essays on the "objective conditions" of history, the dialectic, the "means of production," the stages of proletarian development. He often elaborated his own orthodox Marxist-Leninist 'thought' to the cadre. So from what medieval pit had such superstitious inklings emerged? *It was all crazy, utterly insane.* With all his strength, he resisted the celestial pull, fought its grip on his Chinese soul. Yet more often now, the ancient gnosis was winning.

PART THREE

20

Shanghai

WHILE GENERAL SECRETARY Ren was having his doubts and reveries in Beijing, Peale and Ho were in their Shanghai hotel. They had waited through the night for a call from Castelli. The next morning dawned sunny and cool. White fluffy clouds hung in the cerulean sky. The city around them was in a roar of traffic and motion. The mysterious Gold Tea, whatever it was, had worn off, and they ordered strong coffee over breakfast.

"Do you want cream in that?" Ho said, cutting short his chances for his coffee joke.

"Straight is fine," he said. Fortunately they'd found a quiet eatery on the block, because now the phone call came through.

"Peale, this is Castelli. We've got a few question for you and Miss Ho. Some plans as well."

Peale put the SAT phone on speaker and they huddled over their table, Ho listening in. "We're ready, shoot," Peale said.

"Our analysts have gone over this six ways from Sunday, and we have a theory."

"Great," Ho said.

"Okay, first this person, Quang Daiyu," Castelli said. "She is apparently the niece of the current general secretary. We don't understand their relationship, but her diary, read by our psychological profilers, gave us a picture of who, or what, we are dealing with."

Reading from the profile, he said it was conducted by two experts at Quantico, home of a Marine base and the FBI. One expert was American and the other Chinese-American. They had an interpretation of the Quang woman. "Probably in her mid-to-late forties, and of uncertain family background," Castelli said. As Peale had already found, she had been in America studying art history. The diary noted that she'd returned to China soon after the 1989 Tiananmen Square events. Her entries looked back. Some revealed a deep anger, a confusion.

"She seems to be striking out at both the West and her own government. The profilers call it cognitive dissonance. Sort of what some Americans felt after the First World War, the so-called 'lost generation.' Further, Quang's scribbling showed a resolve to make a mark of some kind. And of course, she speaks a lot about Empress Cixi. The profilers say this is a kind of empress complex. Apparently rare, but known in some Chinese women."

"Interesting lady," Peale said. He'd seen psych-profiling before, its categories sizing up criminal minds as organized, paranoid, or obsessive. It was often a lot of mumbo jumbo, but always interesting. On this front, something else came to his mind, a memory from his youthful days of reading English course assignments, *Madame Bovary* and *Anna Karenina*. Very long novels. Two willful, unhappy women. They had followed their fickle hearts, filled with ambition, planting the seeds of their own destruction. Peale recalled the picture he had seen of a young Quang Daiyu in the Harvard yearbook.

As Ho listened to Castelli, she had an image of Quang in her mind as well. She knew the dowager type, but didn't comment. As Castelli had breezed over the profile, he'd said something else like, "it talks here about shame culture and guilt culture," but passed over it. Ho picked up on the point. She knew what that was all about, and thought about it often.

In the West, it was guilt, the sense of sin that had driven so much behavior, so much belief and even art. Asia was different. Chinese were driven by shame, the acute embarrassment before the group, a 'loss of face.' Guilt revealed the individualism of one culture, shame the collectivism of the other. Both cultures had found solutions to such psychologically troubled voices within. For the West it was confession, contrition, turning away from sin. For Asians it had to be reconciliation with the group honor. If saving face went to the extreme, it required suicide.

Ho was not sure what this told them about Quang Daiyu. Nor was she sure what it revealed about herself, a child of China.

"So that's some profiling," Castelli said. "Now the real business at hand, the Gardner heist. From what we see in the paperwork, there is quite a lot of artwork in the two Urumqi facilities, though it's not perfectly clear. The paperwork has facility A and B. Nothing more clear. One of them has items that we can trace to the Gardner stuff, and a reference or two to the 'American collection.' We're assuming that's Gardner. So what did you see when you were there?"

Peale described the two facilities, the industrial park office and the tea farm.

"Yeah, our satellites have picked up electronic activity at both sites, but it's not intelligible," Castelli said.

"My hunch," said Ho, "is that A is the main office, B the tea farm."

"And B is where the Gardner items seem to be listed, according these papers," Castelli said. There was a pause for a while, all three thinking it over. "I tell you what," he said, "you head back to Urumqi, we'll do some more work on this. We want to be precise."

"And in Urumqi, what?" Peale said.

"There are options," Castelli said. "One, we go the diplomatic route. Take this as a complaint to the Embassy of China. 'Hey, you've got stolen goods of ours, and we know exactly what it is and exactly where it is.' We may be wrong, and I'm sure they'd have it covered up within the hour."

"Okay," Peale said. "And second?"

"Or you two get in there somehow, pin this down, you know, photos and proof and then we take it from there."

"I say we do it," Ho said and Peale agreed.

"Ah, let's see, one more thing," Castelli said, apparently looking at his notes. "Those eight-digit code numbers you gave us. Nothing we can find in bank records. However, there's a page in the diary with columns of numbers. The diary says, 'Fours by twos," then there's columns of four numerals, parts of eight digit numbers."

"We noticed that," Ho said, her mind re-engaging the puzzle, but with no answers.

"Anyway, that's the diary," Castelli said, moving on. "We've got an asset over there to help you."

Both How and Peale were wondering whether this was getting too complicated. Would a human asset hiding in China be a third wheel, or just what they needed?

Peale asked. "And what are the benefits?"

"Well, for one thing, this asset knows how things work between

Shanghai, Beijing, and out there in Urumqi. His name is Sam Brower. He's assisted the CIA for a decade."

Before they asked more, Castelli was passing it on. "He's an American and works as a journalist, a well-known travel writer in China. Published everywhere from *Fodor's* to *Lonely Planet* and often a stringer for the *Wall Street Journal* and several British papers. He's got very good eyes and ears."

Castelli would make the appropriate contact, then pass on how they'd meet.

The next morning it came through. Brower would be in the lobby at the Shanghai Blue, a fairly run down hotel west of the Huangpu River. "Just say to the man with a newspaper, 'We have reservations at the Garden Inn.' Then he'll take it from there. You can compare notes, get on the road to Urumqi."

"From the airport?" Ho asked.

"No, the bullet train."

"That's a long way," Peale said.

"About two days," said Castelli. "But you'll see why."

PEALE AND HO had packed their things, light traveling as usual. They found that they could actually walk to the Shanghai Blue, just a half mile toward the river. Their hotel, fortunately, was also not far from the main train station.

It was a nice walk past old residences, some new high-rises, the pyramidal towers of the old Soviet-designed Exhibit Grounds in view, and then the stone gatehouse district with its narrow streets. The Shanghai Blue had a lobby. A few parties were checking in and out. And there was a man reading a newspaper: maybe forties, square jawed, balding at the temples, and dressed casually. Peale and Ho approached, said the magic words. Brower said, "Right this way." He led them back out on the street.

They ambled along for five blocks, found a run-of-the-mill

restaurant with a patio and took a table outside. Brower suggested some light food, beer or tea. They settled in.

Brower first explained that the train would help them avoid the tighter security at the airport. "You can't hijack a train," he said.

"They've got airport hijackings?" Peale said.

"A couple attempts within memory," Brower said. "It's happened with flights out on the frontier where they have problems with Muslim unrest." The Beijing government also blamed the Tibetans, but that was mostly propaganda.

Brower said he would travel with them as far as Lanzhou, where Peale and Ho would make a connection for the final half of the trip to Urumqi. Brower was there to get them oriented, offer any advice. The train was by far the safest. Plus, they had some time to kill. "From what I understand, Washington is making up its mind," Brower said.

"So, you've been given details," Peale said.

"Some."

Ho, being an old China hand like Brower, always enjoyed hearing other's stories—though she never told her own. She found Brower, a putative spy, fairly talkative. But then again, that was his benign profile in China. A known quantity who published articles that helped tourism. He was a common companion of travelers, official and ordinary.

Brower said, "How's your stay been?"

Ho looked at Peale. They both wondered how much minutia to go into, such as breaking and entering, shaking down a Chinese millionaire.

"Funny thing," Ho said. "Over at the Quang office, we picked up some samples of the tea that the Silk Road Company markets. Two kinds. Have you ever heard of Gold Tea?"

Brower laughed. "That's opium tea. Why, do you want to buy some? It's black market."

"I knew it was something," Peale said. "We drank some with our Chinese takeout."

Brower laughed again. "Are you okay?"

"Fine, fine," Ho said. "Just a little buzz last night."

"Let me explain," Brower said. "China has a very medicinal culture, a long history, lots of strange herbs, lots miraculous claims. Tea is part of that, not just plain-old tea. The Black Jade is a connoisseur's tea. An aura of royal tea, only for emperors and the like. Doesn't taste any different to me, but it does wake you up."

"So you've also had some Gold," Ho asked.

"I've tried everything in China once," Brower said, "and often lived to regret it. Some care is required. Take for instance poison tea. For centuries China, especially in imperial matters, had a kind of honor code. If you betrayed the emperor, well, you had to die. In one scenario, you were given a white silk cloth and expected to hang yourself. Or you could drink poison tea. Other times it was given to you, and you didn't know until it was too late."

"Classic case is Empress Cixi," Brower went on. "In her final days, she poisoned her adopted heir. That was Guangxu, the next emperor in line. They say she used poisoned tea. It could be legend. They did find traces of cyanide in the boy's bones."

"Wouldn't you taste it, spit it out?" Peale asked.

"Not if the cyanide tea is grown properly. You put the cyanide in the soil. You get a mild dose with each cup."

"Gruesome," Ho said. "Let's talk about Gold Tea."

"Very expensive stuff," Brower said. "A hybrid of a tea plant with the opium poppy. Illegal in China, but if you find the right night club, or back alley. . ."

Ho angled her thumb at Peale and said, "Our genius here went for the gold."

Eying Ho, Peale replied gently. "And we shouldn't forget the genius who shoplifted the tea." As Brower's face became a question mark, Peale said, "Anyway, it tells us something about the tea farm. Maybe Silk Road Company deals in exotic herbs or drugs, an illegal trade. Probably a source of revenue."

More than most countries, Brower said, China had a drug regulation problem. On its south was the Golden Triangle, with Burma as the hub. It was there that heroin production entered China or was navigated by Chinese smugglers abroad. Opium also came over from Central Asia, Afghanistan in particular.

From his time in Afghanistan, Peale knew that country's story. The U.S. had failed to persuade or even pay the Afghan warlords to close down the poppy fields. They'd take the cash, drop off for a season, and then resume production. The poppy was as old as the ancient Silk Road, just one of the delicacies among all that tea, silk, jadestone, and spice.

One of those roads, the Wakhan Corridor, had been trodden for centuries. It was a thin arm of modern Afghanistan that reached over to touch China. It was so remote and beautiful, on par with a U.S. National Park, that it was deemed one of Central Asia's nature conservation areas. Below snowcapped peaks, the green valleys were home to farmers and herdsmen, young Afghan girls with bright traditional dress. Sadly, it was also a population often addict to the opium that smugglers brought through. Peale once heard it called the "Appalachia of Afghanistan."

Brower broke his train of thought. "Out where you're going, Xingjian Province, it's pretty quiet. The farmers grow fields and fields of hemp, but they make rope from it. They use its oil as machine lubricant."

"Huh," said Peale. "Half of San Francisco would walk a mile for that axle grease."

"Probably so," Brower said.

They agreed to meet at the train station that evening to catch the regular overnight express. They could buy tickets on the spot, which required a passport and visa, but that was fairly routine, Brower said. As they traveled across China on a two day trip, Washington was still figuring out what they'd do in Urumqi.

PEALE AND HO passed the rest of the day in their separate hotel rooms. In their line of work, both were used to tedious waits. When the sun was low they all met again at Shanghai railway station. For the first lap of the trip west, they'd take the Shanghai-Lanzhou train, occupy a "hard sleeper," a private compartment with large reclining seats. With tickets in hand, they boarded the train. They found their sleeper and settled in. Ho found it was not bad. Comfy enough and shades of the Orient Express. The train began to jerk forward, pick up speed, and then a smooth ride began.

The sun would be above the horizon for another few hours, and through the night the train would make nineteen stops before Lanzhou. Brower explained that this leg of the trip was across a densely populated area, passing through the China heartland, approaching the origin of the ancient Silk Road, which had begun in Xi'an, city of the terracotta soldiers. Beyond Lanzhou was the second lap. It crossed between some low mountains, edged against the Tibetan Plateau, and then reached a flat desert path called the Hexi Corridor, all the way to Urumqi.

"We'll wake up to the Lanzhou sunrise," Brower said. After de-training in Lanzhou, they'd have another several-hour wait for the next train to Urumqi, which left in mid-evening. "The second lap is a true bullet train." Brower would leave Lanzhou before Peale and Ho, catching a train over to the terracotta soldier site. "A large group of Europeans, some archaeology students, are showing up there."

"A story?" Ho asked the journalist-spy.

"Maybe," Brower said. "I keep on the move but like to hang out around Xi'an." He pulled some folded papers from inside his jacket. "I'm tight with some of the provincial leaders, including in Xi'an. They've given me letters of recommendation."

"Not bad," said Ho. "Support for the home team."

"Very helpful for interviews. Foreign tourism is more powerful than the Party in some of these places." Brower began his life in China writing travel pieces, then got gigs as a tour guide. He began to specialize in VIP tours, eventually got a license in China for that kind of work in addition to his press credentials—and his other sub rosa gig, as Castelli had intimated.

DURING THEIR WAKING hours, the setting sun cast its pink glow over hills and valleys, but also countless ramshackle neighborhoods, many with incongruent modern structures cropping up as if the urban planning was a throw of the dice.

Peale was watching it all pass by, thinking that by dark he would have gazed upon the dwellings of a few million people. Then something surreal entered his vision. It was a vast construction site with orderly streets and nearly uniform structures. It looked like a Hollywood movie set, empty and quiet.

"Sam, what's that?"

"That's a small city. The government is building small cities from scratch. High rise offices, public housing for several thousand, roads, buildings for warehousing and manufacture. It can be spooky to visit one of these places. Someday there will be a mass population transfer into that empty city."

It was all about population control, Brower explained further. "China's vast, but it's overpopulated. The farm in China is essentially still a food garden, not some big enterprise. Every year a few million people from the outskirts press in toward the cities. That's the main job of the police in China. They keep everyone in their place. So, these ghost cities are waiting."

Ho said, "I have a new appreciation for suburban sprawl."

"Ha," said Brower. "Now think of the sprawl beginning a few millennia ago." Shanghai was established as a fishing village at the Yangtze River delta around five hundred AD. Then that habitation sprawled out.

"A century after the fall of Rome," Ho said.

"Barbarians will do that to you," Brower said.

He explained that China had recently been making claims that it found "writing" on stones five thousand years old. Despite those claims, they'd still have to strain farther back to get the world record. That was held by the Middle East, the Egyptians coming in second.

For anyone who'd read the history, Ho thought, it was not hard to look out on the landscape and see the dynasties coming and going, the Shang, the first well documented one, than the Zhou—where her own name originated—and then the Han and Qing spread in the same direction that the train was going.

Brower broke her spell and said, "Just think how many armies fought for this land over how many centuries. It boggles the mind." During a few historic episodes, the slaughter, the wars and revolutions, the forced movement of populations and the starvation cost tens of millions of lives. "And that's each time."

"And the Cultural Revolution put the icing on the cake," Peale said. That was another twenty million.

"You won't read that in their grade school textbooks," Brower said. "Most of those things are whitewashed now. They prefer to emphasize the times the Westerners came and ruined everything."

They finally slept and as the next day broke the train pulled into

Lanzhou Station. Even under the fresh yellow light of morning, the city looked cursed—some of China's worst smog and traffic. It was a main crossing on the upper Yellow River. Peale and Ho could whiff the refineries, which were hissing and belching out their byproducts far over the horizon.

"The river has always been a golden brown," Brower said. "Silt washes down from the highlands along the Tibetan Plateau."

The train station mimicked many in China, a kind of modernist take on a temple, a broad curving façade with giant red calligraphic letters. They took a taxi into the city, as modern as any in China. It had been a hub of the northern Silk Road and was now being built up as a link in the Belt and Road Initiative.

The downtown was a hubbub. Ho noticed the large number of Chinese who wore the traits of Muslim attire, scarves and caps. These were the Hui, a good part of the population. The largest mosque in China stood near the river. The city had once been part of the Tibetan Empire, and those influences showed in some old architecture and clothing choices.

Brower took them to a restaurant near a city square for breakfast. After that they strolled around, Brower keeping an eye on his watch. They soon were in the thick of the urban streets. And they began to notice something odd. Groups of young men in dark clothing, even leather jackets, had gathered at street corners and moved down side streets. As they moved, flurries of street peddlers were scooping up their rickety kiosks and running in the opposite direction. On one corner, they saw the men, as if a police patrol, knock apart a food stand and take its owner off by his collar.

"What's going on?" Peale asked.

"Cheng Guan," Brower said. "They're gangs hired by the police to clean up street vendors and move vagrants out of the city. A lot of people outside the city are coming in. This is more population control. These guys are both hated and feared, more than the police in the blue shirts."

Suddenly one of the groups began coming their way, clearly having the three—two Westerners and a Chinese woman—in their sights. Peale asked, "What's this about?" Brower was surprisingly calm, it seemed to Peale.

"We'll just head the other way," Brower said. "There's a trigger out here. This is the countryside in many respects. When these Chinese guys see a Caucasian guy with a Chinese woman, well, they get kind of triggered." A Chinese man with a white women was acceptable.

"I've heard of that before," Ho said. She'd seen it before.

They processed to a larger street and hailed a taxi. "I've got my train in an hour, so I best get back to the station," Brower said. "What's your preference?"

Peale and Ho exchanged glances and Ho said, "We'll hang out in the city." Neither of them could imagine sitting in the train station until evening.

"That's fine," Brower said. "This is the China experience. Good to have. You've got your phones, right?" They did. "I'm going to give you a number, one of our people in the city."

"Your people?" Peale said.

"A sleeper," Brower said with a wink. "I have a few out here."

The term was becoming archaic, but still made sense. During the Cold War a sleeper was an in-country person who was loyal to American interests, either monetarily or ideologically. They were especially valued in the old Soviet Union or the Eastern Bloc, but now it seemed they were a resources in China as well.

"His name is Gao," Brower said, taking out his notepad and writing down a phone number.

As they lingered a bit too long, the taxi that stopped for them drove off. They'd have to hail another. Just then another group of Cheng Guan came around the corner. Brower gave a small laugh, the bemusement of a street veteran. "At least it's the Chen Guan and not the Jiwei or the *Hei shehui*."

Ho understood that Jiwei were Party police, plain clothes thugs who could take anyone away for detention, usually on corruption charges. "What is Hei shehui?"

"Exactly as it translates. Black society thugs," Brower said. "The police hire them, too, when they want to rough you up a bit." He shook his head as if simply annoyed. Their group of Chen Guan, which numbered about twenty, looked as if it was going to surround them, now thirty feet away. They were at a corner, so Brower said, "Look, you two skip around the corner then walk off. Call that number it if it makes you feel more secure."

"And you?" Peale said.

"Routine. Remember, I've got a million credentials." Brower padded his coat pocket where he carried the letters of recommendation and who knew what else. "Things happen in China, and we just find our way. Now scoot."

Peale and Ho flitted around the corner. Ho glance back to see Brower walking toward the group of Chinese, almost with a wave of greeting, pulling out his paperwork. Around the corner there was a restaurant, so they went inside. They saw an exit in the back and headed there, coming out on another street. They covered several more blocks at a brisk pace, then stopped at a small park with a few women and children taking in the late morning sun.

"What do you think?" Peale said. He was still a little surprised that this was happening in a city known for its scientific research and its modernity. They were seated on a bench, no gangs in sight. Three of the children approached, curious about the tall man. As they stared, Peale gave a little wave, put a funny expression on his face. They giggled and scampered off in search of more mischief.

"Well," Ho said, "my best guess is that we're in the sticks and the American-guy-with-a-Chinese woman thing is being taken poorly." She thought a moment, looked at the paper Brower had given them. She was always game for a little intrigue. "Why don't we call Mr. Gao."

21

Lanzhou, China

MR. GAO TOLD Ho that they should go to the south side base of the trestle bridge, where there was a park. He would be in a light blue truck which had a tarp over its rear cargo frame. He could be there in thirty minutes.

By now, Peale and Ho had rummaged through their carry-ons, not to ferret out guns and knives, but something to work with—just in case. Peale slung his bag over his shoulder and offered to lug Ho's on its rollers. They knew the river was to their right, to the east, so they padded off through the geometrical maze of streets, leaving behind the business and shopping district for shabbier sections, many related to commerce on the river. The traffic over here was mostly small and large trucks, but some streets were hauntingly empty even for this time of day.

"Which way?" Ho asked at an intersection. "Keep going toward the river, or up some blocks?"

"Up some blocks," Peale said. He could see some pedestrian

traffic that way, versus industrial blight toward the river. Soon, he wished he had changed his mind. Two blocks up, a dark gray panel truck was parked with three inhospitable characters in black leather jackets loitering by its open back doors. They kept their pace in that direction, and Peale said, "We turn right again at the next street."

He was trying to remember the term that Brower had used for the third kind of thug that the Chinese police let wander on their own, dispensing street justice, or just mayhem. It was something like "black gang."

Ho said, "Looks like Hei shehui, the 'black society thugs.'"

Ah, yes, *that's* the name, Peale thought. "I was thinking the same thing." Like a replay from earlier, one of the three swaggering men closed the panel van door, and the trio began to walk toward Peale and Ho, picking up their pace.

"I think we have another case of triggered Chinese goons," Ho said. A Caucasian man with the younger Chinese women—that seemed to do it in the backstreets of Lanzhou, a supposed university city.

"Okay, we turn the corner, kick our luggage into a doorway, out of the way, and stand around looking at our watch, or maybe pull out a travel brochure. We'll talk first, let them make the first move, and hopefully they'll go away."

"Got it."

"I charged my Taser this morning." It had traveled in his shaving kit and generally looked the part—a black shaver.

Ho had tucked a mini-can of pepper spray in her back pocket. It looked like deodorant if it was ever checked by curious customs types.

As expected, the three men came on like muggers, two on one side and the third to their left, not five feet away from them. The apparent leader spoke to Ho, but he was staring at Peale. Ho calmly replied, as if there was nothing unusual about the situation. Then she heard the lead guy say in a low voice, "You get the luggage after we handle them." One covered Ho, and two approached Peale, their hands up in fighting position, whether as fist fighters or karate wannabees, Peale could not tell.

It was all telepathy now, for Peale and Ho did not exchange words, but they were in sync—Ho suddenly swung wide with her leg, giving her nemesis a round kick, then she grabbed his arm and kneed him in the groin. For a split second, this turned the heads of Peale's quarry, and he gave one of them a lunging fist in the jaw, knocking him back, tumbling him on the ground. Peale sprung back, anchoring on his left foot to refocus his right fist. The man still standing lunged at him, swinging, even clawing, and Peale took a strong hit on his shoulder, but he moved with it, managing to land his fist on the back of the man's neck, making him stagger.

The three regrouped and seemed ready to try again. This time, as the two again came at Peale, the third went for their luggage. It was time for reinforcements, Ho decided. She pulled out her pepper spray, leaped to the man at the luggage, and with his collar in her hand, hit him square in the face with the foaming toxin. He screamed as his hands came up to try and scrape the burning sting from his eyes and nostrils. Ho gave him a punch in the kidneys, then a sidewise kick to his knee, just short of dislocating it.

Again, the two on Peale—one having and arm around his neck as Peale swung at the second—were distracted by the scream, and this gave Peale time to pull out his Taser from his back pocket, find the switch and jam it on the torso of the guy putting him in a headlock.

"Ahhhh." The man shook for a second, then stiffened and staggered. Peale jolted him one more time and he crumpled to the ground.

The second man on Peale had by now turned to catch Ho from behind. "You bastard," she screamed before his arm put a strangulation lock on her throat. Ho's leg was flailing, trying to get a back kick to land somewhere, but she was getting only empty air. Peale rushed over and jolted the man in the back of the neck, giving it some time, and amid a few spasms, gravity took him down.

Ho gave him a kick for good measure and said, "Those bastards. I hate oversized juvenile delinquents."

"You okay?" Peale asked.

"Once I get the smell of him off me," she said, straightening her hair and blouse.

He eyed her neck closely. "You've got a nasty bruise there."

"That's why I carry cosmetics," she said.

They quickly checked the luggage, which was jostled on the street, and kept an eye on the man on the ground who still had some wits about him. They hadn't considered whether these guys had guns or knives, but regardless, Peale tried to land one more blow on the thug who was down, nursing his injured leg. Quickly, though, the adversary limped away toward the panel van.

"Let's split before these guys regroup," Peale said, already grabbing the luggage. He looked at his watch and could see the time to meet Gao in his blue truck was just five more minutes. "Can you jog?"

"Do birds fly?" Ho said as they moved on.

"Do fish swim?" Where did that come from? Peale wondered, a bit hyper.

"Thanks for covering my back."

"And you mine." He was still catching his breath.

"Glad we brought some extra toiletries," she said.

"Yeah, I'd hate to get caught with a gun in China."

"How about stolen art worth millions?" she said, keeping pace alongside.

"Oh, I could explain that. No problem." He was still a bit winded, showing his age.

They were approaching the river. The buildings became more staggered, blocking clear vistas up and down the street. They tried to use these blinds as they sped along, now just a block from the river. They could see the span of the old steel bridge rising above the flat rooftops. So they hugged the riverside road at the soonest turn. Two blocks ahead they could see a kind of park with trees and, at the curb, a light blue truck with a frame back covered by a tarp. Both were nearly out of breath. Peale's old wounds made his side ache a little, but next to the exertions of their past military training, all this sudden rigor on the back streets of Lanzhou was nothing to tell any wide-eyed grandkids about.

AS THEY APPROACHED the bridge, Peale and Ho saw a man standing by the light blue truck, which seem to be that of a fruit vender or something farm related. The man saw them, waved them over, and got into his driver's seat. He was in his fifties, tall and graying with an oddly professorial bearing despite his rough work clothes—that was Ho's first impression.

She went to the cab window and said, "Mr. Gao, I'm Grace Ho." They spoke in Mandarin.

Gao nodded almost sagely, calm despite the flushed looks on the woman and her older Caucasian companion. He spoke slowly.

"Go around and sit up front." It was a wide cabin so the three of them had plenty of elbow room.

"Mr. Gao, thanks for the ride," Ho said once inside. A conversation ensued and Ho translated occasionally for Peale. Gao also spoke pretty good English, which he used liberally. In that regard, Peale was mostly in the loop.

"It's getting worse," Gao said. "A city of strong arms." He meant thugs.

Brower had called this man a sleeper, so he was obviously operating under some kind of understanding about how Americans circulated covertly in Communist China. What surprised her was his apparent profession. A fruit vender? A farmer?

Gao put things clearly from the start. "You have a train this evening. You can either wait at the station, or I can take you somewhere out of the limelight." He paused a while, then said, "Or I can drive you to the next station, which is Xining."

That surprised both Peale and Ho. That would be up the Lanzhou-Urumqi line a couple hours' drive to, as the Gao noted, a smaller city called Xining. Gao was turning out to be a full-service sleeper-spy, Peale mused.

"What do you recommend?" Ho asked.

"I have a trip to take in the direction of Xining," Gao said, pointing roughly northwest. "A delivery."

Peale and Ho noticed that the truck's bed was covered by a tarp and full of something. Ho and Gao began a conversation and the situation became clear. Lanzhou was a locus for agricultural goods from the region. Gao had a delivery business, picking up in the market exchange and taking it to outliers. Today he had a truck load of tobacco, peaches, and melons. His delivery was in the direction of Xining. "It's only a half hour out of my way," he said. "No strong arms in Xining."

Again, Peale and Ho traded glances, comparing a seat in the rocky truck with one in a train station for several hours.

Peale shrugged. "A little more eyeball on China."

Ho caught the sentiments and said, "Mr. Gao, we would be very pleased to drive with you. We have some resources to contribute."

She meant cash. Sleepers had expenses, and it was a job also undertaken for pay, especially in thread-bare sectors of China.

The fruit truck made for an odd contrast in downtown urban Lanzhou. But as they looped through the city proper to get on the great trestle bridge, its kind was more common. They crossed the bridge and began up the river valley between the mountains. The curiosity was killing Ho. Who was this man, so reserved, yet so intensely focused?

That answer came as she prodded in conversation. It came reluctantly at first, then flowed. "There was a time, a couple decades ago, when we could talk in China," Gao said. "But, as it turned out, if you talk too much . . ." He trailed off.

By the term "talking," he meant doing academic work and writing about it as a university professor, Peale and Ho soon learned.

"Which university?" Ho asked.

"A major one," Gao said. "In Shenzhen. On the mainland, across from Hong Kong." Ho's eyes widened, and Gao noticed with mild alarm. "You know Shenzhen?"

"My parents are from there," Ho said.

A nearly imperceptible smiled crossed Gao's melancholy face. "A good place to come from," he said.

Ho was tempted to mention more about her family, her three uncles and many cousins still on the mainland, and about her own genealogic research, but wisely held her tongue.

The road ahead became a two lane highway, not too crowded, and modern in its maintenance. The terrain from Lanzhou to Xining was still a warren of mountains with narrow lowlands. The railroad and the highways navigated the valleys, which rose higher toward the Tibetan Plateau. The truck was solid, moving at a good pace. By his SAT phone, Peale had found that the distance to Xining was less than one hundred forty miles. They'd arrive well before the

Lanzhou-Urumqi overnight train made its stop there. They had their tickets from Lanzhou, and could board with a little explanation. "Sightseeing, and what do you know, we're already in Xining." All aboard!

The three passengers were familiar with the protocols of meetings such as theirs, under the radar in a foreign country. Neither party needed to explain what they were doing or why. They already agreed on the unspoken basics: mutual help to complete a task for the good guys. Ho's Shenzhen connection, however, touched a spot in Gao and he became a bit more forthcoming. He was speaking to Ho now in Chinese, and Peale put his mind on the scenery, knowing Ho would brief him during the rest of their long train ride.

"It's what you would call political science," Gao said, explaining what he formerly taught at the university.

During the liberalizing mood of the early 1980s, he and others were writing about the intersection of Confucianism, a philosophy for governance, and modern Western democracy. The two systems often clashed, almost opposite in some of their premises. But there were openings. At first, their academic writings were popular, of interest to both intellectuals and some Party leaders. Then came the Tiananmen Square episode and nationwide martial law. For what he had written, Gao was forced out of his university. He was assigned to a small struggling college near Lanzhou. He was still inclined to argue with Party officials, and with such a personal temperament, he worried about risks to his family's future. So he resigned from academia and took up his transport business.

"They follow the family," Gao said and Ho understood.

"So what are those openings?"

She referred to what he had said about Confucianism and Western systems. She translated sporadically, giving Peale a sampling of his answers. Gao asserted that the Confucian system, built on earlier philosophies such as Taoism, or "the Way," still underwrote the Communist system. That is because Chinese are what they are, Confucian by dint of a long cultural experience. And still, there was much debate on the essence of what Confucius taught. Even the sage contradicted his own words, but a repetition of some ideas were unmistakable.

"His was a time of royalty and common people, a sharp divide, and of warlords as rulers," Gao said. "So any refinement was an improvement. Confucius ranked types of humans, commending the 'good man,' the 'complete man' or even better the 'gentleman.' Such a man was the chun tzu. Above these was the sage, but Confucius said he'd never met a sage, suggesting that it was a kind of impossibility. To be these kinds of persons required two things. First was proper etiquette and rites, called li. The second was to be an excellent human being, or ren." Gao chuckled at this, since that was the name of the current general secretary. "We're not sure which came first for Confucius. Does etiquette make a good man? Or does a good man naturally show the etiquette? At worst, the etiquette can disguise a bad man."

That's what is called face, Ho thought. Even for her it was a bit abstract, as often were the Confucian Analects, a long collection of pithy sayings and answers to questions.

Gao was concentrating on driving for the moment. The air was getting cooler and thinner as the elevation rose. He cleared his throat. "But if you take the essence of Confucius, like your golden rule . . ." Gao paused to quote the sage exactly: "'Do not impose on others what you yourself do not desire,' for yourself."

The word for that was shu, or benevolence, he explained. He and his scholar colleagues believed that Confucius was flexible on the etiquette, the structure, as long as shu was motivating people. This lent to a democratic approach.

Gao's face brightened, as if reliving his youthful excitement at such ideas. "But, then there's other contradictions. Confucius was very strict on the patrilineal family, both small and large. Filial piety. That meant loyalty to a parent or a ruler, or an eldest son, even if they were wrong or evil. That's what we call the mafia today. Sometimes government in China can be like the mafia."

Peale was catching glimpses of the discourse, thanks to Ho. It brought to mind the classic study of the Italian and Sicilian mafia, a study of "amoral familyism," something seen many times in history. Its strength was its family-like bonds, backed up by severe penalties for betraying family secrets and loyalties.

Gao went on. "Confucius said if your father steals the neighbor's cow, you mustn't tell."

Ho recalled the dictum, an example of filial piety. Peale was in his own thoughts, eyeing the scenery.

Gao added, "What if the Party is stealing cows?"

Ho thought, Maybe you protest in Tiananmen Square, but she said, "I see the dilemmas. And how did your group reconcile them?"

"First, we agreed that the essence of Confucianism is two things, chung and shu, which are doing one's best and doing unto others . . ." He used the Western version. "We also argued that family bonds could at times be conditional, and political loyalty was always conditional, as is often required in a democratic approach. We are loyal to what is good, or benevolent, not simply to a ruler who has power or to our self-benefit only."

"I can see why this might get someone in trouble," Ho said.

"It's not exactly Marxism-Leninism is it?" Gao seemed to enjoy the recollections, ones he perhaps had not shared for some time. He chuckled again. "Confucius, you see, could never find his perfect man and seemed to retreat into wise indifference. He was born of royalty, orphaned by war, was a worker, and then a policeman. He was no revolutionary, maybe a reformist. But he never argued for success, only that virtue was its own reward."

Peale got that tidbit. "Confucius was a cop?"

"Police commissioner," Gao said. "But finally just a philosopher. What remained in China is the idea of rank, ritual, etiquette, which has its good parts. It keeps order and keeps face, as we say. It created the Chinese bureaucracy, the centuries-old exam system. But it does not allow for change or evolution to better ways. That's why Mao preferred utter revolution, I suppose. As a youth, I was taught to wave Mao's red book. We were also taught to report on our parents if they didn't wave the red book. The Maoists not only perverted ideas about family, but adopted, then corrupted the Confucian ideas of rank, ritual, and blind loyalty."

Beijing must have squirmed at such writings at a top university, Ho thought. The professor had found his own indifference it seemed, and perhaps safety for his family.

Gao scratched his forehead and gave a small ironic smile. "If only we had waited twenty years. Chinese Marxism is dying. Even the Politburo is reviving Confucianism, something for a society to believe in."

The time was passing. With long bouts of silence among them the two-and-a-half-hour drive was eaten up by their thoughts. They were well ahead of the train arrival. They'd have a few more hours to kill. Without much ceremony, Gao dropped them near the modern station, which looked a lot like the one in Lanzhou. The city was a flat, a well-defined matrix of high-rises designed as utilitarian rectangles, each about fifteen stories. They reminded Peale of white and gray Legos, so uniform were the structures.

"Now I must make my deliveries," Gao said. "It was a pleasure to meet you."

They said the same. The short adventure reverberated, and the next hours of waiting seemed to pass quickly. They purchased some food to take on the train, and when the time arrived, Peale and Ho showed their passports and visas, converted their tickets, and were soon in a private compartment. This time it was a soft sleeper.

"Sleepers," Peale said. "Like beds, right?"

"Right," Ho said and added, "I didn't want to show off, but I vividly recall one of the sayings from the Analects. Confucius said of himself, 'I set my heart on the Way, base myself on virtue, lean upon benevolence, and take my recreation in the arts.' Note the recreation part."

"Duly noted," Peale said.

"A relevant link to our exploits, don't you think? And a nod to Confucius."

"I know one too. 'The fish rots from the head.'"

Ho looked puzzled. "Confucius say?"

"No, that was Giuseppe at the Fulton Street Fish Market." That was in lower Manhattan, where Peale had worked for a few years.

She laughed. "You can be so sublime."

They had a good night's sleep. On their morning arrival in Urumqi, they would seek out a discrete hotel. A few had been recommended.

Before they left the train, Ho had taken out her billfold, pulled out the card. She had been thinking about the PLA kids. They'd grown up in Urumqi. She still had the lieutenant's phone number. Confucius had apparently downplayed dumb luck, even the stars. But maybe there was some luck in the next few days. She shared her notions with Peale. There was the slow way, and there was the direct way to check out the tea farm, and maybe even a very direct way—with PLA help.

22

Urumqi, China

IT WAS MID-MORNING in Urumqi when Peale called through to Castelli, too weary to calculate the time differences. For Castelli it was before midnight, so good timing. "If we find the Gardner stuff, what then?" Peale asked over the SAT phone. They already had some ideas, and one in particular.

After years in the NYP, Castelli had his own indelible instincts, despite what diplomats up the chain might be thinking. In the old days, if you found stolen property, you confiscated. You cuffed the perp, if there was one, and sorted it out down at the station. "Diplomacy" was not in that dictionary. The same goes with being an independent contractor, Castelli thought, one of its simple pleasures. "I suggest you secure it," Castelli said. A bird in the hand and all that. "I'll cover for you. Once you've secured it, the higher ups can decide what to do. Leave that to me."

With that, Peale and Ho turned to their plan A and tried to ignore all the hotel clocks, all on Beijing time. They had to be coordinated with Washington-world time. From their hotel, Ho phoned the young lieutenant in the PLA unit. Peale listened to her side of the conversation, in Chinese. It was turning into friendly banter, just like out in the desert.

She ended the call. "Okay, they'll help."

"Just like that?" he said.

"I can be very persuasive. It's a good story, retrieving stolen property. I mentioned that we might look a little different. Anyway, he likes us. He's on our side. You know, 'Ya Bee Gees, hu, hu, hu, hu, stayin' alive.'"

A few questions remained. First, how did they get into the storage area—with keys, a coded lock as in Shanghai, or by busting down a door? As they considered the options, Peale said, "I've got an idea. We'll wait to see."

After that, if they got the cache, then what? They could hide out in Urumqi with the cache and await orders. Or they could ask for a pickup, some operative, another sleeper in China. Maybe they could take it to the Embassy, or someone could be sent in for retrieval.

"So what did you tell the PLA kids?"

"I didn't mention the entry issue to the lieutenant, but told him there's two possibilities once we get the stuff. Hang out in Urumqi, or take a very long drive. He said okay, either one."

"Just like that," Peale said, almost to himself.

"Like I said. Persuasive."

They planned to enter the tea farm during Urumqi's busy end of the day, when the city acted like it was five or six p.m. Beijing time said seven or eight p.m. Minus the two-clocks controversy, Peale decided it was a good time: not yet dark, but the busy roads would give them cover. At that hour, the tea farm's workday would presumably be ending. The sun was telling the time, still high on the horizon, but dipping downward.

If they found the goods, they'd call Castelli and confirm. Hopefully, he'd tell them what next. Peale had meanwhile grabbed the day's copy of the *People's Daily*. As it happened, a picture of General Secretary was on the upper front page, and he was pleased to see its date on top was bold.

What else? he thought. They code numbers were in his wallet if needed. Even so, they'd have to tell the young lieutenant exactly how to handle getting them to the door of the right facility. He was thinking hard now. At last resort, they'd force the entry. The jeep must have a tire iron or crowbar, he hoped.

At the evening hour, Peale and Ho packed their travel gear and trooped across the city to meet the PLA jeep by the Bazaar. A man waved, standing there with two others.

"Okay, you're my interpreter, pretty lady, lead the way," Peale said.

Ho spoke first, everything in Chinese.

The young lieutenant did a double take, especially at the mustachioed Peale.

"Bee Gees. Stay Alive," Peale said, is if the password.

The lieutenant now smiled. "Welcome back," he said, introducing two others, both of whom Peale recognized from the desert. The two had rifles swung over their shoulders.

Peale pointed, concerned.

The lieutenant said, "Just for show."

At the covered jeep, Peale, Ho, and a soldier climbed into the back seat. The lieutenant was up front by the driver. The jeep's rear was empty space. Enough room for a cache? If they found one, Peale speculated. The engine started up, sounding brittle, and they headed for the north of Urumqi. Beyond that was the tea farm, tucked up against some Tien Shan hillsides.

A cold breeze had descended late in the day, and the sun, passing through clouds, cast light and shadow, flickering across the tall buildings and then on the mountain slopes. A distant factory let out a deep bellowing sound. The smokestacks of the northern industry, now behind them, were disgorging their pillars of fire—plumes of gray, white, and orange in the late-day sunlight.

The jeep came off the highway and turned into the paved entrance road. As they approached, they could see the tea farm, the sun glinting off the glassy surfaces among the rows of green houses, the other buildings in a dull gray and tan. Wires and lights were strung on poles across the property. The tall chain-link fence enclosed the acreage. Behind the compound's main office was a paved courtyard, then a modern, higher-quality building.

"That newer building is probably where we need to go," Peale said.

They had stopped at the gate. Now, Peale went over what the PLA boys had to do. It was a kind of complex negotiation with whoever was watching the tea farm. Once the strategy was clear, and the lieutenant nodded his head in comprehension, Peale and Ho ducked low in the jeep. The lieutenant went to the gate and pressed the intercom button.

"Yes," a voice said. A camera was aimed at the entrance, and the man inside the office gave a start at what he saw. Three PLA men, two armed.

"This is Lieutenant Huang-li, PLA regiment," he said. "We would like to enter."

The gate buzzed open. The jeep pulled over to the side of the front building, out of view. Then the three soldiers headed for the office. Peale had the crowbar, so he and Ho slithered out, heading for the backside of a nearby shed. Once the PLA boys had everyone secured in the office, Peale and Ho would snake their way to the target, the newer building.

On the office front steps, the lieutenant flashed a badge to the tea farm worker, perhaps unnecessarily with the rifles so obvious. Then he waved a paper, like it was an official order. "We need to inspect Madame Quang's inventory."

The man hesitated. It was only him and another civilian guard, who was walking the grounds at the moment.

"We're in a hurry," the lieutenant said. "Do you have the keys, please?"

"There are no keys," the man said. "A key pad."

"Please, then, give me the code."

"Only Mr. Liu Hui has the code."

This is what the lieutenant was prepared to navigate, and he was winging it. "You are an honest man, as Madame Quang said. I have the code. Please take us to the entry."

The man looked relieved, a bit confused, but got up and led them toward the newer building. On the way they met the other watchman, who was signaled to join the group, and he came along. At the entrance there was a small atrium and then the main door with its key pad. Against the wall, there were a number of air conditioning device, all humming, feeding pipes into the building wall.

"Okay, we take it from here," the lieutenant said. "Take them back to the office." One of his team pointed with a rifle and the two security guards got the point. The second PLA kid, rifle in tow, stood watch in the courtyard. With the tea farm staff constrained from seeing anything more, Peale and Ho joined the lieutenant.

"Need code," the lieutenant said.

"Good work," Ho said, evoking a smile from the soldier.

Peale took the paper from his wallet and went to the key pad, his mind racing. He looked at the list of numbers. First he tried the two most obvious, the full dates of the birth and death of Empress Cixi. Only a weak beep resulted. He reversed them, but nothing. As expected—a different code. He took a deep breath.

"How's it going?" Ho asked, now looking over his shoulder.

"No luck yet." He glanced back toward the security office, thought about the crowbar at his feet, and then began to guess, mixing years with the months and months with days.

Suddenly it came back to Ho—turning bad luck fours into good luck eights. They had forgotten their dreamy insight back in their Shanghai hotel. "Julian, take four digit segments and start putting them in twos." She gave an example; the possibilities were many.

Peale gathered his resolve, as if in the field of fire in Afghanistan, when he had to believe things would be easy enough. Except this had to be systematic. His hands tried to move as quickly as his mind.

Ho was beginning to worry.

"Huh, okay," he said with exasperation, having tried a few combinations. It still seemed like throwing dice. After more failed attempts, he said, "Now these two buggers," typing them in—and the door clicked. "God, I should've got it the first time." He heard Ho sigh with relief.

They pushed in the door and the lights automatically came on, revealing a tidy warehouse, crates stacked everywhere, some draped with tarps. In the back was a zig-zag corridor with scattered boxes. It wasn't getting any easier. There were a lot of closed crates. The room was cool and dry, indeed, museum quality humidity control.

"Hew boy," Peale said. "Okay, look for anything that might look like the Gardner."

Ho conveyed that to the lieutenant, and they spread out. All the crates had some kind of markings, mainly in Chinese, some German and some English. Some were hard fiberglass, others rough wood, as if for industrial shipments. Five minutes later, there was finally some luck. "Here," the lieutenant said.

Peale and Ho came over. Peale said, "Bingo." The lieutenant smiled.

The crate was fiberglass, large with hinges on the top. The label had the words "American" and "Gardner."

"I've got to get photos," Ho said.

"I'll look through," Peale said. The lieutenant picked up on the routine and helped him. They brought over another crate. Once the artworks were out, they carefully poised them against the two crates in fairly good light. Then Peal took the *People's Daily* and put it in the scene. Ho began taking the photos. That done, they put the works back.

Looking around, Peale said, "We're taking it. Is there a dolly somewhere?" Two were over in a corner. Ho signaled and the lieutenant brought one over. Ho continued taking pictures of the scene of the crime, the warehouse interior and any distinguishing marks. Soon the crate, which was not heavy, was on the dolly. They headed for the door.

They brought it through and across the courtyard, Ho still taking pictures of the scene but not the people. Near the front office, Peale and Ho separated from the lieutenant and glided into their former cover at the shed. The lieutenant rolled their quarry to the front of the office, then marched inside. He began giving instructions. The two civilians were still cowered.

Suddenly, Peale said, "The phone wires." They had not considered this. He hoped the lieutenant was taking his time. At the back of the security office, wires from telephone poles fed into an outside metal box. Peale maneuvered, then dashed over, flat against the wall. He flipped open the box and was happy to see there were two fuses. He popped them out, put them in his pocket, and was back to the shed.

One of their uniformed PLA soldiers was still in the office, rifle in hand. The lieutenant and the other guided the dolly over to the jeep. It just fit into the back. They slammed the cabin shut. The lieutenant went back to the office, thanked the men for their cooperation, and said he would put in a good word.

"The Party will be in touch with Madame Quang," he said. "All has been arranged." He couldn't tell if the subdued men were skeptical, but now it was time to go. He pivoted and strode back to the jeep. Outside the gate, Peale and Ho got in, and they sped off. Peale peered at his watch: world-time in Washington, it was early morning the same day.

"Well done," Ho said to the lieutenant, who smiled, looking a little nervous.

"Okay, we head for the back alleys of Urumqi," Peale said. "I'll put in a call." He pulled out his SAT phone, punched the connection, and waited. Soon he heard, "Castelli."

Peale said, "We've got the package. What now?"

"I was hanging by my fingernails," Castelli said. "Secure the package and yourselves. A final decision's coming. They're juggling this over at the White House. I'm here, so you can call through if anything breaks. Up to the minute, if necessary."

Time was running and Peale wished a decision was already in the bag—either by Washington's orders, or by a strong recommendation that he and Ho could agree on. "I will signal when we're secure." He was making a mental checklist of what "secure" entailed.

"Roger that."

The evening traffic was light on the way back to town. As they skirted its urban edge Peale said, "Wait, I think we need something." He weighed the risks, saw the downtown passing to their left. The sun was still up. "We need one more photograph."

"Worth the gamble?" Ho said. She knew what he was thinking.

Peale directed the driver to swing the jeep by the People's Square. They nosed into that part of the city, saw the square with its obelisk, Party headquarters, and park.

"Okay, let's do it quick."

The jeep pulled over and Peale jumped out, Ho following. He went to the back, jiggered the crate so it partially opened and took out the Vermeer painting and the Shang Cup. He still had the newspaper. Ho was in position, and when he set them out, with the landmarks of the square in the background, the newspaper visible, she snapped the photos. Peale's eyes were fliting around, as were those of the driver. No pedestrians seemed to notice, or probably felt it was not their business to stare at a PLA jeep. Peale returned the two items to crate, and in an instant they were inside the jeep, which turned into the road.

The PLA kids were slightly bewildered, but Ho explained the need for documentary proof. She apprised the lieutenant of what they might need next. The rapidity of instructions made the young soldier's head spin, but he took it well, even felt the thrill. Clearly he was on board.

Now Peale said, "We may need to lay low in Urumqi for a while." Ho was translating. "Or, we'll need to drive this jeep somewhere, maybe far." Obviously, Shanghai or Beijing were out of the question. But some place. "We're waiting to hear from our people."

Hearing this translated, the lieutenant nodded again. "Just need gasoline."

"We'll cover expenses," Ho said in Chinese. "Your team also gets a reward."

The lieutenant smiled and nodded his head. "We like Americans," he said. Ho wished Peale understood Mandarin at moments like this. It made it all worthwhile.

What Peale did understand was that their operation was running on a knife's edge, but he was ready for either option. Hold tight, or back on the road? His mind was racing, conflicting thoughts sloshing around as he tried to sort out the best one—and make his own decision.

FOR TWO HOURS, the Jeep with its tense crew laid low in a park area by the red-rock cliffs at the south end of Urumqi, also where the highway broke for the desert. Everyone was hungry, but they waited on Washington. Ho was looking at her map, Peale was pacing around outside. The PLA boys willingly sat tight. The wait was tortuous.

Ho signaled to Peale to come over by a large overhanging tree in the park, away from the PLA team.

"I'm thinking we slow down."

"What?"

"Look, we've got the goods. That's the main point. I don't know what Washington has in mind, but we can always call through and recommend that we stash the crate, let some time pass. There must be other ways they can get this out of the country, less risky ways."

"Now you're being Cautious Karen. I don't get it. You used to be Gung-ho Grace."

"Funny. It just seems best. What's the urgency? If we can secure this box somewhere, we can get ourselves back across the border. Make a better extraction plan. There must be some other assets who can take it from here." She was already thinking how the goods could get to the Embassy in Beijing, then out of the country. Or contacts like Gao—and there must be others—who could sit on the cache until things cooled down. They didn't know what tripwires they may have hit up to this point. At this juncture, she couldn't imagine how the U.S. could come in like gangbusters.

She said, "There's no reason to think the Chinese authorities know anything about this box. It was all under the control of the Phoenix Group."

Peale couldn't believe this was the same woman who'd started a fight in London, just for the heck of it. "I can't believe this. Look, we know their weighing the two options in Washington. They want our recommendation, and I say now or never. I've seen this done before in Afghanistan, these in-and-out operations. They can handle it. I think we should call that through. Come and get us." He had weighed this during their tense hours of waiting. It was more logical. The more time they delayed, the more likely something unexpected might crop up.

"I thought you were Cautious Kevin," Ho said.

"What?" Peale couldn't process that right away. "Very funny. Well me . . . you've probably tagged me as Judicious Julian, but that's not the case right now. I say we go for it." In the first year of Navy Seals training, Peale had excelled in the long jump, prompting the drill instructor to call him "Jump'n Julian"; classmates ribbed him as "Peale the Projectile"—but he wasn't going to go into that with Ho. Through the whole episode of the day, he'd been gathering up foregone feelings, the immediacy he'd often experienced in his battlefield career. A more youthful zeal of the past was overshadowing his late-age wariness.

"Are we at an impasse here," Ho said.

"Not for me."

She gave him a long look. What's the hurry . . . she was insisting to herself, then she relented. "Okay, you're the boss."

"Castelli's the boss."

"But he's letting us decide, or recommend."

"We've decided. It's now or never."

They shared a long look, then Peale broke his gaze, looking over at the jeep and the PLA team, feeling their anxiousness as well.

"Call it through then," Ho said.

"Good." He dialed up the SAT phone, and was on with Castelli.

"What's the situation?" Castelli asked.

"We recommend immediate extraction."

23

Washington D.C.

THE URGENT BRIEFING for President Hughes was just ending. With him in the Oval Office were the CIA's Lucy Anderson and Ronald Frey, the National Security Advisor. Time was ticking in Urumqi, they had informed him.

"Those sneaky rascals," the president said. He was speaking of the Chinese. "Right under our noises. They must think we're pretty dense."

Details of the Chinese operation at the Freer Museum were not new to him, but now there was something additional, a second provocation. That was the stolen Gardner Collection, just located in China. He thought he could see a pattern, and it crossed his threshold of patience. Several options were being put before him, and they couldn't have been more contradictory, though groundwork for both was being done.

His decision would pull the trigger, or holster the weapon for now.

The CIA's Lucy Anderson was subdued in thought. "I think we go for it," she finally said. This was option one, grab the Gardner cache and run.

Sitting by, Frey objected. "Look, Mr. Peale and Miss Ho have sent in the documentation. We have pictures of the stolen items, the newspaper, a lot more. We shouldn't be rash. There are other ways we can play this. Take this to the China Embassy, make a protest."

"And what about the Gardner cache?" Anderson said. "Are we just going to leave it out there? We should bring it all back home, pronto."

"And our people?" the president asked. "What's the recommendation from the field?"

Just then a call came through to Anderson. "I better take this." It was Castelli. "Yeah, okay. Right. I'll pass that on."

She hung up, took a breath, and addressed the president. "The field recommends immediate extraction." Everyone knew this was the boldest plan, one option already on the drawing board. "Everything can fit in the Black Hawk, plus the Marine Band," she said.

Frey jolted back in his chair. "I disagree." He'd already made his case.

The president had chuckled at the Marine Band allusion, and was now drifting to another thought. Life at the Oval Office desk could be tedious at times, a cog among cogs, dulled by the machinery of administration. His golf game was a disaster. This could be a hole in one. At this instant, he was still at the point of plausible deniability. Peale and Ho were lone wolfs, a cabal of mercenaries, Washington could say—if found out.

Then he thought about local politics. *All* politics was local, went the phrase. The Gardner heist had been a punch in the nose for Boston and proud Massachusetts. As any Boston Southy would agree, between that slight and the Freer Museum espionage, it would be natural to punch back—take the consequences, probably keep it between himself and the secretive leadership in Beijing. If the U.S. government got caught, and Beijing had a fit, he would counter with his aces in the hole, the well-documented evidence of their crimes. These were cards in his deck. Plus, two Massachusetts senators in his party were up for re-election in the fall.

"If all else fails, we've still got one of the most powerful weapons on Earth," the president said.

Alarm crossed a few faces. One of his advisors said, "Mr. President, I don't think—"

"A leak to the press," he said.

A sigh of relief rose among the staff.

The president knew he could do a lot overseas on his own authority, even though Congress had passed the 1973 War Powers Resolution to curb excesses of those executive powers. Of course, the word "war" was now rarely used, replaced by terms such as "intervention" or peace-keeping force. In this case, the president liked the term "rescue," and felt that it was well within his purview. It was not going to lead to war with China, and if done well, China would never find out—very soon, at least. And if they complained, well, he had the evidence.

"Marco Polo," the president said.

"What was that, sir?" Anderson said.

"Operation Marco Polo. Send the Black Hawk."

24

Urumqi, China

PEALE WAS LOOKING up at the red-rock cliffs of the Urumqi park, their colors changing in the setting sun. He was attentive to the sounds of a city winding down. Dogs barked in the distance. Ho was hanging out with the PLA boys by the jeep. She was trying to keep up morale as time passed and uncertainty was in the warm air, thicker than the smog.

Finally the SAT phone rang.

Peale was on for a few moments, said "Okay," and turned to Ho and whispered. "We're a go. Instructions coming." Then he was back on the phone, its screen lit up. He was alternating between its microphone and a satellite coordinate image on its screen—looking, then speaking, then looking. Ho had come over quickly, leaned in to hear what she could.

"Okay, got it," Peale said. "Highway 314, down to Kuqa, got it. Okay, Polo Bravo out."

From the phone came, "Marco Bravo out."

Pealed signed off and hoped for the best.

"Polo?" Ho asked.

"Yeah, White House idea. They're Marco."

"And we're Polo. Very cute," Ho said. "One for the history books. So what's up?"

Peale signaled everyone back into the Jeep, where he explained the plan. "We're headed for Kuqa, a desert town. They're picking a spot and will get back." Peale turned to the three young soldiers, said to Ho, "Okay, please translate. We're going to drive into the desert, to about here, Kuqa." He held up the tiny map illumined on the SAT phone.

The lieutenant said, "Ah, Kuqa, yes."

Ho said, "Let's use a real map." She already had it out, and now folded it so the evening sun coming in the jeep made it visible to everyone. Having fixed the point from Peale's tiny screen, she traced her finger and then stopped. "Here." With a little calculation, also using the SAT phone, they had some numbers.

"About 470 miles, maybe less," Peale said. "They want us there well before dawn, want to fly under nightfall." He figured the sunrise came in less than ten hours. "We better go."

The lieutenant looked up, said to Peale, "We'll need gasoline." The lieutenant was thinking again, staring into space. He looked back at the two other soldiers and spoke to them. They exchanged glances, then nodded to the lieutenant in agreement.

"What did he say?" Peale asked.

"Two of them will go with us. That will look normal."

"Which?" Peale said.

"The lieutenant and his deputy," she said, patting that young man's shoulder.

Peale regarded the young man, decked in his PLA ball cap, and got a grin in return. Peale put out his hand, and the two shook.

Peale was a bit of a diplomat himself, he liked to think. "Okay, let's get started. It looks like we're going to get there in the middle of the morning, still dark. I'm still waiting for an exact time from our control in Afghanistan." The daylight hours had grown a bit longer as summer approached, with sunset, at world-time, around 9:30 to 10 pm, sunrise around 6:30 a.m. They had to hit the dark spot in between.

"Well, if we've got to kill time, better out there than here," Ho said.

The remaining soldier got out. He knew his way home, family relations in town. Ho thanked him, gave him a mock salute, and they began to drive. The south edge of the city was getting dark. Some streets had a few paltry lights. Others were gloomy with shadows. Strangely, even heading south, they could see Urumqi's tall northern smokestacks. Their billowing smoke caught the disappearing sunlight. The industries ran nonstop.

They drove into the desert, along the ancient Silk Road. The route followed the southern contours where Tien Shan Mountains met the desert, and cut through rolling desert hills.

AT JOINT SPECIAL Operation Command, lodged in a glorified Quonset hut at the NATO base in Marmal Mountains and adjacent to the legendary Hindu Kush, General Maxwell looked over his own maps, advised by a wing commander.

"This will be tricky," Maxwell said, simply calling the pickup "a package," though he'd been told the details. A bunch of art, which was puzzling. But the president has spoken. The grizzly old warrior was actually a bit thrilled; an order right down from the Oval Office.

The wing commander was giving latitude and longitude for the city of Kuqa, using a military grid that pinpointed within a mile. He pointed to the national highway that came down over some high desert, then crossed into spotty foothills at the north edge of the city. "Best is somewhere here, above the city."

Maxwell then said, "Get the bird ready." The base had several Black Hawks, and as with other mix-and-match options on the versatile air machines, this one was specially fitted with stub wings and two extra fuel tanks. It could also put on sound dampers. This way it could fly relatively quiet one thousand two hundred miles before refueling. It also had chemically treated skin and windshields to evade radar.

"Okay, we'll have to take a first hop, get out near the Wakhan passage." That's where the copter would again top off its fuel tanks to achieved maximum range.

The Wakhan Corridor was one hundred thirty miles long, squeezed between Tajikistan and Pakistan. Once the chopper got going at top speed, it would be a toboggan ride over a wild, mountain-woven nature reserve, then like a cliff, they would hit China's vast desert stretches. With the desert came the winds, and that was one more reason to fly in the calmer cool of night.

The two-man crew boarded and the copter warmed up. The pilots put on the helmets, plugged their headsets into the ceiling. "Check," one said, flipping switches and reading gauges. Two dozen dials lit up with green luminescence. The roar began to build as the four blades, a whirling circle fifty-four-feet wide, begun to pull on the fifty-foot fuselage. The vertical blades on the tale were up and running. By now, the copter was slightly bouncing between its two front wheels and the one far in the rear.

The wing commander was still at the maps, the radar screens, and the radio. Maxwell always liked to view a takeoff, even from a window a hundred yards away. The Black Hawk rose tail first, the pointy chopper angled down. It suddenly bolted forward, leveled off.

It leaned for a starboard turn, and then sped off in the early sunset, the sun to its back.

Godspeed, Maxwell thought, as always.

THE PLA JEEP was on a steady clip down the two lane highway, the sun in their eyes. Some clouds muted the glare. The trucks that populated such routes seemed to be coming in great number from the opposite direction, into Urumqi, which gave Peale's jeep an open highway.

The Tien Shan peaks were to their right, still visible, many heavily snowcapped, despite the spring thaw. An hour into their drive, to the left was the vast Taklamakan Desert, one of the largest shifting-sand deserts in the world. Hundreds of miles wide, its dunes were carved in giant waves and furrows by the northern winds. Some rose to six hundred feet. Many were the burial ground of ancient cities along the Silk Road. As the sun lowered, the winds started coming in, buffeting the jeep.

"I always wanted to travel the Silk Road," Peale said. He was in the back with the lieutenant, while the second soldier was driving this first shift.

Ho was up front for translation duties. "Thank God we're not doing this with camels," she said in Chinese. The soldiers laughed. Peale wondered what was so funny.

The lieutenant said, "All of us came out here when we were kids. In those days, bandits. So scary." Ho was translating for her partner. As a child, the lieutenant once saw the desert covered by a layer of snow. He didn't mention the dust storms. Most were small, but some were historic, large enough to fill the lenses of weather satellites.

Ho was a deft translator, working it off and on. Many times it was only English with Peale. She had her travel book out, not military issue but for tourists. "Where we're headed was once an ancient Buddhist kingdom, went by the same name Kuqa," she said. "Lots of monastery cave ruins in the foothills. They go back to the Han and Tang dynasties. Buddhist armies ran things back then." Those peaceful Buddhists and their rapacious armies. A different time.

"Lots of caves out here," Ho said. That was, after all, the cultural legacy of the area. For a century archeologists and plunderers had done their work out here. A good number of the paintings on plaster were in museums around the world.

"Good, if things go south, we can find a nice cave for a while," Peale said. "Meditate on the meaning of all this."

"And get this," Ho said, reading from the tour book. "An ancient chronicle says the first city out here was built by Alexander of Macedon." That was Alexander the Great.

"Now we're talking," Peale said.

The city of Kuqa was founded at this site for its Tien Shan watershed, with two rivers forming an oases. The prefecture population was nearly all Uyghur, farmers and herdsmen. Today, the travel book said, it was known for its production of wheat, corn, rice, and cotton. It had orchards of pears, apricots, melons, grapes, pomegranates, and figs.

"Exotica, too. Fine lambskin and thin-shelled walnuts," Ho said. "Plus, some bombings, back in the nineties." This part of China was almost entirely Uyghur.

Like many stopovers in western China, it was also being prepared to serve the Belt and Road initiative. Already coal and oil factories were at work.

Peale's stomach growled. "We forgot our lunch," he said. "I could use a few dried apricots."

Somehow the soldier understood. He reached into a hollow in the jeep and pulled out a rucksack. Ho translated, "Food. And water."

"These guys should go into tourism," Peale said, and Ho passed on the compliment.

"They've got that down also," Ho said. "They know all the Buddhist sites out here."

"They can check us into a nice cave if things don't work out." Peale was otherwise trying to be optimistic.

The hours passed. The jeep rumbled at a steady pace. The passengers had grown eerily quiet as the sun began to set and the winds picked up. To the Jeep's left, over the dunes, a cloud began to form, not of moisture, but of sand and clay. It began to rise up, expanding like a blooming flower, as if in fast motion. The driver became animated and a bit alarmed as the crackling of sand began to spray the windshield.

"Sand storm," he said, gripping the wheel.

"Uh oh," Ho said.

Peale was just beginning to relax, and now this. The windows were all rolled up. He watched helplessly with the others as the cloud grew closer to the road. Its winds came in pulses. The jeep was speeding up—outrunning the cloud, if all went well.

"Should we pull over, sit it out?" Peale said. Ho translated, but the driver maintained his speed. For an instant, Peale pictured them buried in a dune, like an ancient ruin.

By now the cloud of dusty yellow sand was illumined by the red sunset. It was engulfing them on the left side, hissing and swirling under the jeep, around and over. The driver turned on the headlights and slowed. The windshield wipers ground back and forth as if on sandpaper. Peale thought of a demonic car wash.

They continued on, the dark road and its white line barely visible. The air inside grew thick. The soldier driving began to cough. Everyone else had a sleeve to their face. The sun had given way to the dark, and the headlights cast their long dusty beams through the sandy fog—a fog that was finally dissipating. Fifteen minutes later, it was as if they had abruptly surfaced from a body of water, crossed a line between a nether world and fresh air. The sky was turning velvet black. After a time, letting the dust fly off the jeep's exterior, they opened the windows. Fresh air flooded in. Now the sky was a dark dome filled with stars, a million pinpricks. A desert sky if there ever was one.

"That was close," Peale said. He withheld his joke about a new kind of car wash, the kind that removes paint. Through all of this, his SAT phone was silent. When they were closer to their destination, he'd say the ridiculous words, "Polo Bravo." At least the president had a sense of humor.

At The Refueling station in eastern Afghanistan, the Black Hawk crew was standing down, waiting for the signal to relaunch. Back at Joint Operations, the timing was going to be ragged, but it was set. Round the clock, it already had a communications plane circling the Afghan border. This allowed Peale and the command to share a frequency. The Black Hawk could also pinpoint their location on its radar.

Peale's SAT phone had been quiet for some time, and then a call came through.

"This is Marco," the operations voice said.

"Bravo Polo," Peale said.

The command explained that the Black Hawk flight to Kuqa would take three hours. "Do you have an estimate of the drive time to Kuqa?" They knew where his jeep was, but couldn't tell its rate of travel.

Peale did some calculations, then said, "It will be tight, probably a bit more than three hours for us, so you may want to hold off." He could barely hear himself over the rumble of the jeep and the whoosh of the night air.

"Bravo Marco," the joint-ops voice said. "We'll watch the timing, just keep your pace. We'll be getting back at 0200 hours with a coordinate on the highway." That was about two in the morning on everyone's clock. If all went well, the Black Hawk would be in an out before sunrise on the China border.

"Bravo Polo, got it," Peale said.

After the sandstorm, they'd stopped at a truck depot to gas up. The lieutenant took over the driving duty so his partner could rest. The jeep had seen better days, but they were good in the fuel department. Time passed. The dead of night enveloped the weary travelers. They'd eaten the food, passed around the water. Ho flashed back for a moment, recalling family road-trips, traveling into the night, a thrill to a young girl. Before long, she and the soldier next to her were nodding. Peale was an insomniac, on top of his tightly wound nerves. Time was passing in a strange way even as he looked at his watch.

Eventually they saw a glow on the distant horizon. Maybe little Kuqa was a city of lights. Lively Uyghur nightlife? It was probably the industries pounding away.

The SAT phone beeped. "Bravo Polo," Peale said.

"Bravo Marco. We have you on our radar. You're nearing the city, and about five miles outside, there's a turnoff. It should be marked, a tourist crossroad for some Buddhist caves up in the foothills."

"Got it."

Marco continued giving directions. "At the crossing, turn up that road and then it's about fifteen miles. There's an open area, fairly large. Something called the temple ruins. Find a spot at the edge. Leave your SAT phone on. When you get there, keep the headlights on, good also if you've got rear flashers."

"Got it. See you there, Bravo Polo out."

Fortunately the crossroads were well marked. There were

roadside turnoffs, probably for tourist buses. There were also some signs, written both in Mandarin and Uyghur Turkic, which one of the soldiers knew. The jeep slowed, angled so the headlights illumined the words. One of the signs said Subashi Temple Ruins, and Ho passed that on.

"That's the place," Peale said.

Wasting no time, the jeep sped up again, turning off the highway, following the branch road. In twenty minutes they drove into an open desert area. On its far side rose many odd shapes, the haunting profiles of an ancient ruin, once a city. The archeologists had done a thorough job. Shades of Stonehenge even.

As directed, they pulled over to the edge of the area, turned on all their external lights—and waited. "I could really use a stretch," Peale said. He opened his door and slid outside. He leaned back, twisted sideways a few times. "Ah, that feels good."

Probably twenty minutes passed and the desert was still. There was only the squawk of some dark birds passing through. It was easy to imagine the worst, but it was no time to lose faith. Any minute now.

Finally, they heard a low whoop over the horizon, growing louder. The Black Hawk was hidden in the dark, its sound preceding it. Getting closer, its ground search lights went on, casting beams over the ruins, gold and orange earthen works. It was circling in tight. Finally positioned, the chopper descended straight down, dust picking up like a storm. Its rear wheel touched down first, then a heavy bounce on the front. The blade decelerated rapidly.

Peale's SAT phone beeped. It was the pilot. "Ready to load. Drive on over."

They had already jumped back into the jeep. The lieutenant, awed by the sight, directed his driver to head that way. The jeep pulled up ten feet from the chopper. Peale and Ho were quickly out, Peale going to the back to open the hatch.

"We can do," the lieutenant said, and Ho translated.

Peale nodded, and the two soldiers hefted the crate, brought it over to the large side door of the chopper, its blades lazily spinning, some dust still settling. Peale was ready to go, done this before, grabbed his things.

Ho was feeling anticlimactic. There was no time for hugs and kisses for the PLA boys. She did her best to express gratitude, the two soldiers standing there mute, ready to run for the jeep. She still had a large packet of money. The plan was to dole out a certain amount, which she mentioned already to the lieutenant. She gave them the whole wad.

"Won't be needing this," she said, handing it over in Chinese style with two hands and a slight nod. Then she turned and jumped in the chopper's wide side door. It slid shut with a slam. The rotors were already revving up, the dust rising. The two soldiers turned away, covering their faces as best they could, and sprinted to the jeep. Looking out the window, rising up, Ho could see the lieutenant giving a wave, then slamming his jeep door. The jeep backed up and headed down the road into the night.

IT'S NOT OVER yet," Peale said. The pilot hollered back, "Piece a cake." He brought the low flying bird on course and got it up to cruise speed, praying that the dawn was still three hours off, and that the steep Tien Shan foothills would continue to block Chinese radar.

Encompassed by the Black Hawk's muted roar, a steady hum mixed with desert darkness, Peale and Ho retreated into their own stillness. The copter jostled at times, keeping them alert despite a descending fatigue. Ho was still thinking about the PLA kids, what their lives held before them. She would later check to see if Sam Brower was okay after the Lanzhou run-in. She recalled the tiny picture of Brower with toothy grin in the back of *Lonely Planet,* "our correspondent." The old Professor Gao had found his place, a disinterested philosopher, like Confucius. All of this was a common reflection after a mission. It was technically called "collateral dam- age." She hoped there was none. She always assured herself of the same, each time a job was completed. The target was achieved, the innocent unharmed.

Peale watched her face. It usually hid any sign of emotion. "What are you thinking about now?"

"Oh, just everything," she said.

"No collateral damage that I can see," he said, reading her mind.

"Yes, I suppose so," she said. "You never look back, since you never know, right?"

"A good rule of thumb."

What mystified her still was Quang Daiyu, a woman whom they had gotten to know intimately, yet a live human they'd never seen. Ho still wondered about her fate. Perhaps it would be good as ever, perhaps not. No use looking back.

THE HOURS PASSED but not with the speed of the chopper it- self. The interior darkness was broken by the flicker of cockpit lights, splashing at times on the crate, still dusted by the yellow grime of the Taklamakan Desert. Peale stared at the boxy object, a totem of sorts and the fruits of their adventure. The value of the thirteen artworks was half a billion dollars, and oddly, for the first time that began to sink in. He tried a few ways to grasp the amount, first by simply dividing it by thirteen. That was about thirty-eight million each, which seemed absurd. Most of the value was in the Vermeer and the large Rembrandt paintings, those three having been cut from their stretcher bars.

What in fact was a half billion dollars? he pondered. It was a pittance compared to the GDPs of nations, and he recalled one comparison—the thirteen pieces were worth the annual GDP of the Tonga Islands in the South Pacific, an archipelago with a hundred thousand residents. A Black Hawk, he knew from losses in Afghanistan, could cost from six to ten million each, depending on the specifications. Back in the 1950s, the price of "blue chip" art had begun to skyrocket for the first time, acting like a feverish stock market, especially with modern and contemporary art—and traditional art followed suit.

Despite his five years working at an art restoration studio in New York City, the mystery of pricing art had always baffled him. In the high-end global art market, there were only about fifty collectors—now including Arab princes, Russia oligarchs, and perhaps some Chinese tycoons—who would spend at least one hundred million dollars on a single artwork. Then there were a few thousand more who could plunk down a million or more for one coveted artifact. This concatenation of wealth gave the Gardner cache its value. As if a sport, the world's fat cats competed, pushing prices up and up until the highest bidder won. Nobody knew those heights, of course, but in the Gardner case, art authorities put it at half a billion—like a rabbit from a hat, and who was anybody to question that?

Apparently, and oddly enough, Communist China and its vast gray market was catching on, turning Marx and Lenin in their graves—and Mao in his mausoleum, Peale thought. His mind continued to wander in the flickering darkness, his ears almost numbed into silence by the copter's even roar. Even the force of traveling one hundred eighty miles per hour had equalized in his body.

Now he pondered how crime raised art world stakes. He'd never been to the Gardner Museum. Yet the story of the 1990 theft was legend. Back then it had relatively low security, and a ruse was easily foisted on two museum guards late one night. Then there was the famous pilfering of the *Mona Lisa* in 1911. The French king who employed Leonard da Vinci brought it to France and thus finally to the Louvre, where the painting would have no particular acclaim for a few centuries. Then it was stolen, and the theft gave the *Mona Lisa* its world fame. The works of Vermeer had similarly slumbered in obscurity for a couple centuries, at least until a noted art connoisseur called them works of genius. Now having been stolen a few times—first by the Nazis and now China—anything by Vermeer was deemed incomparable.

It was all very bizarre how it worked, Peale thought.

More incredible still, many such famous works were now in museums with the caveat that they must never be sold; they were a patrimony for the world, never again to be in the grasp of private collectors. Those same museums, meanwhile, were always hard up for cash, despite the virtual gold that hung in the galleries. And the Gardner Museum was probably no different—it had perhaps a billion dollars on its walls, but besides a trust of some kind, the museum got by on $15 admission fees from visitors—and anyone named Isabelle entered free. It was a Fort Knox whose gold bricks could never be sold.

And now here he was sitting next to the crate, its contents worth half a billion dollars—but in what real sense? A strange world indeed, but one in which so many intangible factors determined the value of things.

Peale was staring ahead, lost in his thoughts, and Ho noticed in the dimness.

"So what are you thinking about?" she said.

"My love-hate relationship with the art world."

"Don't worry. It is what it is. We done good."

Peale gave her a generous nod. A small catch rose in his throat, and he felt a rare moment of deep satisfaction.

The time of crossing out of China had arrived. Below, the valleys on China's side of the Wakhan Corridor were still dark as pitch. Eventually a thread of light appeared on the eastern horizon behind them. China gave way to Afghanistan. In the valleys the farmers and nomads, and not a few opium smugglers, were starting their day as the Black Hawk passed over.

"We caught some headwinds on the way in," the copilot hollered to the back. The timing had been just right, nevertheless. "Now you get the tour," he said, pointing down at the window. The Wakhan Corridor was three or four strings of mountains, valleys between, running perfectly east and west. In an hour, the morning sun was casting its yellow light on snow, pine covered mountain slopes, and silvery rivers in green valleys.

Peale looked down, momentarily speechless. Then he let out a slow breath and said, "So that's what the Silk Road looks like." For them, the famous route from the heart of China through the westward hills and deserts was coming to an end. Ride the Silk Road, he said to himself. Once is probably enough.

25

Beijing

As The Black Hawk was landing at the Afghan base of operations, the sun was rising in Beijing. Madame Soong Wei was fuming. The day before, as the PLA jeep began its journey into the Taklamakan Desert, she was for the second time on the phone with Ren Jinuah. He was still adamant that she meet face-to-face with Quang Daiyu, her rival.

Some etiquette was finally required, so she agreed, hiding her acute displeasure. "Yes, Chairman Ren, this could be appropriate, as you suggest," she said. "Though I have difficulty with the way your niece is operating, I suppose I must show respect to a member of your extended family." Accepting the directive gracefully, Soong otherwise boiled inside. Both women preferred that Ren simply take their side, throw down the gauntlet, but to the contrary, the general secretary had spoken.

As Soong was ending her call with Ren, Quang Daiyu was taking an afternoon walk in Beijing's parks, preparing for the encounter the next morning, a Tuesday. Her mind was still in a flurry over the break-in at her Shanghai office six days ago. By early evening, she settled into her Beijing hotel, and in time, was sipping her Gold Tea. Its calming effect took hold, and it was beyond even her suspicious imagination that in far off Urumqi, a PLA jeep was breaching the gates of the tea farm.

Her sleep was fitful, but the morning grudgingly arrived. There was no backing out now. She we would meet Madame Soong Wei at one of her urban homes in a tony neighborhood, and Quang loathed the fact. She'd thought it through carefully, calculating. Her strategy was to humble herself before Soong, her elder. She would imply that they had no rivalry for the top position in the China Global Art Museum and that, indeed, that it was Madame Soong's due. Quang felt quite the opposite. But things were done this way in the cloak and dagger history of royal politics.

Until now, Quang had been able to avoid the labyrinth of Beijing's politics and its social scene. She'd never even met Madame Soong Wei. Her only impression came from the news. Having been wife to a former general secretary, Soong Wei was a known quantity in China, even in some society pages. To Quang, she was clearly of the old school, a hangover from the revolutionary days. She'd seen pictures of Soong in her Mao outfit, the green tunic. As time passed, Soong's appearance changed with the times. She showed her age, but was still a stern woman, now presenting herself in the conservative business attire appropriate to modern China.

Quang was mindful of such matters, for a woman was known by her choices in dress. In the years immediately after the Cultural Revolution, dress had become a target for persecution. Party women cut their hair short. They donned the uniforms. Women, especially the young—who sported jeans, high heels, Western fashions, or even the older colorful long dresses, too ostentatious for the revolution—found their belongings thrown from their homes into the street. The world had never seen such a rapid fashion revolution. It had gone uniform-green almost overnight.

Things had changed since the late 1970s. Although the youth were sporting name-brand clothes, serious women of business like Quang herself fell into a standard conservative wear—pastel business suit or dress buttoned to the neck, flat shoes, no visible makeup, and at most a gold brooch. Always, though, a gold watch on the wrist. Quang still liked a little flair in her wardrobe. She was not going to peddle backwards even for Madame Soong.

Some traditional etiquette was to be followed, however. From her artworks, Quang selected a choice gift, a Ming silk painting, for Madame Soong. It was sure to impress. She had a second gift as well—a beautifully wrapped a package of her best tea, a superb selection from the Gold Tea. She carefully packaged it herself, putting a little Gold Tea on top, though it was actually Bronze tea throughout. Its fate was still undecided; Quang would wait to see whether to give *this* gift or not.

The crucial day had arrived, and by mid-morning Quang was well dressed, ready to call for a taxi. She put her cell phone in her purse along with the gift tea. With these, she carried the wrapped painting down to the entrance of her hotel. The taxi was on time and it began through the Beijing traffic, past the Imperial Palace and government complexes.

Then her cell phone rang. She listened.

"What?" she exclaimed, alarming the taxi driver. "When?" A long pause followed. "How could that happen? You idiot!" Her manager at the tea farm just told her that the night before a PLA regiment had arrived at the tea farm. They took a crate from the warehouse. He wanted to let her know that, according to her wishes, it had to been done—though he did not mention his tardiness, due to a dead phone line and the constant trouble getting connections in the desert on a cell phone.

"My wishes!"

"The PLA showed us papers, Madame, they said—"

"Idiot! Was anything else taken? Only the crate? Which crate?" But he would never be able to explain it to her satisfaction. The questions were coming fast, and the manager did not have all the answers.

"Nothing else was taken," he said.

"Secure everything," she said. "Call Mr. Liu Hui and tell him everything. I have a meeting now." She hung up the phone, her mind in a furious state. So this is what Madame Soong does on the eve of their conciliatory meeting. It was time to play her final hand. She would indeed give the Soong dragon lady her gift of tea.

AT THE DOOR of Soong's residence, a house of French design from the Nationalist period, a concierge in uniform let her in. Madam Soong did not answer her own front door. Politely, the doorman offered to carry Quang's package, but she demurred.

"Thank you, I'll take this in," she said.

They passed through a front room, then a short hall with artworks tastefully hung, and finally entered a room that reminded Quang of a small, well-appointed, comfortably warm audience hall back in imperial days. By a window in the corner, with an empty chair at hand, sat Madame Soong Wei. A small ornate tea table was in place. Madame Soong stood as Quang entered.

They approached each other with cunning eyes, assessing the other's choice in style.

Since the Cultural Revolution, "feudal" styles of dress were frowned upon, though today, short hair had given way to something more natural, if not too showy. As Quang could see, a woman like

Soong, who once wore the Party uniform daily, had evolved a somewhat imperial taste.

Quang was an admirer of the traditional, the splendors of Ming dress, the colors and couture of Empress Cixi. Even so, Soong's appearance took her by surprise. The woman's hair, long and dyed black, was tightly pulled back, giving her full face a stern aspect. She wore a white embroidered Chang-ao, a wide sleeved wrap around, slit at the sides, with a multi-layered collar. It was as if Quang had drifted into a royal court before the revolution.

Madame Soong's eyes had the darkness of the darkest jade, and she would often open them wide in her expressions. Her modest smile greeted Quang, and her eyes flicked up and down taking her in, probably disparaging her "Shanghai look."

As was the custom, the supplicant Quang spoke first. "It is a great pleasure to meet you in person, Madame Soong. You have many important duties, I realize."

"It is good that we meet. General Secretary Ren Jinuah has made it possible." Soong was precise in raising that name from the start.

"I have been honored by the attention given by both of you," Quang said. "And in honor of our meeting, I have brought you a valuable present, a painting."

Soong nodded, a small smile.

Quang put her purse on her chair and unwrapped the painting, a wonderful work on silk, now mounted, from a large Ming folio, blossoms and birds. "For your collections," she said.

Soong was impressed, though she kept her dour look. She sat back down and gestured at the empty chair. "Thank you," she said. "Now tell me about yourself. We are two women of business affairs, but quite different backgrounds, I believe. Your family background is vague, and I've heard you were adopted."

"That is correct," Quang said. "I've taken that family name

Quang. I believe it's the name of an ancient emperor, and a city in the Zhou Dynasty."

"And you are very independent, aren't you?" Soong said.

"By necessity, and probably nature."

"Tell me about that."

"Well, as you know I studied in the United States, but on return had enjoyed a rich re-education at the Party School in Shanghai, a very large school. My love of China's art and civilization, perhaps like yourself, led me into this field, a very good business decision, as you know."

"But you tasted America, did you not?" Soong said. "American ways?"

"Oh, but there is no comparison, Madame Soong, none at all. Their civilization is so young, so immature. Ours has endured for centuries. As I said, my folly was only for a moment, and then I came home, truly home, where I belong." She offered an old Chinese proverb, said, "You can cultivate the seed, but you cannot predict the blossom."

Unpredictable, Madame Soong agreed. "And you grow tea."

"Yes, I have a tea farm in the west, a very good soil. It specializes in high quality teas, some mainstream, others exotic. We like to think of them as teas suited for emperors and empresses."

"Do you now," Soong said, with a small cough. The questioning continued and Quang played along, gingerly choosing her words. "Who do you admire, then?" Soong asked.

"The great men and women who built China, of course." Quang thought a moment. "I've always been impressed by the 'Thought of Deng Xiaoping,' and now our current leader." She decided not to mention Empress Cixi, about whom she knew much more, and had more admiration.

Madame Soong seemed to soften, thinking of her own days

rising from youth, to middle age, then seniority. She felt a strange empathy with Quang, which she had not expected. "I too admire Deng, and before him Mao, but that early time had gotten out of hand, too much anger and chaos. From ancient times, Chinese have been an orderly race . . . proper etiquette, patience, looking at the long term."

"I agree totally. Building a business takes patience, as your successes have shown."

"Well, it is true. Nothing does quite compare with Omni Art Global. It is a leading group for culture."

Aiming to impress, desiring to take attention away from her Phoenix Group, a rival of Soong's, Quang turned to explaining the art of tea growing. Tea and its hybrids still had future potential in the world market, despite the commonality of the drink and the abundance of growers and companies. Quang reached into her purse. She gracefully removed the package of Gold Tea. "This is our specialty, and a gift for you. May we have a cup together? May I make it for you?"

Soong wondered for a moment, doubt and even suspicion in her face, and then she suddenly agreed. She called for a staff woman to boil water and put it in a porcelain tea pot to be delivered to the table with two fine cups. The women continued to talk, Quang putting forth her best obeisant foot, and Soong warming to the younger woman's humble attitude.

They were two women of China, two generations, two different experiences. Soong was of the revolutionary time, her youth intersecting with the Cultural Revolution of Mao. Quang had been reared in a less violent milieu, surrounded by relative privilege. Her time was one of social uncertainty, though. It was China's "hide brightness, bide time" period, beset with its internal cultural and political confusion. Then came the economic boom, the capitalist chaos, as it was known. Only Quang's native instincts had grounded her. This sort of self-reliance impressed Madame Soong, but with it came a generational misgiving.

The conversation continued. Soong suggested there might be a way that Quang's Phoenix Group could become part of Omni Art Global, a branch, a valuable tendril into the Western art world, with all its complexity.

"That would be wonderful," Quang said.

They discussed how it might work.

By now, the steaming pot of hot water had arrived. It was placed on the table, and Quang took off the porcelain lid. She opened the Gold Tea package. During the taxi ride, after the alarming phone call about Urumqi, she had hurriedly worked with the bag of specially prepared Bronze Tea, cultivated in cyanide-laced soil. On the top, she put a large pinch of the opium-based Gold Tea. It was this that she pinched into the steaming pot. The two women could smell its sweet aroma.

Quang said, "I drink this several times a day, very medicinal." She discussed the aches and pains that older women develop, and how soothing the tea therapy could be. After a while the tea pot had brewed. Quang poured the golden liquid into two cups.

Soong waited, a sphinx. Etiquette required that Quang let Soong have her tea first, but at this point, Soong's preference was unspoken, but clear. Quang took her cup, and sipped. She smiled, then she sipped again. "This is my special brand, very good for my health."

After Quang had taken several sips, Soong leaned toward the table with a slow grace. She took up her cup and sipped. The flavor was remarkable. She sipped again. Time passed and both women felt the uplift, the hot liquid, the unusual quality of the tea.

Soong said, "This is quite unique." She sipped again. "And you say it improves your health?" She was feeling in a light, airy state of mind, with an unusually friendly outlook on life.

"Very much so," Quang said. "I have some whenever I can. Many times each day. It's very soothing."

Soong took the package from the table, contemplated its elegant label, smelled its pungent sweet aroma and recalled her many aches and pains and how little the doctors could do. "I will try this, and thank you for the gift."

The women had a second cup from the pot, and in time it was clear that their briefing meeting was over, and that Quang was willing to work with Soong, an arrangement to be ironed out soon enough.

"Before you go, let me show you my personal collection," Soong said.

She asked the concierge to call a taxi. Then the two ladies rose from their chairs, and Soong led them into another room, replete with ancient Chinese scrolls, vertical and horizontal, vaporous landscapes in ink, dappled blossoms and birds, many brightly colored. Soong spoke with a light enthusiasm, a mood quiet opposite to the one Quang had encountered on arrival. They next passed through a hall with even more variety on display. At the entrance, Quang praised the older woman's tastes, her ability to collect, the endowment this would give a future China.

"And thank you for the gifts, the gift of the tea," Soong said. "I do need to improve my health." She smiled and almost gave a self-effacing laugh.

26

Boston

FOR TWO DAYS the Gardner Museum in Boston was closed to visitors. Some of them were surprised to find the sign outside, "Temporarily Closed for Repairs." It had suddenly rained FBI.

Inside, the museum authorities, FBI agents, and a team of expert curators were at work. Some of the art, lost in the "art heist of the century," could simply be placed back in their original spots, the Shang Cup on its pedestal, the Vermeer painting, still in its frame. Likewise with the smaller Degases and the Monet. The larger Rembrandts had been cut out of their frames by the original burglars, a mystery that might remain so forever.

Whoever they were, and wherever the paintings had lingered, most likely in Europe, it had been more than thirty years. Fate had conveniently gathered all the pieces up, apparently the doings of a buyer in China. Whoever that was remained a secret of the White House and the agencies. All that was known remained simple: the artworks were found. They had gathered themselves up, like a flock of birds once scattered by a storm.

At the museum, the experts merged the cut paintings with new canvas. State-of-the-art glues and touchups were applied. Before long, everything that was lost was back where it once had been.

"I think this is the right way to go," the museum director said to FBI Senior Special Agent Hargrave, who had come up from Washington. For all Hargrave's frustration at being cut out of the China operation, he at least was being given credit for the end product. The final cleanup of the museum was nearly finished. "We appreciate that this won't be the normal FBI press conference," the museum director concluded.

Usually, the FBI summoned the press to a headquarters building. With the contraband on display—tons of cocaine, heroin, stacks of currency or firearms—the bureau would detail everything, feed it gleefully to the press. In those cases, the daring seizure would be described, the agents lauded, and most questions from the press answered. Not this time.

"Orders from the top," Hargrave said. "For a museum, this kind of thing, well, it does seem more appropriate. Everything back in place. A dramatic touch, I have to agree." Plus he was there, the senior cop, overseeing the victory lap—and why not, after all the grief and public doubt that he and his agents had endured for a few decades.

For over three decades, the spots where the art had once been displayed had held empty frames, explanatory plaques describing how "on the night of March 21, 1990, burglars stole thirteen works of this marvelous collection." Now, after the press conference in the lobby, the press and the public would be allowed to wander the halls of the Gardner Museum, like an Easter egg hunt, to see glowing new signs telling of the homecoming for each lost treasure.

Except that what they were told was really nothing. The White House, saving up ammunition, had wanted it that way.

"Today we are happy to announce the return of the stolen Gardner Collection," the head of the Boston region FBI said at the press conference podium. "It's a great day for Boston, a great day for America's legacy of art collecting. It's also an assurance that the FBI and its agents are working around the clock to solve crimes, to make our nation, and Boston, a little safer."

There were some introductions, a few other remarks, and the announcement that now the Gardner Museum was open to the press and public, back to normal, just as it was a short lifetime ago. The reporters were beginning to grow restless. Some made false starts by raising a hand during the somnolent pronouncements.

"Now we'll take a few questions," said the Boston FBI head.

Several voices began to clamor, but the loudest took the floor.

"Was this an Irish Republic Army heist, as first suspected?" the reporter asked.

Boston's FBI chief was unruffled. "We're not at liberty to comment because of ongoing investigations," he said.

"Did FBI agents recover these in a raid, or did you work through a third party?" another reporter asked, with a quick follow-up: "Did you get them one by one, or as a group? Can you say?"

The chief was getting a bit wound up by now. He stuck to what he was supposed to pass on. "We're not at liberty to comment because of an ongoing investigation. I think you understand." A fog gathered in the media pack's collective eyes.

After a few more similar questions, a reporter hollered, "Is there any detail at all that you can give, Chief?"

He said, "What we have for you is all there in the press release. I think it's great news for Boston, for the FBI, for the country." He looked at his aides. There was nothing more, so he said, "Thank you." The officials left the podium area, and the museum was officially back open, its legacy intact.

As things were breaking up, two dark town cars pulled up outside the museum. The back doors swung open and two men stepped onto the curb, one tall and thin, the other well built with a crown of thick gray hair. They were the two U.S. senators from Massachusetts, members of the president's party, late for the opening event.

The press noticed, and a scrum of cameramen, adept at pushing through crowds, headed in their direction. Another small press conference had begun. The senior senator from the state was saying, "This is a great day for Boston, a great day for the great state of Massachusetts." When asked about the mysterious recovery of the art, the junior senator said, "You'll have to ask the FBI about that."

27

Washington D.C.

FROM THE WHITE House President Hughes watched the press conference. He was satisfied. The FBI did its job by keeping its mouth shut. "Okay," he said to his chief of staff. "Now, how do we handle China on this?"

"As you said, we've got two strong cards now, the Gardner and the Freer, Mr. President. I think you'll want to play this hand with China carefully."

That meant making the two incidents one big issue. They could either take it all to the Embassy of China, navigate a direct line to Beijing, or hold their cards.

"A complaint will be tricky," the advisor said. "We have documented everything, irrefutably. But of course, China will deny everything. At least for a time. When they do concede, it will surely be by secret diplomacy."

"We have them in an embarrassing situation, in other words," the president said.

"That's correct. They won't want to be embarrassed in public, a media storm. Especially now, after the National Gallery just treated Beijing like a princeling. The red carpet treatment."

"That celestial face thing," the president said. "Is that over?"

The advisor said, "Celestial Face of China. It has just left town. As I understand, it now exhibits on the China mainland."

"Their victory lap," the president said.

"It seems so."

"The cagey bastards," the president said. He asked for more on the Gardner incident, having just seen the press conference.

"It was a rogue operation in China, an art buying operation. They tracked down the Gardner stuff. A relative of the general secretary, a niece apparently, was involved. The stolen art had floated around Europe for some time, then it was scooped up by the Chinese. The way it works, the Party has a hand in everything, so we can assume their involvement. Some level of complicity, at least provincial if not Beijing itself."

"So it sounds like we can get someone in trouble over there, local at least," the president said. "For now, I don't see that as a particularly strong lever with Beijing. We'll keep it under wraps. Someday it may be useful at the bargaining table."

"Yes, sir, I agree."

"Draw up a plan, put it on a front shelf."

"Yes, sir. Ready for use."

28

China

ON THAT SAME day, Beijing was getting an unusually early taste of summer. Some of the flowers had bloomed, others were already wilting on this particularly hot afternoon. On the latitudes of the Earth, Beijing was no higher than Athens, Rome, or Marseille in the south of France. But its winters could be stark, weeks of dry frozen air, cold winds blowing down from the flat lands of Mongolia.

Some of the windows in the Zhongnanhai offices, overlooking its imperial gardens, had been opened to welcome the fresh air; one nice day of the short spring, a day to enjoy before the sweltering heat of later months. It was often only the weather, in fact, that could brighten the severe mood that dominated government central.

General Secretary Ren, balancing China on his fingertips, was also being hit by some cold political winds, but nothing, he believed, he could not handle.

The night before, the Politburo member in charge of International Relations, and thus the embassies abroad, had come with the strangest news. There might be an incident in Washington, still being assessed, but potentially an unwelcomed embarrassment to the general secretary.

"We have acted quickly and, as always, we will deny all accusations," the official told Ren. "After hearing from our ambassador, I ordered an internal investigation. With no delay."

"And what have you found? Is this true?" Ren asked.

"Unfortunately, we believe so. From what we can tell, a deputy attaché was directing his small group of five curators in a conspiracy. They were, it seems, stealing original China artworks at the Freer Museum, a famous institution in Washington. It seems that they were replacing them with perfect forgeries. The attaché is under detention."

"Does Washington know, or know that we know?"

"We do not believe so."

"And our ambassador?"

"He had just found out about this, and took immediate action. He's very embarrassed that it might cause trouble."

"Do you believe him?"

The minister paused, his face a puzzle. "We believe him," he said, elaborating further. "The guilty man, a mere deputy at the embassy, is apparently tied to the Yellow Faction. This was not known before. He was stealing the art to give to Madame Soong Wei, leader of Omni Art Global."

"At Soong Wei's direction?" General Secretary Ren said, slightly enraged. He was wondering whether the ambassador himself had loyalties to the Yellow Faction. The sands were always shifting.

"We don't think so. The guilty man was lining his own ambitions, it seems."

Ren Jinuah sat back in disgust. Not only was this incompetence, but it could have blowback on Beijing. He told the minister to take all the appropriate actions, get to the bottom of it, and definitely keep it quiet.

Ren said, "Keep me apprised," before ending the session.

THE NEXT DAY, other business was pressing. Ren Jinuah tried to push the Washington problem to the back of his mind. If the U.S. government found out and then complained, China had its tried-and-true responses. In truth, China had relished every chance it had to stealthily acquire intellectual property from the U.S. That was one of Ren Jinuah's chief interests. It was to be encouraged, in fact. The only sin was to get caught. The fools in the China Embassy were not clever enough. And now this. Washington would actually welcome an incident, if it played to their advantage. The chess game was on.

He rose from his desk, strode to a window, and pondered the imperial grounds. He shifted his thoughts to the next private meeting, somewhat impromptu. Earlier that morning, a member of the Yellow Faction, head of the Leading Group on Party Building, rang through on the red phone. Now a knock came at the door. The secretary let in the man. By Politburo etiquette, Ren was merely "first among equals." Yet his visitor knew how it really worked.

The man was taller than Ren, his shoulders crisp and wide. He was older than Ren, too, known for his cunning, a silk glove over a bronze fist. Not a leader in the Yellow Faction, but a player.

For Ren Jinuah's part, he had always seen Madame Soong Wei as the unseen controller of the Yellow Faction. And he still wondered about the Freer Museum matter. Was she and her Omni Art Global involved? Again, he pushed aside those thoughts. The issue today—and everyday—was the Yellow Faction's votes, and for this reason he treated his peer from the Politburo Standing Committee with serious respect. The man had come with a serious offer.

Once seated, the minister said, "Chairman Ren, I wish to make a proposal. I think it will solve one of your problems. And, I must admit, it will also benefit my family. My family has served loyally for many years in the Party."

Ren was interested. He had already calculated why this man from the Yellow Faction had sought him out so quietly. But he wanted to make sure, be blunt from the start.

"Is this at the behest of Madame Soong?" Ren asked, a knowing look in his narrowed eyes.

"It is not," the minister said. "The faction has been very loyal to her, because of her husband, for a good while. But it is time that we move on, in my opinion."

"Yes, your proposal then."

The minister cleared his throat and straightened his posture in the chair. "I have an older son, a very good man, loyal to the Party. He has been in real estate and construction for some time, in Shanghai, a little in Beijing, also Macao."

"Yes, he is known," Ren said. "One of our Party entrepreneurs."

"And always with Party supervision and cooperation," the man said. "My son believes that his company is a very good candidate to receive the government contract to build the China Global Art Museum here in Beijing. It's a job that needs such talents as his." A pause floated between the men. Often in these discussions, what was not said spoke loudly enough. Faces also told the story. The two men had seen each other plainly.

"I will have the votes I need?" Ren asked.

"Absolutely. It is time for our faction to move on, have its own mind, if I may say." Respect for age was a given, and Madame Soong had that elder stature. But still . . . "For the sake of the future, I believe we should move on, and solidly support your leadership."

And gain your son a very profitable, and prestigious government contract, Ren thought. It was the norm. "I have no doubt that your son's company can do the job. We never like to move too fast. We want to make sure." Now Ren was thinking of the autumn Party Congress, the crucial vote, a preparation that could not tarry too much longer. Madame Soong had become a nuisance, too persistent. She was unusually reluctant to make any promises to Ren, not until she had everything she wanted.

"Minister," Ren said, "I think your proposal is a very good one. I do have the final authority on this. My mind right now can agree with this proposal."

The minister would have liked it in writing, something formal, since the political landscape often felt tremors, even small earthquakes, in the weeks before a Party Congress. He wanted to say so, but was holding back. Ren seemed to read his mind.

"Minister, my decision is as good as if we were signing the final documents, I assure you. I can see many advantages to this proposal, not least a rapid and high quality building project."

"Yes, Mr. Chairman. My son's firm is well known for its prompt and quality work. And may I say, it will be a pleasure to see you continuing as our general secretary." That was the minister's promise, his one Yellow Faction vote, a promise unwritten but now inviolable.

"I am very glad that we met," said Chairman Ren Jinuah. He rose, as did the other man, who gave a slight bow. As he did, Ren was thinking about Madame Soong Wei, a slippery situation. Yet one he could certainly handle.

A DAY OR two later, Ren was discussing with his deputy some alternative roles that Madame Soong Wei might serve in the soft power cultural initiative. The office secretary knocked. She was summoned and peaked in the door.

"A very important call for you, Mr. Chairman."

He picked up his red phone and said, "Yes," and listened. "And does anyone else know?" he asked. "Yes, thank you. Nobody should know." He hung up.

He sat back in his large chair. He put his hands in a steeple and thought deeply for a time. His deputy kept his eyes on the floor, waiting for his overseer to pick up the discussion.

Ren Jinuah said, "Madame Soong has fallen very ill, in a comma at the Party hospital. I will be making some other plans. As decided, the contract is going to the company we have selected. The election will be assured. You may go now."

The man stood, gave a slight bow, gathered up his papers and left the room.

What Ren did not mentioned was that Madame Soong was not just unconscious. She had died in her hospital bed, and apparently had been poisoned. Whether it was accidental or intentional was not clear. Immediately, he had to take steps to quell any rumors, such as that he might have been involved. Beijing's insular politics were hard to predict. On his red phone he called the Party leader who controlled the medical system and gave an order that was perfectly clear. The medical report was to not mention poison. There was not to be the slightest hint that the death was unnatural.

Things were moving fast now, but Ren was a man prepared for the unpredictable. He always thought ahead, and now it was time to take that step. He was thinking of that one particular member of the Politburo Standing Committee who was in the rival Xinfeng Clique, a pliable man who often caught his eye. That man was currently on the Zhongnanhai grounds, working today at his office. Ren picked up his red phone, made the call.

For some time, already, Ren had used a mediator to begin an inroad to this man. Over the weeks, he carefully watched the man's face, his eyes, sought his inner thoughts and ambitions. He'd learned every detail of his family. Now was the time to talk business.

The man soon arrived at Ren's office.

"Chairman Ren, thank for your personal attention," the man said.

"It is my pleasure," Ren said. From the outset, Ren was honest, showing that he was well aware that the Xinfeng group—he did not now call it a clique—was not his greatest supporter, and indeed, it had long held a different view about improving China. "I have learned of your daughter's great work in our state manufacture," Ren said. Specifically, he was speaking of the woman's chairmanship of a state-owned clothing enterprise, mostly basic staple, but also fashion, the high-end market where great profits were made for the Party. "I understand she is a great woman of taste, a person of the arts, if I'm correct."

The member of the Xinfeng Clique was indeed proud of his daughter, his eldest. He could feel that something was about to be offered.

Ren continued. "I do this because of her good record, and that is of utmost importance. But I must also note that you have long and loyally served the Party." The man also had a powerbase in two of the key provinces. He was a controller of China's growing coal and natural gas industry. He was the kind of man who might, one day, swing the entire recalcitrant Xinfeng Clique to Ren's side.

Ren said, "Therefore, I would like to appoint your daughter as chairman, that is, as leader, of our great state enterprise Omni Art Global. We need a new and loyal generation for our future."

The man could barely hide his emotion, yet he did. He was not where he was today without being able to hold a stern countenance under any circumstance. "How can I possibly refuse such a benefit for China and, indeed, for my firstborn?" the man said.

Ren knew his colleague could not refuse. Ren himself marveled. In a single day, he had swung at least one member of the Yellow Faction to his side, and also cemented a new ally in the Xinfeng

Clique. The first was an outcome he had long sought and constantly fretted over. It had worked, and now the Xinfeng Clique, too, would supply a vote, previously an impossible quest. The path now seemed cleared for his highest ambitions.

The meeting was over, and Ren's thoughts turned back to Madame Soong. If she was intentionally poisoned, he was uncertain by whom, for surely she had enemies in the marketplace or among the political factions—and he couldn't imagine it was Niece Quang. It was the Madame's time after a long life. Now it was time to decide about his niece. Much was going his way. The entire mess had to be cleaned up. And that was a specialty of the Party.

A FEW DAYS later, as Urumqi was coming to life, two contingents of green-uniformed police led the way, one to Quang's main office in the industrial park, the other to the tea farm outside of the city. Part of the People's Armed Police Force, they were often tapped for logistical operations, strong-back work. In this case the direction from behind was given by the Ministry of Public Security, often likened to China's FBI, but with extralegal powers. It was often deployed to intervene in serious border or customs violations.

Since the order had come down from the Politburo, indeed from Ren Jinuah himself, it was first assessed by the Ministry of State Security. It monitored anything bordering on "counterrevolutionary activities designed to sabotage or overthrow China's socialist system," as the statutes said. After a careful assessment, the order was passed to public security, which had its own soldier-police. These units did not ask questions. They only followed orders to the letter.

Dark blue vehicles made up the two convoys, which included trucks for the confiscation. They arrived almost simultaneously at the main office of the Phoenix Group-Silk Road Company, and at the tea farm. The few staff at the two locations were alarmed, worrying at their own complicity or guilt by association.

"Where is the merchandise?" a public security captain asked the supervisor at Quang's main office.

"Downstairs," the man said. "Is there a problem?"

The captain did not reply, but said, "Take us there. Is there a loading area?" There was on the ground level. The uniformed men began their work, down to the basement, through the security door, and into the subterranean storehouse with its many crates filled with works of art. "Take all of it," the captain told the workers. "All of it into the trucks."

He was now going to locate any files and records. They too would be confiscated while he was interrogating the supervisor, specific to his orders. By the end of the day, Quang's main Urumqi office was cleaned out, a hollowed-out shell as if the building had long been vacant.

The same was happening at the Silk Road Company tea farm, several miles to the north, with its large fenced-in enclosure. As the grounds were being inspected, the uniformed squad breached the inner doors and began to load boxes and crates into the trucks. The office files were boxed up as well. At first, the leader of the intervention could not make sense of the greenhouses, so numerous and various in their ground plan.

"Take samples," he told a subordinate.

"You mean the tea plants?"

"Yes, just throw some from each different place in bag or box. Make an evidence record, I don't know, just by number, sample one, sample two, like that."

The work began, and as the day passed, the tea farm, too, was eviscerated of its valuable stores and its horticultural mysteries. By evening, the vehicles in the two separate contingents had met up at the Urumqi International Airport. A large PLA cargo plane was waiting in its special loading area. A few hours later, everything was securely ensconced in the cavernous freight bay, itemized on sheaves of papers. The pilots set the course, a one-way flight to Beijing—where, long ago, Emperor Qianlong had also gathered China's treasures.

29

Shanghai

QUANG DAIYU HAD awoken early that day and greeted the Shanghai morning. She was preparing herself, nearly out the door, when a loud knock came from its other side. Then a demanding voice: "Miss Quang Daiyu, this is the Ministry of Public Security. Please open."

Quang froze. *What could it be?* She scanned the room, irrationally thinking there might be a way to avoid the nuisance, so common in China, always officials coming to your door. It was no use. She pulled the door open.

"Quang Daiyu, we have a warrant for your arrest. The charge is suspicion of corruption. You will please come with us." The man speaking was clean cut. His deputy had a wolfish appearance. They were the plainclothes Jiwei, the Party police. "There will simply be some questioning," the man in charge said.

Quang stood placidly, thinking. The criminal codes of China, liberalizing slowly over the past decades, had begun to recognize the rights of the accused, though with severe caveats in practice. China's legal system ran on two tracks, the public face—the public courts—and the hidden face behind, the Party apparatus. It could detain at will. She'd be lucky to get a public trial, which, anyway, was designed for public humiliation. For Ren Jinuah's purposes, a Party verdict had surely been reached already. As was the custom, political interests nearly always trumped family ties in China's millennia of history.

"I must take my things," Quang said, insistent.

By now two younger police, a plainclothes man and woman, were on either side of Quang, ready to follow the directions of the two arresting superiors.

"There is not time," the lead officer said.

"I am niece of the general secretary," Quang said. "Do you want him to get a disrespectful report?"

The officer glowered at her and glanced at his second. A slight nod was returned. "Okay, that is fine. One travel bag is allowed."

At this stage, with this kind of arrest, the Party police system had a few options. Typically the subject would be taken to a secure facility and placed in a holding cell. Matters were executed perfunctorily. Common enough was the short-order ticket to the penal system. Or the re-education labor farms.

Everyone involved knew, however, that this was a different kind of arrest. While the police did not know everything, the charge of corruption was made explicit. That had become somewhat routine these days. It often reached into fairly high levels of society. With millionaire CEOs, and many lesser souls, there was always something to find about graft, banking, or taxes. The outcome was not always a court trial. By Party calculation, trials were only a political tool, a way to make a front-page example of a rival official, or a family that had pushed the limits.

"Go with her," the superior told the female officer. "One travel bag, and no delay."

The female officer accompanied Quang deeper into her residence. She stood by as Quang, her hands shaking, and wishing for cup of Gold Tea, threw an open travel bag on her bed. She began to gather things. There were the clothes, some toiletries. Her makeup she left behind. Then as inconspicuously as possible, she retrieved her two electronic devices, a cell phone and a computer pad on which she wrote and kept records.

"Excuse me, Madame," the young female officer said. "No electronics."

Quang faced her and tried to divine her mind, thinking quickly. "If I am to be held, I still have work to do. I am a businesswoman. You understand. I keep a diary, which is essential to me. Am I expected to ask for pencil and paper?" The two women held gazes with each other. The younger woman's eyes wavered.

She said, "Please, go ahead. They may ask you about this later."

Quang smiled, as she would to a daughter. "You are very kind. I'm sure this is some kind of misunderstanding."

From out by the door came the superior officer's voice. "What is keeping you?"

The young female officer said, "We're coming." Then she said in an officious, audible voice, "Madame Quang we must go."

Quang again smiled at her, with a slight nod. She was taken back to the entrance. The apartment was locked, to be searched later. The police team escorted Quang downstairs. On the street were two dark cars with dark windows and with drivers. She was put in the back of the second with the two young guards, and with the superiors inside the front vehicle, the security detail broke into the Shanghai traffic.

The ride was like any through Shanghai's crowded streets. But by the officious look of the vehicles, with their peculiar license plates, most of the traffic knew, instinctively, to give right of way. At one intersection, an alert young traffic cop, her pretty face belying her robotic, uniformed motions, stopped traffic to let the two dark BMWs pass quickly.

Before long, the cars had crossed the Huangpu River, caught an elevated expressway, and were headed inland, somewhere between Shanghai and Nanjing, a city to the west. The landscape, heavily populated, never became countryside to the eye. There were instead clusters of hovels, small factories, some office centers, even a few negligible farms. They were all part of the uneven texture that made up the edges of the expanding metropolis. After some navigation, now on smaller roads, Quang could see a more open, barren valley ahead. The cars kept up their diligent speed. They soon passed the guard house at a wide entrance that penetrated a screen of high fencing. The cars began turning into a facility. By appearance, it could have been a resort complex, stripped, however, of anything decorative.

Quang was taken to the foyer of a kind of police station lobby with somber guards. The emblem told the story, the red within the golden wings—the Ministry of Public Security, always at the service of the Jiwei, the Party's secret police. She was greeted by a man in uniform. He wore some kind of business suit merging with army police attire.

"Madame Quang, we are pleased to have you as our guest," the man said. "We recognize your standing. We have arranged for comfortable lodging during the process."

He did not say what the process was. For most of the others who were delivered to the compound, the detention lodgings were not comfortable, designed to instill a fearful cooperation. As they spoke, Quang from a distance saw two men, their shoulders rounded, clothes askew, faces distressed. Guards shepherded them into another building. She could not believe her eyes. But for the shaved head, she could swear it was her deputy Liu Hui. Surely they would extract a confession. And what of her soldier, her loyal Zhang Wei? He was nowhere to be seen. By the time someone was delivered here, Quang could tell, neither family nor lawyers were going to receive a call.

The dragon plays with fire, Quang told herself. She had aspired to be a dragon in China. And as the ancient tales always showed, the dragon is eventually slain, sooner or later. In other ancient tales, there were women whose lover died in battle, whose families fell into dishonor, or who betrayed an emperor. They had all found a way out. She could not read the heavens. But only two things were possible. Either Madame Soong had won, or she was gone. In either case, Quang herself, whether under suspicion or a mere victim of political expediency, saw only twilight.

She resisted her desire to protest, play her cards and argue from her family ties. Instead she hid brightness, bided time. After this many years in China, she understood the process. She knew the odds. They weren't in the favor of a detainee like herself.

An hour later, she inhabited a spare living quarters. It was a two room apartment with a heavy door along a long hallway. Her two guards from the vehicle had escorted her in. On their parting, the young female gave Quang a melancholy glance. To this, Quang smiled and nodded.

"Is there a tea pot here?" she said.

The young woman crossed the room and fiddled through a set of cupboards above a faucet and sink. "Here is one," she said. It was an electric boiler. "Here are cups." Meals would be served at particular hours.

As soon as they were gone, Quang reached into her travel bag and took out the Gold Tea. Her hands quivered. She began to brew some, ready to calm down. She'd try to achieve the meditative state she knew so well in her special room. There was no art to surround her, no more future plans to make. Only the worst to look forward to. The prospect was unacceptable.

Quang took out her other tea as well, and her two electronic devices. Surprisingly, they had not been screened upon entrance to the golden prison. Her name, her niece-hood to the powerful, had counted for something after all. She checked the devices, her skills still intact. Once they were up and running, it was more than she'd expected—she did have an Internet connection. They worked, those satellites and IPs addresses she had known for years.

There was one couch-like chair in the room. She sat in it, testing whether she could recreate the mood of her inner room. It would do. The water had boiled, and she sipped the Gold Tea, sipped again. It soon had its effect. She put out her other tea, the Bronze tea, the mysterious tea of royal politics and intrigue. She would meditate on what was to come. She would decide. First she found on her computer her files with the genealogy, the complex family tree that showed her blood line from the household of Empress Cixi, from Deng Xiaoping's wayward love life, and her illegitimate birth by the seed of Ren Jinuah. Then the line of adoption, of her faux relations. In all, her more than royal inheritance.

Before deciding, she meditated. She sipped more tea. The ghost of Empress Cixi came to her. They began to speak. It was the time, Quang realized. Time for her to let her myriad followers, the countless readers of her "Ghost of Empress Cixi" blog, know the yet unknown. It took some doing, some careful arranging. She pulled up her files, preparing to cut and paste, attach, and send. It all seemed in order.

She made one more cup of Gold Tea, strong this time, enough to elevate her mind, numb her to her willing fate. The effect was welcomed, satisfying, a mood in which great things could be done.

The art of China would live on, would have its day, its human admirers coming and going, generation after generation. She thought of Qishu, the Wondrous Brush. Her life had been like that. Both bold and subtle, like the ink floating in the water, telling an inner story, dazzling to the eye. Inscribed in memory.

Then she did what was necessary on her computer, posted her last message from the Ghost of Empress Cixi. Her hands trembled, but they were sure. The Bronze tea did not take long to brew. She made enough for three cups, which would bring the desired effect, the lazy drift into nothingness.

Maybe she would meet Empress Cixi on the other side. That would be enough, enough to make her life worthwhile.

30

Washington D.C.

PEALE PUT ON a dress shirt, the first in a while. From his pic-ture window, Annapolis was the same as always. It was noon on a Sunday, and the bay caught the sun, refracting brilliant flashes of light. As always, the mid-Atlantic humidity was rising, and spring-time by the Chesapeake had been a mere bleep of blossoms and pollen.

Time had passed slowly since he and Ho had touched down with the Black Hawk in Afghanistan. They had made their way back to the United States, and returned to their personal lives. A week of extra sleep, then the relative doldrums that follow an unusual amount of stress and excitement, not unknown in military service. As one First World War wag had put it, this life could be "months of boredom punctuated by moments of terror."

Now dressed for the occasion, he and Priscilla drove over to Northern Virginia. They would meet up with Grace Ho at a Chinese restaurant, a kind of cap on the whole affair. Priscilla had recommended the gesture. "You're not going to just say bye-bye at the airport, and leave it at that," she had said. Why not go out for Chinese as a final farewell?

In the time since getting back, Peale and Ho were close-mouthed, catching a breath and paying utility bills. Washington was handling everything from this point onward. There was nothing in the newspapers, at least about their foray into China. The *Wall Street Journal* was reporting on the opening of the "Celestial Face of China" exhibit in Wuhan, detailing how for months the city had transformed itself for the event. The airport had been expanded, as were many roads. For a week before the opening, the industries in Wuhan closed down their smokestacks. The air was to be clear, blue, and clean.

The Peales parked near the Apex Martial Arts gym. As they entered, Peale whiffed the sweat and Lysol that was the gym's trademark. Nobody was in the lobby this time. Soon after entering, they heard a loud Womp! in the gym room. Peale wondered whether Ho was in her sweats for dinner.

They entered and saw two men in dojos, one pulling the other up by a friendly hand. Over to the side was Ho, nicely dressed, saying, "Good one, you've got to watch your left side." The man who had just toppled his opponent was the same guy that Peale saw Ho knock to the matt on his first visit, ages ago, it seemed.

Ho waved and walked over. "Hi Priscilla," she said. "How's the big guy been since we got back?" She eyed her partner, winked.

"A little grouchy, I guess. Suffering from boredom."

"Bored as an English duke," said Peale. "I miss the rantings and ravings of New York City." Plus, New Yorkers never liked to be told what to do. Those were his lessons after nearly five years in that city.

Priscilla continued with, "I say to him, well, clean up the house, mow the lawn. Paint that old fence. There's plenty to do."

Peale took it on the chin gracefully and just shrugged.

Exiting the gym, they jumped into the Peales' car and drove over to their former haunt, the Golden Harvest Restaurant. The manager recognized them. He gave them a good table—no private room scanned for bugs—and they ordered.

"You know, the Chinese food over here is just as good as in China," Ho said.

"Really," Priscilla said.

Peale said, "She's been over there, what, a dozen times, so she should have a good reading."

"That many?" Priscilla said.

"Long story," said Ho. Peale didn't really know the number, for she'd never told him. He was just throwing out a big number to egg her on.

The meal arrived. Peale was hungry, as the two women noticed. He dove in, better now at chopsticks.

The two fair weather spies shared some updates. "A guy came out from State the other day and had me sign the papers," Ho said. "How about you?"

"Yeah, I went into town, cleared that up." These were the State Secrets Act documents, promising that the details of their work goes no further than their private thoughts.

Ho was putting a chopsticks full of stir fried in our mouth, eyes wide. "Hmm, this is good." Then she said, "Anything new from Castelli?"

Peale said, "I spoke to him the other day. He said the White House believes it has 'two cards to play,' the Freer and the Gardner stuff. Not sure what they have planned." Castelli also passed on that their escapade opened a number of small windows on China's soft power initiative. The government was also more closely watching that curatorial program being run by Beijing. There were still a few hundred Chinese curators checking around in U.S. museums.

"What's interesting," Peale said, "is that Beijing still doesn't know about the Black Hawk."

"What Black Hawk?" Priscilla asked.

Peale smiled. "Classified."

"Fair enough," she said.

"Castelli also told me that the brass is interested in this 'ghost of Madame Cixi' thing, and that it might be a third card they can play."

"How can they play that as a third card?" Ho said.

"I don't know," Peale said. "He's asked to meet me tomorrow, so maybe I'll find out." Before him on the table, Peale had his choice of the next dish.

Ho ruminated on her next comment for a moment, then continued. "Speaking of ghosts, I've actually just started to read a biography of Dowager Empress Cixi. Should have read it before we headed out. Not quite a Catherine the Great, of course. Mostly involved in palace politics. I must admit, though, she'd be a great person to spin a fantasy around." Accretions of legend always formed around small kernels of truth, she was thinking.

They sat for a while, discussed a possible desert—maybe vanilla ice cream with green tea powder. Ho moved on to another topic.

"Also in the news," she said, "my fiancé has been transferred to the U.S. Embassy in Beijing, a good step up." She looked at Priscilla and said, "An American guy."

"How's that working out, overseas duty and all?" Peale said.

"Not a problem," Ho said, "We're really stuck on each other, no hurry. You know what they say about Chinese, thinking long term and all that." Except that her beau had German and Scottish ancestry.

During the few weeks of working together, Peale had never broached these kinds of personal subjects, nor had he offered

intimations of his own family life. Nor had Ho ever raised such top-
ics. An all-around professional, if sometimes seat-of-the-pants, mission, they had to admit. Priscilla, however, was not so circumspect.

Peale had already told his wife plenty about his past, his work
in Navy intelligence, how a roadside "improvised explosive device"
nearly blew him to pieces in Afghanistan, how he convalesced for a
year, his first marriage going down the drain. Priscilla's late husband,
on Peale's team, had died in the incident. Over time, that was how
Peale met her. The whole episode had generated a strong mutual
sympathy, and happily, too, a marriage that was bound to last.

"Did Julian ever tell you about his family?" Priscilla asked Ho.

Ho glanced at Peale, gave an odd smile, and said, "Oh, you do
have family. I was wondering."

"Tell her, Julian," Priscilla said.

Having taken a last mouthful, Peale was not paying attention,
but then signaled he was listening. "Nothing special," he said.

"Then it's not a state secret," Ho said. "You can tell me."

"Okay, think American art history. Have you ever heard the
name Peale, I mean, before my incarnation?"

Ho thought a few moments. "Someone in the colonial period,
right? Say, Philadelphia, the Continental Convention."

"Close enough," Peale said. He then explained that the Peales, an
immigrant family from England, were an artistic dynasty in colonial
times. They founded the nation's first art museum in Philadelphia—
not related to the political conventions. Some of them painted portraits of early American political figures. "A whole brood," Peale said.
"My goodness. The patriarch was Charles Wilson Peale. He married
three times, so he had eighteen children. Three sons and three daugh-
ters became artists, painters, the three granddaughters after that.
Named all his kids after Renaissance and Baroque painters. Anyway,
my family line, with the patriarchal name, starts somewhere in there."

"So that's where you got the genes," Ho said.

Peale didn't want to go into his own amateur exploits as a painter, and more expertly, as a restorer. "I think my grandfather got most of them, and it probably stopped there." His grandfather had been among the "monuments men" who recovered European art during the fall of the Third Reich. "True, though, it's always been a strong interest, even an inclination. An odd instinct for a soldier, well, a Navy man." That was also his father's trade.

"And what about you, Grace?" Priscilla said.

"It's complicated," Ho said. "I should admit, though, that I've been researching my family's genealogy for several years. Hobby only."

"Very interesting," Priscilla said. "Does the name Ho go back, like to emperors or something?"

"Probably to some Dowager Empress, a dragon lady," Peale said. "That's a compliment." He finished his next bite, and smiling said, "All those past times you were in China, what was that about?" He was again putting his partner on the spot.

"The genealogy is more interesting," Ho said. She still wasn't going to apprise them of her past China adventures, the tracking down of the hacker with Defense Department secrets, aiding the escape of a dissident's family, making contact with a prefecture leader, and more. "What I can say is that my travels in China allowed me to do research on my parents' family lines."

"What did you find?" Priscilla said.

"Well, to start with, there's no country more difficult to track genealogy in," she said, giving a number of reasons. Most basic was how names were used, women keeping their father's names even after marriage. China had only about five hundred surnames, so it was also hard to separate one Ho or one Cheng or whatever from another.

"Then there was a century of turmoil. Fall of the imperial

house, two civil wars, the Japanese occupation. Then the Cultural Revolution. With all those deaths, family lines ended. People changed their names for safety. Records by the millions were destroyed and lost."

"Sounds like an impossible task," Peale said.

"Not if you're smart," Ho said.

"I knew you could do it," Priscilla said, giving Peale a jab with her elbow. "What did you find?"

"It's interesting. You begin with your parents, of course. My father had three brothers and one sister, my mother two sisters. As Julian might have told you, my parents, in effect, fled the mainland, but their relations stayed."

"Huh," Peale said. "You never mentioned that."

"Not work related," Ho said. "So on my side, of my many uncles and aunts, there were more children, and there were marriages into other families. Here, it's helpful that the women keep their patriarchal names. You know, you can follow those back."

"Where did it lead?" Priscilla said.

Ho went on to explain what she knew of the relatives, some her parents' ages, her age, and younger. Some of it she had tracked down during her visits to China. "Off hours. Not on the taxpayer tab."

Peale didn't believe it, about the tab, but kept listening.

"Well, before my parents, the Ho name did have a kind of regional lineage, south China, mid-China. It was also spelled HE. From what I can tell, it originated in the Zhou Dynasty, maybe a minor emperor or two. I'm proud to say"—she elevated her chin theatrically—"it ranks twenty-first in the 'Hundred Family Surnames' of an ancient poem."

"Royalty, no doubt," Priscilla said.

"Actually, now it's a commonplace," Ho said. "About the twentieth most common name in China."

She paused for a sip from her water glass. "As to recent gene-alogy, the interesting part goes over to one of my uncles, who was in the military. Unfortunately, he was purged for opposing the Tiananmen crackdown."

"Oh, dear, where is he now?" Priscilla said.

"He was sent to a camp, but no word since," Ho said, a somber look on her face. She paused stoically, then continued. "Well, any-way, he had a daughter. She was a bit independent. That's usually noticeable in a Chinese clan. So she married a man in another family, a well-connected one. It had survived all the fires of the rev-olution, and apparently Tiananmen as well. So, this man from the well-connected family was also a kind of black sheep. Anyway, he entered politics, and his wife, my cousin, with him. At this point, it's hard to track. Once you're at that level, in China at least, your family becomes a black box."

"A kind of mystery," Priscilla said.

"In a manner of speaking, yes. Someone knows all the facts. What I can say, from research, is that this fellow rose pretty high in the Party. The evidence suggests that he's risen to the Politburo, the larger one, the twenty-five people."

"That *is* hard to know," Peale said. "Even the Sinologists can't find the names, let alone their family ties."

"I did make some headway," Ho said, her usually placid face momentarily animated. "Apparently, this male relative of mine, you know, a first cousin by marriage, or some say cousin-in-law, became part of something called the Xinfeng Clique. He's not in the Standing Committee, the top nine, but in the twenty-five full Politburo. So this so-called clique formed after Tiananmen, a kind of underground opposition party among the military and politi-cal cadre. Clique is a derogatory term, but that's what it's called. Otherwise, it's a bit of a mystery, part of the secret world of China's elite." She wasn't sure she wanted to convey all of her certainties to the mixed company.

"Xinfeng," Priscilla said. "What does that mean?"

"It can be a surname, or a symbolic name, like in the late dynasties. Ming means 'bright.' Qing means 'clear.' Either way, as surname or a symbol, Xinfeng means 'fresh wind.'"

Peale leaned back. "So let me see," he said. "Your long lost cousin will someday rule the Politburo, and then, say, in a couple decades you'll be head of the CIA." He gave Ho a questioning look, jest in his eyes. "Hollywood couldn't make this up."

"Stranger the fiction," Ho said, worried that she had said too much.

Peale was thinking, I wonder if Castelli knew any of this?

Then the desert arrived.

EPILOGUE

Beijing

THE STERN GRAY building near People's Square, its facade of the old Soviet vintage, was a hive of activity. It was hard to get into China by the Internet, but the Leading Group for Propaganda and Ideological Work, Beijing's cultural arm, had every means possible to herald the message, getting it out. The staff were scouring the Western press, collecting the 'rave reviews' of the "Celestial Face of China" art exhibit that had astonished the world.

The deadlines were tight. The traveling exhibit had returned to China. Now it was being expanded. Many new works had been suborned from the PLA's great trading arm, Omni Art Global. The government also confiscated an unexpectedly superb collection of art from the now disgraced Phoenix Group, which had stepped out of bounds with the Party.

The staff at the leading group for culture was collecting all the news clippings to present to General Secretary Ren Jinuah, who was widely rumored to receive his third term, and after that—no one spoke of it openly—a tenure for life. It did seem the Chinese way, after all. China always did have an emperor. The propaganda staff, often privy to such insights—routinely withheld from the public—felt the importance of their work. A new booklet was being produced. It showcased the "Celestial Face of China" exhibition in Wuhan, emphasizing that it was the birthplace of Ren Jinhua himself.

Over the previous months, the city had been transformed, as if a Potemkin village on international display. Traffic moved swiftly, buildings gleamed, and the skies were blue for the day that General Secretary Ren Jinhua arrived to cut a great red ribbon.

A WEEK LATER, Ren was taking stock of recent events. Every aspiration of Beijing had been fulfilled. The world took notice. In the first days of the Wuhan exhibition, hundreds of people of great notoriety, from countries far and near, were seen wandering the exhibit grounds. They admired the sheer scale of a China production. It was unprecedented, a foretaste of what was to come. They admired not only the ancient works of China, but just how rapidly China was ennobling great Western Art, now as its owner, a stewardship for more than China, now even for the world.

On return from the ribbon cutting and media spotlight, Ren Jinuah had moments of profound reflection. He recalled what a military leader in his faction had once said: when you guide an aircraft carrier through narrow straits, unlike a fishing junket, you have to smash some coral and make gigantic waves. Ren was a visionary, not a sentimental man. While the demise of the two women had been sad, it was a casualty of history, a history he was making for the Party and for China. His loyal security minister ensured that nothing appeared in the media or escaped the government's blockage of the Internet, and anyway, who would take seriously silly rantings about the ghost of Empress Cixi. No further investigation into the deaths, meanwhile, was required.

The rise of China was so large, Ren could not imagine anything larger that could possibly halt its progress.

In that generous mood, he gave his eight associates in the Politburo Standing Committee a day or two off. Time to relax, bask in what was accomplished. Unfortunately, though, this was not possible for Ming Zhou, the Minister of Culture. Ming Zhou was aging. Through a normal year, the cold winds of Beijing took a toll on his health. His headaches and difficulty breathing were now very different from his previous colds or bouts with the flu. He was rushed to the hospital.

The doctors were puzzled. It's not a flu, not even pneumonia. They kept their inquiry quiet. It seemed that the elderly Ming Zhou was suffering symptoms similar to what doctors saw a few years back, a rather terrifying medical mystery, which was finally called SARS. It took the lives of many in southern China, yet with time, the population developed immunity. It was defeated. Still, what was this with Ming Zhou?

The doctors carefully isolated some of the virus. They sent it to the top national research center, which too was in Wuhan. That laboratory had earlier pinned down the identity of the SARS virus. The new sample was sent just to make sure.

The lab's work was done in a few days, as always, analyzed in the hermetically sealed inner rooms. By mid-morning, the lead researcher came out of the air-tight enclosure. She removed her gear, placed it in the disposal area for incineration, and took a special shower. Only then did she don her lab uniform. Outside, in a small conference room, she gathered her team of three other doctors.

"It looks like SARS, but it's somehow different," she said. "We don't want any panic, but we should find out more about the patient's travel in recent weeks."

Even though she said that, about the travel, they all knew

that the cultural minister had just been in Wuhan, opening the great "Celestial Face of China" art exhibition alongside the general secretary.

"Don't call Beijing just yet," the lead doctor said.

THE NEXT DAY, Ren Jinuah received a call on his red phone. The news came like a sudden gale, chilling his bones. Ming Zhou was dead. That vote was lost. He worried that this would divert the focus of the Politburo. This was supposed to be a time to celebrate and unite under him. By the next morning, the news about Ming Zhou, despite his order for secrecy, would be spreading. Tongues would wag, minds might change.

Ren took a deep breath, but the air seemed thin, and did not rejuvenate. He'd gone on all six cylinders for the past two weeks. He felt worn down, some chills, a headache, but that was in the body, not his spirit. His stamina was always strong, as were his ambitions, and to these he once again resorted. Now for action.

He called in his two top deputies and his ally Hua Yang, a brilliant strategist at times like this. They were uncharacteristically slow in arriving, nearly an hour. They finally came in carrying newspapers, full of glum apologies.

"This is urgent, why so slow?" Ren said, wound tight. He presumed the newspaper reported Ming Zhou's death, a punishable breach of secrecy.

"Yes, Mr. Chairman, we agree," said Hua Yang. He apologized further for holding his deputies back. "We had to make sure."

"Sure of what?" Ren asked, motioning them to take their seats. He sank back in his chair.

"Mr. Chairman, there are news stories out, the world press, Taiwan, even creeping through the disloyal scribblers in Hong Kong." He handed Ren Jinuah one of the newspapers. On the front page was a story, "China Attempts Theft at American Museum in

Washington." Under the headline there was a photo of five Chinese curators, bearing their satchels, filing out the back entrance of the Freer.

"What is this?" he gasped. He was going to say he knew nothing about it, except he did. He had buried it, pushed it aside. Even with this, he knew that most news stories were short lived, then died quickly.

Hua Yang wouldn't dare ask if it was true. Yet it was now a world topic, a blow to China's soft power integrity. The thick bundle of newspapers under a deputy's arm seemed to groan with foreboding. Hua Yang handed Ren a second one. The headline read, "After Three Decades, Famed American Art Collection Found in China. State Theft or a Smuggler's Game?" There was a photo showing two Gardner items, a newspaper with Ren pictured, and the backdrop of the People's Square in Urumqi.

Below the fold of the newspaper, Hua Yang pointed to another related article. The headline said, "Illegitimate Daughter of China's Top Ruler Involved."

Ren scanned the reports with mounting incredulity. "This is a lie," he burst out. "Slander!"

Hua Yang frowned. That's all he could do. "We are investigating." He was withholding perhaps the worst news of all. He looked his old comrade in the eye, then glanced to the floor, unable to bear Ren's inflamed gaze. "I'm afraid the woman, daughter of the Xinfeng Clique, has withdrawn her interest in leading Omni Art Global." Its name had been tarnished unfairly in the news reports. The woman had become reluctant.

"How could she?" Ren demanded. "That is not done. She must obey."

It was too complicated for Hua Yang to articulate in the moment.

He sighed and said, "There is not a good feeling, apparently. We are still working to bring this around."

"You must," Ren said. He'd not heard anything from the man in the Xinfeng Faction, the man who had promised to give his vote. Ren could see it was another family fiasco, like so many, so endemic to China's rulers. He calmed himself. Much was still going in his favor. The bright light of the past few weeks would wash out these petty nuisances, this trouble-making by the Western media. The China Global Art Museum was to be built, the votes he needed a certainty.

He stood up, put his two outstretched hands in his desk and said, "We must not show weakness." He paused. "Do you understand?" The three men kept their eyes down.

"Of course, Mr. Chairman," Hua Yang said. Yet he knew that, for the moment, the bright sun had dimmed.

"I will handle this tomorrow, when we meet," Ren said. "Do not show a doubtful spirit, do you understand?"

The three men stood, signaled that it would be so, and left the room.

The next morning Chairman Ren was more determined than ever to present his optimistic message. In his office beforehand, he had prepared carefully. His mind whirled furiously. He knew he could win the day. It was his fate, his feng shui, his good luck. *I am under the Snake, passing into the Horse* . . . "Foolishness!" he said aloud, slamming his hands on his office desk, straightening his thoughts. His "thought" for China was his good fortune, not mythical creatures in the heavens.

In the conference room, the seven other members of the Politburo Standing Committee were assembling. One chair would be vacant, the chair held by Ming Zhou only days before. As Ren Jinuah entered, he went to each member and shook hands, though it felt like a forced ritual now. He had arranged for a less formal format, around the great table, a symbol that, after all, he was merely the "first among equals." He had felt tense all night, as if ill, but he knew it was only the challenge that weighed.

When all were seated, he poised himself and began to speak. A few sentences in, he began to cough convulsively. "Excuse me," he said after it was over, his eyes watering.

Some of the men at the table looked alarmed, a few discretely lifting a hand to cover their mouths. Ren continued, but his voice weakened, and then he expelled a few more coughs. Sitting to his right, Hua Yang said, "Chairman, perhaps we can break for the day?" Others nodded.

Ren wanted to strike out, throw off whatever was holding him back. Yet the energy to do so, the feng shui, did not come, for the Snake had not yet crossed into the Horse, the "thought of Ren Jinuah" was not yet in the celestial time of good luck.

"Another day, then," he said, suddenly overpowered by weakness and coughing again.

The meeting was breaking up, and as Ren was ushered down one hall to his private apartments, the seven remaining members of the Politburo Standing Committee went down another corridor toward the entrance of the Zhongnanhai. Outside a line of black Mercedes was waiting. A low rumble rose from the idling cars. Doors were swinging open, the black-haired men briskly getting in and doors slamming, the engines at the ready. One by one they drove through the parkland, out the gates and past Tiananmen Square, splitting off in different directions.

One car in the motorcade had turned a sharp left, passing directly in front of the great Ming gate, where an outsized image of Mao, a celestial calm on his face, looked forever down on Beijing. Suddenly, a siren approached, as if from nowhere. An ambulance swung around the side of imperial grounds, its tires squealing. It sped forward, causing the Mercedes to swerve out of the way. The ambulance lights were flashing, and their red hue, for a brief moment, caught the great face of Mao, and then passed by.

ACKNOWLEDGEMENTS

For the factual background of this novel I am indebted to a range of excellent books on China and art history, with a particular thanks to authors Richard McGregor (*The Party: The Secret World of China's Communist Rulers*), Martin Jacques (*When China Rules the World*), and David Shambaugh, ed. (*China and the World*). For the story of China's art history there is none better than Craig Clunas' *Art in China* and Karl E. Meyer and Shareen Blair Brysac's *The China Collectors*. I am grateful for sage advice given by colleagues who read the early manuscript: writer/editor Robert Selle; fiction editor Jacey Mitziga, and novelist Chin-Sun Lee (*Upcountry*), and to Lindsey Alexander of Reading List Editorial and the team at Archway Publishing.

Printed in the USA
CPSIA information can be obtained
at www.ICGtesting.com
LVHW050225110324
774111LV00021B/85

9 781665 749060